Jack O'Connell
Seattle
25 luglio 1994

QUARTET ENCOUNTERS

SANSEVERO

Sansevero is a monumental novel in five parts, published here in two volumes. The first comprises the first three parts, the second the remaining two. In this edition the final part appears in English for the first time.

The novel is narrated by Giuliano Sansevero himself, the younger son of a Neapolitan ducal family. The era of the great aristocratic families has passed and the Sansevero family, besides having lost its role in society, has lost its fortune: Giuliano is destined to revive the family finances. He is unable to shore up the ruins of his dynasty and leaves in order to discover more of the world. He goes to Milan, Ferrara (where he is stationed while serving in a cavalry regiment), Rome and Paris. In the third part he attempts to find the peace he has sought in a remote village in Calabria. Here life continues as it has done for centuries, but the twentieth century is pressing in: the villagers want a road to connect them to civilization, and Mussolini has come to power in Italy. The first volume ends with Giuliano's departure from this idyllic life. The second volume opens and war has come. Having found that he cannot retreat from the world, Giuliano rejoins the army. When the Republic of Salo is established, he refuses to serve under the German command and is taken as a prisoner of war to Germany, where he witnesses the destruction of the Reich. The novel describes modern European experience but, as Paul Scott has observed, 'the book's drive is inward to an elusive centre of private martyrdom'. The final part sees Italy rise from its ashes and Giuliano resume his search, travelling within Italy and to England, then returning to accept his fate in Sicily.

ANDREA GIOVENE

Andrea Giovene was born in Naples in 1904 of an ancient ducal family. He graduated in law from the University of Naples, but his interests were already wide-ranging and he also attended courses in mathematics, literature and medicine. He soon abandoned law as a career, and founded the literary periodical *Vesuvio*, thus beginning a lifelong association with journalism as contributor to various periodicals and reviews. From 1950–1 he was vice-director of the *Mattino d'Italia*, and in 1955 he was chief editor of the Neapolitan edition of *Il Tempo*. During the Second World War he was a cavalry captain and served in Greece, Poland and Germany, where he was present at the fall of Berlin.

He has travelled extensively throughout Europe and the length and breadth of Italy, but now lives much of the year in London. He has published a number of short works, ranging from poetry to a small book on typography. His many other interests include bibliophily, architecture, painting and antiquarianism.

ANDREA GIOVENE

Sansevero II

Translated from the Italian by
BERNARD WALL and WILLIAM RIVIERE
With an Introduction by
VALERIO DI BALVANO
in Volume One

Quartet Books London New York

Published in Great Britain by Quartet Books Limited 1987
A member of the Namara Group
27/29 Goodge Street, London W1P 1FD

British Library Cataloguing in Publication Data

Giovene, Andrea
Sansevero.
2
I. Title II. L'autobiografia di Giuliano
di Sansevero. *English*
853'.914[F] PQ4817.I814

ISBN 0-7043-0035-4

Reproduced, printed and bound in Great Britain
by The Camelot Press plc, Southampton

TRANSLATOR'S NOTE

Readers may be helped if one or two points of background are filled in for the period when the events told by Andrea Giovene took place. The Allied Forces landed in Sicily and threatened the Italian mainland while Sansevero was in Greece. In July 1943 King Victor Emmanuel called in Field-Marshal Badoglio to take the place of Mussolini who was arrested. More than a month later the King signed the Armistice with the Allies (September 8). Mussolini was liberated from imprisonment by German parachutists and founded the 'Republic of Salò' in North Italy under German control. Meanwhile South Italy was being conquered by the Allies and remained nominally under the control of the King and his government.

In Greece as elsewhere there were partisan movements, and the Greeks knew their left-wing group as the 'Andartes'.

THE DICE

(*From fragments of my diary: Bay, November 10, 1940.*)

To Denise Digne, of course, I am an enemy. Before the war I would have been a welcome and favoured guest in this small hotel in the Upper Durance. On rainy evenings I would have drunk muscatel wine with her and the others – the muscatel fragrant with spices and spirituous to the nostrils – that she makes from a secret recipe. In the afternoons I would have played bowls outside here on the rectangle of flat earth greened by the damp; I would have played with the other guests – a family, an uncle, the daughters. But though the war weighs down on me and crushes such memories like footsteps on grass, they always spring up again, which is all the more surprising as these quiet homely activities never really happened.

An abstract but impenetrable curtain has been erected up here, just where another equally immaterial barrier – the frontier – has collapsed. And because of these unrealities, my life and that of Denise Digne have become crystallised into hard and fast systems, rather like substances that are transmuted at a temperature below freezing-point: I on my side am an officer of the occupying army billeted by a requisition order; she on her side is a member of the oppressed people. And above us towers the castle of the situation, as high and confused as the scaffolding of a building whose form and purpose are unknown.

Denise is large and silent with white skin and black hair and eyes. Her choice of clothes up here in the mountains is surprising. Her voice is soft, perhaps because of her reserve. I know nothing about her except that in those first weeks her husband was reported missing on the Maginot line. It is said that misfortune draws people together. But I think that Madame Digne – who detests me for wearing the uniform of a despised enemy – is drawing hermit-like isolation from her misfortune and making this its first direct consequence. Pain has closed up her spirit as cold closes the pores. Given such conditions, she does her very best not to see me at all, which does not worry me and also lets me out of a difficult confrontation. The wall of irreconcilability erected between us also protects us by dispensing us from explanations. As for formal relations, she manages the little hotel with exemplary efficiency, and apart from the orderlies and the telephone personnel I am in any case the only occupant. In the evenings, though not till then, they all gather together round the kitchen fire downstairs, dark shapes, smoking and drinking; but they all immediately stop talking if for any reason I have to put my head round the door.

I carry out my military duties with the scrupulousness of one who knows that in certain circumstances routine is the best pain-killer. On June 22 a fragment of stone left a romantic scar on my face from my chin up to my forehead – very noticeable though superficial. This happened in Mentone. So for more than four months I have benefited by exemption from taking a similar risk. Ever since that first huge flare-up, hardly thinkable in the austere folds of these mountains, the sector up here has been not merely quiet, but dead. The whirlwind then moved off elsewhere and we hear pale echoes of it only in those uninformative news bulletins that hardly hold the attention. My unit is divided into several small groups and is guarding the bridges, tunnels and passes over a span of five miles as the crow flies. It is exhausting work and might even seem superfluous, but I carry out my inspections all the same, not only by day, but getting up at dead of night and in all weathers. The men receive me as if surprised that anyone should bother about them, even to inspect them; they stand to attention in the silence of their thankless task. I do not raise their morale, but neither do I take any action against them even if I find one of them asleep at his post; I just shake my head. 'Then why on earth does he come at this hour of the night and in such foul weather?' Of course they say this sort of thing to each other – in undertones. And it is good that Madame Digne, too, talks as softly as she does. Perhaps we all need silence, like a weary herd when evening comes.

I usually get back to the little hotel at nightfall, when all is quiet. The few men attached to the Command are out, except for the one sitting resignedly at the field telephones which at that hour are silent too. Now and again shadows pass beyond the kitchen window – men who whisper a few words to Madame Digne and then move off. But a few days ago I found a man sitting in the vestibule at the small round desk that must once have been used for checking in visitors; he was holding a cup between his hands and playing a solitary game of dice. He seemed utterly engrossed, as if wanting to read in the little black and white cabala something he already half knew. And when I drew near I saw with surprise that his dice were not the usual sort but the tarot dice of the ancient Greeks, the sort I had seen and examined in my days at Licudi – the knuckle bones extracted from a lamb's heel that the boys used to play with.

'Does fate exist?' he asked me with such ease of manner that he might have known me already and was going on with a conversation we had already begun. 'If I could put these little bones in exactly the same position in my hand, throw them from the same height, at the same angle and with the same force, then they'd hit the surface of the desk in exactly the same way as before and give me the same score. Dice don't escape the laws of physics even for an imponderable, and a mathematician could give you a precise calculation of the result if you provided him with the data. But the data aren't known, or rather we're not in a position to ordain them in advance. Would you call that fate?'

This man was lean, unkempt and very poorly dressed, with a rough but melodious voice and dark eyes embedded in deep sockets. He wore a small ring in his ear like a gypsy. As I looked at him without answering he came round to the front of the desk and introduced himself.

'Demetrio, the Seer,' he said. 'I'm here with my medium Priscilla to give a show to the Armed Forces. I'm honoured to make your acquaintance.'

Then his eyes went back to his dice lying brightly and enigmatically on the desk, the symbols showing a pair of fives.

'No!' he went on, giving me a long purposeful look. 'There's no such thing as fate, so there's no such thing as chance. It's just our incapacity to foresee circumstances. It isn't by chance that you came into collision with that fragment of stone in the Mentone cemetery. It's that you didn't know on what day and at what point that bit of stone was going to fly.'

That the incident had happened at Mentone he could have learnt from one of the soldiers, but I felt sure I had said nothing to anyone at Bay about it having taken place in the cemetery. He foresaw that I would hesitate before replying, and with perfect timing shouted loudly towards the kitchen as if someone had called him:

'I'm coming!' And off he went.

If one of the shadowy figures beyond the kitchen window was

his mysterious Priscilla, then it was possible that through her he exercised some faculty or other to transmit or penetrate thought. But what surprised me was not so much that he had identified a place – the cemetery – lodged in my memory, but that he had entered into my secret yet vivid sense of being guided not quite by the fortuitous nor yet perhaps by my own will, but by a power always intent on putting me to an ever more difficult test and obliging me to accept it.

And, indeed, what but this power could have made me flee from the deep South, and from an adventure as intense as life itself? What had wrested me from my melancholy picking and choosing among Uncle Gian Michele's bookshelves, and brought me up to this exact spot, to lie with my face against a tombstone in the Mentone cemetery, while shells from the French Lebels were smashing those sacred marbles to pieces?

It was from the cemetery that the attack on the town began; so there was nothing illogical about Demetrio's words. I had arrived at the Naples District Command, my trusty assignment card in my hand, at a moment of violent upheaval. The Office for Directives needed a liaison officer as requested by the Cosseria division, and they found just what they wanted and from the right corps (not to go into subtler points). Liaison officers nowadays have nothing in common with Risorgimento messengers galloping through gunfire. And it was certainly not on horseback that General Gambara would dispatch me into the babel of the advance line, nor on horseback that I would have to remain in the thick of the attack. It seemed an ordinary affair of chance. But between the Gothic-style reading desk used by my uncle to pore over his infoglios, and that tombstone momentarily preserving my life, there lay a link so strange that it called for interpretation. I looked for one: and I read – with some difficulty, for my cheek was pressed against the stone – I read out of the corner of my eye: 'Marianne . . . 191 . . . Pari . . .'

Where were you, O gay Paris, raised like the pennant of a medieval knight on tourney day? I no longer wanted to stay with my face pressed against that stone; I wanted to get up and run towards France, not to conquer her, but to become part of her. But that loose fragment of stone (which, this time, even I could have foreseen), kindly joker that it was, had torn my 'buccinator' and 'masseter' muscles (as I learnt later at the Base hospital), and I could feel blood running down inside my collar. What had ordained that my spirit would find solace in all this as if I had paid my debt to that piece of earth? I would never tell anyone, not even Uncle Gedeone, that I had tried (though without success!) to lift myself up a little, so that a drop of my blood would fall on the tombstone of 'Marianne . . . Pari . . .' An offering rendered all the more absurd by D'Annunzio's harangues, and one which would horrify our rulers today, and embarrass their descendants, who by then would have other names. So I willingly followed the stretcher-bearer who took me behind the lines; the advancing troops saw me, and perhaps my spectacular appearance both disturbed and elated them. 'The others were coming back all covered with blood,' they would say on a latter day, 'but we swept on regardless!' No, Demetrio is right. It is rhythm, not chance, that governs all this. I let myself be put on a stretcher and no longer felt remorse for my participation in the capture of Mentone – unseemly as it was so to disturb its cemetery . . .

As I write, following the vagaries of my thoughts and memories, a strong consoling aroma wafts in from the kitchen. Though rare in Italy, coffee can easily be found here at Bay – they say it is contraband from Switzerland. The same applies to the aquavit, very strong; and to the tobacco, which is excellent – that, too, comes down from the mountains. At fixed hours Madame Digne sets the table for the non-commissioned officers of our Command; and for me in a little separate room. During the day she also serves tea or muscatel wine, and puts them on the mantelpiece without either of us uttering a syllable. But the other day I was not alone. The military police commissioner from another little village higher up had come down here, and a second lieutenant from the Alpine regiment had come up from the valley to join us. It appeared that one of our planes was missing above the slopes of the Assiette.

'It's a single-seater reconnaissance plane,' said the commissioner with his bureaucratic attitude to daily horrors, 'and we don't know whether the pilot was able to use his parachute at the last minute or not. He's a sergeant, married three weeks ago in Savona.'

Madame Digne, coming in at this point with the tray, must have heard. I made a sign to the other two that the news was for our ears alone. But to start a search for the plane now, and in that area, would be a desperate undertaking. It was nearly eleven, and only four or five hours of daylight remained. Yet were the pilot alive, and no help brought to him before nightfall, he would have to bivouac up there at fifteen degrees below zero.

From the field telephone we put out monotonous calls to all guard posts, getting benumbed replies from them all. We began again with the same words, while the Tyrolese clock beat out the minutes during which, it could be, that young man's life was draining away – the young man who had left his wife of three weeks' standing and gone and crashed on the 'sacred mountain-tops' to kill himself, as some would think, 'nearer to God!'

Having received some rather vague information, we set out leaving the doors open to the cold (as I now remember), though the house at two in the afternoon was empty and the telephone silent among the coffee cups. But our help was no longer needed. The boy must have spun down and fallen like a stone, and it was tough work disentangling him from the wreckage by torchlight, wrapping him up in the tent canvas and dragging him down the steep slope. At one point the bundle slipped and broke open. No one dared to look.

Then we went to the little church at Bay, and stayed there till the approach of dawn with the second lieutenant and the chaplain. A part of the boy's face, and the chin, were almost intact. The chaplain had left the young lips uncovered and pure between the bandages. We knew that his wife would have a safe-conduct from Savona the following day. I returned in the icy dawn with the cold biting into my bones. I found Madame Digne in the kitchen in the half-darkness.

Before going to work, when it is still night, the labourers come in here for their drop of absinthe; that is why she always gets up so early, and I realised that my return had coincided with this habit of hers. Coffee had been prepared in a large pot for a lot of people. The gesture with which she gave me mine was, as usual, dictated by duty. I was drenched in snow and mud and had not had a clean-up for fifteen hours now – the hours spent searching on that mountain and then the rest of the night in church. I had an indefinable smell sticking to me which I myself noticed. I knew that my recent scars had reddened under the lash of the icy cold; and that she was covertly looking at them.

'Yes,' said my conscience with irony, 'we played you a dirty trick pouncing on you just at that moment and gutting with cannon-fire the little tourist shops at Mentone, complete with their beauty products. And you certainly didn't run out to welcome us! Mussolini "needed" I don't know how many dead; but from his own people, to make them pay his debt! Not from your people. Yet it was you who gave them to him.'

The silence between us was as smooth and cold as a sheet of glass. Her duty as a woman was to show care and solicitude, as it had been with my Aunt Francesca when I went to stay with her, and as it had been with Incoronata when I returned from the sea. But with Denise everything that she ought to have done and did not do became an act of hostility. Oh, no doubt, if one of those two dictators had made an offering in Rheims Cathedral, and the other had been present at the elevation of the Blessed Sacrament in St Stephen's in Vienna, they would have understood that the nations that venerate similar monuments can perhaps submit to occupation but certainly not to subjugation. What is happening at this moment is an outrageous mistake; but have those suffering under it thereby earned the right to throw in yet a further portion of pain and evil? Why do I leave my soldiers alone, when I should really send them before a court-martial? But I look at their peasants' faces, sweet and serious in sleep, and I see the thoughts passing through the dark chamber of their minds, a woman, a field, a village. And this is also why I consent to withdraw from the pleasant drowsiness of that corner by the oven – so that those others can come in: the French workmen whom I know to be outside the door waiting for me to go.

I woke up late and saw snow outside the window, bluish in the mist. Yesterday I was thinking about Rheims, so I fleetingly dreamt about it last night, and now it is in my mind. I remember that when I was there in my Latin-America travel agency period I also saw snow from my inn window. 'Rheims is the pride of France' was inscribed on the walls of the communal room, and round the ornamental scroll was a gay composition of ribbons and rosettes in blue and vermilion. That inn was a rustic affair with large wood-burning stoves smoking day and night as in a woodman's hut. But soon after waking I would be brought a goblet of that famous champagne, the flower of the region and of the best vintage, sparkling and limpid like an enchantress's eye. And as I looked at the snow and thought about Catherine I savoured that exquisite essence that shakes off indifference, opens out your spirit to the day, seduces you and beckons you on.

It was in this mood that, shortly after, I stood looking at the fantastic mass of the cathedral, magnified and deepened by the thick surrounding mist. A most heroic structure, protected against the breath of evil by holy dragons, gentle monsters, and mighty devoted claws. These heavenly legions welded into the stone not only acted as a barrier but sprang forward to threaten and disperse. Wings, symbols and saints proclaimed that this was an impregnable bastion, the Word in stone, consecrated in virtue and by the power of God.

Yet Rheims cathedral was empty that morning, and very cold. Far above me I could hear the fluttering of the pigeons living in the vaults. I saw more leaves than flowers in front of Our Lady on the second altar to the left.

'In winter, in weather like this,' explained the pious old woman, keeping her distance, 'we can't get the money to buy flowers . . .'

If Rheims was the pride of France, why should it have been granted to me on that morning – just to me, a mere travel agency employee – to provide for the dignity of worship in her cathedral, the most famous cathedral in the world? Certainly not as a result of chance. The Seer is always on the right track. No, it was so that at some future date I should be able to be tolerant towards other men – men of that very same country – when, without even wanting to get to know me, they refused to enter the room where I had paused for a while in a state of total exhaustion. And so that I should then be able to go to sleep with no bitter thoughts.

I stayed in my room when the airman's young wife arrived, but far away as I was I heard her cries: 'Dino, my Dino!' They must have been trying to hold her back so that she would not touch that shattered body. 'How many others must weep,' I asked myself almost angrily, 'because people have paid with their lives even before they have loved?' Shaken and stricken by those cries, I felt that the whole war should serve only to atone for Nerina's death so many years ago, for the perversion of Licudi, for the rough red hands of Arrichetta who had become a scullery-maid in Milan. Then I felt ashamed and would almost have liked to take the dead airman's place if only that girl would stop crying.

I have spent the whole day on tours of inspection and got home late to find Bay silent again. The little church was closed as I came up. And as soon as I entered the hotel's communal room everyone stopped talking; but this time I sat down, with the result that the others got up one by one and made off. I was left alone with Denise Digne.

To my amazement she said something. 'Surely in the course of the war,' she said, 'you must have seen others . . .'

I noted her emphasis. By 'others' she implied only those who had fallen on her side and at our hands.

'Yes,' I answered, 'but I didn't hear the weeping.'

Why did she not weep now? Openly, without hiding her face? Perhaps I have not said that I feel pity even for Denise. Was she so frozen in her grief for her own dead man that she had no thought to spare for that other man smashed up at the age of twenty? Does she want to reserve all compassion for herself? How did such hatred come into the world – a hatred that refuses to recognise even someone who is absolutely equal to ourselves?

Now the days are slipping by, for I shall be leaving here shortly. For some time my left eye has been giving me trouble, the one that only just escaped the stone. There has been a burning sensation ever since that night on the mountain. The military doctor has been up to examine me and has ordered that I should return to Italy for a while . . .

Going down towards the valley I saw the little hotel high up above getting smaller and smaller and then fading away among the brown and white streaks of trees and snow. But I shall remember it as an agreeable place. In my imagination I have played bowls on its small rectangle of beaten earth, played bowls with a charming family that came up on a Sunday trip. One of the girls (or so I fancied) was called Nicole. And she gave me a mischievous smile when she left.

*

To tell this part of my story I have used a fragment of a diary that I kept at that time, a habit I had started in my youth. The flames of war were spreading over everyone now, just as the unknown sea of life used to flood in over the young boarders at my school. Things were assuming such gigantic proportions that the only safeguard against them was the quiet work of the individual mind within its own chapel, somehow filtering into its own small world the complexities of the great world. Most of that diary was lost as a result of subsequent events, but the fragments that remain bear witness to thoughts and feelings I would otherwise be incapable of recapturing. Both logic and theory have established that our past is irrecoverable. But my mind grieved for reasons other than these buried ones.

Standing in front of my makeshift easel – a board propped up against the back of a chair – I looked out from the long window of my Uncle Gedeone's house (where I had gone for my convalescence) and watched the evening dissolve in a haze of light over the Riviera di Chiaia, beyond the tall hotels of the Villa. Painting was all very well; but where did one start? How did one circumscribe those throbbing depths within the space of a piece of paper and on only one plane? How include the Lerici palace in that filmy trail of houses, given that it too must only be a tone of colour? Certainly that low glint of the sea against the light, and the rapidity with which it changes and darkens, do not exactly lend themselves to prolonged contemplation or searching meditation. But it's the intention that counts. And a man who has made so many attempts to shape his life, and has found himself each time left with something stunted or incomplete, will be able – by questioning every line of a stretch of landscape – to draw close to the discipline that will encourage him to try again.

'Don't strain that eye,' advised my uncle.

At first, and after such a long lapse of time since those ears and noses done with charcoal at school, my unpractised hand floundered in the void. In seeking the initial line on to which to hinge all the rest, my unruly pencil traced on the white sheet of paper not what I saw externally but a tentative inner vision, one that brought the line back on itself, crossing it with strange arabesques from which hung drops, festoons, lanterns, sinuosities of all kinds: a strange harlequinade of shapes springing out from its own self: arrows, plaster mouldings of roses adorned with pistils or little wings – all exploding round a composition which, though at first out of perspective, seemed finally to converge on an invisible point in space round which balance was finally achieved.

'Marinetti isn't in it!' was my uncle's comment. He had regarded Futurism as a mere joke and was incapable of even conceiving what had subsequently taken place in the figurative arts.

Yes, painting! Even before song, even before the spoken word, the drawing on the wall with flint was surely man's first means of self-expression. Nature had already endowed each animal with its own mark, so the cave-man traced his sign on the walls of his cave, the product of some dim aspiration that already harboured his creative urge. It was from that moment of absorption, dedicated to the sketching of that shape, that man's duality had sprung and art was born.

My uncle did not contradict my theories. He was too sensitive to look on these interests of mine as anachronistic, though as soon as a gust of wind arose his nostrils caught the faint odour of the dust-cloud hanging motionless over the bombed-out quarters of Naples – almost half of the city. But it was perhaps better to pretend to forget the war rather than live it in terms of vengeance and remorse; like an insect that seeks protection under a leaf in a storm and takes no notice of anything else.

I had left Naples tumultuous and excited under the June sun, and I had hardly recognised it on arriving at nightfall at the station square nine months later. There had been talk of a ship loaded with munitions that had exploded in the bay in the San Giovanni area; but even worse was a blast that had flattened more than a mile of the Rettifilo and hollowed out all the surrounding hills. The huge thrust had gone right up the Corso and towards the centre, ripping thousands of fixtures from the façades of those two hundred five-storey buildings; and the fixtures, held up by the framework of the balconies, had stayed dangling over the void like faces without limbs; sinister witnesses to a tragedy that had already been played out. An indefinable smell permeated that yellowish gloom and an acrid dust-cloud hung motionless like a chunk of impenetrable air.

As I walked towards the distant Riviera di Chiaia along the almost unnegotiable road, I could not help thinking of my father Gian Luigi as he was fifty years ago – the passionate young man who used to walk along this very road every day so as to save his tram-fare and build a city that others were to enjoy and yet others destroy; while he dreamed of the young Annina, my mother. (It was so long since I had seen my mother and my brother Ferrante and Checchina! They were safe in a country villa between Sulmona and Aquila in the Abruzzi. Only the common people had remained in Naples to be pounded by the war, the people who had never believed even half the ideas of the Fascist regime, and whose small portion of well-being ever since 1860 had perhaps only come to them from foreigners!)

Here was the piazza Nicola Amore. And only a mayor bearing that name of Love could have ridden the tempest of Naples between the filth of the poor quarters and the dreaded spectre of cholera. Yet from that mezzanine floor over there, I had heard the crowd in a frenzy of excitement watching the young Belgian princess passing by – the new bride of Umberto of Savoy. It was a national holiday and the window where I was standing belonged to a representative of a cloth firm. Ten or twelve tired and badly-dressed employees were crammed round it in a circle, so that I could see nothing. But I heard the thunder of applause swelling and then fading. At one point all those poor people shouted in one voice as if to split their throats – especially the poorest of all: 'Maria José! Maria José!' Should the stupidities of the well-to-do rebound on such poverty as this, capable as it is of such an ecstasy of imagination?

My uncle and I exchanged very few words that evening. He drew me to the light of the long window to examine my wound, and for the first time I saw a dark flame flashing in his mild eyes.

'When you think of all that goes to make and produce a man!' he said. 'Nights of suffering because the baby has coughed, is feverish, has come out in spots, or anything else. Years to send him to school, negotiate with his masters, supervise his lessons, preach at him, take him a hundred times to be examined: his eyes, his stomach, his glands, his tonsils. Then with a hail of scrap-iron without anyone knowing who is firing or at whom, the work of half a life is ruined for the next half – that is, if all goes well.' He stopped to take a better look at me. 'With time it won't show so much,' he went on. 'Good God, they might have killed you!'

Might they? No, I think not; at least, not yet; not if the Seer had correctly intuited what I myself already knew: that the flow of my life would not come to an end until I had discovered its meaning. And this was why, in those tired days that passed idly by, after disturbed nights when enemy planes loomed from the darkness and explosions blindly tore at the womb of the city – this was why, as I stood before the new canvas propped against the back of the chair, I tried to find some basic line in the vast landscape, some point that would then carry the whole thing after it.

Tucked away in our graceful churches, defenceless against this insane persecution, the dark canvases by such painters as Stanzione, Cavallino or Preti were surely intimations of life, hints, guide-lines. . . . In the orchestration of their composition I saw research and wisdom together with marvellous results and solutions! Each mass, or plane, or shape, and the tones, and the various shades of light were interlinked with all the others down to the tiniest detail. They were the fugues and accompaniments of innumerable fanciful perspectives: each one resting in its own harmonious place, yet reaching out towards imaginary spaces. Though drawn from truth, this fantastic vision was capable of creating a different and even more extraordinary truth – one that came to rest in a sweet modulation of colour and a motionless lake of light, presented with a serene certainty dazzling to the mind. Was it not perhaps in this way that we ought to understand and shape our lives?

I noticed the noise coming from the anxious and tormented city – like a wave that breaks on the shore then draws back and spreads out, seeking its new form; then breaks again, and so on *da capo*, following the invincible rule forced upon it in perpetuity; yet ever-changing. And beyond stretched the whole country with its undulating coastline, exposed now, like bared breasts, together with the fabulous heritage of its way of life and its monuments – but putting a brave face on the assault and chaos. It was this smiling spirit that had inspired so many great paintings, measured the beat of so many poems, erected so many miracles of architecture, and it was this spirit that would in time restore rules and measure. But a spark of that spirit could meanwhile measure things within myself; putting them in place, separating this from that, making distinctions – in the linear clarity of judgement managing to redeem disintegrated and sorrowful material.

Gradually, I regained my serenity. Mentone and Bay had both helped me in their different ways. I would never have thought along these lines at first, when, after my uncle's telegram, I had stayed with him for about a week before leaving for the French front – in that little sun-drenched villa of his where he spent the summer. He had seemed rather distracted at that time. The huge calamity engulfing his people was too much for him; his modest life based on the canons of goodness and dedication was being turned upside-down; and his resignation, as a believer, to the unknowable Will, did not spare the suffering of his human heart. My neglect of him during those years and then his realising – as a result of my silence – that Licudi was lost to me and that that sacrifice had been in vain, meant that I had added to his other sorrows; but he felt he could not reproach me now that our lives, like everyone else's, were lying heavy on our hands, darkened and stripped of all meaning.

Now and again he would refer to the war, but I think only to test me; and his traditional ideals, which had also been those of many of our ancestors, suffered humiliation at the silence that immediately crept between us. He knew that in one way or another I would become involved in the war; but he did not like to think that I would involve myself for the danger rather than for the glory; not so as to bring about the triumph of an idea but so as to annihilate my thoughts and submerge myself in union with them.

It was my uncle's very affection and uneasiness on my behalf that made him so excessively agitated. But my confession would perhaps have upset him still more; because when I had heard those irretrievable words bawled over the radio in that little station at Celle, and when I realised that they put an end not only to my time at Licudi, but swept away everyone's time in one huge hurricane, something resembling a cruel joy had slid into my heart. Many many years before, when Nerina had died, I had found refuge in renunciation and uncertainty – the very opposite, in fact, of the affliction and fear which it had seemed to the others. I knew that almost nothing remained of the tension by which the First World War had been sustained; and that this time the army would not be only disunited but reluctant, embarking in its turn on dark currents that could only lead to danger and pain. Nevertheless, as I had fallen from my Paradise, I felt these two to be necessary to me.

The ambiguous atmosphere that was to surround the whole of our intervention freed me from even my last scruples – not so as to exempt myself, which I would not have done, but for reasons I would have carried within me even when wearing my uniform again. It was no longer a question of a few poor Licudi fishermen being indifferent to the Abyssinian enterprise; this time it was the vast majority of the Italians who felt the war to be extraneous to their genuine feelings and impulses; they did not want it; they had not even believed that it would happen. Their shouts in the piazza had been theatrical lapses, flashes in the pan, decorative formalities for downing tools in the lunch hour; and the country, tormented by doubt and chastened within this ambiguity, resigned itself with difficulty to living the most open lie of its history.

As for me, I had been estranged for so long from a society I could not feel to be mine that just as I had not shared its enthusiasm – whether true or false – so now I did not share its arguments and fears. I did not see the war as a fact involving this people or that, but as a crisis investing as protagonist simply and solely mankind; and, with mankind, myself. If my first challenge had taken place in the tiny world of my school, and later of my family; then in the Milan pensione, at the Palazzo Grilli and in the regiment, and recently in Licudi where a whole village was involved, this time the context was excessive, and I had to prove myself in a river swollen to overflowing. But just as I had never feared living, I knew now that I had no fear of dying. If there were danger, then I was ready, the more so because I was alone; and the unexpected reversal of situations and values and of what has so often been a very heavy burden, was now my best protection. For years everyone's life had gone on calmly and serenely in its customary comforts, but now it was struck at its very foundations. Huge sacrifices and huge sorrows were indiscriminately awaiting those who possessed the most, those who were bound by the deepest affections: the underground revenge of the unattached who, if even against their will, had stored up their strength for a greater ordeal. These were stern and somewhat ruthless thoughts, and I did not impart a word of them to my uncle for fear of hurting him. But my mind was confused: I believed that I had wrongfully tried to make an Eden on this earth and for that reason had lost it; I believed I was old and weighed down by the sorrows of many years; and I had only presented myself so as to have a look.

When I got back from the District Command with orders to join the Cosseria Command within twenty-four hours, my uncle looked down and said nothing; then gently made a sign with his head as if consenting to a grief but also to a duty and accepting both. With his characteristic industry and forbearance he helped me with my preparations. But at a certain moment, and as if lightly telling an anecdote:

'There's a cripple in one of the little streets behind here,' he said, 'a cobbler. Yesterday I heard him laughing and singing for the first time. I asked him why. "It's the sound people who are going off to the war this time," he said. "When my turn comes, I'm stopping here." '

He did not take his eyes off me. If he had read my thoughts he was telling me that they were unjust; that I would not affirm my valour merely because others were weak. After the Mentone episode which passed like the wind, that is to say during the boredom at Bay and then two stupid months wasted in infirmaries and hospitals, I had written little to my uncle. But when I saw him again, though only two or three seasons had passed, he seemed to me much changed. Thinner, and hence taller. As he sat with his absorbed look and his now quite-white hair, he reminded me of

Gian Michele and perhaps of my father too. Without wanting to admit it to myself, I found him rather frightening. Once again, and even in those terrible days, his Christian stoicism did not desert him. I went down to Paola and asked the old solicitor, who had handed Gian Michele's estate over to me, to administer it for me for the duration of the war. When I got home my uncle was out. My ill-starred sister Cristina, who had been in a state of mental breakdown for sixteen years, was on her deathbed. He had deliberately gone off alone, wanting to spare me those dreadful hours. 'If we'd had to suffer together,' he had written in a note, 'we'd have suffered more.'

Alone for the first time in my Uncle Gedeone's house (as I had been in the past in Uncle Gian Michele's), I was uneasily aware of a ghost that seemed to weigh on me more heavily than the man himself; for in the style of each object, and its placing (however subtle this was), and in the habits and niceties of taste to which each bore witness, I found all the virtues whole and intact that lay beneath his kindly air and gentle reticence; his loyalty, his respect, his constancy. Indeed, even at this moment he was fulfilling his heroic duties. Where were all the others? Why, from all the branches of the family tree, was it always he who was called upon? – always he who was ready to get up and go?

Oh, Cristina, who will ever again give me such anxiety as you gave me when you went away, or such joy as when I found you in that smart little tea-room, wearing your prettiest clothes, your small jewels neatly stowed in your bag?

Yes, the magic of painting! That slow rethinking in which memory flows without jolts, as smooth as the oil on the brush, stripped of everything that has tainted it with bitterness and dross, made bright and clean even where things were dark and hostile before. And the whole blended and harmonised like the colours on the canvas: half-tones, fleeting fusions from which yet further images and thoughts (whether very old or new) spring forth from all the depths. Yes, memory! But not as it is shown in Joyce's chaotic deformations; nor yet as presented by the debilitated and debilitating Proust, a series of flashes, now frequent and vivid, now slow and blurred, within an endless night. And still less Freud's kind of memory, heavily marked with his race, a doughy mess of sex. But memory as explored by the Saint. The memory by which Saint Augustine came to know God.

My uncle returned well after nightfall, and in the darkness of the balcony gave me the simple yet bitter details of Cristina's end.

'But it wasn't the day before yesterday that she died,' he said. 'She died many years ago. She didn't notice anything. There was nothing left of her.'

After I had finally given up my impression of the Riviera di Chiaia landscape, a complicated network of forms came to life on my new canvas, shaping itself by spontaneous germination. On a crystalline background fringed with white like a fresh September sea, there sailed two erect and fantastic apparitions: sailing ships or gigantic swans, as white as mountain peaks. On one side there appeared a veiled face going downwards and enveloped in a sort of fire; and this in its turn became concretised in a massive dark object, almost like a boulder which at the same time suggested the form of a heart. On the other side there was a wing with a mighty bunch of feathers over muscles as strong as limbs. The whole blended within a tone of hard enamel: the perfection and flawlessness of crystal or marble.

When my leave was over I left this masterpiece with my uncle who examined it through half-closed eyes, moving his head and his hand this way and that as if he wanted to follow its movements.

'The strip of blue,' I suggested to myself, 'is the sea at Licudi. That veiled face up there is Nerina. The sightless chimeras are Cristina who has passed all unseeing into the beyond. And that cold grey surrounding the base of the wing is for Denise Digne. And that fine touch of scarlet is for Catherine: today I have finally forgiven her just as France and Paris must forgive us and me.'

'What'll you do now, Uncle, alone in Naples?'

'I was alone at first, when no one needed me. Now I have people to look after, as many as I want, so they will keep me company. With these air-raids, we have to evacuate the homes and hospitals and hostels run by charitable organisations. Do you know how many there are? A hundred and six. The Prefecture has made me responsible for this.'

By now our last evening together was drawing in over the Riviera di Chiaia. The already-pale shadows had quietly disappeared as if absorbed into the earth. Soon it would be night; but the mighty landscape would not sleep; it would await the howling of the sirens heralding the air-raid. The homely lamps would suddenly be extinguished. My uncle would light his candle. He had not ended that day's work. He would not go down to the shelter.

That bridge over the Crostolo! A majestic edifice made entirely from river flint like a fort in the days of the Gauls, with huge pillars shaped like castle-keeps or keels, and bizarrely adorned with cast-iron balustrades of an exorbitant weight and posts made in a single piece with initials and crests. And needless to say it was not done by public, but private, enterprise and merely provided access to a vast villa – the property, so it seemed, of a single eccentric individual. What that bridge was doing in that desolate place where the Crostolo loses its shape and sprawls between a wilderness of crumbling banks and impassable bramblewoods, and what we were doing there, only God and Major Nappa (my new commanding officer) knew. The lancers, trained for quite different type of work, endured with humiliation the imposition of this incomprehensible service (as those others had done at Bay); but they too must have understood that the war, though in the early enthusiastic days proclaimed as being short and victorious, was in fact only just beginning. I myself had had no more than a glimpse of its endless and murky theatre, like a peeping-Tom at a chink in a wall; and this new pause could neither displease nor deceive me. Others, meanwhile, were playing their parts, and owing to the distance we carelessly followed their mime though their voices never really reached us. But the stage would soon open up for us all.

I liked Reggio Emilia very much, judging by the short period I was able to stay there at first, and then the times I had to go there to report to the Command. Today it is almost impossible to rediscover the texture of our lesser cities before they were turned upside-down by the whirlwind of urbanisation, the consumer-goods civilisation, and the grotesque proliferation of the motor car. A strong and independent race, the people of Reggio are by nature frank but cautious. There were so many gratings in the city, gardens closed by high walls, and an infinitude of silent courtyards behind barred gates. The architecture was modest for the most part, with plain shutters flush with the walls, simple roofs, belvederes, dormer windows. However, the shades of colour, quickly weathered to perfection by wind and rain, provided delightful backgrounds and romantic flights interspersed with little porticoes or trees. The last mists of March increased the unobtrusive sweetness of the place. At certain hours of the evening when the weather was fine, the brick churches of Reggio took on the colour of flesh: they came alive.

'Not suited for foreign service.' It was with this viaticum that I resumed my posting in the homeland. The oculist-captain had urgently prescribed that I should avoid damp, sun and dust. He evidently believed that such things existed only beyond the frontier, and that our national territory was immune from them. Reggio Emilia? A city as comfortable as any other, so they assured me in a fatherly way. But the group of dismounted cavalry which, on the map, was stationed there, in fact only maintained its Command there; the rest were dispersed on the usual sentry service as far as the Cerreto Pass on the heights of the Apeninnes. Almost immediately I found myself surrounded by snow again, under Mount Valestra. A couple of weeks later I was at Albinea in connection with that already-mentioned bridge over the Crostolo in the foggiest, muddiest, least sheltered place in the whole valley, rich in such places though this network of rivers is. 'A bad throw of the dice,' I said to myself.

In those months the war was fluctuating uncertainly but virulently, like a disease spreading through th- deepest and most hidden of ramifications. The Germans were holding down half Europe, but the destruction of the Alpine Julia division in the Greek mountains, grievous naval losses and an element of insecurity and ambiguity in our military and political conduct, and, above all, the nation's silence and those closed faces down to the poorest man in the street – all this said only too much. Yet, so unlike Naples, the country from Modena to Piacenza still seemed to be calm. Germans were seen very little and they kept themselves to themselves. Food rationing was more formal than real. My new commander and his underling – a priest-like type very old for the rank of Second Lieutenant – both lived in the age-old Albergo della Posta in the centre of the city and kept a good table at the Cannon d'Oro – where they only came under the fire of highly spiced sausages, chicken soup with the best possible parmesan cheese, and all served under the patronage of Lambrusco wine. For form's sake it sufficed for the cutlet to be hidden under the spinach and, halfway through lunch, for them to stand to attention with an aggrieved look while the radio poured out a bulletin so watered-down as to make one reel.

Age apart, this Major Nappa was an officer of the Reserve like ourselves; but it was said that he owed his rank to service done the cavalry squadron of Nitti's Royal Guard in 1921. He was a small *rentier* from Caserta, the kind who possesses a strip of land for growing hemp and an agency for agricultural machinery or fertilisers. He knew nothing about drilling, book-keeping or arms; but his stupidity could become dangerous because it went with an irritable and distrustful character. In that first week, because he was unable to read maps, he had sent my detachment from Carpineti to a place he judged to be three kilometres away. But that was as the crow flies, because in fact the men had a seven-hour march so as to get round a tall cliff that reared up in mid-course. At dawn next day the major ordered them to return at once, hoping thus to make good his mistake. Owing to my opposition to this order he conceived an aversion to me from the start, and my posting to the Crostolo bridge was the immediate outcome of it.

It is only a few kilometres from Albinea to Reggio and they can be quickly covered even by bicycle. Disguised in civilian clothes against the regulations, I went to Reggio as often as I could. Not that I knew anyone there, but I felt the same secret life vibrating behind those great walls as I had found in Ferrara. I discovered certain accents, certain faces, familiar in that earlier world of the De Michelis and Mavì; and for reasons difficult to explain, it delighted me to brush up against those secrets – which I had violated once but were now closed to me.

Accustomed as I was to large cities, in Reggio I had the feeling of being in a house, but a huge and fantastic one – a Renaissance residence, say, where everything belonged to one lord and master against whom some conspiracy was always afoot. Those big archways giving on to the central square, and the way this square led into that other smaller one, secret and austere and dedicated to San Prospero, suggested forums or theatres where the stage is set for different events; and those Emilian arcades like military communication trenches, and those churches square like citadels . . . But it was kind of the churches to keep their doors open, so that the street reached right up to the altar and the altar right down to the street.

Partly with a view to avoiding undesirable encounters, I would go in the evenings and dine in little working-class taverns, elbow to elbow with people of every kind. They were always courteous to me yet always kept to themselves; an amiability towards the foreigner that in fact serves to set him apart and hold him at a distance in some indefinable way, precisely through singling him out for polite attentions. Most of these people were workers and all were avowed socialists – despite the efforts of the Duce and Balbo (whose Fascist squads had failed to force the 'Perma Voladora' torrent in Parma, a little to the north, in 1921). Perhaps these people sensed in me the officer, the foreigner, the master, and that was why they kept to themselves.

The majestic medieval aspect of the city's bonework, which becomes poorer and peters out in the jerry-building at the tail end, showed how wrong the Fascist regime was in wanting always to rebuild in the style of the ancient Romans, and skipping the Communes (the real roots of our times), the Renaissance and all the rest. It might just be possible to imagine the solid full-blooded people of Reggio with Roman swords and tunics – perhaps because of the Roman via Emilia; but in reality they come from the age in between, from the six lines of castles rising around the Po at Bismantova. Their mythical heroine was Matilde of Canossa; their biggest hate was for tyrants who had lasted seven hundred years. And like those tyrants, and with them, Fascism was obliged to pull in the reins with the same ends in view. At the time of the Ethiopian enterprise I had grasped the extent of the opposition of the 'deep South' to the Duce and the other Fascist leaders; I had seen it in Uncle Gedeone's silent but implacable protest, and there lay the voice of Naples. Here, in Piazza Grande, there were a few sacks of earth to protect the cathedral statues; a sort of trench beneath the San Prospero tower to catch the pieces that might fall; otherwise, to all appearances, nothing; except those reminders and reproaches. For the hour of reckoning was not to come until later.

So we all waited . . . my only occupation being the inspection of my guard posts – of which the most outstanding was the one on the Crostolo bridge. And on Major Nappa's orders I gave uplifting little talks to the lancers to keep up their morale, and meanwhile did my best with my paints. For which diversion I was reproved by the Major: 'In the middle of war . . . to pursue such schoolboy occupations!' But Major Nappa had nothing to say about the long hours his subalterns spent in certain houses on via Cavour and via Cravezzerie. Perhaps he didn't like me keeping to myself.

'Look, Sansevero,' he said, addressing me in the second person singular and thus showing off an ancient habit of our regiment to which, incidentally, he did not belong, 'Look, we've got difficulties in the administration of the group and in the collective expenses to which you, like the commanders of the other squadrons, ought to be contributing with your funds made on the "black".'

He had already sounded me on the matter before. The 'black' fund was made up of those sums earned by every commander by irregular if tolerated methods, and were then used for indispensable disbursements, in their turn not recognised by the administration. It could seem strange, for instance, that the shoes issued by our stores were always in natural-coloured leather, whereas according to regulations they should be black. Whenever a recruit arrived he had to be forbidden to go out in pale shoes though there was no way of providing him with dye: result, no exit permit. So after three or four days most of them got busy solving the problem in their own way: soot, black polish, even ink – which produced deplorable gradations of purple and red. These and many similar amenities were acquired by selling or exchanging surplus foodstuffs, or by promissory notes on long-term understanding with quartermasters, master-shoemakers, saddlers and so on. In the golden age when colonels were of the type of that good soul Count Dati, no officer would have dreamed of taking advantage of the black market for his own benefit. But from indiscretions on the part of the orderlies I knew that at Group Command things were done differently; and that Nappa had received from a sympathetic colleague of the same rank, attached to the accounts department, a friendly tip-off that there was to be an inspection of the books. This was why he was trying to get in money and recalling me to the solidarity I had neglected.

'In my squadron,' I replied, 'the fund isn't administered by me but from the orderly-room direct. Everyone knows what there is and what it's used for down to the smallest detail. How can it be transferred?'

Nappa seemed annoyed. 'I don't see,' he said, 'why you have to inform the lancers about what is a commander's duty. It's against the regulations.'

He had been scrutinising a map when I went in, but he quickly whisked it away because he found it painful to remember that time when he had made the men march for seven hours owing to misreading it. I felt that my antipathy to him, coupled with his initial ill-humour, was again shaking the dice-cup. But how could I be reconciled with him? There was yet another aspect of the situation, that of bringing together and mixing very diverse kinds of men, so as to make them live and perhaps die together, without their having a single thought or affection in common. That very large section of current opinion which had first applauded and then profited by Fascism was now shown up as disunited, cowardly, and untrustworthy. It was always this section that held the reins of command, and used them to evade its own responsibilities while at the same time procuring further privileges and profits. The call-up was governed by a system, as it were, of 'draft sections' – that is to say, not according to age but to the heterogeneous needs of the armed formations in the water-tight compartments of the administrative areas; and this favoured endless abuses, substitutions and evasions. But at that precise moment the system was operating in the opposite direction. Once a man like Nappa, who was a real non-entity in civil life, was assured of a lucrative and risk-free assignment, the call-up brought him respect, means, and power. From nagging quarrels with his wife about who had had the last word, he rose to the intoxication of command and to the possibility of absolute power over many lives.

The same thing happened with the rest of his officers. War, like all upheavals, throws up what lies underneath, and buries what is on the surface. The selection board in the cavalry courses in which I had participated in my days in Rome and then in Ferrara was extremely severe. Out of nine hundred applicants who each year aspired to rank, only about thirty were accepted. Thus in fifteen years the courses had selected five hundred officers. Subsequent regulations readmitted an indiscriminate number of those excluded and they constituted the regimental lists of the corps at home. In Nappa's entire group, hardly anyone had attained regular promotion; a further motive for keeping me on the Crostolo bridge.

So my so-called comrades in Reggio and, I suppose, in all the rest of the peninsula, endured military service as one endures flies in summer, and the countless Nappas who afflicted them as logical counterpart of the situation enjoyed things to the maximum: they had the soldiers serve them as though they were patricians while they were always deep in debauchery or sleep. A spectacle all the more depressing for the troops in that they, for their part, had sacrificed a lot and had not the faintest idea of the super-strategy of the Rome-Berlin axis. So what could the lancers think, lying in their tents in the deep mists of the river, and born, like the people of Licudi, in some village bounded by its own Calitri? Their only real enemy (like mine) was the inflamed Nappa who was drunk with the undreamed-of possibilities of being able to command nearly a thousand men, and having the right to be swiftly obeyed by them. Intoxicated at being taken a drive in a truck among everyone's smart salutes, Nappa enjoyed now and again playing 'the martinet' and holding those poor devils at attention for half an hour at a time.

I was pondering over these things towards the end of May while swarms of new-hatched mosquitoes were buzzing over the green puddles scattered on the gravel. Other news echoed on the quiet from the Olympus at Reggio. It was certain that the major had decided to entrust my squadron to one of the officers loyal to him (they were said to serve him as pimps) and had in mind the twofold intention of getting his hands on that 'black' fund and of undoing me; but he was frustrated by that 'unsuitability for extra-territorial service'. A couple of requests – one for assignment to a camel-transported squadron in Africa, the other for a liaison officer in the Genoa cavalry taking part in the expedition to the Russian front (where did the dice intend to fall?) – had passed within range and he was unable to profit by them. Indeed once, having missed his blow against me, he had risked losing one of his most cherished underlings. But he, too, like nearly all the others, turned out to be 'unavailable' outside the country. This was not the same as 'unsuited'; but it formed part of the interminable casuistry which put nearly everyone under a different rule and a different obligation. And now the phonogram summoning me to the Command at eight o'clock was the prelude to some other trap. But what?

As I free-wheeled down from the smiling hills of Albinea, radiant in the Sunday light, I was thinking about Uncle Gedeone. He had not needed call-up papers, a uniform and still less any pay to stay in his city and do the work of a General as well as his own cooking and housework, whereas Nappa had assigned himself three batmen. The bombardment of Naples was getting worse, as reply to our vain hammering of Malta. My uncle wrote that the requisitioning of iron gateways for armaments had caused incredible damage to very little constructive effect. Disembowelled by attack from the sky, ungated and unguarded, with insufficient and inadequate air-raid shelters, with surpluses and shortages, Naples had heavy crosses to bear. Whereas here, where I was, such thoughts were overlaid, blurred, put out of focus by the sight of two-wheeled carts coming down to market; by bold women on bicycles generously displaying their legs for the joy of eyes and thoughts; and finally by the low line of the Reggio landscape suddenly coming into view, with its houses and little suburbs and steeples spread merrily out, and so rosy and young-looking – even after so many years – that the war seemed like a fairy-tale; and Nappa, and all the others, non-existent.

'The major isn't in,' the adjutant informed me in his priest-type way. 'But in view of the fact that he's twice reported you to Area Command as not indispensable to the group, they've now given orders to second you to the local Propaganda Service. Here's the order paper: a real stroke of luck!'

And indeed, once I had handed over the squadron (and the 'black' fund) to the lieutenant who came to replace me (a thoroughly debauched man who immediately started looking around), I found myself transferred from the little inn at Albinea to within the comfortable walls of Reggio itself, and for a much lighter service. This time the markings on the dice were in my favour.

Propaganda: that 'sale of words instead of things', the monstrous development of which Balzac had foreseen a century before! In our time its law-maker and prophet was Goebbels, a character darker than any Shakespearean Iago, a sort of malevolent spirit, Hitler's other half, to whom Hitler had entrusted the forked tongue of the serpent while reserving to himself the deliberate cruelty of one of La Fontaine's carnivores, but in a professor's clothing. After the dress-rehearsal of the Berlin Olympic Games and the colossal Nazi parades, Goebbels had invaded half the world with his diabolical creed. Though the Allies did their best, they were a far cry indeed from the satanic inventions of this resuscitated Dantean 'fraud'. It was incredible – what he managed to make people believe, and not only in Germany; above all, what he managed to conceal. Events involving millions of men and extinguishing millions of lives slipped by almost unnoticed, and many never really came to light even later. Following in the footsteps of this example, and in chameleon-like imitation of such a powerful ally, the Fascist regime gesticulated as best it could; but it was uphill work, given the ill-will of the Italians; and the avalanche of satirical stories that circulated at that time, even if they were the unwarlike reaction of a country that did not know how to offer opposition by deeds, coupled with the passivity and ill-will of a vast number of individuals, provided excellent ballast to the high kicks of the famous 'Roman goose-step'. It was in this climate that I was called upon to expend those gifts of oratory I was said to possess (heaven knows why) in favour of the war and in stimulating the frozen spirits of some of those whose duty it was to wage it.

The General in command of the military area was a regular officer but on the administrative side, and he received me in his requisitioned villa – with small cement columns and floral stuccos. He indicated certain themes I should develop in addressing the troops, the first of which had as title 'The Justice of our War'. He told me that I would be able to work on them under the direct supervision of the commanding officer of the Propaganda Office. Should there be serious grounds, he authorised me to come and report to him.

Leaning against the marble lions of Verona that keep guard over San Prospero, I turned over in my mind the subjects the General had proposed – interspersed, I may say, with not a few contrapuntal notes of irony. It had not entered that good man's head that when a country resolves to go to war it no longer asks itself if it is right to do so; just as when one is at a dance it is better not to cast doubt on the expediency of the merry-making. And supposing I failed to convince someone – had he therefore the right to take off his knapsack and go back home? Those were the days when Aimone of Aosta was nominated King of Croatia, no less. Showing the rightness of such an investiture was no joke.

From the deep shadow of the main nave, I was looking at the colours of the little market in the smaller piazza, chock-full of fruit and vegetables under the bright summer sun, and the people going about their harmless pursuits. That square, dedicated to the good saint of Aquitaine, protector of Reggio, itself seemed like the fresh clean heart of a lettuce or a cabbage; something healthy and fragrant in the plexus of the town: to be looked at, smelt, lived. Who could have elaborated the themes provided by the General out here? Who could have summarised the reasons why there was sadness on the kindly faces of these people who till now had been happy with their vines and their way of life? And who was going to disseminate so much evil in that mild provincial water-colour as to produce first a drop and then a torrent of blood?

So it was under such auspices – while General Geloso's army was installing itself in Athens which had really been conquered by the Germans in that headlong march on the Vardar; and while Ethiopia was returning to the velvet paw of the Lion of Judah – that I prepared myself to play my third hand in a game that was to produce so many others. But this time, who was it against?

The Propaganda Office of the area (or the P. Office, as it was called) was at that time in charge of a certain Captain Toia, a man from Bergamo, who lost no time in letting me know that he had been called up by mistake and from one moment to the next was expecting the phonogram order that would restore him to freedom. For Toia was, in fact, a functionary of the Department of Finance, and out of due respect for the higher bureaucracy was exempt from the call-up. Perhaps there had been manœuvres against him on the part of his colleagues, in that network of intrigues on which careers thrive; but Toia's counter-attack was now in full swing and its result was certain. The captain was a big man with a barbarian's loud voice and shining eyes – an exemplar of what in common parlance is described as 'coarse blooded'. But he had no idea he was one of those figures that people make fun of when having a jolly evening together, for his self-assurance was the outcome of his rapid advancement. Already in the fifth grade of the civil service, though still in the springtime of life, he was about to be promoted to the fourth: which, in military life, corresponded in rank to a Divisional Commander. Hence, as a mere officer, Toia had reverted to the tenth grade, so it followed that he was supremely uninterested in the Services and passed his time in his comfortable billet in via Ariosto – with a lovely view over the churches of Cristo and San Giorgio – consuming a notable quantity of the famous local cheese washed down by the best Trebbiano wine.

With those bottles around him he was always telling me stories about his splendid position in Rome, and about the Department of Finance, one of the three omnipotent departments of the Administration, the other two being the Exchequer and the Council of State. Hitler, Mussolini, the war, Italy's feared disasters – all seemed of scant interest to him, irrelevant facts, compared with the continuity and stability of the Department of Finance; and his promotion to the fourth grade seemed to represent the only important and certain event in the years to come. Toia's hidden enemies – but he must have known them well – were putting up a certain resistance to his counter-offensive, perhaps so as to achieve some sought-after aim during his absence, or to combat things that he had planned or intended. So they managed to keep him in Reggio for a few months, and thus I had to enter into some measure of familiarity with him.

Luckily, the General made his voice heard too; and as the area was enormous and the detachments numerous I was out of town for a week at a time. I became accustomed to being received surlily by individual commanding officers, and had to study a type of attitude that would mollify them. I was dealing with officers of the Reserve, not unlike Nappa, and to many of them it did not seem right to rattle off endless tirades to troops obliged to listen against their will. Pretensions to oratory are a national characteristic with the average Italian, like vanity; and whoever manages to obtain any kind of audience tyrannises over it as much as he can. Many of the officers were petty Fascist officials who had attracted attention by following the great example of Ciano and Starace and, accustomed to the 'plenary meeting', felt cut to the quick.

'You,' they said to me with some ill-humour, 'you've been sent here to tell our soldiers what evidently we are not thought capable of telling them ourselves!'

And on the whole they were right, because in fact I had not devoted myself to the study and exercises of Demosthenes. However, after much reflection, I carefully set aside the subjects proposed by the General, and tried to find something convincing in all that moral morass. Our reverses in Africa and, towards the end of 1941, the threat of German reverses in Russia, allowed me to draw certain conclusions. If the Licudi fishermen had taught me about their way of conceiving the motherland and the magnetic force that always kept them turned towards home, Nappa and Toia had clarified the rest. So it seemed to me that to speak of 'crowning glories' or 'incontrovertible victories' was to put water instead of wood on the fire. Better confine ourselves within our human condition and the pains and obligations this involves us in. So, basing myself on Plato's *Laws*, I encouraged those poor devils to obey and, given that they had been sustained by the law in civilian society, have patience now that the law was against them. I explained that the policeman who now accompanied the deserter to the military court was the same man who had defended the boundaries of their fields; and if they had been called up because their names were on the register, this was because their names had been recorded there as citizens on the day of their birth, thus entitling them to civil rights, a lawful wife, recognised children. Truth to tell, the peasants from poor villages had never had much else; but my fifteen-minute talks seemed to be acceptable and did not appear to disturb even the commanding officers predisposed to be hostile. As for the General, he was a thousand miles from imagining what rather unorthodox conclusions were passing in the name of Socrates – who had talked in this way precisely while one of the many inexplicable crimes of history was being committed against him, as now against us. On the reports he received, the General congratulated Nappa on an 'outstandingly good man', thereby giving Nappa both pleasure and discomfort. Toia, on the other hand, laughed loudly, and made round jokes about me as he did about the General; and so openly as to make me suspect that he perhaps wanted to try me out.

My buried but deep aversion for Toia which I had observed from the start (much greater than for Nappa who was too miserable a creature to be considered for a moment on the moral plane) helped me to detect in his apparent sociability and ease of manner some sort of intention concerning me, and one which must have come into his mind when I first presented myself to him, as if at that moment he had found what he had long been looking for. Little by little my conviction about his dark purpose grew, and I felt it probing me, pressing on me, though I had no idea what it was. But when Toia sent for his wife to join him during his banishment in Reggio and introduced me to her, and for no good reason showered rather outspoken remarks on both of us, I began to get an inkling.

I had imagined the wife of that tedious individual would be one of those provincial women of little beauty or wealth who marry their husbands in the days of their obscurity and hence remain well below the career-grades subsequently attained. I found myself confronting a strikingly beautiful woman, still very young, and with manners so polite as to seem almost brittle. And when I noticed the exquisiteness of her dress revealing the minutest attention to detail, it was no surprise to learn that she was born in Parma, for that seems to have been the hallmark of the court of Maria Luisa as though in reaction to the glorious but murderous imperial display of Napoleon. At that first moment I was unable to get any further, but I felt that Toia's dark intention involved his wife, me, and above all himself.

As I needed a billet not far from the railway station – my daily starting-point – I had found one in the neighbourhood of the church of San Pietro, on the edge of a quarter of ill-repute but teeming with eager life. Reggio comes to a rather unexpected end in that direction with those aulic palaces in via Toschi and via Fontanelli; and having put up a final resistance with the majestic walled garden of the Levi Villa, it suffers sudden shipwreck in a maze of little streets and houses that are highly questionable where customs and hygiene are concerned but incomparably touching in other respects – such as the colours of those dead leaves, the yellows, the purples, the russets, all steeped in a sense of time and irremediable decay. I occupied a ground floor, very large and high, with the possibility of access on to a great walled garden full of age-old trees – ilexes, planes, cedars, and even eucalyptuses, as in our old home at Monte di Dio. There the long dark cry of the turtle-dove could always be heard, so unlike the graceful bird that emits it. I could almost imagine the reappearance of the tortoises of time gone by, after an absence of twenty years, and the very same ones at that.

For the sake of convenience, and without paying much attention to the other customers who were mostly from the locality, I sometimes made use of an old tavern opposite my billet in the via San Gerolamo. On the evening that I had been introduced to Signora Toia (Albertina, as her Christian name was), I arrived rather late at my tavern, so that it was almost empty, and the first person I saw on entering was the Seer of Bay, the dice-man, Demetrio, sitting next to a sleepy-eyed girl.

He showed no more surprise at seeing me on this occasion than he had shown on the last. He rose, shook hands, and having introduced the woman with the single word, 'Priscilla,' he said with his usual gravity and ease of manner:

'We're wandering around more or less like you, and today we've come from Gualtieri. By now, again more or less like you, we're militarised and dependent on the Propaganda Office. We're giving two shows here at the Rossini theatre. Will you join us for supper?'

But here the innkeeper intervened and said he had got to close. 'But if you'd be satisfied with a cold supper I'll leave it here and go on upstairs. Please shut the door behind you when you go. That's all. You don't need to lock it. There are no treasures here.'

I scrutinised the Seer more closely: he was very thin; dark eyes, ill-shaven, dirty threadbare clothes. Priscilla was a listless girl with vacant eyes and a spotty skin. She was weirdly dressed – something between Levantine costume and bits and pieces picked up at village markets. She was wearing a long necklace made of shells. Despite his gold ear-ring, Demetrio was not a gypsy. For a while he had been bandmaster in his native Verona; and God alone knows what a neurasthenic from that city can be like.

We said little during supper, Priscilla not even a syllable, as though she saw nothing and no one. That day they had given a show in a barracks on the Po: straightforward conjuring tricks. But now Demetrio was in deep meditation. Then, like an artist who is forced by circumstances to live a life alien to himself but at certain moments recognises that the time is at hand for genuine creation, he seemed to come to a decision. He looked up at me as if for a final reassurance and appraisal, then, without further ado, said:

'This time let's try an experiment in levitation. The disposition of the forces is favourable.'

Without adding a word, Priscilla stood up with her sleep-walking look, removed every single object from the table and carefully wiped its surface. She then removed the chairs around it and placed them against the wall. We were all standing, Priscilla and the Seer opposite each other, I on the third side of the table, which was square, solid, and very heavy.

Demetrio concentrated for a fairly long time, then almost unexpectedly, and as if he wanted to hold on to something, he rested his wide-open hands on the table in the attitude of a master pianist about to take possession of the keyboard. Priscilla did the same, synchronising her movements with his down to a split second, as if the impetus of Demetrio's brain were operating on her nerve centres too. They remained motionless, but the gradually-increased tension made their bodies tremble owing to the impossible effort to which they were being subjected. Priscilla's eyes opened and radiated a sort of light; the spots had disappeared from her highly coloured face and she looked strange and beautiful. Drops of sweat beaded the Seer's forehead; for a moment I thought he was going to collapse; but he gritted his teeth and held out. Slowly under their naked palms, the arms of each taut and apart, the table rose.

This unreal scene in semi-darkness lasted a few seconds; then those two strange creatures gently relaxed their arms and delicately lowered the table on to the floor. They removed their hands by sliding them along the surface as if they had difficulty in disengaging them from an adhesive substance. Priscilla's eyes went out and now the repulsive spots reappeared on her face. The Seer drank a big gulp of grappa straight from the carafe and withdrew into the darkest corner where he collapsed into a chair and fell silent.

I have no idea how long things stayed like that; but I was brought to my senses with a jolt by that funereal yet slightly sardonic voice saying:

'You mustn't despair, Signor Sansevero!'

I thrust myself forward in an effort to see his face; but he held it completely hidden in his hands. I was disconcerted and would have liked to regain my grip on reality by looking under that table, now returned to such normality.

'No,' he went on in his melodious uncouth voice, 'Madame Digne up at Bay knew nothing about you, and couldn't have given me any information; in fact, it was I who explained you to her. And if you want to look under the table, or make sure we haven't any resin on our hands, then do so. But why don't you want to believe in the Powers? I did that experiment for myself alone, certainly not to take you in. I know you don't believe in the brute domination of matter; I know how often you've expended yourself' (those were his very words) 'and that you are going to be warned again, and that shortly heavy demands are going to be made on you. If you've an energy swelling within you, it's because you must give it. That's much more than lifting a table.'

We went out into the darkness of the alley. Air-raids throughout the country were multiplying. My uncle had written me desolate letters from Naples about the nightly hammering. The blackout was humiliating to a country renowned for its lights and sounds.

'I don't know how you intuit these things,' I said after a moment of self-questioning, 'but a difficult interlude has indeed come to an end. It's true that things will now change. And it's also true that I can make a fresh start.'

And without another word we parted.

The winter came early that year. It found the Germans deeply entrenched in Russian territory, but at a standstill, and the English once more pressing on Libya. The P. Office was under pressure too. My trips became *tournées*, so much so that I found I was indeed in the same boat as Demetrio. The General ordered me (even though with Socratic words) to go for two weeks to infuse fresh zeal into the troops stationed from Santa Lucia di Tolmino to Lublin, from Montenero to the Bainsizza and even to the Carso, those mountains that had been the theatre of blood-soaked trench-warfare back in 1915–1918.

Toia was extremely annoyed by all this and regarded it as an unseemly interference in his own invested command. However, he calmed down after a few angry vocal outbursts. Perhaps the plot he was weaving in his mind needed time for development; but however that may have been, he inflicted an interminable evening on me just when I had to be off again at three o'clock in the morning – an evening in which he zealously divided himself between his wife (towards whom he feigned great solicitude despite her air of indifference) and me, whom he bombarded with satirical praise. Albertina was amiable but strictly formal; yet at times I thought I intercepted certain quick glances from her at him. In my private opinion she was thinking of facts and feelings far away; and Toia's attention was concealed yet tense precisely so as to spy out her secret together with my capacity to penetrate it. He was forcing her openly to observe me, hoping to see from her reaction those hints that he felt to be perhaps essential.

I left the city in darkness, with the train coasting along beside the black castles and flashing fires of the Reggio factories, then still intact, and almost in a dream I heard the hammers of the factories over and above the clang of the train. The ground was an undefended land, oppressed by the sword. And Albertina's delicate face came back to me like something that had been stricken but was now static.

In the low kitchen nearby the women were chattering in a language to me incomprehensible. Stretched out on the warm Jugoslav *pec*, in that household in the rainy valley of the Idria, I felt the cold and exhaustion gradually melting from my limbs; and smooth soundless thoughts and images floated in the deep waters of my memory.

When morning came over the high desolate plain, the commanding officer named in my service orders – a lieutenant of the Alpine regiment, athletic but with a child-like face – took me to visit one of the ancient redoubts of the first war: a little cavern not much taller than a man, dug into the rock from which mountain water dripped. Through the slit you could see a small valley; and to capture that post guarded by a few machine-guns, two thousand soldiers had fallen. Was it the image of the motherland that pushed these ignorant infantrymen to the assault – men who had grown up with their herds on the remote slopes of the Apennines? Or were they subject to some spectre, much vaster and at the same time much less identifiable? The obligation proper to combatants, not only in a war, but in reality as a whole; a debt taken over within themselves, and paid to the whole of life?

That was a strange luncheon with the lieutenant. He had ordered two large hares to be prepared in two monumental pans, with nothing to follow but coffee in milk bowls and murderous slivovitz in coffee cups. The feast went on till darkness fell; and the lieutenant, in his fortress of alcohol and melancholy, talked endlessly of the odyssey of the Julia division and the march on Mekowo; of the famous retreat and the sinking of the ship bringing home the only survivors, those of the Gemona battalion. And he told of the high seas in which the dead were floating held up by their lifebelts, and how it was impossible for the rescuers to tell whether there was anyone still alive among those hundreds of bobbing heads.

'I was the only one alive,' the lieutenant went on, 'and for nine hours I fought against the sea and the current that prevented me from reaching the shore. Towards the end I saw a torpedo boat pass by, but they didn't see me. I had to come to a decision: either a huge effort to reach it or, failing that, surrender to the waves. But at last they saw me and came to my rescue. I was caught beneath the hull so they threw me a cable to haul me up, but by mistake I grabbed at a rope fixed to the side of the boat and hoisted myself up with my own two arms – to their astonishment. After that I went down with pneumonia for ten days, and that was another brush with death . . .'

To die for one's country: an ambiguous concept today. In the First World War the men of Cadorna had fought with their families and possessions just behind them. After Caporetto, beyond the Piave, the land that the men had fought for and lost was their own church tower. There still persisted the memory of that almost legendary past among the little detachments I sought out in the folds of the mountains – a past that seemed a remote nostalgic paradise of honour as seen from the ambiguous present. The rains, beating down on the bleak mountain-sides which twenty-five years earlier had been contested foot by foot with a mighty enemy, were constantly uncovering hidden traces of that long-ago battle waged for four years and at infinite cost in blood – the blood of poor ignorant people and all mixed up with that mud from which, after all, man was made: a dark and doleful amalgam whence nevertheless voices were reborn.

'The other day,' so the lieutenant told me, 'the rains washed away a pile of stones and brought to light the bodies of a whole squadron – they must have been buried by a landslide after an explosion. You could even see the postures of the soldiers, and one of them still had his ninety-one in his hand.'

Their identity discs, numbers and names would be unearthed; the long-ago procedures of presumed death would be ratified; the tears of widows – now grandmothers – would be renewed. While down below Nappa was working out his petty ways and means and Toia was conspiring even within his own household. Between these two extremes lay human life: between the absurdity of self-sacrifice and the absurdity of self-aggrandisement, both equally inexplicable. Italy's lucky star would rise when she had found the balance between these two: the conscience of the more generous part paying the price for the meanness and indifference of the other.

'Up there, above the Goliko,' the lieutenant went on in his hollow voice, 'that's where our hero, Dolfo, met his death. There was only a small clearing between *us* and *them* and there had been so many skirmishes that some detachments knew one another. And when Dolfo emerged from his position one of *them* shouted in Italian: "If you've got the guts, come out!" And he . . .'

That was the way it was. I felt I'd have preferred the story not to go on, I'd have preferred what I was going to hear never to have happened. The rattling of plates in the kitchen had stopped; a young man must have come in and every now and then I heard his grave voice mixed with the cheerful interjections of the women.

'So Dolfo advanced in full daylight,' the lieutenant went on, his face raised and his eyes tight shut, immersed in memory, 'he advanced with a grenade in each hand, followed by his orderly, machine-gun at the ready. It was pure suicide. Even the Greeks just stared at him without shooting. Then he cried out: "We've got guts and to spare!" and he threw the first grenade. There followed a scuffle over his bullet-ridden body.'

Few things have persisted in men's minds like the idea of a hero, from Hector to Henry IV of France and our own first-war air-ace, Baracca. But has a hero ever been defined? Has he needed to be?

I had gone to the war willingly because I had lost everything, but I would never deliberately seek death because deep within me

I felt my life to be bound up with Uncle Gedeone. Yet Dolfo was young and loved life. Perhaps he thought he wouldn't die? Perhaps he was thinking of the glorious honours he would receive if he survived? Or was he being downright vainglorious, wanting to show the others what, in his view, a man was; wanting to prove that a man is only worth something in life if he is ready to give his life away – like a coin which only counts when it is spent? Or was he thinking of Italy at that moment, and placing himself through his action among the names that in due course she would venerate, inscribed on marble tablets or encased in little bronze wreaths?

No, no, nothing of the kind. As Demetrio had said: 'I did the experiment for myself alone.' And why after all should he have wanted to take me in? He had never met me before the war and would probably never meet me again after it; I had given him neither applause nor money. He and his dreamy Priscilla had left at dawn on the morning after making the table rise. So his motive was very like the one that drove Dolfo to throw his life away on the Goliko. For no one: not to convince or deceive anyone; not to obtain anything; and in return for that nothingness, to give everything. It was the height of arrogance, a defiance of the geometrical mechanism of the Universe, where everything is linked by cause and effect, so that whatever contrives to set itself up outside the chain, whatever turns out to be without motives or aims, partakes of the Divine. Producing water from rock, suspending weight in air, dying while loving life. The new epoch was trying to vilify heroism; but this had to do with the heroism propagated by the newspapers or prompted by the P. Office. It was not that other heroism of the soldiers who, without knowing anything about claims or aims, stuck darkly to their posts through their sheer quality as men (which is precisely what distinguished them from the beasts of the forests); and still less that of the lieutenant of the Alpine regiment (now fallen asleep with his baby face on his chest) who, when exhausted with the cold and his battle against the waves, had gambled his life on the efficacy of his spirit. In last analysis, the final trappings of the hero had disappeared along with the Fascists' regime; but not the impulse that lay behind it.

This contributed to an understanding of the elements of the war. The Julia division, like Dolfo himself, was operating on foreign soil, and this fostered that sentiment of primitive man when he finds his enemy where migration has pushed him and wants to get the better of him – like a baby who thinks that what he can reach with his hands is his; and, being men before soldiers, they had another irrepressible instinct, the one that exists in the cubs of wild animals with claws. But more certainly still, they were led along by a thread of illusion. Life shone before them like a perpetual act of imagination, outside any positive theory. Those who listened to my Socratic reasoning, whether beneath the peaks of the Predil or in sight of the stone dam of the Tagliamento, were left resigned and discontented, for there was no getting away from it. Only the 'winged word' was capable of moving them: precisely because it was designed to deceive them.

I got back to Reggio halfway through December. With Pearl Harbour the Japanese had set fire to the other half of the world; and the Rome-Berlin Axis went so far as to extend its war against the United States. The city was covered in snow driven by a tormenting wind beneath the dark porticoes of via Emilia. I saw frowning faces, people walking quickly, warily. An elegantly-dressed woman passed by me staring in front of her, her face slightly withdrawn, like someone who has been offended.

Great changes had taken place at the Command, especially for Nappa; very probably he was one of those who had negotiated his call-up and the best assignment. But his group, which according to the administrative structure was still mine, had suddenly been 'mobilised' – the prelude to a posting as mysterious as it was dangerous. Up till then, the only squadron to suffer had been that of those poor fellows on the Crostolo, for the other three had been quartered in the city. Mobilisation, involving as it did different equipment, weaponry and training for the whole detachment, presented Nappa with many problems, considering how incompetent he was. His subalterns knew even less than he did but, as was to be expected, just as they should have been getting down to work they slipped off to every sort of hiding-place to escape from a body which felt itself to be already under fire. All except four or five of them had ready and prepared some 'provision' or 'circular' capable of releasing them. In the end they dispatched a collective memorandum to the War Ministry then waited the result with folded arms. The major, who earlier had recommended me in glowing terms as a first-class orator, was now urgently pressing to have me restored to him. But he met determined resistance in stubborn Toia and perhaps also in the General, who was against him.

In this uncertain situation, not for any merits of my own but for reasons connected with the defects of those who made a show of caring about my services, Toia dispensed me from almost every task. His dark intentions must have come to fruition in those two weeks, and he did this under cover of the uncertainty of the situation. On the other hand, as he himself was in the last stages of his exile and ready to flee back to the Ministry of Finance at any moment, he did nothing but propose card games, musical pastimes with the gramophone, little meals and diversions, all day long; and always in the compulsory company of his wife and myself. I could not evade these orders, at least for ten hours a day, however unbearable my uneasiness became; but between us was Signora Albertina, a double-edged blade in whatever way I might have tried to take her: for I could neither help her nor abandon her; and my instinct told me I had to pass through those dark Caudine Forks. Even Demetrio's prophecies came back to my mind, for they chimed in so well with what had happened and what was going to happen. 'Before long you will be warned, and then great demands will be made upon you!' Was this the 'warning'?

Though I had observed Albertina closely I barely received a hint that she had so much as noticed me. As an individual, I mean; because of course she treated me with the respect due to an officer held in high esteem by her husband. Toia was about forty-five, Albertina little more than twenty-five; they had already been married for some time and had a small baby who was always ailing and whimpering. When, on Toia's orders, I telephoned his house at a specific hour, it was always Albertina who answered; and I could always hear the baby screaming wildly, so that Albertina hardly managed to get out brief phrases of instructions or receive my report. Then Toia would take over (I imagined him always beside her garnering every word!) and behind his coarse voice emitting the usual outbursts of protest and reassurance, the cries of the baby would fade away into the distance. I could see the impatient wave of the hand with which he would order Albertina upstairs with the wriggling baby in her arms. Once I had seen the baby. He was fat and almost repulsive; I felt Albertina was in some way sentenced to his weight and his appearance, both so like the father's; and, moreover, had to love him; as with a wicked spell in a fairy-story, or like something in a cruel and incomprehensible dream.

Stretched out on the *pec* in those days, I had come to various conclusions concerning Albertina, Toia and myself. Everything about him was so appallingly commonplace, even his captiousness. If he wanted to test his wife's fidelity or, worse, positively push her into betraying him – either so as to get rid of her or (a more probable hypothesis) so as to rage against her, win a victory over her, settle some long-standing account – then his choice of me as guinea-pig, and the abuse of his rank involved in forcing me to comply, indicated the abject level of his mind and his incapacity to penetrate the thoughts and emotions of others. It must have seemed to him that the double-rhetoric of my coat-of-arms and my ancient name, reinforced by the subsequent rhetoric of my romantic scar, my supposed oratorical talents and, now, my probable imminent danger at the front (for otherwise Nappa would not have been so eager to have me) – it must have seemed to him that all this added up to the right man at the right moment where his nefarious aims were concerned; for his was a bureaucratic mentality that judged people according to their 'character notes' which had made me seem a dandy along the lines of the *Segretario Galante*. But even if he did not know me, and had seen me only through the spectacles of his preconceived idea, it seemed strange that he knew Albertina so little. Did he really think her capable of some servant-girl's lapse between the kitchen and the pantry, or of an affair in a train with her neighbour in the next bunk? And, if so, did he then want to cheat with himself and bring down vengeance on her whole life for some casual sensual slip? It was a contemptible game that ought not to have been played, so as later to blame fate for the outcome.

Meanwhile a gust of hope and enthusiasm was sweeping through Italy in the first months of that year. The Reggio paper *Il Solco Fascista*, which up till then had done everything in its power to conceal our many misfortunes, now proclaimed over eight news-print columns that the Axis had broken through in Africa and that our tanks were eighty kilometres from Alexandria. Those armies had made a huge and generous effort. With their litre of water a day in that parched desert, with petrol a priority over bread, in-adequately armed and with nothing to back them up, they had managed to beat an enemy with unlimited resources at his disposal.

In the other hemisphere the Japanese were simultaneously pouring into Singapore, the Philippines, the East Indies and Burma, and we were assembling an army to play our part beside the German effort in Russia. This latter item caused Nappa burning anguish for he did not even dare to envisage a destination such as the legendary steppes that had brought even Napoleon to his knees; he did not even dare to envisage it for his troops or for himself. His difficulties with his unreliable subalterns were already real enough. The General had to resign himself, and I now found myself reintegrated into the Command of the squadron, one unit of which had left the Crostolo and passed with the other three beyond the city gates. It seemed that my perplexities over Albertina would get into focus in the frightful confusion afflicting the squadron and in which I was intimately involved. The adjutant, no doubt foreseeing the need for future good relations, whispered in my ear that the documents dealing with my promotion to the rank of captain – which had lain for five months on the major's desk without his doing anything about them – had been sent off a week earlier with recommendations for urgent attention.

'Here, things are going badly,' he added. 'Nearly all our officers enjoy special exemptions and will make use of them. There are no sergeant-majors and very few senior sergeants left. There are a few second lieutenants, and then there's you who will soon be the only captain and thus second-in-command of the group. But I've noticed that you're declared unfit for service abroad. Nappa will ask for a revision of that – you wait and see!'

Thus things emerged from their earlier confusion. By appointing me his second-in-command despite his antipathy towards me, Nappa managed to throw the whole weight of the mobilisation on to my shoulders. He had seen me spend a winter on the Crostolo, the unhealthiest river in the province, so he had every reason to suppose that I could serve in the devil's own house should this be necessary. But the rush to have me promoted revealed a more far-reaching purpose: that of having a replacement to hand when he himself moved off, as he would when the suitable moment came. In the meantime I had to spend murderous weeks dealing with the troops whose physique and morale had both been seriously impaired by over a year of pointless sentry work. Drawing on poetic memories of Ferrara and the noble shade of the colonel at Pinarolo, Count Dadi, I was just able to pull myself and the lazy discontented troops together. My appointment (that anxiously-awaited glory of a career!) arrived almost immediately. I had to drop in on Toia who had repeatedly asked to see me, and I was met by an ostentatious, almost aggressive cordiality.

'At last we can talk to each other in the second person! This calls for a first-class celebration!'

'I think it'll be the last,' I said. 'Nappa's preparing some trap for me.'

'Nappa won't do anything!' cried Toia, with a threatening eye. 'My case has now been settled. Within a week I'll be going back to Rome and then I'll take care of your Nappa!'

I tried to change the subject for I disliked this way of talking. I had hoped not to have to see that man again. It was difficult to address him in the second person and I did not like him doing so to me. I had to accept his invitation but refrained from mentioning Albertina, even to send her my formal greetings – and nor did he mention her.

Events followed thick and fast within the next few days. On the military transmitter that repeats the same line in triplicate to avoid all possible doubt came the order assigning our group to the Athens Command, thence to proceed to some further destination on that chessboard. The General summoned me. He was a decent man and seemed to be divided between various lines of thought.

'Now that your Command is being sent abroad it wants to retain you at all costs. I don't know what the Medical Board will decide; but in any case I could have you seconded to Captain Toia's post which will be vacant when he goes back to Rome. I've asked him for a full-length report on the work you've been doing in these last months; and if it's favourable, as I'm sure it will be, we could keep you here. You've done your bit in the war as it is.'

I thanked the General; but I felt an ironical happiness stirring within me which presaged a change in my fortunes, as my scars showed a change in time. The following evening was to be Toia's party: a knot in that depressing tangle.

This time the venue was a large room made from a converted courtyard – such as one sees in the provinces. There were dozens of bottles of every type and origin ranged on vast tables; everything was too big, too little used, and too uncomfortable. The Captain had mobilised the whole of the P. Office and a small group of women, evacuated from Milan or Bologna, one or two well-to-do, but most of them of very uncertain means; though it was not actual hunger that would make them potentially dangerous. In defiance of rationing, there were large quantities of mille feuilles gateaux of translucent whiteness; and as for the Trebbiano wine, this time Toia had really excelled himself and bottles were displayed by the dozen. In a rather ill-lit corner of the huge room a corporal was operating a gramophone by hand, but very quietly, for, in view of the war, every kind of entertainment was forbidden. So all those present took on an air of complicity. By the end of the party no less than half of the guests had discreetly disappeared.

Toia deliberately took no part in the dancing. He seated himself at the far end of the room, almost in darkness, behind the cake table, and set to work on his bottles.

For a while at first Signora Albertina seemed to want to stay near him; but as his absorption in the glasses prevented him from paying any attention to her, she gradually started looking after the others – who were after all her guests – and with her formal and slightly weary politeness patiently handed round cakes and Trebbiano. Every now and again she was invited to dance and she accepted with an ease that removed all value from her consent. But she only exchanged a few words with her partners, and certainly generalities at that; no one seemed really interested in her as they all had their own intrigues in hand and were doubtless intimidated by the presence of their immediate superior.

However much it might have pleased me, I did not want to dance with Albertina. Shyness, always the sign of some affection, prevented me from asking her; but most of all I felt that our relationship, which had been rendered impossible by circumstances, would only suffer in such cramped conditions. Moreover, some kind of keen intuition, if not sheer fantasy, warned me that in that almost funereal room only Albertina, her husband and myself were involved in some business relating to real life; this flashed across my mind so insistently that it was impossible to ignore it. After a couple of hours Toia seemed so heavy with wine, and so quiet and inert in his corner, that I could scarcely see him from the other end of the room. At that moment Albertina, who happened to be beside me, put aside two unaccepted glasses and smiled at me wordlessly with her air of gentle patience. I was seated and she sat down beside me. It was the first time we had been able to talk alone.

'Are you tired, Albertina?' And an echo within me seemed to say: 'Are you tired, Vincenzina?' – words of years ago beneath the olive trees of Licudi on the night of that moonlight barbecue. And from that echo sprung many others, as many as the years, and they made me feel sad.

She kept her head down. I expected her to give a timid glance at something or someone, just as Vincenzina had done on that previous occasion. It occurred to me that if I had asked her to dance she, too, would have refused with a 'No, no, that's not for me!' – although she had danced with everyone else. I said nothing. In that attitude, with her delicate skin, her fine hair, her ears unpierced, Albertina looked like a young girl hardly yet awakened.

Our conversation was long, hesitant, uncertain. No one took any notice of us and we forgot everyone else. I knew that she had married very young; and I surmised that for complicated family reasons – of the kind that so often form the dramatic undercurrent to what goes on in certain households – she had been unable to extricate herself from what others had decided for her, and that Toia's overbearing personality had been able to impose itself in some way. There had been no one to save her from someone who, though better disguised than Dr Carruozzo, certainly came from the same stable. Following this thread of reminiscence – she having said nothing – I knew what she would not be able to admit even in confidence, given that she had tried so hard to close her mind to it.

The doors of our big room were firmly closed, with the result that the air had become heavy. Someone had the idea of lowering the lights which were already pretty dim; and in the semi-darkness one could only just make out the couples gliding along in slow dances. All that swaying and squeezing seemed to be causing Albertina more than mere boredom. And now no one asked her to dance any more.

'What do you think about it, Albertina?'

She tightened her lips and shook her head. I could sense her thoughts so well that they might have been words; I saw her as an innocent young girl led lovelessly into the arms of a man whose weight must have crushed her. I stood up and offered her my hand. As I steered her towards the centre of the room I again caught sight of Toia, now almost besotted with wine, his head down, his eyes blank. But I knew how he could disguise his tensions. That he should have wanted to inflict this new kind of anguish on himself; that he should have wanted his sin against Albertina's life to rise up before him again, whole and entire, with all the suffering it entailed; that he should have wanted to be sure that she was completely free from him, who had broken her without even touching the surface of her – there lay the mysterious side of his character. As for me, I was convinced that I ought to obtain the answer to this conundrum, and from him; an answer that he had spent so many years denying to himself but which was now demanded. And she wanted the same thing, though she abstracted herself from me. Like all deeply wounded people, she had an intuition that I was wounded too. Our sympathy for each other was of the kind that has always obliged the world to feel in bad conscience when confronted with those whom it ill-treats and yet battens on. It was necessary that the ulcer of a problem that he had no right to disregard (and he was the first to know it) should reopen within him. Yet I was afraid of reviving those lacerating wounds for Albertina's sake. Meanwhile she appeared to have awakened – perhaps for the first time for years. Colour had come into her face; her eyes were afire. As for me, I realised it would be useless to pursue her, because such pursuits had already taken their toll in my experience, and it was a risk because Toia would certainly enter into the game finally. Yet it was impossible for me to hold back, not because I was unable to, but because I did not want to: I thought I was fulfilling some kind of indefinable duty towards her, some right over him, and at the same time challenging what Demetrio had said should not be called fate.

At a certain point Toia got up and staggered from the room. She did not utter a syllable, but sat down beside me again and waited a long time before following him.

In saying goodbye to her I felt that the moment was over, and that there would be no tomorrow.

As I had foreseen, there was no further summons from the General. Toia's report on my conduct as a propaganda officer must have been a masterpiece; he knew very well what I thought about the state of things in Italy and of the war in general; hence his praises, tempered with ministerial wisdom, were certainly wrapped round in impenetrable veils of doubt. Then something else unforeseen happened: despite Nappa's assurances, the Medical Board insisted on classing me as 'unsuitable' for service abroad. Together with ninety per cent of the other officers in the group – their collective memorandum had won a victory – I was exempt from going abroad with the detachment and was sent back to my original area for an assignment to some other unit at home. The dice, having rolled capriciously over the table, had stopped on a blank. I was free from risk and able to set myself up again as I wanted.

Mobilised in February, our unit had been reorganised as well as could be expected in two months. After so much labour we were as good as ready, when suddenly the men found themselves without officers; worse, they knew their officers were privileged and exempt from common duty. A wave of unrest bordering on rebellion ran through the ranks. In his despair Nappa sent for me.

'Listen,' he said, 'all reason is on your side. But I have nine hundred and sixty men, with six second-lieutenants, and not one regular officer. Who's going to put them on the train? If you leave me too, it will be the signal for mutiny. We'll have the military police. For God's sake, Sansevero, come with us!'

We were outside Reggio in some school buildings in the direction of Sant' Ilario, having had the torment of several successive mobilisations. We were pacing back and forth over brick paving that crumbled beneath our feet with age and use. The sky was already bright with the beautiful colours of the new season. My thoughts were a thousand miles away from the Major and what he was saying, so that I was only giving him formal attention. I knew perfectly well that I would not abandon the detachment, and the Medical Board had no importance for me at all. The only thing that irritated me was Nappa's insistent appeals, for what I really minded was having to fall in with his wishes.

On returning to Reggio, I ran into a poor-looking man who stared at me from beneath the shade of a battered old hat: it was Demetrio.

'Captain, sir,' he said almost humbly. 'May I offer you my congratulations?'

'What for?' I wondered. And his eye gleamed from deep in its socket, made darker by the brim of his hat.

'There's an evil force against you; but it will be atoned for in the future by whoever harbours it in his soul. All you have to do is to carry on.'

'According to the force of things? Or against the force of things? And who will be able to stop it?'

'That's just it,' said the Seer. 'That's just it! No one will be able to stop it!'

On the eve of the day fixed for departure the group's morale was at zero. It was four miles from the village to Reggio station from which our train was to leave at eight in the morning. At the last minute the depot had sent us nine officers, of every age and type, and picked up from every branch of the army, but only so as to accompany the troops on the perilous journey through the Balkans. The staff would be reconstituted in Athens. At the Divisional Command in Bologna the lieutenant-colonel who had received my declaration renouncing my 'unsuitability' looked at me quizzically but countersigned and stamped the form without comment.

At ten in the evening I gathered together a handful of sergeants and one or two other reliable men. More than half the effective troops were missing from the billet. The lancers – whether scattered in wine-shops, huddled in ditches with girls, shouting in bars, or taking refuge in private houses – seemed to be in the grip of a sort of collective neurosis and were giving vent in a thousand unreasonable ways to the nervous crisis into which I had managed to throw them – Socrates apart.

'I am the only person here who belongs to your own branch of the army! I've been at the front already and I'm going back. It's a thing between men. You'll see that, too!'

By four in the morning, under a full moon of fantastic beauty, the trucks had rounded up most of the men and delivered them back to camp. We took the baggage of those still missing, as rumour had it that, by hook or by crook, they would be at the station in time for that train. We came across quite a few of them on our way to Reggio, some in shirtsleeves, some in a feverish state of excitement, some plain drunk. We picked up those who could no longer stand on their feet, and told the others to follow along behind us. The trucks had to shuttle backwards and forwards until the frantic work of picking them all up was finished. At half-past seven the military authorities who were to give us a formal send-off began arriving on the departure platform. Nappa was among them, as yellow as a lemon, and it was to him that I was able to report that the men had rejoined the ranks – which gave me feelings of pride as well as irritation.

From the large group of territorial officers and city authorities – totally unaware of the situation – came sounds of greeting and applause. Fascist women dressed in black clustered round the train bristling with bright or gloomy faces, and from their little plaited straw baskets distributed carnations in token of good luck.

Then the train set in motion. The gentle countryside, already marked with the sweet footprints of spring, fled past us – our comfortable motherland; warm kingdom of waters, of greenness, of peaceful mists. But the pleasure-sadness that soothed my heart came from understanding my country better now that I was about to leave it: understanding how its very essence lay in expressing itself in a continuous emanation of its power and love; but a voice that is not heard unless it is raised, unless it breaks out of the breast and flies upwards.

'Splendid!' I said to myself. 'You were looking for communication with men, weren't you? Well, here you've got an army! Come on now, Sansevero!'

THE SCREECH-OWL

The village of Krano, in Arcadia, seems to hang over the southern edge of the high plain that forms the heart of the Peloponnese, once known as the Morea. From up there you can look down on an endless landscape sloping into greenness, criss-crossed by sky-blue rivers and fading away in torrid haze towards sunburnt Messenia – all that famous land which legend and poetry tell us was traversed by the horses of Telemachus. At that height, what with the steep gulleys and unnegotiable stubble, even malaria loses something of its hold; and the parched heat hanging over the low plain is somewhat calmed.

After moving about for some months, first in Attica, near Megara, then among the pink and graceful little villas of Corinth, it was in Krano that my Command was finally established just as the new season was beginning. During that time the group had been subjected to almost continuous changes and upheavals, but there were no engagements and life was uneventful – it was rather like that period of duty inside Reggio. Major Nappa and his boot-licking adjutant had finally managed to land a soft job in Athens, leaving me in provisional command and with a sea of woes. But after nearly a year, the arrival of a new commanding officer brought about a move to a new destination, and I saw my small battalion of scarcely more than a hundred men extended even further than at Bay in the early months of the war. At Bay we were hardly beyond our own frontier, and nothing very dangerous was happening, whereas here our perilous redoubts were miles away from each other, and covered an arch of gorges from the centre of Tripolis as far as Kiparissia on the coast; they represented not so much efficient defence positions as attractive prey for the guerrillas who were hungry for food and arms.

There were seven of these redoubts, each with ten or twelve men, and their job was to guard the viaducts, tunnels and bridges of the long thin railway line which twists and turns interminably among the folds of those mountains, winds through the entire peninsula, spanning it from the canal to Kalamata. Thus the few lancers who remained at the Command with me had to supervise the stores, the arms depots, and the means of transport – when not replacing the sick or those on routine leave. An impossible task, even if they had not been incessantly on their rounds (as they were), first drawing food from the central stores then distributing it to our guard posts. The roads were bad and dangerous and often blocked; the trains had unpredictable timetables and only went by day; so that once the men had gone, they could disappear for two or three days at a time, and a second distribution of supplies was required before the first had even been completed. Then it was one thing to load sacks or hampers with supplies for a hundred men, but quite another to divide it all up into seven parts and send it off in cans and bottles; a ludicrous undertaking, especially as with the arrival of summer many provisions soon went bad in the heat. I had noticed that up till then the remedy for this untenable situation had been the tolerance of the various Commands towards raids operated by the troops on the Greeks' poultry-yards, orchards and sometimes even markets, each group thus more or less providing for itself on the spot. But times had slowly been changing as the clouds grew darker and darker over the destiny of the Axis. To embitter our relationship with the Greeks and sooner or later to incur reprisals was a risk with which I had to concern myself as a personal matter.

As for my own life, I found myself yet again reduced to almost absolute isolation, though for ever bound down by duties that broke its continuity but not my meditation. From the very first I had been moved by the striking resemblance between the natural features of the peninsula and the natural features I had known in Licudi. There were the same bare austere mountains, the same sparse but impressive vegetation, olives, vines, the reddish sand and, everywhere, the dazzling light and the distant shimmering of the sea. The strength of the plants was amazing; the geranium hedges were as tall as houses and as long as streets; the eucalyptus trees spilt cascades of dusty foliage which became all entangled with the exuberant undergrowth. The sun's silences were hallucinatory; the nights magical and withdrawn.

This filled my spirit with a secret delight, enfolded it in a sort of wide toleration, separated it off. If the Commands in Athens were living in a state of reckless euphoria, for us the war was ceasing to be an inward-looking affair (in which we had nevertheless to defend our essential if minimal positions) and direct and distinct experience was taking over, reaffirming that we alone were responsible for our actions and our lives. Nothing could have been more relevant to my thoughts and my intimate ratiocination than to be led to the places that I myself would have chosen; while my long-ago youthful affections – coupled with the sediment of culture instilled into me by the monks at my school – could be sustained by the sheer word: Greece. And in my fancy transform the whole dangerous business into a pilgrimage back to my origins – a pilgrimage rich in toil and fatigue, like the one I had made to the top of that mountain with the poor people of Licudi.

We had a Group Command too, at least in name. But if I had seven redoubts in my care, scattered over forty-five kilometres, our new major had seen his four squadrons dispersed – one to Patras, one to guard the bridge over the isthmus of Corinth, one to Nauplia on the eastern shores of the Morea, and the fourth (mine) almost to the other end of the peninsula. He was a nobleman from the Marche, a fine fellow with a strong sense of duty but already advanced in years and unsuited for work of this kind. He was decorated with the little black disc of the Cross of Malta and had had too much self-respect to evade the call-up; but his moral stamina was inadequate to the sheer physical exhaustion of his post. Besides which, he suffered beyond measure from the lack of those comforts he had always enjoyed. He had only about a dozen men with him and not a single heavy machine-gun; his liaison with us was very unstable through the spider's web of field telephones; and had he wanted to inspect the thirty redoubts of his group it would have taken no less than six weeks. Then he was in some way linked up with the higher Commands at Tripolis, but these left him in peace. When he had torn himself away from his native Jesi to come and put himself in the lion's den, the good man had provided himself with a case of Lambrusco wine which had been improvidently consumed in the twelve days' journey through the Balkans. So his hope lay in the celebrated Greek wines; though he was well aware that even the water would fail him.

I felt Christian compassion for the Major (that nobleman Costa Oliviero – hence consecrated to peace, if my schoolboy memories do not deceive me) and I relived the anxieties that must have led him to run through his precious reserve of Lambrusco during his (and my) railway journey through the Balkans. From the chaotic sorting-out at Mestre under an African sun, and then across the wild mountains of a primitive people, the disturbing spectacle became more and more apparent, that of a situation manifestly on the verge of total collapse. It was the Germans who kept guard over this railway, the only link between Greece and Central Europe; but as they were more logical than us, they were not going to waste their troops keeping guard over the thousand kilometres of dangerous railway-track separating Klagenfurt from Salonika – the seat of their High Command which was watching over the movements of the Turkish army and the chessboard of the Middle East. The Germans had merely placed large deposits of material and adequate groups of men at various key points, deeming it more practical and expeditious to repair the railway every time it was damaged rather than mount guard over its whole length and throughout the whole year. Thus there was a progressive increase of partisan activity in that barbarous country where war and brigandage were still a normal way of life, so that countless troop trains were burnt, overturned or derailed. Along the track was an unending succession of black and twisted carcasses; the night was broken by gunfire; and during the hours of darkness it was obligatory to stop, take up defence positions and pass weary hours under arms. But what had been worse was our encounter with the first Italian detachments sent to Macedonia – the strange spectacle of those soldiers crowding on to all the stations just for the fun of it and wearing the oddest assortment of clothes sometimes bordering on the grotesque: for there was hardly anything to be seen of their uniforms, nor of anything that a sane person would wear. Clad in shorts of every colour under the sun, pomaded, and chatting away like women at the market, those soldiers seemed to have lost all contact with the dangerous realities among which they lived. Our detachment, composed of veteran lancers accustomed to the iron discipline of war, seemed to belong to another army and another nation; our men stared in silent amazement at those others, while they in their turn stared back at us. It was the period when the African units were fighting in the desert with insufficient arms and their famous litre of water a day. Here was another aspect of the unfathomable vibrancy of our race, the way not only different men, but the very same men, could change direction, be transformed, be stimulated anew, according to their mood, or the situation, or the point of departure. These men were not really different from the valiant fighters in Giarabub or Tobruk; it was just that their malleability had exalted one lot to heroism and pulled the others down into licence. The duality of Italy . . . almost incapable of ordered government, yet harbouring in its bosom the most extraordinary governmental structure the world has ever seen – the Vatican. A marvellous conundrum that I love to try to solve.

As I was overwhelmed with the work of having to watch over all our men – of having to see that they did not leave the train at a halt, or barter any of the squadron's property in exchange for the cockerels or tobacco that the Bulgarian or Serbian peasant women came to offer us at every stop, or run after those easy skirts – for the time being I had almost put my own thoughts to one side; just for once, I had sunk into the way of life of those who no longer work to live but live to work, and finally lull all self-awareness to sleep in the ceaseless grind of an engine turning in a spiritual vacuum. But fortunately Nappa was now making no more demands on me; he had barricaded himself in his reserved first-class compartment, where the red velvet upholstery was, nonetheless, shiny and almost black as the result of constant wear; and anyway he knew I was looking after everything. So that compared with that troublesome business I had become involved in in Reggio, I preferred this risk and weariness for at least I could breathe within it as a man. Greece was about to be revealed to my avid eyes, my spirit knew it, charged as it was with such fantastic expectation as to vindicate even a trace of rhetoric: for it was dissolved and submerged in an utterly genuine wave of emotion. Free from the fear of death, and frequently on the watch from the observation-post at the very back of our train among the trunks and barrels that cluttered it up, I felt ready to rediscover the myths.

But our arrival in Athens excluded any such rediscoveries. Though May was only just beginning, the city was already dazzling white in the sun. Swarming like a beehive, mercantile, disordered, tumultuous, it lay like a vast theatre in which at any moment any type of show could take place. Once the first tragic period of hunger was over, a very complicated network of interests and collusions between the Italian army and the subject people had been established in the capital: a licentious and improvised Mecca of pleasure and intrigues was milked by a veritable myriad of personalities and half-personalities eagerly pouring in from Italy as from Greece itself. Of course those unfortunates who were keeping up the occupation on the rough mountains of the north or the grim plains of Trikkala and Larissa were suffering torments of melancholy and malaria; whereas our central Commands each formed a little court shot through with privileges and secret understandings, where people trafficked either openly or under cover in a hundred ways, and order and conscience were alike disintegrating beneath the hot Mediterranean sun.

For three months our group remained encamped as well as may be on the dusty verge of the road to Piraeus, in other words until the dog days of summer. We were waiting for the outcome of Nappa's manœuvres as he moved towards his twofold objective of profiting by the Command for the time being and remaining in the capital till the end; but great though his skill was for manœuvre in this type of terrain, all he achieved was to stay in Athens alone with his precious orderlies and let the four other squadrons take the road to Megara; and a few months later he handed the group over to the good nobleman Costa Oliviero. He then returned to his old love, the military police, in which he must certainly have provided superlative proof of his abilities. Once we were delivered from his hands we found it much easier to endure the killing labours forced on us by the circumstances. But the moonlit nights up in those mountains were supremely lovely and peaceful. The moon threw back the reflection of her rays as if in a triple mirror, from the one into the other two seas and above the deep shadow of the earth, and she moved in her bright course as if resounding in the skies; or was this Diana's silver bow? Or her mysterious voice drawing events and ideas up into the divine procession?

The sun was rising, its light vibrating on the bare mountain peaks in a blaze more dazzling than the sky behind them. The air was a deep ochre colour. The dark green of the vegetation was pierced by blue shadows. Up there were the heroes; Cybele's drum rolled in the forest. Immediately afterwards the sergeant on duty came to call me for the distribution of the rations, and I spent interminable hours engrossed in the endless crates of preserved foods, margarine and coffee.

The affinity of this landscape with that of Licudi (as it had been before it was corrupted) again held me spellbound in a complexity of thoughts and emotions. At certain times and at certain hours of the day a wave of that former bitterness swept over me as I beheld those lovely aspects of nature whose secret sweetness was already so familiar to me. But the unjust sufferings that we were inflicting on

Greece – we, who should have venerated her – put my own sorrows to shame and helped them to fade into proper perspective; not that those sights and scents that moved me so deeply ceased to have their effect, but I felt that through this unique ordeal at least a part of the past wanted to be restored to me.

A similar thing happened in my relationship with the lancers. I had thought that in moving out of my caste I would re-establish a pact with the common people, but even this had failed. What it did was to distance me from the soldiers. In their servility and devotion I could read the same deceptive appearances that had deluded me in my early years at Licudi. And indeed the same type of nature was to be found in the lancers who were modest country folk like the people of Licudi, obliging and respectful until circumstances – or simply their whim or inconstancy – drove them against me; then nothing would make them revert to our previous relationship. In our ambiguous position it was quite on the cards that there might be a turn or reversal in our fortunes that would put me in their power as, now, they depended on me. But even that thought was insufficient to guide me – either towards making them my friends or towards suspecting and hating them. What obtruded and put up a resistance was that thing deep in my nature which even I was unable to fathom. Thus a scrupulous carrying-out of duties, prompted by my methodical habits and instinctive love for order, produced on the plane of reason what my emotions urged me to deny; and the result was a meticulous concern for which they seemed grateful. The feeling that I had fulfilled my day in a perfect way, like the monks on the Virgo, and was achieving a busy life in accordance with a schedule that I did not even need to follow, but had prescribed for myself, brought peace to my evenings when the pure breath of the breeze touched the Krano hills. Then I stood watching the sun go down, in that same motionless and almost animal happiness with which I used to wait for the sunset in Licudi, surrounded by my household and the animals and the trees; and breathing in unison with them.

Then, though not forgetful of the past, I tried not to think about it. The difficult situation we were in, and the concealed yet certain danger that was now imminent, gradually cauterised wounds which perhaps wanted to be healed. The salt of adventure, the pepper of necessity, the ferment of obligation and action drove away the black turbid water which had stagnated for so long; they spurred on my energy; calmed my diffidence. Now I again wrote to my uncle with some hope; and he understood and answered, also with hope. In this way the slack season came to an end, and the standard of May was again raised in the heavens.

(*From fragments of my diary: Krano, February 1943.*)

One of the soldiers, a peasant from near Sinigallia, needed some tool or other, a billhook or a pitchfork, so went to borrow it from a group of Greek peasants standing a little way off and staring. And since they could not understand him, and remained silent and almost expressionless from his very first words, he began to wax eloquent, explaining that certainly he would bring it back, that labourers should help one another in all situations, that they should try to be friends: and it never entered his head that those poor wretches were unable to understand a word and that the world contained a language other than the dialect of Ancona. This soldier has a happy temperament; his name is Adorno.

Twice a month the local Command offers hospitality to a small group of applicants who are not at all military. The higher authorities, with the pious intention of 'providing for the needs of the troops', have set up a network of brothels all over Greece, and have more or less handed over their order and discipline (a very bright idea, this) to the individual Commands. In Krano the job falls to me.

The local institute is not very well provided: three girls is the usual number; but when the change takes place, between those who are arriving and those who are leaving, four or five present themselves at the appointed hour. Looking as stern as I possibly can, I examine the documents and with a glance satisfy myself that the photographs correspond with the originals. Then I sign.

In the normal way it is young women who come and not at all displeasing ones. The great hunger which followed immediately on the occupation led thousands of needy people to queue outside military messes and offer themselves for a loaf of bread. The extent of the offering explains the good quality of the product which, in normal times, would only have been found in luxury places and now is for the soldiers. But this morning there was an incident.

It was a morning of heavy gloomy sirocco and the whole place seemed frowning and taciturn under the squalls of dust. I thought I heard a sort of insistent wail between the gusts of wind, and soon I was forced to realise that it was a human sob. And we saw a woman slowly walking along against the wind, under the shelter of the wall, in the direction of the church square. It was she who was making that lament to the locked doors and windows and receiving no reply but the swirling of the dust.

Later I discovered her in my orderly room. Her daughter is one of the girls stationed here and according to service orders has to remain a while longer. She was in the room too, standing with her back to the window so that I could hardly see her face.

She had written to her mother telling her she was in regular work – as they often do to hide their real situation – never dreaming that her mother would get a pass, heaven knows how, so as to come and visit her. And the mother had found her (so I heard) in the very room where she plied her trade; which was why she had come along in that distracted way and with that wail that sounded animal as much as human.

And while I was stamping the papers, I saw her raise such a harrowed face towards her daughter, full of an indescribable look of love, shame and pity. The way I looked into my own self. And perhaps the way Mary had looked at her Son's wounds when they brought him down from the cross.

When I was at Megara I exchanged an old cloak for a sucking-pig a few days old. I decided to call him Ciccio, gave him over to the soldiers and more or less forgot about him. But he has not forgotten me. Every time I pass anywhere near his sty I can hear him running out and grunting, almost shouting. In my days in Ferrara and Largita the horses were perfectly aware of a man's rank, and if Lieutenant Binutti was in sight they stopped kicking and biting each other. But who has told Ciccio that he is alive because of my intention and patronage? And does he grunt out of jubilation? Or does he sense the immensity of the dangers, and being so alone in the world, is he trying to make his presence felt and ask for help?

*

If the surrounding woods recalled Cerenzia, and the bare mountains behind recalled Palanuda, Krano itself was not unlike any of the little villages round about Licudi. Built on the final spur of the mountains, it was like a prow over the huge valley spreading out as far as Kalamata and the sea, and an adventurous little road ran through it which, after leaving the church square, ended vertically over the void. From the two rows of houses, each backing on to the precipitous slope, there stretched a few lateral paths, not much more than goat tracks, and then a leap over the gorges. The railway passed about half a mile beneath the inhabited area. My little Command, with its small contingent of men, lived in a fine house just outside the village, and it looked out over the endless panorama below.

As my rank entailed my being local commander of civil as well as military affairs, I had established the immediate contacts demanded by protocol: the mayor Theodosius, a kind of cattle-dealer who only knew his own dialect hence could only reward me with smiles; the orthodox priest Zagara who also acted as interpreter; and the policeman, who was little more than a pig-herd and recognisable mainly by his ancient muzzle-loaded shotgun which our authorities allowed him to keep.

The ban on holding arms of any kind was in fact one of the most brilliant vexations of our Command, because at one time the Greeks, as keen huntsmen, had equipped themselves with excellent guns from the famous manufacturers in Belgium and England; commandeering them became a splendid business and the trade resulting from it flourished on the Athens market. If the Greeks concealed them, this had very little to do with the activity of the partisans; but the guns were the subject of equivocation beyond words if someone interested in keeping them wanted to, and could, get the lion's share. Even in Krano there had been an obscure incident concerning a situation of this kind a short while before.

Standing in front of my customary chair-easel in the small square in front of the church, a matchless vantage-point overlooking the valley, I had taken up my painting again after more than a year. The fear and resentment caused by my uniform for once kept urchins and other inquisitive people at bay. As drawing-paper was unobtainable at the local store, I had obtained some, after a certain amount of insistence, through the good offices of the Krano schoolmistress – a lovely young girl but obviously very frightened of me. When she suddenly withdrew she left me mortified by her fear and my power. This was why I felt it almost an obligation to let my paint-brushes be seen in public, knowing that I was being attentively watched. It was another reminder of Licudi – except that now I was watched with the prejudice and acrimony of a Denise Digne.

Through the half-open door of the church came the voice of the priest, Zagara, conducting his service. He was still young, strong, muscular, with intense feverish eyes and long greasy hair. He spoke adequate French, a little Italian, and sometimes helped himself out with Latin. He and the mayor had been cautious at that first meeting; they had examined me with the keen penetration of Mediterranean people. Evidently my predecessors had left unpleasant memories, and I realised I would have to bear the weight, not only of that past, but of a situation that was altogether unacceptable. Zagara, the priest, was endowed with a fine baritone voice, and when he raised it in front of his square altar it could be heard far and wide.

After that first formal visit of exploration, the priest returned alone to see me. His first requests were on behalf of the village and its outskirts because the troops stationed in the area were continually raiding the chicken-runs, gardens and orchards. Zagara was respectful but not obsequious. His bright heavy eyes – like those of a Circassian or an Armenian – were continually alight with requests, hints, concealed irony. In the previous November there had been a tolling of church bells throughout the whole of Germany over the Stalingrad catastrophe. Hitler seemed possessed by incredible contempt and bitterness, almost as if the Russian resistance to his armed forces was a base revolt of slaves against their rightful master. But now the Axis troops were also having a hard time in Africa. The unheard-of strength of the American armies as displayed in Morocco was to lay them low by sheer weight. Each combatant on any given front seemed to disregard, if not positively forget, all the others; though it was common knowledge that once the fire had burnt itself out in one area of war, it moved on to the next. This time it was coming in our direction.

The priest surveyed the whole scene with calculated prolixity and tenacity, but his spoken discourse was accompanied by an important unspoken one. He pointed out that though we exacted a levy on Krano for a certain number of commodities, it lacked enough supplies for its own needs, and it was impossible to go and get them from areas under partisan control. He asked me to hand them back. I told him I needed time to think it over, then sent him away. If I decided to act in the interests of the village, and put an end to extortion and raiding, then this meant scarcity for the soldiers. Yet if I continued to be harsh towards the Greeks, then I would be risking something worse later. The conclusion, after consultation with the senior orderlies, was that we should extract by trickery from our military stores what, out of blind adherence to the lists, they were not assigning to us. As far as the Administration was concerned, the seven redoubts were scattered over three different districts, and I could get provisions in the one I viewed most suitable. We drew from all three the supplies for the whole detachment. With a triple quantity of rations, it was possible to assign double to the redoubts; and with the other third, through the priest, to set up a progressive system of exchanges between our dried foodstuffs and the fresh ones the village was able to barter. Naturally, at the first overhaul, everything would come out into the open. There was no need of the divining power of the Seer, Demetrio, to foresee the epilogue: not a single tin can would we salvage from the African armies; and hardly anyone had survived the tragedy of the Expeditionary Force in Russia, for our hundred thousand fellow-soldiers had been swallowed up by the Russian winter. The same thing would happen here. Cheered by our initial success, we drew extravagantly from the divisional stores at Tripolis – camp-beds, mosquito nets, kitchen-ware, supplies not really meant for us. The redoubts became comfortable, except for the heat and the malarial mosquitoes. Zagara was satisfied. In the village I noticed various signs of relaxation. The way had been opened to greater confidence through the guarantee of man's first need, bread.

'Commander, do you know the case of Spiropulos?' This time the mayor was there too. As I had only two chairs, I was sitting in one (compelled by protocol; I was in an official position), while Theodosius had taken possession of the other, with that wide smile of his stuck on his peasant face. The priest was standing, darting glances at me from his glinting eyes; and his wonderful vocal organs made the walls of the little room vibrate as if by magnetism. Outside, evening was drawing in.

Yes, I did know the case, alas. The house in which our conversation was taking place had previously belonged to the unfortunate Spiropulos before being requisitioned by the Command; I had been shown the walled-up niche in which the anti-partisan authorities had found four valuable fowling-pieces hidden by the Greek. Spiropulos was now in the Derveni prison.

'Spiropulos's wife and daughter,' went on the priest, 'are now at Kalamata. Second-Lieutenant Cedda of the Nuoro brigade, which used to be here, is having them protected, or so they say. And hence their position is dangerous. This would be worrying enough in itself.'

'And what else is there?'

'Look!' Zagara explained. 'Spiropulos was a rich tradesman who had retired after forty years' commerce in the Greek-Egyptian colony, Alexandria. He was totally indifferent to politics. He hid the guns because they were valuable and because he was fond of them, yet he's been imprisoned as a partisan. They say he was subjected to prolonged interrogation; it isn't clear who denounced him, and then . . .' (here the priest dulled the liquid fire of his eyes and lowered his voice) 'and then he had a way of keeping a sizeable reserve of gold in his house, and there's no trace of it. In cases of this kind the Resistance end up by intervening, even if they've been uninterested at first; and they can do that in many ways.'

'And what could I be asked to do?'

'As you know, it's almost impossible for us to move around without passports and authorisations. But someone ought to be able to help Spiropulos in his prison and make contact with his women folk at Kalamata. We know them and we don't view them as bad but only as misguided. For me these are the duties of my ministry. And I must ask you to put me in a position to carry them out.'

My visitors had been gone for some time and I was slowly reconstructing Zagara's words in my mind, retranslating and perfecting them from the mixture of languages in which they had been said, and with each examination they seemed more demanding, more persuasive; compared with this, Carruozzo's intrigues in Licudi hardly existed. Here the stakes were high: the lives of the two women who had followed Second-Lieutenant Cedda to Kalamata (and were certainly marked down in the partisans' black list); the life, the freedom and certainly the possessions of the old man; the complicated relationships between all of us and the Greeks, not only Zagara and not only in Krano; and finally, my obligations; not the ones that I could feel spontaneously as a man, but the ones thrust upon me by my function and rank. These latter were the most tiresome, and I realised that even against my will the natural effort of my mind was intent on evading them.

Our war against Greece had been unjustifiable from the start and had subsequently become a monstrous imposition. The Greek army had fought very well, and ours had been badly led, though the sacrifice of the Julia divisions had saved the honour of the flag. But in fact it was not Italy that had given Greece 'a kick in the behind' (to use Mussolini's brutal and rhetorical phrase), for we had descended on Athens to reap the fruits of the German victory. As earlier in France, public opinion could hardly be on our side.

But according to the flood of gossip in the Fascist news-sheets, this was the first experiment of high civic value ('imperial' was the word used) that Italy was facing as she presented herself as leader not of a colonial country but of age-old Greece. What was not said was that the experiment was being carried out with such disorder, abuse and corruption that it was hardly tolerable even for people who had behind them four hundred years of Turkish domination. Thus slowly the Resistance was building up round a Command situated somewhere among the rocks of the Taygetus, backed by English aid and strengthened by remnants of the Greek army that had taken to the maquis, as happened in Italy in 1943; and the spirit and rights were identical in each case. But there were also political groups who exploited the situation, vaguely-defined bands or sometimes mere brigands who subsequently fought one another. The natural forbearance of the population, the interplay of interests, and the endless web of erotic relationships (which had given our army the nickname of the Sagapò – the Love Army) cast a dangerous fog over everything. Once involved in an intrigue, it was difficult to get out of it. The Greek Spiropulos, whether partisan or not, was very badly off in his cell in the Derveni prison. And it was risky to try to get him out.

I went on to the balcony from which the master of the house must have enjoyed the beauty of the valley heaven knows how many times. At the moment the valley was lying in deep darkness. The sky was veiled by the vapours of summer and only the larger stars could just, dimly, shine through.

How could Spiropulos be my enemy, and not just a man who had fallen on adverse circumstances, even though these, if I wanted to help him, were adverse for me too? Zagara must have been thinking along the same lines because he was a priest. The motives and arguments that had led us to oppress a people with the same sensibility as ourselves and with the same, if distant, origins –

motives incomprehensible to the majority and arguments non-existent to everyone – signified to Zagara no more than one further injustice in the world to be fought mainly for the sake of the justice of heaven. As for me, who had had the rhythm of dactyls and spondees beaten into my head with the master's rod at school, how could I reject that other kind of universality enshrined in the myths which are the seed of all world history? After his life of toil, that aged merchant must have wanted to retire in peace with his women folk and his sacks of gold. He must have lived in well-deserved content until the iron hammer of war came and swept away his home. I looked at the fine olive-wood table that had once been his and I was now using. He had probably poured his precious coins all over it to count them and look at them, coins of every sort, coins such as I had seen being passed over the counters at the *bureau de change* in Athens, but with the unmistakable glint and ring of gold. I had examined the whole house, object by object, detail by detail, recognising the signs of the same labour, the same patience, the same love as had brought the House of Houses into being in the olive groves at Licudi. A sensitive hand, a mind capable of many thoughts, a fulfilled and complex life – all these were written in the choice of objects, the distribution of spaces and the skill of the furnishings. He was a man like me, who had built and lost a house like mine. Perhaps so that I should be forced to remember it? Or so that I should find the answers I needed in the sense of desecration and perfidy that breathed over this half-despoiled and dishonoured place?

Two days later the most distant of our redoubts, a few kilometres north of the ancient Venetian fortress at Kiparissia, was attacked at dusk. It was the first time; but the men were engaged for almost two hours against invisible people shooting at them from the darkness. One lancer was wounded. When morning came they found the footprints of mules in the brushwood and traces of men who had perhaps been hit and carried away. I was on the spot when the 'anti-partisans' arrived in their dusty trucks.

They were a motley crowd of the worst types, the refuse of the detachment; but according to the Divisional Command gazette their duty was 'to make the weight of reprisals felt wherever guerrillas had put in an appearance'. Dressed like real gypsies or brigands, and living in extreme licence, they had no other task but to turn everything upside-down. But this time the nearest populated centre was Kiparissia, the seat of one of our fairly important Commands which had no intention of being disturbed. So these wild men, who arrived ten hours after the skirmish when not even a vestige of the assailants remained, threw themselves at random around the cliffs, shouting and shooting. They crushed a few unlucky vines belonging to God knows who, and ended up by falling on an old peasant who was going down towards the beach with his donkey and knew nothing about anything. The cries of that ill-starred man, who was thrown from his mount and trampled underfoot like a carpet, reached even our ears. Then the trucks went swaying off though not without taking aboard, in the interests of those executors of justice, a couple of nanny-goats found grazing in the neighbourhood.

Some silence followed this episode. Krano seemed to be deserted at an early hour when I resumed my habit of painting in the little square in front of the church. Zagara came straight out of the door and sat down on the low wall beside me. After watching for a while he started to speak, and his voice coming from behind my back made my eardrums vibrate.

'We're happy that you like our village. The schoolmistress had no idea that she'd receive so many exercise-books in exchange for a piece of drawing-paper. We're grateful to you.'

The school at Krano, as I had discovered, was a fit rival to the one at San' Giovanni, above Licudi. But for a couple of years the mistress had failed to obtain even a minimal allowance of teaching materials. So the lancers, feigning a sudden love for evening classes, had got hold of a case of them from the Divisional Command: not bartered against a single sheet of drawing-paper, as Zagara had so courteously suggested, but against sheep's cheese of the most delicate quality.

'I feel sure,' the priest went on, 'that as you're living in Spiropulos's own house, our pressures on his behalf won't be forgotten. We have faith in your Command, and we are sorry to hear that there has been an incident, though it happened far away from here.'

'If it had happened here,' I answered, 'we would have had a lot of trouble in the village. But even so, the redoubt down there belongs to my Detachment; and the fact that I've done my best for Krano hasn't spared me the attentions of the Andartes.'

'Oh!' Zagara answered, 'there are bands and bands; war is war; and there might perhaps be some ill-feeling towards you about this Spiropulos business. But, all told, we didn't suffer any loss of materials or arms, and only one slightly wounded man. And then...' Here the priest's voice stopped.

'All right,' I said after I had made three or four brush strokes that seemed to me good. 'The Command of the Nuoro Division has summoned me to Tripolis the day after tomorrow because they want a first-hand account of certain details. There'll be a place on my transport; but you must find some plausible reason.'

The sun was beginning to get hot, submerging the valley in a bright haze. And later, when I was in my room looking at that olive-wood table, the priest's powerful voice came to me every now and then as he sang lauds inside the church. It was the voice of prayer but so warm and sunny that you'd have thought it was a love song. And the war seemed absurd, and to have vanished.

(*From fragments of my diary: Krano, March 1943.*)

Yesterday morning I went with a section of my men to one of the redoubts to change the guard. On our way we stopped at the foot of a hill whose slopes were covered with beautifully-tended vines. Though the grapes were bitter, there were plenty of them already showing.

Then a woman came towards me with a look at once timid and determined, as though she wanted to make some very bold demand to which she had no right; and she begged me to order my men not to damage or strip her lovely vineyard.

How many weeks have I been here? I have not yet spoken to a single child; our dealings are only with the tradesmen who come to negotiate the exchange of foodstuffs. I spend my days in trains, on dusty roads, in the dirt of open trucks, among hairy men with disquieting eyes who do the work on the railway lines. I never hear gentle voices or laughter. Only Zagara's golden voice raised in song, and the responses from his silvery choir; though I have never seen what this consists of. The frightened schoolmistress who gave me my drawing-paper is always disconcerted if we meet, and tightens her lips. She is afraid the Partisans will think she is friendly with us, and shave her head.

Below lies the hump of the Taygetus. When I go down to the plain towards Meligalà I get a glimpse of it: solid, compact, and with leafy woods lying thick over its red cliffs. Later when the colour gets darker and stiller in the motionless enamel of the early evening, you would think it was a mythical animal covered by its woolly coat and exhaling deep warmth and scents. It is somewhere buried in there that the Greek guerrillas have their headquarters; somewhere there lies the hiding-place of the bands and the sum of all hatred. But all the same for me it exhales 'the odour of lambs and milk' – just like Licudi in the past.

*

General Coi, commanding officer of the Nuoro Division garrisoning the central Peloponnese, was one of those men who had risen from the ranks (as they say). He had attained his lofty position through uninterrupted service since the Libyan war in 1911 (when he was a volunteer before he was twenty) up till the war in Spain, always picking up semi-official but important posts. There were six rows of ribbons on his chest, the first one – blue – bearing witness to his courage under fire. Though short in stature, he was robust and pulsating with life; and vigorous but friendly in manner. Thus did he receive me, later placing me beside him at the mess (like the colonel in Modena so many years before).

Now I have to go back a little. When we reached the Morea our group had had to halt near Corinth, and here a General even more highly placed than Coi had decided to review the troops – who had seemed to him fairly fresh on arrival but were really utterly worn out, what with the Crostolo, mobilisation, the troop-train and the Athenian suburbs. This General was a heavy ponderous man compared with Coi's liveliness and athleticism. Weighing well over two hundred pounds, flabby, of yellowish complexion, and squeezed into a uniform that tried in vain to bestow on him a military outline, this incredible condottiere was unquestionably living in a dream-world of vanity and euphoria. Even from a distance you could catch whiffs of the strong scent sprinkled on his person – a sure sign that he must have taken full advantage of the erotic adventures that the situation permitted. I was reminded of Omobono, of happy memory: had fate assigned him a Command, he would have interpreted his position in very much the same way. And the General had in his power nothing less than the Army Corps and the magnificent headquarters at Derveni.

Having assembled the men on a dusty plain, he had ordered a rostrum to be improvised from a triple row of benches placed one on top of the other; and from this he intended to address us. But first he wanted a full-size military review, a ceremony that ended in disaster. The lancers had been thoroughly instructed in horsemanship in peace-time, and ever since the war they had mounted guard so continuously that they had positively put down roots. But if they were unprepared for this manœuvre on foot, so were the officers, and more so; and the pitiful disorder of the whole affair culminated in a gaffe as innocent as it was ridiculous – for our major, the nobleman Costa Oliviero, in bringing his troops up to the rostrum where the General was standing, told them at the crucial moment to present arms before he had ordered them to fix bayonets. So while Oliviero, his back towards us and carrying out the order he himself had given, was standing stock still with drawn sword in the regulation position, behind him a farce worthy of a French film was taking place. One man was hurriedly fixing his bayonet, another presenting arms without bayonet, while the majority were consulting with their comrades with their arms held anyhow. The very important General contemplated the whole scene with bitterness, but it did not rob him of his speech.

Unfortunately his words were not only thwarted by the wind which raised high waves of dust (and, anyway, in a vast open area such as this he would have to be a Stentor to be heard), but no sooner had he begun than a column of German tanks passed nearby, drowning all his attempts at eloquence in the infernal clatter of their caterpillar tracks. True, with an air of great arrogance, he dispatched an Ordnance Officer to halt the tanks, but as the emissary did not really believe in his errand it was ineffectual, for the Germans first stopped a moment to listen to him, then pulled down their shutters and continued on their way. So it was our Major Costa who had to bear the brunt of his superior's anger, while the lancers looked on in the worst possible humour: they had seen this kind of thing often before and knew what would follow. The story of our hopeless performance spread far and wide and finally reached the ears of Coi himself; but he assured me that it was when under fire that soldiers proved their worth; that the little guard post had behaved admirably under attack; and he gave me to understand that he was thinking of coming to visit us. I left the mess somewhat relieved. It was impossible to recall the scene at Corinth without laughing; and yet it is in that type of farce (as in the days of that Fascist boss in Milan) that the germ of our misfortunes as a nation lie; even Coi, who was not really a bad man, seemed mentally ill-equipped for a post involving responsibilities that were not purely military. Like the Fascist bosses, the Generals were none of them trained to a complex or political vision of the facts (and how were they selected?). And yet the low rank from which my Coi had risen, and of which he still had a pretty strong smell, was much better than the perfumes of that other man, which made one think he was disguising some horrible disease – following the custom of the ancient Persian satraps.

I went to call on my good Major who had established himself in a withdrawn dead-end of Tripolis, and had even found a way of avoiding the communal mess at the Divisional Command. Alone with his ten or twelve lancers and the only second-lieutenant who remained to him, the Major was living a miserable life, bewailing his Lambrusco wine and his little girl-friend whom he had left in a small apartment in Jesi, well outside the city gate, he said, with a view of the hills and the quiet Esino valley. He was much thinner and the whites of his eyes had become duller. They told me it was hard to find any food that would tempt him; and as for the wine, treated with cypress resin, he found it disgusting. So the poor man was letting himself literally pine away with sadness and starvation, like a prize animal removed from its native surroundings.

'I've heard you're behaving in a thoroughly imprudent way, Sansevero. Yours is a dangerous area, as you've seen. According to regulations, you should go around with an escort, but they tell me you go around alone. What's got into your head?'

'But I assure you the Andartes have no earthly interest in me as a person,' I explained. 'They're looking for shoes, food, and arms. If I go around with four men, that means four rifles, a certain amount of ammunition, a good supply of bread, and quite a lot of clothing. Ten or fifteen of them lie in ambush for us and it's for action. But if I go alone and unarmed, and if they get me, they will only have one pair of boots, while condemning the village of Krano to flames as reprisal. It isn't worth their while. So I go around as I do, not out of bravado but common sense.'

'You mean you go unarmed, Captain? There must be something wrong with your head! I don't even want to hear you say it!'

'Please let me explain. A gun is the main bait and I don't like taking it with me. But I've got two hand-grenades of the pine-cone type from the other war, and I take those with me. Some Alpini gave them to me on the Bainsizza. I don't exactly go around with my eyes shut, and I could place them all right. They're not recoverable afterwards; nor are the men who were in their range. And you can be sure the partisans know.'

Wearily, in a soft voice, the Major gave me explicit orders always to go out with an escort of four men armed to the teeth; and with that we parted.

Meanwhile, General Coi's little court had noticed the distinction with which he had treated me, and inferred that I had personal links with him. Thus the captain in charge of the military information service at the Divisional Command thought he had to receive me effusively; and he was even generous with information that he should not have communicated to me had he been carrying out his duties seriously.

'The Spiropulos case,' he confided to me, drawing me to one side, 'has brought Second-Lieutenant Cedda the distinction granted to those who identify elements of the Resistance by their own zeal. Cedda was more than a year in the Krano redoubt, where your men are now. Perhaps he found a way into the good graces of Spiropulos's daughter, or his wife, or both; perhaps he found out from them that there were guns in that wall, or perhaps he discovered the hiding-place himself. We don't care about details, but results; and the guns really did exist, four of them, and well provided with ammunition for boar-hunting. The law is explicit; Spiropulos is at Derveni, and now it's up to the people there to make him talk.'

The captain exerted himself so far as to look up the dossier himself.

'Here we are! Cedda later brought to our notice that the two women were suspected by the partisans so were in danger at Krano, and this was why he obtained their transfer to Kalamata, where he is now, and it's a big city. I wonder if I could ask you why you're interested in this business?'

'I'm in command at Krano, and things that happened in the past can reflect on things now. I've even mentioned it to his Excellency the General who told me to watch out. I'll let you know.'

I left my friend satisfied with this promise, and became a provisional collaborator of the Information Service as I had previously been of the Propaganda Service. At the appointed hour I met Zagara where I had put him down in the morning, outside the city.

'The archimandrite asked me to thank you,' he said. 'The visit has been useful.'

Those were almost the only words we exchanged during the interminable return journey. We had been told that the roads and railways of the upper Peloponnese had been built by Italian firms over the past ten years. But as they had been paid for by the mile, those thoroughfares twisted like snakes between the folds of the hills and seemed always to stay more or less at the same point. When I got back to Krano I noticed that I did not say to myself, 'Here I am at the Command,' but 'Here I am, home again.' And it was Spiropulos's house that was giving me this sense of comfort.

These events occurred in the spring; but with the advance of summer the fortunes of the war came to a head. The defeats in Africa were now definitive and had closed that round of the match; the Allies were now in Sicily and their control over the Mediterranean could no longer be contested. The fate of our army in Greece – an enemy country, difficult to defend and almost isolated – was becoming precarious indeed. An intolerable heat fell on the country and with it there was a premature outbreak of malaria. The soldiers manning the redoubts in the lower areas of Messina were particularly afflicted but it was impossible to remove the men owing to lack of reinforcements. Then suddenly partisan activity increased. The reckless euphoria of the Athens Commands collapsed at a stroke. The Germans, who had hitherto kept only a few troops in Southern Greece and the Morea, got on the move. But they did not come to Krano because it was hardly more than a village.

And now when I came out on to the church square to contemplate the valley as it disappeared among the fiery eventide mists, I had Zagara and the mayor Theodosius as my almost constant companions. I had performed various other services for those two. I had enabled the priest to recover some paintings on wood from an enterprising colonel who was already getting them packed up to take away; it was said that as a good southern Italian he wanted to offer them to the Madonna of Pompeii for favours received, but a sudden transfer had interrupted this charitable operation. Though the paintings were only a few decades old, the antique style had been recaptured to perfection – so much so as to remind me of the patient work of the novices at the Virgo. As for Theodosius, I was not grudging about permits for his trips to Laconia, Attica and Messina; 'cattle' he always gave as his pretext, while Zagara said 'churches'; but in fact they both unquestionably belonged to the Resistance. A current of secret thoughts had been set up between us as participants in the vast understanding of the Mediterranean, and my classical imagination enabled me to appreciate all that lay behind the mayor's shrewdness and the priest's zeal. Though extraneous to them in practice, I felt myself within their complex of words and deeds and vowed to interpreting them.

'The government,' Zagara was saying, resuming a conversation begun some while before, 'the government made use of a study prepared by an Englishman named Cockerell for the restoration of the temple. But these days the Paulista mountains are inaccessible; a pity, because the monument is wonderful.'

'Why inaccessible?' I asked, for I had pored over maps and taught myself about the area from an old guide-book. 'Our redoubt at the end of the Kiparissia beach is near the mouth of the old Neda. If I went up that valley I would soon find myself in the heart of Phigalia, between Cotylium and Asum consecrated to Black Demeter. And if I couldn't go from that direction, I could try the other, set out from Megalopolis, and reach the high plateau like that. It would only take a day.'

'Perhaps Signor Commander,' said the priest, when he had translated the gist of my remarks to the mayor, who looked on with curiosity, 'perhaps you haven't a very precise idea of the nature of those mountains, and don't realise that to venture into an area controlled by the guerrillas, and without any roads, would require considerable forces – out of all proportion for an archaeological trip.'

'Considerable forces,' I replied, 'or else one man alone. That's how I see it. The Divisional Commander wouldn't loan me a regiment, but you two could find me a guide.'

For both them and me there were good reasons for reverting to this discussion about the temple of Bassae. The emotion that had once impelled me to discover and make contact with Uncle Gian Michele's woods, was now driving me towards this new project; it was a direct challenge to circumstances and good sense, but seemed to me to combine the exercise of a right and the fulfilment of a duty. We were in Greece as an enemy occupying force, and had totally disregarded the obligation to venerate the land that had nurtured every particle of our culture. In the name of Art and Truth I was hoping to redeem the collective sin by this single unknown offering: and thus refuse to accept the sin. If Dolfo had given his life on the Goliko for the sheer exaltation of his power; if the Seer

Demetrio had used up the vital energies of perhaps a whole year of his secret existence so as to dominate weight under my eyes and thereby prove himself as worthy of life; then I should climb the mountain consecrated to myth, and place my being at the foot of Ictinus's monument and do so unarmed. The chant of the nuns uprooted from the world, as I had heard it on that distant Christmas night in the Roman basilica of Santi Quattro Coronati, became fused in my memory with those other melting chants on icy mornings at my school. There was no doubt that the devout voice of the saint alone in his cave had the power to atone for sin in God's eyes.

To these lofty flights of fancy were added other thoughts of a similar kind. A conjunction of things was coming into being, and the moment it reached completion, at that moment precisely, then I would be ready to go; like an astronomer who, at a specific moment in time and point in space, and only then, can perceive the interconnections of a star. I convinced myself that I had perhaps come here for no other reason but to seek out and achieve that unique pilgrimage; and that when I had done it everything would be decided, everything settled; and that I would be able to move off towards other points of rest. These thoughts flowed thick and fast. As night spread over the valley my interlocutors fell silent, and we could hear men's faint voices, and cowbells; and the damp twilight breeze sprang up to blow away the scorching day.

'I've heard,' I went on, continuing the same conversation, 'that Napoleon Zervas is interested in Spiropulos. The old man's fate is in the balance; but if Zervas intervenes it would indicate that relations really did exist between Spiropulos and the Andartes.'

'It's a very confused situation,' said Zagara, 'and Zervas's intervention could mean any number of things.'

Napoleon Zervas, the leader of the Greek Resistance, was naturally much discussed; many people thought he was living in Athens itself under the aegis of the highest protection. The captain of the Information Service at Tripolis had let me know 'on an absolutely private line' that someone had seen to it (heaven knows how) that Spiropulos was at least left in peace in his Derveni cell. At first he had been subjected to the string treatment (a piece of string with knots in it progressively tightened with a twisting movement round the temples) but he had given nothing away. No more was known; but perhaps Zagara was better informed than the military office.

'We've already spoken of the gold Spiropulos may have hidden in his house,' the priest went on, 'but nothing has been found except the guns. It's possible that it was, or is, in a place known only to the old man . . .'

There was a silence in which our thoughts confronted each other, trying each other out like combatants who pause for breath. Then the priest resolutely threw himself into the risk he had to run.

'Let's suppose,' he said, 'that Spiropulos promised those funds to the Resistance which certainly needed them. It would be a good motive for Zervas; and he would then have a way of getting the old man out of prison. But the difficulty lies in getting into his house, which is at the moment your headquarters as commander. The partisans would only be able to do it by force and that would involve reprisals on Krano. Of course these are only theories of my own!'

'Zagara,' I immediately replied, 'I want to visit the temple up at Bassae. Give me a guide. If I get back we'll carry on this conversation.'

The priest got up with a bow, and Theodosius did the same. And they went off without exchanging a word with each other. Mosquitoes came to buzz irritatingly round my face. On the mountain peaks, towards the north-east, an overpowering brightness announced that the moon was rising. And in my imagination there rose the noble sanctuaries sacred to Apollo Epikourios.

Acts prompted by impulse, acts that far outstrip the limits imposed by authority or convention but burn with instinct and passion, acts that challenge us to set out on an adventure, if not to achieve the impossible – these are the ones that stand out in our memory as vivid, real and unquestionable certainties. That was why, in the past, I had so often wanted to go into reverse, wanted what was forbidden, because only there could I find the authentic taste of life, something I almost owed to all the shades that had prepared its course, and to the thoughts that had consumed me. And now, in the torrid glare of July, I felt I was again entering the absurd, if only within myself and before myself; I was again being drawn to that shining point, there to anchor a great moment of my life.

I knew I could be assured of Zagara's protection, but it was he who had told me that there were 'bands' and 'bands'. He could pass the word to the regular partisans, to Zervas's lot, and to the ones under English command in the Taygetus; but he could not safeguard me against the outlaws infesting the area, nor against the small bands carrying on guerrilla warfare on their own account, and those were the most ruthless. So I was committing an action with risks on two counts; first, I was setting out on that unknown journey without really being certain of the priest's guarantee, and at the same time involving myself in helping him as if he had given me this guarantee; and second, by making it possible for him to find Spiropulos's gold (and he had not concealed from me that it would go to the Resistance), my action had the ring of treachery owing to my uniform; and this could rebound against my own soldiers, if not against myself. The final knot in the tangle: the life of a man who had been cruelly stripped of all his possessions and whose desecrated home I had hourly under my eyes.

Moreover, I had to bear in mind that our military structure was on the point of collapse; and that, when it came to the reckoning, we would find ourselves alone; and each man of us would then have to choose and provide for his own destiny. Here there were no roads to enable the defeated soldier to escape home. Our army had already yielded the island of Sicily to the Allies almost without a blow, so it would certainly offer them no resistance on the coasts of Greece. Everything was uncertain, and had many facets. And everything could lead to a crisis of conscience, to yet greater danger, to useless sacrifice, or to searing dishonour.

These were the arguments put forward by reason. But a secret instinct accompanied by almost childish lightheartedness and unconquerable joy, made me realise that these evaluations did not really count with me. My sense of honour was profoundly moved by the priest's trust in me. He had placed himself in my hands and, what was more, he had tested me with the tinkle of gold. As master of his secrets I could have betrayed him; whereas the pride of the Sanseveros made me, in my turn, respond by placing myself in his hands. Moreover, I wanted him to understand the motives of what must have seemed like a senseless action; the votive act whereby I felt I was asking his people for spiritual forgiveness, at least as regarded myself. It was a reconciliation for which it did not seem excessive to risk my life, and one that should show that neither Spiropulos's gold nor anyone else's meant anything to people who really wished to come together over and above the prevailing hostile circumstances – that is to say, circumstances that required men to be enemies when they themselves wanted to be acknowledged purely and simply as human beings.

In the middle of July, after a brief visit to headquarters at Megalopolis, I returned as far as the bay of Karytaena by a military transport luckily going in my direction; and when that had pushed off into the distance I saw in front of me the little shepherd boy who was to be my guide. In the silence that enveloped us my bonds with my country, with the Army, with the whole war were suddenly severed; it was a silence so fresh and free within the scents of the wood that it seemed to belong to another world. I had been warned that the going would be extremely difficult, as all well-trodden paths, roads and villages would have to be avoided. I would have to follow cattle-tracks hidden in the folds of the mountains, and Zagara himself had given detailed instructions to the boy – a kind of Arab with bright bold eyes. And so we walked hour after hour through those deserted expanses. Sometimes I heard the rushing of a stream, the rolling of a stone; and then only the faint rustling of leaves. But as we never met a living soul we were usually surrounded by enchanted silence, and again it seemed to me that I was travelling towards another planet; and always with that indescribable feeling of happiness, so that sometimes I smiled as I went along while the most disparate memories flooded into my mind – prompted now by a hornet, now by the shape of a rock, now by a flower. It was the evening walk at the monastery on the Virgo; it was the cart high against the sky bringing the stones to build my house, with the dazzling sea lying below; it was the people of Licudi hurrying towards their Madonna over the rocky shingle of the torrent-beds, between the gleam of the water and the darkness of the shadows, in the light of the moon.

In the afternoon we rested and only began walking again with the approach of evening. Sometimes my guide paused and listened; and I too sometimes thought I heard the sound of footsteps or of distant engines down in the valleys; or sometimes, perhaps, the echo of a shot. Then silence returned and reached out ever further as the evening slowly spread around us.

And as daylight faded, an immense radiance beyond the horizon heralded the rising of the moon. It was under her guidance and in a sparser undergrowth that we climbed the final slopes; and the temple appeared before us.

We stayed concealed among the trees for a long time without

going right up to our goal, as the place was obviously used as a reference and rallying point and also as a shelter. But later, when the moon withdrew up to the heights and grew smaller and spread her gentle light evenly over the milky landscape infusing it with peace, then we crossed the clearing and installed ourselves in the deep recesses of the temple. There were the remains of a bivouac and a lingering smell of smoke, but the embers and cinders were cold. The boy signalled to me gracefully to be on my guard with both ears open for the slightest sound – and on such limpid nights sounds carried from afar – then rolled himself up in his blanket and fell asleep. But I communed for long with that silence, that darkness, that void. On the dark mass of the low pillars I saw no blossoming of shapes or designs, but I felt the emanations of the heavy heat that they had absorbed from the sun during the day. And perhaps because I was so tired I had a dreamlike sense of being nowhere; of being suspended in some extraordinary entity which was the sum of all my days, and where I had to lie motionless – like my little guide, in sleep.

It was then that the screech-owl suddenly let out its shrill cry. First with that double top note, almost an angle of notes, followed by a quaver in a minor key, a plaintive echo of the first cry. Through the chinks in the walls I saw the scorched and holy landscape spread out beneath the radiance of the moon, prostrate before the altar of God, whence in return it awaited its own redemption. But the ominous and most noble cry of the bird of wisdom brought home to me the pull towards ideal abstraction found in its devotee. Eyes that see in the night, and the call of a solitary voice – to make you shudder, yet to set you boldly on your way.

The return was exhausting, an interminable trek through the desert lands that had once formed the territory of ancient Phigalia. At last we saw the rim of the high plateau over towards the mountains above Krano; and we arrived there almost at dusk. The lancers were waiting in some anxiety though I had told them when I left that I would be away for the night. Zagara was not to be seen, but my little guide – who had disappeared the moment the village came into sight – must have informed him. Before I fell asleep – and for a while weariness held me suspended in a sort of elation where sounds and lights appeared to be multiplied – I seemed to hear voices calling me by name. But though I could not distinguish them I knew they belonged to people I had loved and lost, people who were watching over me so that I should not lose myself.

About a week later, at the end of July, the Fascist Regime in Italy collapsed. King Victor Emmanuel, who had decorated Mussolini with the Collar of the Annunziata and called him 'cousin', had no hesitation in arresting the man from whose hands he had accepted the crown of Emperor of Ethiopia, and this inside his own palace where a guest should be looked on as sacred, under the sign of Jupiter, and in accordance with a rule that would be followed by the poorest shepherd of our mountains.

General Badoglio – an ambiguous figure for long suspected of treachery, for many years in charge of the army, and to whom were unquestionably due its lack of preparation, its disorder, and that underground disintegration bordering on sabotage – took over power and ordered the armies to 'continue the war'; an absurdity that could not stand up to the most superficial examination. I unfolded a map of the region in front of my mournful major and pointed out the reality of a situation which was precisely one of geography.

'Our links with Italy along the Balkan railway are as tenuous as a hair. Between Morea and Attica there is only the Corinth bridge – another hair. If the Allies appear on the beaches, the Athens Command will have its hands full dealing with the bulk of our army in the north up to Salonika – no more than that. Not one of our group will get back past the canal.'

'So what do you want to do? And what do you want me to do? You're a captain with ninety men and I'm a major with twenty-two. Leave the map alone and let what will be be.'

The good man was suffering badly. To compensate for his loneliness he had found a little Greek girl who could remind him of the one he had left behind in Jesi – at least this was the gossip of the Orderly Room. And this new affection now redoubled his woes by adding infinite fears and anxieties. Furthermore, as a declared monarchist and convinced aristocrat, he saw thick clouds gathering over the throne of the House of Savoy, and at the same time had to turn a deaf ear to the mutterings of his men who were becoming increasingly red and less and less subject to discipline.

'Look,' I went on, 'you're in a better position with twenty men backed up by the Division than we are with ninety divided between seven redoubts in the middle of the mountains. If the Allies disembark they'll take their usual few weeks to reach the high points from the beach; and if the bridge is closed behind us we'll have the partisans on our backs, and we'll have to fight, ten men at a time, against a whole country in revolution. With the Andartes, that's all right; but with the Communist bands, or worse, the brigands, you know what lies in store for us. It's my duty to say this because it concerns the lives of them all.'

'So what? What?' he said restlessly, clutching at the rosette he wore as a Knight of Malta. It was already pretty bedraggled on his dusty jacket.

'And then keeping the men scattered like this means condemning them to a nasty end. There's nothing more to guard now, no bridges or anything else. Get permission to round up the detachment here, where at least there'll be a lot of us. Or let me get mine together at Krano. The General would certainly understand this kind of talk!'

But two days later Coi calmly came up to 'inspect' the Krano redoubt, as he had promised. He inspected it minutely, made the most apt observations where it seemed suitable, then gathered together the little platoon of twelve in a heat that was melting the rocks, first to regale them with a talk and then to make me exercise them so that he could judge their training (he, too!). The platoon, worn out with malaria and the heat, carried out the General's orders but left him dissatisfied (like the other one!).

'Are you trying to spare your voice?' he asked me. 'Just you see how a detachment is commanded . . .'

And that Divisional Commander, amused at returning to those distant times when he was in the ranks, displayed a splendid voice sending those twelve up and down, while all of us (including himself) had a hatchet at our throats. It would have been vain to repeat to such a man the arguments that even the good Oliviero would not have put forward.

The lancers looked at me pitifully. But what could they hope from me?

That evening I told Zagara that I had to carry out some repairs in the house of the Command, and could he find me suitable workmen. Especially as the repairs seemed urgent.

That August was one of anguish. There were persistent rumours that the war would end soon, and the silence of the Greeks was heavy with implications; but for them too the hope of liberation was accompanied by fear of the problems involved; countless was the number of those marked out by the Resistance as collaborators with the enemy, if not outright traitors. Our army on its side was enfeebled and corrupted by two years of collusion and malversation and had no power to pull itself together: a mass without a soul, heavy with burdens and destitute of energy. General Carlo Geloso, rumoured to be King Victor Emmanuel's natural brother, who had been living luxuriously in the princely villa of Cape Kavouri among incredible dissipations and secret extortions, found himself succeeded (after a sensational and discreditable inquiry) by a good man, but not much more; a man, in other words, of the type of my Major Oliviero, who was far indeed from that greatness required for taking control of situations which by their very nature called for the mind and spirit of an ancient Roman consul; and there were hundreds of higher officers who, like Nappa, had intrigued for a post in Athens for their own profit but were now trembling in their shoes; it was they who had reduced our army in Greece (the Super-Grecia) to the weak and bloated monster that it was. The Germans, on the other hand, far from showing signs of doubt, every day brought fresh and powerful troops to Morea and the beaches; on the one hand foreseeing our defection, and on the other determined to hold the country. A new and unexpected danger, as the conflict between these two forces – of which ours was superior in numbers, theirs in readiness and close-knit structure – would have given rise to chaos, especially with the unpredictable attitude of the Greeks thrown in.

From the fragments of the diary I kept at that time, I have found the following:

Krano, August.

Malaria has struck down two-thirds of the men; it is impossible for me to replace the sick at the guard posts; and, consumed with fever in a heat that has reached 40 degrees down in the valley, we live in a sort of hallucination, our arms reaching out to the machine-gun. Most of the troops have been away from Italy for about three years; the desire to put an end to it all has assumed the force of an intention. Fed up with the absence from their families, with inertia, with their own deterioration, the men look longingly towards the oasis of home so as to rest at last and find themselves again.

My contacts with Zagara are rare now. I have given him a mule and it may be that he visits the chapels in the mountains and makes his golden voice heard there. As for myself, I am doing all I can to stock up the redoubts with food and ammunition so that they will be able to manage as well as possible when they find themselves isolated, as I foresee they will.

Lying on a piece of tent canvas drenched with my sweat, in the infernal heat of the valley where I often have to spend the night, stunned with quinine yet aware of the hum of fever in my ears, once again I am faced with a mysterious haze, an enigma of arguments, an obscure turn of events in which no single thought can get the upper hand and no intention really formulate itself.

A few days ago, at a specified hour, I sent four of the nine men remaining at the Krano Command out on a fatigue; three to the redoubt on some pretext; the rest to the village. Then two Greek workmen turned up to do the repairs about which I had consulted Zagara, and they carried them out in less than half an hour in one of the store-rooms, while I remained alone in my office. One of the two saluted me with a nod of the head on departure, and I had to admit he had a certain style. His shining eyes and lean taut face, coupled with the deep eye-sockets, bore witness to a harsh life; but his noble bearing was not that of a peasant. Perhaps the partisans thought I wanted to make friends of them, now that our cause was lost. I know that I was not thinking of myself at all, but of things as they appeared to me, with myself removed: of the ninety men whose fate lay more or less in my hands; of Spiropulos's freedom, paid for after all with the gold belonging to him alone; and especially of Greece, and its ancient face of wisdom which I had glimpsed that night behind the screech-owl's cry. Doubt as to the motives and justice of my actions – that is the highest price I ought to pay. So my glance answered the glance of that man. In the evening Theodosius brought me another piece of drawing-paper on behalf of the schoolmistress. He begged me to do a watercolour of our headquarters which had formerly been Spiropulos's house: to keep, so it would appear, among his records.

Shortly after this there was another incident: the fifth redoubt guarding the railway bridge over a remote ravine can be reached only by the railway itself. I often go there in an antiquated steam train which puffs away when climbing and goes too fast when descending. Sometimes there are crowds of Greeks in the goods trucks; I am often alone with them, in an unlit truck and at night.

Then I have to order them all to huddle up on one side of the truck while I sit on the other side with my torch pointing at them and those two famous hand-grenades within reach. Those faces, white with exhaustion in the beam of the torch, worn out by their wretched lives, return to my memory like ghosts.

When I arrive I stop at the signal-box lying in that remote corner of the mountains, five minutes away from the redoubt and the bridge. I return there to wait for another train to take me back up the line and sometimes the wait is long. The signalman is exactly like our Calabrians; massive build, highly coloured complexion, moustaches like King Umberto, cheerful loquacity. It all reminds me of those little stations on the line rising from the Ionian Sea towards Melito di Portosalvo, around Tropea. I had already got my tongue round a few words of Greek – or perhaps, without knowing it, of dialect. In any case I talked as best I could with that man.

Last time the train was late and deep night had fallen; in the increasingly solemn silence we, too, ended up by having nothing more to say. When at last I reached the Command two hours later a telephoned message from the redoubt was awaiting me. Aroused by gunfire, the lancers had gone down to the signal-box and found the signalman shot by people who had already got away. It was said that the man was involved in some sort of denunciation or spying, but the people who killed him must have waited for me to leave, with the deliberate intention of not touching me. Perhaps I am already in Zagara's debt, and this weighs on me.

Towards the end of August Spiropulos was released; it seems that he is safe in Athens and that his women are now with him. But Lieutenant Cedda has fallen victim to an ambush on some country track, beneath one of those tall geranium hedges that blend so nobly with the cypresses of the Peloponnese. Why is it my destiny to be involved in the destiny of others, when I feel it to be so extraneous and remote?

Yesterday a lancer arrived here from the redoubt on the beach at Kiparissia which has already been attacked once; he had fled from his post. He was trembling violently as he told me a tale of assaults and deaths; and yet nothing had in fact happened. This stifling heat coupled with the delirium of fever fills the silences of the midday sun with frightening spectres. And the night, infected by the malarial mosquito as it may be, is not long enough.

Athens, September 3.
At noon on the last day of August I dropped in unexpectedly at the military command at Meligalà. It had for long been in the hands of a captain who disposed of a whole company of infantry in this small town of little pink houses basking in the sun; he was a stupid man who had committed countless abuses earlier on and now could not conceal the panic that beset him. He had shut himself up in a real and proper redoubt and one had to wind one's way along a trench to find him. My visit and his good manners were decisive for his destiny and certainly had a modifying effect not only on mine but on that of everyone bound up with mine at that time. Fate?

When I left after lunch the captain took it into his head to accompany me outside the trench and towards the apparently deserted square lying in the burning midday sun. We were hardly in the open and taking leave of each other when I saw a dark object plunging towards us from the top of a roof. I leapt into the trench. I saw him fall, and it was certainly to him that the attention of the Resistance had been directed. A few hours later, before making contact with my own men again, I ran into the good Major Oliviero at Tripolis station. Patiently and without irony he made what would also have been Uncle Gedeone's comment:

'You see! They used a hand-grenade on you this time!'

That night I reached Hospital No. 536 in Athens wearing only trousers, boots and a shirt. With commendable perseverance a tiny splinter of metal has again lodged itself in that battered left eye of mine. The other wounds are not much more than bruises. As for the captain of Meligalà, he is dead.

In the torrid breath of the late afternoon the muslin curtains – which formed a very high, threadbare and somewhat dusty wall – scarcely trembled. From beyond the residences disposed around the king's former palace, from the squares in front of it, and from the low gardens, there rose a confused clamour which sometimes grew fainter and then swelled again to fill the spaces, like smoke from a bonfire which now curls thinly and then picks up and swirls thickly around, according to whether the wind clamps down on it or kindles it. And smoke indeed was rising from distant points in spirals and curtains and clouds, mingled with indefinable scents and continually hanging over and permeating that vast tide of shouts and noises which seemed to come from a countless crowd running through the city; a city, perhaps, with doors and windows thrown open, not because of merry-making and gift-offering but owing to abandonment and fear.

The architecture of the hall was of the majestic Wagnerian school where heavy German fin-de-siècle blends with classical art, but the hall itself, though immense, was denuded. Weighty glass showcases contained bronzes, marbles and earthenware, but the collections had been ravaged and decimated, and though efforts had been made to cover up the empty spaces, the dust made them all the more obvious. Mr Niko was standing humbly before me, waiting. His striking ugliness was redeemed by his discreet but penetrating eyes and his exquisite manners; at first sight one would have said that he was a retired don. His French, which he had learnt from books, sounded very pure in as much as it was academic.

'My cousin,' Madame Theodora interrupted, 'is convinced that you should decide quickly!'

Unlike Niko, Madame was large and masculine and unquestionably suffered from diminished feminine appeal owing to the down that darkly adorned her upper lip and cheeks, but to the entire advantage of her energy. Nor did this deprive her of style; and her interests, in the days when she had had them, would certainly not have been of the kind limited to words.

Imprisoned in my uniform, I felt distinctly uneasy in front of them, so said nothing. The black eye-patch over my ill-used eye must have endowed me with a heroic aura – in very poor accord with the circumstances. It was through the good offices of the Archimandrite of Tripolis and Zagara's unexpected solicitude that I had my letter of introduction to these two people. I was meeting them for the first time; and cards needed to be put on the table.

'Look,' Mr Niko went on affably, 'it's impossible to know what's going to happen, but it's certain that the alternatives to be faced will be serious. At least you're in a favourable situation, even if it's against your will, because you have only yourself to answer for and not any troops. That simplifies a lot of things, because nowadays anyone who's alone is lucky!'

'Think it over,' Madame Theodora advised, 'and have the courage of your convictions. We have at our disposal the entire wardrobe of our relations who have taken refuge in Egypt, so why not take a civilian suit for the time being – it could be useful; and then if you prefer to come over to us, who's going to make an issue of it with all this confusion!'

As I was walking up again towards the hospital, the tumult from the city followed me and hung over me, the shouts coming more quickly now with the approach of dusk. The armistice had been announced three days ago and the bottom had fallen out of everything by now; but at least in Athens the outward structures still remained, even if they were tottering and cracking up in unprecedented clouds of confusion and disorder. The huge and already finalised event was crashing headlong all around us, incredibly swift and as if static owing to the immensity of the void: millions of age-old episodes, millions of age-old intentions circumscribed by the occasion. That very simple definition of history – 'how things really happened' – posed the whole problem of it yet again; no mind would have explained, or even registered, a chain-reaction of numbers capable of thus committing the nations. It was so often impossible to verify a single small detail of the communal happening. Who, with such an infinitude of motives put forward to obscure it, who would have been able to bring the truth up from the bottom of its well and lay it bare?

Thus with no regrets I felt my mind turning away from relentless reality so as to find refuge – then as now – in the only authentic history possible to it: the secret, sweet, destructive history of itself; the only one really known in its smallest events, its subtlest motives, its imperceptible links; which was nothing compared with that other history, yet nevertheless was so drawn into the myriad of existences above its own tiny wave that it seemed its source and then its head. An interminable river but made our own again in desire and memory, and if only because of that little trickle of water necessary for our own minimal life.

It was already a week since the eye doctor – a major – of Hospital No. 536 had removed the small splinter lodged in my pupil. As he was manœuvring his instruments he pressed on my eyeball so as slightly to distort it, and this produced a corresponding distortion of everything I saw: a phenomenon usually brought about by nausea, but in me, by association, provoking it. I then fell victim to the well-known chronic pessimism of oculists; it is my opinion that in some obscure way they are infected by the fear and sadness staring at them in close-up from the tearful or bloodshot eyes with which they have to deal; and in any case on this occasion the Major had no particularly cheerful news to impart,

'It's an ill-wind that blows nobody any good,' he said as he went on exploring my eye with his lenses and waving his treacherous instruments about in the air. 'You're now going to get a splendid six months' leave and a visit home before everything here collapses.'

'It's collapsing as soon as that, is it? And what about my men stranded in the depths of the Morea mountains? Who's going to help those poor fellows?'

'Certainly not you!' he said, shaking his head lugubriously. 'You must keep this eye shut for at least two weeks and do as little as possible with the other one. Heaven preserve us from a complication which could lose you both of them!'

Relieved of the splinter but fed up to the teeth with ill-humour and boredom, I had then returned to the darkness of the little room and stayed there for four days like a bat hanging by the feet from the stalactites of a cave. Four days – each one bringing us nearer, though we were unaware of it, to that inevitable collapse. And when the bandage was removed at least from my good eye, I was able to occupy that slender thread of time – having no idea that it would be the last – in writing to my good Major, to tell him it was useless putting me in charge of the baggage as in any case I would first be going to take leave of my detachment. He sent me a phonogram wishing me a good recovery, and before that he had given me an introduction to the personal attaché to the commander-in-chief o our army in Greece. Those were the parting shots of that modest member of the flock of the Cross of Malta, and he wasted them on me whom he was never to see again. It was the 6th of September.

Next day, in defiance of the oculist's explicit orders, I went to call on the attaché. Like me, he was a mere cavalry captain but had avoided military service thanks to protection from on high; he received me in the vast neo-classical building of the General Headquarters, in surroundings that were luxurious but dark owing to thick curtains and lowered lights. He made no mystery of the rumours spreading like wildfire through the town. An important personage had arrived a few hours before on a secret mission from Rome and was still in conference with His Excellency. Something was on the point of happening. I asked him to release me from hospital and send me back to my men.

'Don't move from here!' he cut me short. 'You must leave your detachment to others. Where do you imagine you can go with only one eye?'

So making slow progress through the tumultuous crowds thronging the marble pavements of the main thoroughfares, I set off to find an attaché at the Legation – a contact of my own this time. He lent me a shirt and a jacket, and when I had exchanged the ostentatious hospital bandage for a narrow black band I went back into the street. I was so unused to civilian clothes that they seemed very light, almost as if I had nothing on. But the weight of the heat and the intensity of the noise and lights bewildered me. An enormous sense of freedom invaded my breast, as when one goes out for the first time alone. This detaching of myself from the war, as the product of active desire and an exercise of my sovereign power (an action which my mind had anticipated in conceiving the idea of the expedition to the Bassae temple), was now becoming more clearly defined. And the immense drama into which Italy was about to plunge dazzled me as if it was her very liberation that was in question, whereas really she was about to pass over to the other side, the side of the conquered and the oppressed, and I was about to pass over with her. It seemed impossible that my heart should be so light!

I shall never forget that summer evening! I was as unknown and unattached as in those early days at the Roman hotel up among the swallows, and again I was separated from everything, though not by my own will this time; and with yet another deep dive into my memory I discovered the resourceful delights of the little boy intent on exploring and exorcising the big house at San Sebastiano; the little boy turned into an unknown, unseen spirit, and gifted with nothing save the mysterious power of penetrating and understanding.

The city was noisy and brightly lit and in a great state of elation, hot with the summer heat and feverish with the imminence of a crisis towards which the collective soul was already moving and preparing itself, like a choir about to give voice. Owing to the ready intuition that runs through a crowd when great events are pending, everyone knew that shortly they would be living not as subjected to a demon but as protagonists in an important page of their history; that in the narrow space that was to contain the conquered and the conquerors, their real substances would have to face each other and come to grips with each other and express some measure of absolute value that was over and above force: as a proof of mind and civilisation. And the swelling excited throng was already assembling and forming the first and most certain images of that foreknowledge. One's glance slipped behind the rhythm of the footsteps on the marble paving-stones: perhaps they were stained with crimson as evidence of the many who had fought over them in the final convulsion during the famine. And perhaps there was no stain but only the venerable stone washed by water, the sun and time.

And so in my inner transport and emotion I spent perfect hours mingling in that vast tumultuous concourse, abandoning myself to its vital flow, breathing in the pulsating life of others from which I had been excluded for so many months; and from every word, gesture and look, gathering in the warmth of affections which I managed, as the moments passed and in the mediation of the hour, to welcome as if they were my own. Later, in a crowded popular theatre, I felt I recognised in the participation of the people with what was going on on the stage a sentiment well known to our old dialect theatre. The actors' attitudes, their mimicry, the human and complex expressions on their faces, the propriety and gentleness of the women, they were all a mirror of my South. And I could almost understand the words, so close and akin to me were the situations and the plot.

This immense Mediterranean nation – the only one which under an infinite diversity of laws has progressed through the centuries following the same way of life, and spreading from Alexandria to Algiers, Barcelona and Marseilles – welcomed me as a fellow-citizen in that little theatre, as it had welcomed me already in Omonias Square where a beggar-boy, differing from those in our country only as to language, had beaten his brushes on his shoe-shine box in pride at polishing your shoes – not out of servility but so as to earn his crust of bread like a bird and add to his city's lustre through your elegance. When I went back at night – again wilting under the heavy, almost insupportable weight of my uniform – I was followed from inn to inn by the persistent noise of guitars and the rustle of couples in every house, in every street, among the trees: the implacable advance out of war and towards love.

By sundown next day the Italian State had disintegrated. As for the nation, no one could speak for it as a whole, but individual histories were going to be unfolded for several years to come. Silence and alarm had suddenly descended during the night while from all sides the German tanks could be heard rumbling in – they were looking for an enemy, but no enemy showed itself in the darkness. My thoughts went to Uncle Gedeone, waiting at his post in the light of the tallow candle; and I responded to him with an intensity and vigilance of my own, for my courage was due to his. I felt I was ready for anything, rather like the migrant driven across the seas.

Whereas the German forces in Italy, galvanised by Hitler and determined not to give up a single strategic bastion in the peninsula, acted swiftly and resolutely with regard to the Italian army, and to a large degree were helped by those who remained faithful to Fascism and thought it dishonourable to abandon their ally before the outcome of the war was finally decided – it was all very different in Greece. Here, the Commander-in-Chief of our army, if he had had the capacity and the energy to lead, was in a position to disarm the Germans (at least in southern Greece), to close the roads below Salonika to them, gather together the bulk of his army, and treat with the Allies for a reasonable and ordered surrender according to the terms of the armistice and with a laying-down of arms.

Perhaps some time in the future the calamitous history of the secret pacts between King Victor, Badoglio and the Allies will throw light on why the orders transmitted to the good Vecchiarelli should have served to paralyse our troops, throw them into equivocation and then chaos, and finally hand them over, defenceless, to the very men who, previously, far from hoping for an incredible solution like this, had been trembling in their skins. Between those early days when many Germans deserted or tried to escape towards Turkey, and the last ten days of September which saw three hundred thousand Italians dispatched like sheep to Germany and a fate that was to mow down twenty per cent of them, only two short weeks had flowed through the hour-glass of time; but they were of a passion and exaltation that verged on madness.

Ever since the evening of September 11, and as a result of the mysterious treaties ratified between our army in Greece – the Super-Grecia – and the German command, the men of our army knew they had been abandoned. The Germans were already coming forward in small groups to demand the surrender of whole regiments, and if there were individuals who felt scalding tears of shame, everyone could nevertheless see that the bonds of discipline had broken down, that the military stores had become 'res nullius', and that there was no longer any need to render an account of anything if accounts were not even rendered of the arms entrusted to the flags. A process of dissolution substantially the same in Greece as in France, and to a great extent in Italy herself: because that was the genuine 'historical' result matured in its good time. By collective consent – amazing in a people chronically hostile to any sort of unanimity – it was in fact agreed from Toulon to Leghorn and as far as the Piraeus, that rather than hand over anything to the others (whoever they might be) it was better to use everything for one's own greater good. The black market sprawled over the Athens pavements (where I had imagined blood!) with the new vital urge characteristic of Greece's flexible and mercantile soul. Our peaceful dissolution seemed adequate satisfaction for a breed aware of its deep links with us; while allowing it that smile that demolishes honour and avenges the past better than reprisals.

Then over and above all this, individual passions burst out, the lust for money and the thousand other manifestations of an excessive conglomeration of human beings. The slopes of the Lycabettus were crammed with couples making love – the incalculable coin of forgiveness spent to make mockery of the hate between men – while archives were burning at Command headquarters and disquieting hordes of people freed from prison heralded the looting and general uproar. Meanwhile the Germans in silent scorn looked after what was essential, namely that that dangerous mass of men should be removed; and they did no more than put them on troop trains. Only where there was no forgiveness was there a flow of blood. Relentless news reached us from Italy: the Allies were above Salerno; and perhaps that stretch of olive grove that had once been mine was re-echoing to the cannon.

The second time I went to see Niko he introduced me to an important Greek whose credentials, however, he did not vouchsafe. I found the two of them waiting for me in that stripped room among the dust-covered antique collections. I was still in uniform, but had been totally unable to glean even the slightest news of Major Oliviero or my squadron, all contact with Morea and the Islands having been cut off for some time now.

The unknown Greek greeted me with deliberate courtesy; then, while Niko remained motionless with his thoughtful eyes lowered, he said:

'My cousin has told me all about you. The Germans have pledged themselves on their General's word of honour to repatriate your army; but we all know that the General's authority goes no further than the frontier. It won't be him who receives the troop trains or is in charge of them once they're out of Macedonia. And so . . .'

While speaking he looked me straight in the eyes, as I did him. In his greyish pupil there lurked a tawny glow as with birds of prey. His Italian was correct and yet it aroused in me an inexplicable irritation I would find it hard to describe. Madame Theodora came in.

'And so,' she said, resolutely concluding his remark, 'the Italian army will end up in the concentration camps of Northern Europe. Hitler is raging against you and calling you all traitors. So just when the Germans are involved up to the neck controlling the situation in Italy, it's hardly likely they'd agree to hundreds of thousands of disbanded men arriving . . . The Salerno landings have split the peninsula in two. Where do you imagine all the Southerners in your army going? You must sort that one out for yourself, here.'

'The Germans,' put in Niko in a low voice, 'are offering to incorporate in their own army, with equal rights, anyone willing to make a declaration of loyalty to them. This may be displeasing to your ears, but inside information has it that they won't put any trust in the Italian elements, not in any circumstances. They'll leave them unused in some backwater. But still, it's better than the camps.'

'Then there are always possibilities of escape,' the other Greek went on. 'Not as some are doing, by putting their faith in unknown traffickers, which can bring them assassination on the high seas, or as has happened – robbery and abandonment on some deserted beach here in Greece. But the partisans would be very ready to receive skilled and determined volunteers for their operations against the Germans. Or alternatively it would be possible to treat with them and with their help get through, for instance, to Egypt.'

He then felt like a busy man who has things to do, but as he took leave of me he already knew he would never see me again. A light cloud passed over his face signifying both irritation and resignation.

'And you must remember,' added Madame Theodora, 'that your life is worth something.' She and Niko both insisted that I should take a civilian suit with me and she packed it for me in a knapsack. She looked at me from eyes now slightly opaque and melancholy, and I saw memories pass through them that both moved me and humiliated me although I could not quite understand them.

I went on thinking about those two when again entombed in my small dark hospital room – this time not to please the oculist but in order to concentrate. They knew what they knew through the good offices of the Archimandrite and Zagara. The man I had met was certainly a Resistance leader and would have helped me on this occasion for nothing, or so I believed. But then was this really for the best?

Madame Theodora seemed to value my life, but what did she know about it? I had wasted it three times in its brief span: first in Naples, then in my disorderly youth, then at Licudi; always finding justifications and always without remorse. And what had I to put on the scales to counterbalance these turbulent fancies of my mind? My private sorrow? But this in its turn had become bound up within me as a force of inflexible obstinacy and ruthless contempt. All I had needed to quieten my mind for having allowed the partisans to get hold of the gold that went to pay for the Resistance – the Resistance against which I had been called up to fight – was a solitary pilgrimage to the ruins of a deserted temple. Was it an aspiration to sovereignty, or an absurd flight of the imagination?

Hundreds of thousands of men were now drifting and swarming like bees whose hive has at last caught fire. A miserable horde scenting profit, or a scarred and wounded mankind whose sufferings and despair had to be shared and examined just this once? The vast sediment of differences and contradictions deposited within it by the centuries was evaporating like the last speck of foam on a burning rock. Was there a need to forget charity for this reason? St Paul's epistle did not ask for a judgement to carry it out but only concern and affection. And even if Christian warmth were lacking, man's patience could suffice to take its place.

As for myself, I had not risked my epaulettes so that the Andartes should be my friends, but for the sake of that poor old prisoner whose life I understood because it was written into the walls of his house. If I now accepted some kind of reward then I would belie the nature of my action, I would feel some kind of betrayal within me. The man dressed up as a workman who had come to do my repairs and scrutinised me when leaving the Krano headquarters with his little sack of gold hidden in his labourer's haversack had questioned me with his eyes. And he had received confirmation of the answer I had already given him.

On September 18 I went for the last time to visit His Excellency's attaché. It was ten in the morning and the military police on guard at the gates of army headquarters let me pass as though they had not seen me. The ordnance officer was not there. While I was waiting in the half-darkness of his room I saw a German junior officer advancing silently in colonial shorts, revolver in hand, followed by two of his men, walking stiffly and cautiously with sub-machine-guns under their arms. Without a word those three men entered the General's office. A moment later he came out and I saw him. He was a white-haired man but with a strong pink face; a kind of good country uncle on whose countenance I read little more than surprised vexation. He crossed the anteroom under my eyes, always followed by the three. The military police had disappeared from the gates. The general headquarters were empty.

Back at the hospital two hours later I heard voices outside my small window – a window that had been shut for days because of my eyes, so that people in a little inner courtyard of the building must have thought they were alone. From this peephole I could see a group of hospital orderlies haggling in undertones with some Greek women over one or two half-open boxes.

The sun was still high, and as the light fell slantingly between the white walls of the courtyard it lit up with vivid colours the strips of cloth which were the object of this cautious bargaining. It was a business of flags. The orderlies were carefully sharing out the three strips of cloth, the red, the white and the green, and were making them up into compact little bundles to sell to the purchasers. From without came the distant but intense noise of the feverish Athens sundown.

That evening I took Niko back his civilian suit and he presented me with a spoon, a soldier's prime need but a thing I lacked – he took it at random from his untidy table. No words passed between us, but his eyes moistened when he embraced me. Madame Theodora was silent too, and this time her eyes were lowered.

On an open truck among unknown people, and having adequately tightened the bandage over my wounded eye, I left for the North without any reservations and in summer uniform. There had been an absurd farce at the station at the last moment. Two Greek girls disguised as soldiers had tried to follow an elderly colonel who was their protector (towards Italy, as they thought). They were discovered by the Germans, however, and as we left were leaning crying against a wall, amid jeers and jostling, their hair (which had given them away) now falling loose and long over their too-large army jackets.

THE MUSHROOMS

If the story of a life is to be sincere, it must obviously include the story of its areas of darkness – which, in man's moral world, are so vividly intermingled with light, for not only passion but thought itself lives in a perpetual alternation that permits of no monotony. But when one descends from the realm of fantasy and romance, the texture of life as it appears is grey and drab indeed. Modern society has worked so hard to repress the personality that events themselves are hardly marked, and the fury with which the gossip columns are followed merely indicates the emotional poverty of the masses. So from the point of view of its colouring at least, this story now needs in some way to be darkened; for at that time even great events – events tragic in their causes and consequences – took place in an atmosphere of humble greyness. For though the Germans surrounded the destiny of millions of men in an aura of blood, though they brought death to Russian prisoners and Jews and slavery to countless others, the prevailing atmosphere was one of pallid gloom. An infinitude of mankind was extinguished without beauty and with the help of almost mechanical means. And as for the common prisoners, who were excluded even from the glory of extermination, they were left to rot in a swamp. Nothing was less theatrical than that slow degradation against the background of that mournful northern landscape. But in giving the picture of a life we cannot leave out the dark hours, still less the merely dull and ordinary ones – of which our life mostly consists.

I am not applying these maxims to my own particular life, for neither at that time (nor at others) did it follow the rhythm seemingly laid down for it; but sometimes the history of others has precedence over our own; and in the perpetual duality of the mind – which can participate in events, judge them, but also passively endure them – there can occur periods and events wherein contemplation so engrosses the mind as to make it almost forget itself altogether. And so it was with me then. I had embarked on the communal adventure of my own free will, but this was the first time that I was prepared to resign my will to it. And at once I became aware of how easy it was simply to drift with the current and allow it to carry me along. In the past my life had often seemed to others as one lacking either aims or obligations, but I now saw it for what it really had been: a continual struggle. Conversely, others saw this period of the war as one of bitter pain and appalling danger (and later described it as such), whereas to me it was an endless time in which my thoughts could grow more deeply and my eyes see more truly – owing to my freedom from any complicated involvement of the mind.

At the same time I made a more searching examination of my behaviour. At first I had thought that in sharing the communal fate I was making an act of humility and mortifying my pride, but perhaps this explanation was not quite as genuine as I intended it to be. Like a strong high-flying bird who lands in a barnyard of domestic fowls, I was torn between a certain sense of duty – because I could easily have helped the others with no trouble to myself – and the desire to lie low and remain at the communal level and position. I looked for other points of reference: the saint who is a pastor and figure-head to men yet out of self-abnegation wants to make himself last when he is obviously first; Diogenes in his barrel, yet nevertheless passing judgement on Alexander; Socrates' resignation which brought the worst accusations against his judges – all these examples pointed to the same thing, namely a humility hardly distinguishable from pride. I was not sure whether I should ignore my faculties (and thereby fail to perform the duties they entailed) or exercise them by putting myself forward as a prop to others, and thereby again move into leadership. I felt that in the whole business of teaching or preaching or even setting an example there was a point of balance very difficult to find: between serving good in the abstract and imposing oneself as a person. This was why Christ commended the poor in spirit rather than saints, thinkers or poets. I was familiar with emotional duplicity, with confusion of thought, with the near-impossibility for a cultivated mind to reduce itself to elementary purity – the only kind that has value. I lay inert on the hard wooden floor of the open truck as it climbed with dramatic slowness towards the ambiguous North, and half-masked by my bandage which for want of any other possible treatment I had decided not to remove from my wounded eye, and as I lay all these thoughts passed through my mind; while all the thoughts that were ravaging my companions – regret, indignation, homesickness, hope, fear – were indifferent and extraneous to me. And I felt I ought to reproach myself for this, while realising there was nothing I could do about it.

Meanwhile, having been enlightened by Niko and Theodora, I knew full well that the whole army was on its way to captivity, but I had to keep this knowledge to myself. The Germans had behaved with fox-like malice. Nearly all our soldiers had been away from their families for at least two years so were only too ready to believe the promise of repatriation (which had been given), for nothing is more easily believed than what is ardently desired. The Germans knew this. Thus our troop-trains crossed the Balkans free from any kind of guard; the immense illusion of our men was quite enough to keep them chained to their seats. Tito's partisans came up to the trains and told us that we were heading for the barbed wire in Poland; but no one believed them. And in any case, who would have left a troop-train to all appearances on its way home, and leapt out into those barren mountains to throw in their lot with the partisan bands – as little to be trusted as any other kind of betrayal? Perhaps it was the need to cleave to their illusion that drove many of our men to throw foresight to the winds and get rid of their belongings – food reserves, blankets, overcoats. It was mid-September and still hot in the land that had once been Serbia, and many of the men thought it pointless to hold on to their unbearable uniforms; or was it that they wanted to burn their boats in a vague hope of overcoming their fears? So for two weeks hundreds of troop-trains rolled up towards Austria, and once they had crossed the frontier there appeared the barbed wire, with the searchlights, the machine-guns on guard-towers, the police-dogs; and such shattering disillusion that no one dared to admit it even to himself on that first night. There was silence.

But when morning came the new reality had to be looked in the face. The other ranks were immediately sent off to hard labour in appalling conditions, while the officers seethed with indignation. In Greece – as in France, where things had happened in the same way – they had handed over their arms in return for a promise of repatriation, so they now saw the Germans as betraying the word pledged by their commanders in military honour. But these promises had been made in distant territories by local authorities and no one seemed to have heard of them in the Reich. Here, the Italians were regarded as traitors to the alliance and had to answer for it themselves. Those first assembly camps and sorting-out centres in Lower

Bavaria were run by low-grade troops and highly politicised young officers who tested our sincerity, with typical northern simplicism, by asking us if we wanted to go on fighting alongside them. To our negative reply they responded with contemptuous silence or dark threats, while among ourselves the chorus of argument and lamentation reached the rhythm of Babel. The equivocation was basic, but after pressures and exhortations which sometimes reached the grotesque, a modest percentage was persuaded to join the German cause, and these new collaborators took the way of Innsbruck and North Italy (their lives thereafter to be fragmented in their various destinies); while the others were told that they would have to pay the penalty of their unwarranted obstinacy. This time terrifying trains with sealed coaches moved off towards an unknown destination in the silence of a landscape already grey with impending snow.

The journey from Athens to Moosburg, not far from Munich, had lasted thirteen days. I had known no one personally in my open truck and there had been no one from my regiment. My possessions were minimal both in clothes and money (though I did have one gold sovereign which I had collected for touristic interest in my early days in Athens) – so already in that first period my material conditions had been somewhat harder than the average. But from Moosburg – after about a week's stop spent in complaining and quarrelling – our train ground on for another fortnight during which the cold and other privations became worse and worse. Incomprehensibly to us, our train followed a loop of thousands of kilometres between Vienna and Berlin; we turned off towards Warsaw; we rolled north-east between deserted plains and desolate heaths where we could see nothing but spectral huts on stilts in the marshes; we touched on Lithuania. Then our erratic train decided to reverse its route and it turned southwards along eastern Poland. It came to a halt at Lemberg, the former Lwow.

A journey not easy to forget! But the multiplicity of adventures that have befallen people in the last two wars has robbed stories such as mine of flavour. The episodes that made Pellico's diaries famous a century ago would not interest anyone today. The eccentricities of our guards (and there were some!), the daily incidents of that journey without any knowable goal, the Kafka-like hallucinations of those ghostly landscapes where the frightened prisoners conjured up a new Katyn at every turn, with ourselves as the slaughtered – all this would be small fry indeed in the gigantic explosion of the collective adventure through which the world lived at that time. And yet on that October dawn, when forty-five of us were packed like hens in a coop in our asphyxiating coach, when we had not the faintest idea where we were being taken, and as the train ground relentlessly on with its cargo of fear and lamentation – I have to admit that I felt that silent smile reawaken within me, the smile of elation in danger, of pleasure in experience; a completely irrational happiness, and its keenest moments corresponded with the sharpest craggiest peaks my life had known. My bandage had not been touched since we left Athens. Beneath it I could feel the scab over my eye, painful, and flashing with little stabs of light when I touched it. I had had to risk my 'good' eye being open all this time, and though it had watered and swelled up it had survived over a month of dust, damp and dirt – this time on 'extra-territorial service'. But now, after the second part of the journey, I had no means of knowing whether the sight of the bandaged eye had survived and I just had to trust to nature. When those two interminable weeks came to an end and we realised we had at last arrived, we were at least sure of our lives. We crossed a city inhabited by people whose furtive glances showed us they were friendly; and once we were under cover and breathing freely, without the obsessional rolling of the train, we felt a faint hope trickling into our hearts. That first night we did not stay in the city but were convoyed to various huts put up outside it. Worn out with fatigue, the company collapsed into torpor almost at once, and from that confused mass there rose only the sound of animal breathing. A cold shaft of moonlight came in through the small windows.

My right hand had been burned and was hurting – the result of an incident at the last food distribution. As I had no mess-tin I had had to use a container lacking a handle, and the Russian prisoner on duty had poured in a ladle of boiling soup right up to the brim where my fingers were holding it. He viewed me as an enemy owing to Mussolini's efforts on the Don, and his act was one of intended hostility – what he hoped was that I would drop my ration so as to avoid the burn. But I was determined to hold on, and for once a German corporal came to my help, removed my bowl from my hands and put it down. It was the first kind act I had encountered in Germany. So now I was sucking my thumb like a baby and finding a certain pleasure in it. In fact, I was glad that the pain should keep me awake for I had planned to carry out my experiment in practical medicine, and I didn't want any witnesses. So when there was perfect silence, and the gleam of the moon had slightly brightened, then very very slowly I removed the bandage. It was far from easy as I had no water to soften the crust of blood and dry pus that had formed during the past five weeks and was now as thick as cardboard. I was afraid of tearing away some sensitive part; and knew nothing about what the reactions of the epidermis would be after such a long separation from air. But finally I squeezed my eyelids tight together and, saying goodbye to my lashes, ripped off the scab; then waited, not daring to open the eye.

But a gentle moonbeam came to visit me, and gradually, through a great cloud of joyful tears, I saw it and other trembling forms floating about in the pale blue light. When I used to wake up at night in the dormitory at school I felt hemmed in, abandoned, cruelly sad. Now I was calm, free, and almost happy.

Mussolini never really stopped being a journalist, and in his final polemical essay entitled *In the Days of the Stick and the Carrot* (it was circulated in our prison camps by the republicans of Salò) he described September 8 1943 as the day of the 'pulverisation of Italy' – thereby using a word that implies that the material smashed was already rather fragile beforehand. In the flood of diaries and histories describing that period, this famous event is usually glossed over, due, I think, to a misunderstood love of our country. The event represented a panic crisis of which the military collapse formed only a part. There may be some truth in the infinitude of circumstances brought forward to justify the crisis, but it is also true that 'where many reasons are brought forward none is really valid'! Yet had a returning prisoner pointed this out after the war, he would have found himself reduced to silence by the detailed accounts of all the agonies endured by those who had escaped from the German and Fascist round-ups: as if the fear of something – a fear lasting a few weeks – was worse than the thing itself which had been endured for two years. But the fact that the shadow of that fear still lingered on in people's memory showed that their primary impulse at that time was not the desire to defend their country by risking their lives, but (always excepting the peace of the just) the desire for personal escape, for getting out of it all as quietly and quickly as possible. Though Italy has always been rated very high on the level of deeply meditated values, seen as a national structure she gave clear proof at that time of being dominated by a centrifugal rather than a centripetal force. Indeed, everything appertaining to the State was attacked and destroyed, almost as if it were a question of the goods of a loathed enemy. A lesson little understood by the political levies that have followed, and have been determined to lead a country that hardly knows them, hence so tepidly follows them. And a country that remains indissolubly Catholic because in Catholicism it has found its measure and its rule: 'For,' as Machiavelli said when speaking of the 'antique orders of religion', they 'have subjects and DO NOT GOVERN THEM!'

The most varied remnants of that dissolution met each other in the fortress at Lwow – about two thousand officers, the majority from Greece and France, the rest rounded up by Rommel and Kesselring in Italy. Whereas friendships are natural and spontaneous in war, they were difficult in the camp, because these men – who were a tiny mirror of the decay into which the country had fallen, a country already, and by its very nature, in discord and socially divided – these men had not in any sense found their common denominator. Usually one becomes a prisoner as a result of surrender after battle. Fighting forces have a unity through their common experiences, hardships and dangers, and this homogeneity persists among the prisoners and forms the basis of their dignity and solidarity. This was the case in 1915 with the Italians who honourably endured the famous camp of Mauthausen in Austria. But it was not like that with us.

In Reggio I had seen how the call-up worked: equivocations, confusions, injustices; infinite intrigues to avoid military service or to go into it for non-military reasons, with every kind of equivocation and favouritism. In France and Greece – occupied countries where it was easy to practise abuses – whole gangs of profiteers had gathered who were even physically unsuited to the rigours of war: the tradesmen and businessmen dressed up as soldiers with whom Athens, for instance, had been swarming; and the first people to leave the Greek capital that September were two hundred Field Officers who suddenly became aware that they were 'supernumeraries' simply because they hoped to get back to Italy, and who, in fact, were the first to set foot inside the camp. So the mass was made up of every kind of element: men of a certain age who had wanted to be called up because of the pay and the rations when times were difficult in the cities, and who had occupied cushy jobs in the administrative services; boys from the Leghorn military academy; others fresh from Modena; men with a thousand thoughts and ideas of their own and following a thousand different directions; legal men, ruffians, neurotics, the sick, the rich, beggars and snobs. Yet the Germans pretended to see some kind of unity in this motley crew and stigmatised it as 'anti-Fascist' and 'pro-Badoglio'. Whereas there were as many monarchists and Mussolini-men among us as there were convinced republicans and ferocious haters of Badoglio and the king (I, for instance, was one of these), all mixed up with a crowd of others who had no sense of being soldiers at all; it was these last who complained the loudest when they saw the undertakings they had embarked on with very different prospects in view coming to such a disastrous end.

The stories related by all these men were generally vague or yawning with gaps; and very few of them had actually fought – if only because the Germans, in view of the defection of the majority, had been able to crush the small pockets of resistance and had ruthlessly left few witnesses to the facts. It was said that at the moment of our surrender they disposed of a good 300,000 of their best troops in Italy alone. Now if the legend of Garibaldi (and it really is a legend!) presents him as conqueror of the whole of Sicily with a band of barely 1000 red-shirts; and if it was true that Mussolini took over the country by marching on Rome with 40,000 black-shirts, then the 300,000 very war-seasoned Teutons must surely have been an excessive force even for a country of 45 million souls. But it is also certain that the Russian bear did not exactly find honey when it pushed into stoical and thinly-populated Finland, for ferocious fighters rose up against it from every cove of its thirty thousand lakes and from each of its countless birch trees; and it is also undeniable that, much later (and back in Italy again now), the whole police force and authority of the state could not capture one man, the bandit Giuliano, when they found he was really determined not to be caught. Considerations which I kept strictly to myself, while observing the singular and pathetic spectacle of our tumultuous billet in those first days.

Protected from the winter's cold not by our inadequate little stove but by walls three metres thick – freshly white-washed and equipped with two-tiered wooden bunks – our billet looked like any other military quartering. Contrary to the conditions of those of us who landed up in makeshift huts in swamps, imprisonment in the fortress of Lwow did not for the time being entail excessive hardships – a fortress majestic as to outline and on whose stony projections the snow conferred a delicate moulding rather like the elegance conferred on a human face by a powdered wig. True, our 'detainers' took delight in subjecting us to endless roll-calls and keeping us standing for half a day at a stretch (and once for a whole day) on the sheet of ice that already covered the courtyards – but that was the only real form of tyranny they inflicted on us. For the rest, short of putting his morbid fantasies to practice on them (as, alas, sometimes happened), what could a gaoler do with his prisoners except count them? And that was what ours did.

Food was short too; but we were not subjected to any hard labour and we did not suffer from the cold. The Polish people looked on us as victims of the hated enemy and so were on our side, and it was not impossible to bribe the guards, many of whom were not Germans but came from the areas incorporated into the Great Reich. So it was enough to have some money or some objects to exchange, and many of the men had stocks in their baggage that at that time seemed enormous.

It began with those of us who had come from Greece 'showing' cigarettes, and those from the Côte d'Azur – who had cornered a market in perfume – displaying their bottles of scent. But by degrees everything that had been taken from the military stores at the time of the collapse was produced, ending up with the considerable sums filched from the departmental cash-boxes. These had certainly not been destroyed, as the records relative to them would have us believe. Indeed, in the last days in Athens (so I had heard) the entire funds for the army's needs for a month – 50 milliards of drachmas – had been drawn with praiseworthy foresight only to be mysteriously spirited away at one stroke. Not only this, but many of our men who had been in our army in Greece had substantial hoards of gold coins on them that they had had no time to send home (between two pieces of cardboard); and a certain Lieutenant Quero, an unscrupulous adventurer but a likeable person, had as much as a kilogram of them. He made no secret of the fact that most of his haul came from trading in fowling-pieces – the type of gun that had been at the bottom of the Spiropulos affair.

'With all due respect to your rank,' he said to me, 'I can see you're absolutely destitute. May I ask you, providing you use equivalent articles of clothing as stakes, to partner me in a game of poker against Lieutenants Fabbricatore and Mozzillo? They've already cleaned out two or three of our company. But with your personal coolness and knowledge of the game, plus the strength of my capital, we'll bring them to their knees.'

Such a proposal would have horrified my good Major Costa Oliviero, Knight of Malta, but to me it seemed so ridiculous that I accepted it. Playing poker in partners was absolutely not the done thing but was openly practised by our two opponents; besides which everyone knew that I had no money and would stake minute percentages of an equivalent – in thick socks and Balaclava helmets. So the great game took place but turned out to be a disaster, for those bandits Mozzillo and Fabbricatore, to the dismayed incredulity of the many men standing by, produced 'four queens', a 'full house' and a 'royal flush' – all the best possible poker hands – almost in succession, thereby accumulating on their side of the green baize (unearthed who knows where – could it have been a piece of flag?) a single pile of thousand-lire banknotes of the last Kingdom of Italy, black-and-green dollar bills, slim French banknotes, and gold coins of every stamp and type. What with the heat and the noise and the smoke, you might have thought you were in a gaming-den in any part of our unhappy world. That stolen money obtained once again by theft reminded me so much of Madame Julie's diamonds in my Milan boarding-house. In the matter of men's sins it seemed that the imagination did not range far.

Quero belonged to the second brigade of Grenadiers and was a tall, carefree, very vivacious Venetian. His father was a cattle-dealer and had directed his son's speculations in Athens by means of detailed letters – a fact which Quero himself frankly admitted to me. Attached to the Divisional Command, he had enjoyed the whole golden age of the Sagapò in Greece and knew all about it down to the last detail. But he never passed judgement on the confusions, collusions and malversations of the army, confining himself to merely narrating the facts with a slightly mocking air and facetious tone.

'Every day had its marginal profit,' he would say, 'and now and again there was a jackpot. You see what I mean? There was a fabulous one in Greece. Quinine made of wood! Little wooden pills put into pink sugar! Sold their weight in gold!'

For Quero a situation like ours at Lwow was simply an opportunity for triumphant profit-making, inasmuch (he insisted on explaining to me) as plenty of money could be made from the misfortunes of others once one knew how to go about it. At least I appreciated the frankness of his behaviour, well outside that real sink of complexes within which the others toiled. He gave himself no rest but was perpetually going the rounds in top boots and a three-quarter-length jerkin lined with sheepskin, conferring in corners with people of every kind, then returning to me with a small smile of triumph – scoop after scoop.

Soon others were also taking part in this activity, until it finally grew into a kind of stock exchange where the basic measure was not gold but cigarettes, and on this index were priced commodities such as watches, skin bags, margarine rations, and even diamonds. The richest among us were not necessarily the cleverest, and we knew an airman who arrived with a good million lire in banknotes concealed in the bulges of his jacket, and not long after was reduced to penury through misplaced investments. Before long a struggle flared up (as it would in any society of men) between the rich in order to do each other down or impose their wealth as power; between the rich and the poor for reasons laid down by countless theorists before and since Marx; and between various sections of the economically weak for reasons of greed or jealousy – altogether a disheartening repetition of my last days at Licudi. There were cliques, there was patronage, there was competition; the information services marshalled their forces so that an unexpected distribution of soap or salt should produce immediate variations of price in these provisions and others linked with them, as happens in playing the import market. And the infiltration of foodstuffs smuggled in from outside corresponded both in its risks and its profits to real frontier operations. My mind went back to the rules of Stuart Mill and Adam Smith, laid down in economic manuals in the days of the Pensile. Cut off as we were from the world, we could only listen to each other: complaints, squabbles, deals and, in the depths of the night, fear. Those were the days when the Russians were overcoming the desperate German resistance on the Dnieper and reoccupying Kiev. This might mean our early release, but anxiety stepped up rather than slowed down the rhythm of our lives. I thought of Binutti, who long ago had given himself up as prisoner to a Mantua cavalry patrol so as to 'see better', as he put it. His phrase acquired a melancholy depth. Was it true that he who thinks detaches himself from life? And that there is less pain when one knows no history?

'I'm still convinced,' Quero whispered to me, 'that Fabbricatore and Mozzillo are a pair of cheats. But their trick must be an unknown one if the two touts I put on their track to watch them, and who are two veterans at the job, haven't been able to catch them out. That was why we had that fine "slaughter"; I don't mind about the paper money; but I'd really like to have back the "double eagles" they got off me.'

Like France, Greece hoards gold; but being more archaic and adventurous in business, and situated eastwards, Greece collects the most disparate coins: from the Chilean 'condor' to the George IV 'sovereign'; from the Bavarian 'double thaler' to the Russian 'fifteen imperial roubles'; and sometimes one came across others that were much less familiar and more ancient, such as the Turkish 'mejid', the Tibetan 'mohur', or the Persian 'two tomans'. Quero knew to perfection the weight, relationship and value of all this coinage. The American 'double eagle', worth twenty gold dollars, is a coin out of a Western; and he had lost four of them.

'At home Fabbricatore is a wine-merchant and Mozzillo a shoemaker. But they certainly know how to *do* us. Instead of fighting them we must take them into partnership. I'm getting new ideas!'

These new ideas had to do with drawing into the black market the supplies that the Germans had begun distributing to those who had finally decided to collaborate with the Reich, under the very nose of the rest of us who were kept on short rations: a novel aspect of our eccentric situation. In obedience to Nazi orders, envoys from Mussolini's North Italian Republic of Salò were undertaking journeys up north to try to convince glum and hungry gatherings where their effective good lay. But once the prisoners had weighed up fear as against hunger, their troubled and confused minds got lost in a whirlpool of arguments, tangled emotions and open or concealed motives. If the Germans were to withdraw from Poland, as was now being whispered, we would have to pass over to the Russians: a thing obscurely feared by everyone. To sign on meant the Front once more, in Germany or, worse, in Italy, or even for civil war. To stay in the camp was certainly the best, provided it would not be for too long, but who could guarantee this? There were Fascist bosses among us who were trying to clear their name and achieve political virginity; there were swindlers afraid of being called to account; amateur lawyers who held forth at length about the Geneva and Hague Conventions with an avalanche of facts. Someone unearthed the concept of military honour, and those from Greece shouted to deaf ears about the agreement reached by Vecchiarelli. No one knew that that General had died in obscure captivity. I recalled his face, that of a healthy countryman. God knows how his life must have been broken – like a straw in the terrible storm that he unleashed without even having an idea of what he was doing.

With all this, not more than fifteen per cent of the prisoners had come forward to sign the act of allegiance – or commitment to collaboration with the Germans; but instead of being immediately sent off elsewhere, these men were kept almost next door to us so that we should see the groaning loads of sausages taken in to reward them. Our tough ones spat fire against such blacklegs, while concealing the fact that, in many cases, their spirit of resistance was based on reserves of money. Quero, on the other hand, deaf to any kind of polemic, and without the faintest hypocrisy, looked on those sausages exactly as a Swiss *rentier* (for instance) might nose out an imminent option on preference bonds. He gazed covetously, and in no time had set up a unique enterprise which included the monied and masterful Fabbricatore and Mozzillo.

'You should join us too, Captain!' In addressing me, he always kept up the correct formalities and I believed him to be sincere. 'You haven't got a shirt on your back and you've every right not to die of hunger. As far as your scruples are concerned, remember it's not a matter of you entering into the partnership but just of being employed as book-keeper. What could be more natural?'

I interpreted his words as a possible desire to create for himself the very alibi that has led brigands to do good to the poor, and notable pirates of big business to found hospitals and schools. Or perhaps a darker instinct led him to detect in me, and in my detachment, the witness if not the judge. And then there are those who are incapable of raising themselves up of their own momentum so try to drag those who are above them down – a phenomenon as old as the human race. And a vast quantity of our literature, following the Italian publicist Longanesi, has been based on the idea that a personal disgrace can be justified by a communal one. But Quero was of a simpler breed. The evil actions he went on committing served (I think) to prove to himself that he was still the same man as he had been before; that nothing had changed; that he was not walking in a void – which would have terrified him. Then I thought that being like others meant not having only their weaknesses but their actual baseness. In worthy memory of the bookseller Pagano, and of the card-index of comrade Chiurico's Fascist bible, I accepted the office of book-keeper in the partnership, rather as I had consented to take part in that game of poker.

The strangeness of this type of enterprise brought me in touch with a lot of the prisoners. Hypocrisy was the worst possible sin in the camp, because those who protested against the black market were incapable of freely giving to others even a crumb of what was theirs, whereas had they done so they would have automatically put an end to the black market. The black market could only be founded on an exchange of goods having an initial proprietor, and here lay the root of the evil. For instance, it was said of so-and-so that he had more than a hundredweight of dried foodstuffs in his possession, but he would rather have been skinned alive than freely give away a crumb of it. When one of the young Leghorn students was discovered to have the tuberculosis from which he soon died, it was impossible to obtain the necessary help for him; and that crime to which I was particularly sensitive (in memory of Nerina) passed unobserved. They answered that they had their own lives to protect. But for many of them it was merely a seething hatred for anyone whatsoever. As they were the victims of injustice, why should they not participate in it? But as for myself, I did not agree that we were victims of a really unjust punishment; in my view we had all in some way deserved it. But the majority simply did not want to accept its austere warning or the truth it indicated.

When I retired to the double bunk of which I occupied the upper place – so as to put in order the accounts of the weary day's affairs – I noticed absent-mindedly the sibilant Latin esses of Captain Téolo, Venetian nobleman from Lake Garda, my fellow-tenant, who at fixed hours recited his Office exactly like an ecclesiastic. To this end he had fixed up a little cotton curtain as a kind of confessional behind which he retired when he wanted to pray, and this was often. At first Téolo had avoided me as a man who kept bad company; but when he saw that I went laboriously gleaning a packet of razor-blades here, a tin of powdered milk or a packet of small cigars there, then he unfroze. I respected Téolo's devotions and his spirit of recollection and climbed up into my bunk without letting the soles of my shoes touch his. Though he did not tell me so, I was later convinced that he had included my name in his ejaculatory prayers – among those to be led back on to the straight and narrow path.

By the beginning of December, just two months after our internment in Lwow, the organisation Quero & Co. had realised such profits that the Italian Command of the camp was moved to intervene; but Quero & Co. pointed out that they had introduced into the camp from outside a huge and indispensable quantity of food, and that the collaborators had charged their weight in gold for the sausages so Quero & Co. had done likewise. However this may be, we were surrounded by the hostile whispering, the suppressed rancour, the back-biting and the insults to be found in the needy soldier confronted with profiteers and the new rich. But the partners continued to ladle out the goods. They were in a position to provide a full dinner, starting with some kind of pasta served with butter, followed by beefsteak and fruit, to anyone who could pay a price calculated at around four or five hundred times the ordinary one. Quero also provided a special pasta meal for the partnership, to which I was invited. But owing to lack of space and the inadequacy of the containers, it happened that while he was cynically serving out the *tagliatelle* under the hungry gaze of our companions, the dish slipped from his hands and the total steaming contents fell on to the filthy floor. Then I heard a cackle of laughter which made me realise what the joy of the devils in hell must be; and, looking up, I saw one of our comrades watching us from the height of his bunk with an expression of such malicious glee that I felt myself freed from my scruples – more even than by a papal absolution. Then some of the poor wretches threw themselves on the remainder of the pasta and fought for it. However, the climax of the dinner was still to come, a vast cup of strong coffee which, taken on an empty stomach, produced the same drunkenness and torpor as wine.

Before Christmas the situation came to a head in Poland too. But as the Germans were worried about the local unrest, they were afraid to remove us by daylight under the eyes of a population already cherishing ideas of revolt. This made them very polite during our last days at the fortress; they gave us, for instance, a free hand over our equipment which would otherwise have been left to the enemy with everything else. So Christmas week was lived with an extraordinary intensity in the camp where alternating hopes and fears were reborn; but even this time the wheel of things turned in an unexpected way because the prisoners in their turn – out of fear of being absorbed by the Russians, or into their legendary and interminable country – displayed such a favourable attitude to their gaolers that it bordered on the grotesque. And our departure was truly grotesque. The old German colonel in charge of the camp, a type taken straight from Elisabeth Werner's romantic *San Michele* (Cristina's books!), waved to us almost as a father to his beloved sons; and we replied! We crossed Lwow in full daylight and almost without surveillance, as had happened in our journey across the Balkans. The Poles were looking out of their windows, silent and thoughtful, and every now and again a large white loaf of bread would fall beside us in the snow. The column reached the trains intact. Quero was concerned to find a place in a carriage where he was little known or not at all. He was afraid of some hostile reaction on the part of his clients. I was with him; but my mind at that time was filled with a keen pity for the flock in which I included myself.

The sufferings of that journey were severe. German comprehensive planning for the removal of vast masses of people – through an enemy country and with the Russian army at their back – gave yet another proof of their incredible efficiency; but this did not detract from the hardships to which they, and we, were subjected. This time we were crammed in fifties into sealed coaches for a journey lasting eleven days, getting air only through narrow vents – except for two short halts to take aboard fresh supplies of water and empty the stinking wooden box converted to man's needs. A number of men were ill, and in our carriage a doctor had to operate on an abscess with a penknife. The slightest movement involved a fight with the others, and the sense of suffocation reached such a frightful pitch that there were fits of hysteria. Suitably anchored to Albero's memories and his frequent sallies on the subject of warfare, I persisted in regarding these torments as the natural concomitant of a checkered campaign; after all, we were at least starting our journey back to the centre of Europe: notions not shared by all the others, to judge by the chorus of laments. It is quickly noticeable that the people least able to endure pain and privation are those who at first sight would seem most inured to them. People who have never known comfort or luxury, farm-labourers for instance, give to their physical being an attention that the intellectual disregards in times of trial. The majority of the officers came from the lower middle class, and I took it badly that they groaned so loudly at being huddled together, as if they had previously been used to princely expanses. These personal eccentricities of theirs, echoes of ancient feelings now largely obsolete, helped me on my side to behave correctly; and I was not unprepared when there finally rose up before us the ominous barbed wire fences of Siltau.

If you came to think about it, it was not difficult to guess what would be in store for us. The Republic of Salò was trying to moderate Nazi severity towards Italian prisoners, but the Nazis were standing firm: if we were not traitors to the Axis then we should at least adhere to Mussolini's new government – if not to the Wehrmacht then to our own republican army. Lwow had been the last testing-ground for this end, and in that short period the choice had been made and we ourselves had made it. Those who had opted for the Fascist Republic went from Poland to Italy by normal military transport; the others were now to know the rigours of punishment. Thus with groans and curses that condemned mass of men passed through the spectral gates of the new *Lager*, while both captives and captors prepared themselves for new trials of strength.

There were ordinary pedestrian reasons too, besides the dogmatic ones, but of unhappy augury for us. When we were first directed to Poland, new and adequate installations had been prepared in advance, at least at Lwow: work which had been destroyed after four months and there was no means of renewing it. In German national territory there were no available establishments or suitable sites. But in this the Germans perhaps saw Wotan's hand of justice. However this may be, in that vast camp where up to seven thousand officers of many different origins were gathered together, it was not difficult to 'lose' Quero and all the others from Lwow, except for the pious Téolo who had prayed the whole length of the journey. Together we hid ourselves in one of the most distant huts, a terrible hole where slatted wooden bunks rose five 'storeys' high right up to the bare roof. Almost two hundred of us were piled in here; and I read at the top of my place, cut with a penknife: 'Boris Dragouliub'. And a date.

The flatlands extending from the mouth of the Elbe over the coast of the North Sea and as far as Frisia in Holland, are neither very cold nor very damp; but the low heath spreading out from the undulations of sand is the kingdom of the wind – a strong and perpetual wind that blows over the undergrowth and rips at the fleeting processions of clouds, and at night howls over the desert land as it does over the sea. Everything in that endless landscape, under the high interminable sky, is a dark tiny detail; and the land a network of burnished steel, glinting here and there beneath a shaft of light from the sky or because of a stream. In that space men are less than insects and wander about as if without direction. Seen from above, our huge encampment must surely have seemed no more than a speck of greenish lichen on the bark of a tree.

Téolo and I took it in turns to get the measure of the place, without gaining much reassurance. Siltau, we were told, had a few years earlier been the macabre setting for the death of about sixty thousand Russian prisoners as a result of exhaustion and disease: they had been kept out of doors within the barbed wire until they died. Some French prisoners in the Bavarian camp of Moosburg had told us that Germans never dared enter the Russian camps because those indomitable warriors were ready to die so long as they killed. The Germans had tried to guard them with specially trained dogs, but as the Russians were used to fighting wolves they simply faced them and ripped open their bellies with wooden knives. So the German system for eliminating the millions of men they had captured in the first thrust of the war between Riga and the Black Sea had become more simplified and more cruel. As the soldiers were impossible to feed or use or hold, they were abandoned on the bare earth to a calculated hunger whose outcome was sickness and death. In the matter of deciding on our new billet, the Germans did not make use of the huge gruesome quadrangle over which still loomed the sinister watch-towers, but the huts which had then been for the service, if so it can be put, of the compound. Two winters had considerably impaired them; and they were our home for seventeen months.

Unlike the Russians, we were given old decrepit soldiers as guards, ones with one arm or a wooden leg; so that what with the mud, the disgusting swarms of insects, the abominable *Stube* and the rest, the *Lager*, from the sentries down to the latrines, was unquestionably in the poorest possible working order. As all contraband from outside had ceased, and personal reserves were much depleted, hunger made itself felt at once – aggravated by a psychological factor that hastened its risks and consequences. Anyone who had deluded himself that the war would be over by Christmas, after a mere four months' imprisonment, now had a much longer period of hardship to fear. For many the spirit of endurance now wavered – based as it had been on that early and mistaken conviction – and meanwhile the complex feeling of irritation and spite against the Germans had grown stronger. The Germans were weak in Latin psychology and did not understand this new wave of obstinate refusal any more than they had understood it before. And the camp shut itself up in pig-headed silence, everyone reviewing his forces, anchoring himself to his rights, trying out his obligations, among shattering onslaughts of grief, rage and bitterness.

The interplay of these thoughts and feelings was so complex and changeable that the ironical intolerance I had felt in the train towards my fellow-officers and their lamentations now underwent modification: I developed a genuine interest in their attitudes, rather abstract and scientific though this interest was. The condition of imprisonment is wretched of its very nature (though not worse than the conditions endured by some of the very poor throughout their whole lives). Though prisoners may not have a hand or a foot or both (for good measure!) cut off, as in Plutarch's stories, we seldom hear of prisoners in a state of well-being. With the removal of position, rank, privilege and qualification, there remains only the man, stripped of his identifying marks and sometimes even of his hair – truly naked and how defenceless! The style he has forged for himself so as to become a precise social entity is necessarily swept away, leaving only inborn faculties and deficiencies in adverse circumstances. It seemed to me that in this situation our officers should have constituted a chosen and hence homogeneous élite. But in the September crisis what had literally sunk headlong was the ruling class of Italy, in other words the middle class – and its flower (or what should have been its flower) was with me here in the camp. So just as I had been able to examine the upper stratum of Italian society through my father Gian Luigi, and the lower one through the simple people at Licudi, I now made a minute examination of the middle one as represented at Siltau. What did it reveal?

To begin with, hatred of the Germans. This arose from the particular circumstances, just as it grew up in India against the English and in Algeria against the French. But however theoretical the hatred was, it was much more ulcerating to the haters than to the hated, for it had to be externalised in attitudes of protest that sometimes verged on the lunatic. A few of the officers shaved every day and kept their uniforms decent – at some cost to themselves – for they maintained that you had to put up a façade of dignity and pride in front of the enemy. But most of them went about looking like tramps and were indifferent even to personal cleanliness. Many of them refused to salute the heads of the camp, which threw the latter into a rage; or else they deployed laborious slow motion in bringing their limbs to attention, as they had to do during roll-calls: schoolboy trifles, whereby the Germans managed to discover who would be prepared to become informants on the others. Then there was protest activity in the matter of our barbed-wire barricade. This was over four metres high and five metres wide and could only have been crossed by a bird. In spite of which there was a subsidiary wall of wire two or three metres on its near side – this was called the 'warning wire' and it was forbidden to go beyond it under pain of death. Lacking other ideas, many officers longed with passion to go beyond that wire as a sign of defiance. But the one who put his longing into practice was killed by a burst of gunfire from a sentry on duty for the purpose. The camp went into hysterical fury. They pointed out to the guards that crossing the wire in full daylight could mean nothing at all. But as there were notices along it at every twelve metres laconically announcing that 'anyone who went beyond it would be killed', the Germans maintained that in broad daylight the prohibition was more obvious.

As for myself I regarded these attitudes to be wrong-headed, pointless and often ridiculous, and I found no interest in wasting time with the warning-wire. To begin with, if one escaped into Germany what would one have solved? Where would one then go? Secondly, once I had made my act of presence at the roll-call I had nothing more to do with the Germans, they gave me no more trouble and I forgot them. My difficulties were produced by the Italians themselves, by the circumstances, and preparing for the long haul of the slowly passing months. But on the whole things were not desperate: any intended threat to our lives would have shown itself in Greece (and indeed many had died there); but once we had got to Poland and survived the subsequent crises, it was difficult to suppose that within German national territory a cold-blooded action would be performed openly against us. Yet the Armistice was ambiguous; and if the Allies had not finished the war in a final effort at that time they must have had good reasons, and the war could not be brought to an end so soon. I felt prepared to withstand the winter in the *Lager*, and then more easily the spring and summer, and hold out at least until the following autumn. But it was important to measure out every particle of energy with the maximum of economy, to obliterate oneself so as to be forgotten. I and Téolo – who shared my ideas – and two other like-minded men took possession of an independent four-tiered unit and settled down to a respectable social life modelled on that of the woodworm.

It was a featureless landscape, a confused mass, a monochrome drawing after the manner of Callot, relieved here and there by more sharply defined figures: my Téolo in the foreground, with his book at his breast like the Bestower in altar-pieces now in some museum; then the other two – Pannuzzo, very young, of modest circumstances, brought up by his grandmother who had taught him to sew, hence very good at mending; and Valente, a submarine officer, who had invented a stove that could function with small twigs. If I put the proportion of kind souls in our company at around two per cent, I think it corresponded to what was defined as 'Italy's lucky star' by the more shrewd majority who always knew how to exploit the patient few for their own purposes. Pannuzzo sewed on endless buttons to help the elect to maintain their dignity, though owing to his own small blue administrative epaulettes of a very low grade, and his clumsy ways, he himself remained at the level of an outcast. Valente provided an infinitude of little stoves and no one shared with him the meals they were thus enabled to cook. Téolo did most of all by praying for everyone, but no one even knew it. As for me, I must have appeared a maniac, no less, for I was absorbed in my incomprehensible notebooks for hours and even days on end.

We had acquired a good many of these notebooks from the office of His Excellency General Vecchiarelli on that famous day of his arrest. Blessed foresight, for paper was scarce in the camp and bread was needed as exchange. Another stroke of luck was our lightning decision, on entering the hut, to take over the four-tiered unit at the far end near the small window – the only source of feeble light in the place, for the anaemic little lamps were useless and the hut was more often than not plunged in darkness. Our chosen position was extremely cold, being next to the outside wall and far from the central stove; but wrapped in all the woollies that I had gained through my work for Quero & Co., I was able to write for many hours each day; while the others, lying on their bunks like mummies in their burial niches, could only stagnate, think, and suffer.

From a certain point of view my life now reminded me of my schooldays. But my present condition was much easier. I had been a prisoner then as now; but then I had been a child in need of affection, whereas, as a man, I could do without it. The monks, not to mention the Prefect Cirillo, had seemed much more tangible and frightening than the non-existent Germans. My companions both then and now came from the same class; but now I was prepared to defend myself from them. As a child I had sighed for my medlar tree and my sister Checchina; whereas now Naples, Licudi and Italy were more foreign to me than Germany itself. What else? I found peace of mind; and freedom, because I was removed from everything that had made me suffer so much. Against that there was only the scarcity of food. But no scarcer than the food that the raven had carried in its yellow beak to St Benedict in the desert. No! I saw nothing in imprisonment of what the others were lamenting about. Imprisonment gave me total purity of mind, unlimited freedom of concentration, it absolved me from the past, rescued me from servitude to the flesh and, by obliging me to abide by the rules, it put iron into my will. It made time stretch out like a harmonious ribbon on which no external voice could register a discord; it put me adrift on the water of things; disposed me to the contemplation that gives rise to wisdom and to the recollection that is the mother of poetry. I felt my mind was liberated and safe. And so was I.

(*From fragments of my diary: While travelling . . . December 1943.*)

Our first halt was on the fifth day, at an ordinary station, not far from the main platform. The contrast was striking. On one side there was us, reduced to mere numbers, locked in like wild beasts, grey and hairy inside those animal cages. On the other side a peaceful normal life was going on: students, tradesmen, young people on holiday, decorated officials. We encountered vacuous glances, expressionless faces, uninterested gestures; people moving around, talking, greeting each other as if we did not exist; and yet we were men too.

The troop-train shunted back a little and stopped alongside a civilian one. At the window two ugly graceless girls began giggling at the sight of us, with a kind of ridiculous coquettishness to which only our sad eyes responded. In the next carriage a good German mother was pointing us out to her small sons, teaching them. And further along a solitary woman dressed in black gazed at us with a heartfelt expression of loss and sorrow; she was very pale. She saw the truth; she saw in our faces the pain of her own loved ones, of those who had gone off and were dead, swallowed up by that ambiguous monster that has no motherland: war.

Siltau, February 1944.
The rations so ardently awaited for eighteen hours had not arrived that evening. In the frozen silence of the *Stube* one of the young men suddenly pulled from his palliasse a bottle of rare French scent; he opened it with a malicious grin and then with a yelp of hysterical laughter poured it all over his filthy hair. That was ten days ago, but a hint of that delicate scent still hovers around in the fetid atmosphere of the hut.

Siltau, February 1944.
After our bath they shoved us stark naked into a room adjoining the showers where there were already many other poor souls trying to keep warm at the one cast-iron stove. All those shivering men stood around in circles displaying their under-nourished limbs, their secret physical defects, their forsaken privates; all reserve gone now, but a certain uneasiness remaining. Because their shrivelled arms, their shoulder-blades and breast-bones sticking out beneath their skin, their white lifeless legs and their feet misshapen with swellings and frostbite – all were in such flagrant contradiction with the defiant attitudes that some of them still felt compelled to assume.

And so much wizened emaciation, and the pale sagging skin of the older ones, and the rare grace that still marked a few of the youthful figures, created a strange visual concerto, some mute canticle that passed description: as in those primitive purgatories where the painter's origins and Christian feeling – inexpert though he may have been in design and perspective – bring together naïve ugliness or sheer clumsiness with an instinctive compassion for human frailty.

And we were frail indeed: stripped of clothes, of action and of pride. And thus taken back very far indeed in both time and species by the tepid sickly odour that our bodies gave forth: a human odour and an animal odour, very ancient and yet new. The odour of milk and of the lair; the odour of dung and of the cradle.

If a well-born girl can play tennis, be a beautiful dancer, know in detail the kinship between the 'good' families of a given province, and yet at the same time be devoutly religious, no one is very much surprised. But for the same attributes to be combined in a man is rather rare, yet by chance I discovered that Téolo had not only been runner-up in his regional tennis championships in 1938, and a winner in several waltz competitions, but also had a detailed knowledge of the aristocracy not only of Venice but of many other parts of Italy. As we walked up and down together for the daily fifteen minutes included in our health schedule – between that funereal quadrangle where the Russian prisoners had died and the filthy camp trenches that served as latrines in Siltau – we discussed the work we planned to undertake, I as a civil-court judge and he helping me with his specialised knowledge in matters sacred. Educated by the Barnabites, Téolo came from an old comfortably-off family and had been able to stock a memory worthy of Mithridates in a library such as Leopardi's father, Count Monaldo, would have loved. He could wander back and forth among the genealogies of the Bourbons or the Medici (which are like forests) without confusing a single datum. As my only books were the Bible and the Gospels, I was naturally led to seek some personal theme in these supreme works, the compendium and matrix of countless others; and my choice fell on the story of Esther.

Situated beside the hut's small window, our four-tiered bunk was the only one standing by itself and thus looked as high as a tower. As the most senior, I occupied the bottom place; Téolo was above me; then came the sailor Valente, and then poor Pannuzzo, who got the full benefit of the bugs that poured down from the roof and thus protected the rest of us from them in proportional scale. On the other side, across a narrow space, there rose the wall of the collective bunk tower, ten bunks, each five storeys high, and taking up the whole of that wall. Thus each of us had an enforced contact with the storey corresponding to our own, and to me fell an irritable captain who was always at war with the four who slept above him because they put their muddy boots on his blanket when climbing up to their places. The never-ending sight of feet hanging in the air corresponded, in our town planning, to the operation of lifts in modern buildings. I got used to regarding Pannuzzo's lean dangling legs as a sign of daybreak, for every day at dawn – when a scarcely perceptible gleam of light began to pick out a shape here and there from the heavy evil-smelling mass breathing in the darkness – he let himself down into the gangway, trying hard not to disturb me, so as to begin a strange operation he imagined he was undertaking unseen.

Pannuzzo, one of the poorest and always patiently engaged in sewing on the buttons of the rich, was a figure from a Gospel parable. His jacket had been the object of an incident when nearly a whole bucket of fatty substance had been upset over it, the more unfortunate as it was already too long and almost worn through. Since that time three-quarters of it had consisted of a single blackish grease-stain that gleamed rather like a coat of mail when in the light. He also (as I noticed) possessed a shoebrush, a black one, with its bristles worn down to the wood, and every morning as soon as dawn broke he took his venerable jacket and set to work to brush it with infinite care, especially over the wide surface of the grease-stain, and kept busily at it for a good twenty minutes.

While pretending to be asleep I sank into contemplation of that intent emaciated face seemingly immersed in some extravagant dream, while the hand mechanically sent the brush up and down with a low regular rubbing noise. No part of that jacket was left free from this scrupulous rehabilitation. Then, as the light grew, and someone began coughing or tossing, Pannuzzo would clamber up again to his fourth storey; his legs disappeared and there was no further news of him for quite a while, but meanwhile the whispering of Téolo's prayers would start up.

Attention to needs like Pannuzzo's jacket will give an idea of what the possible occupations in the *Lager* were. The timelessness of time, when one does not know the measure of it, alters all other relationships. The civilian prisoner knows how long his imprisonment is going to last, however severe his punishment; even if he has a life sentence he can measure its hatefulness with fairly accurate precision. But military imprisonment is conditioned by the war being waged and, like the war, can go on for years or end tomorrow. This gnawing uncertainty creates a shapeless spectre in the mind, a mixture of impulses, doubts, crises. The punishment the Germans meted out to us, with a system of shortages, that tested to the utmost our physical even more than our moral endurance, put us into competition with time. Certainly the war could not go on for ever, but neither could our capacity to survive; and if the war could go on a single day longer than us, then it was all over for us.

Thus among the officers there was an obvious confusion of ideas, a lack of method and discipline, a dispersal of reasoning into moods and of moods into reasoning; but the truth lying behind every tiny incident in the camp was that minute calculation between ourselves and time. Each man became very knowledgeable about the quantity of vitamins, proteins, carbohydrates, salt and fat needed to maintain a minimum of life in a body. All knew how many calories they needed and how many were contained in our diet; they weighed up the reserves of their individual organisms and measured consumption down to the last millimetre. That famine in Greece when so many of the civil population had died under our army's eyes returned to people's minds as an experience to be learned from: the Greeks used to remain absolutely motionless on their pallets so as to save up every scrap of vital energy; so most of the prisoners followed the same method, and in the first two months of 1944 the dormitories at certain hours were as still and silent as cemeteries.

'If only they would examine their consciences!' said Téolo, pursing his lips. He had a pretty low opinion of the upper and middle classes; he summed it up by gesticulating with both hands, with a glance upwards: 'If there weren't the police . . . we'd be in a bad way!'

And it was true that there was no talk about examining consciences. The suffering men, wrapped in their rags so as to conserve their meagre warmth, lay in the darkness of their bunks and dreamt their headlong dreams; they thought the same things over and over and over again; they surveyed the whole of their past lives, the intimate memories, the joys, the sins. But no sound ever broke that silence save for egotistical remarks and angry lies: the very ones which, multiplied by millions, had brought us to the present disaster and were keeping us there. The Italians are naturally evasive, querulous, and impatient, and now they were facing a simple challenge: to last out in the camp longer than those others could last out at the Front; a game by no means decided and the zero of the roulette was in our favour, for anyone could get out of the camp at any moment by consenting to work. But as a surviving expression of all human kind, their nature reacted by showing itself obstinately hostile to every explicit truth and they preferred to cling to certain external forms of self-delusion (if not to error) as if it were life itself. Hence, beneath a veil of words and international law and other Byzantine subtleties, and with unending quarrels and litigations and threats of future vengeance, the other fundamental characteristic of our people presented itself, a people believed by half the world to be one of fiery passion and dashing exploits; and it really did possess the former and perform the latter, but always accompanied by consummate diplomacy (so as to be able to 'put into effect', as Machiavelli said) and a very cold assessment of the facts.

Thus, while two per cent – or perhaps five per cent if one took in the whole company – remained inviolate, poor and honest like the hungry Pannuzzo, the others with an eye on the reserves and an ear stretched for the slightest hint of news from the clandestine radio, gave themselves to nothing but scrutinising the calendar which worked through its little two-coloured pages with exasperating slowness.

Though convinced that I was acting differently from them, I did exactly the same but in another direction: I ousted by means of a total chimera the depressing reality that was stifling us. I even refused to believe that I was hungry. Insupportable though my hunger was as twilight fell, I made out that it was non-existent or, if it existed, was no worse than a common headache. Perhaps guided mediumistically over extra-sensory waves by Demetrio the Seer (or even by Thirteen's unforgettable eyes), I set out to detach myself from matter and, by means of will-power and imagination, to replace the degrading spectacle in which my days dragged by with another spectacle and a fantastic one – of the epoch when proud spirits performed great feats under the fierce African sun. Esther held me in her thrall – passionately so – first because she was a woman (and women had been lost to us for some time); then because she represented pity (from which we were excluded!); then because she fought to liberate her people from slavery (of which I now at last understood the reality and not just the concept); and finally because, amid the regal pomp in which Pharaoh lived, she remained genuine and pure: as I myself intended to be.

On that heaven-sent paper, valued in the camp as highly as bread which was life itself, I found my way back to the dignity of writing – like the ancient illuminators on salvaged parchment when they repainted over the invisible trace of the Hebrew, Greek or Latin texts, like treasure upon treasure; texts that would later flower beneath the researcher's magnifying glass, a hundred times more precious than an alchemist's formulae. Once I had started work I never gave up as long as the faintest glimmer of light remained, but went on noting and commenting: real code-writing (in which I revelled) over half a page, while the other half served for footnotes. Indifferent to any kind of annoyance, oblivious of cold and hunger, I relived every smallest vibration of the doings of Assuerus, Mardocheus, Aman, and the unconquered daughter of Benjamin's tribe, the complete heroine, for she combined beauty, courage, sweetness and virtue.

It was certainly the wisdom pouring down on me from Téolo in the bunk above and the extraordinary serenity he derived from his breviary, as well as Valente's patience in making his burners and Pannuzzo's care in polishing his jacket that gave me strength to follow my path in imitation of their fervour and renunciation. But as in my Paris period, when I discovered the Borgognas, the Medici, Rubens, and finally Goya, and experienced them not as external facts (which people still want to call Culture) but as expressions of my immediate feelings and will, so did it happen again now with these new objects of inspiration. I recalled how, when I had decided to leave Gian Luigi's house, Ulysses' 'little speech' to his companions in the *Divine Comedy* meant more to me than any other advice. Both the old and the new circumstances of my life were stirred into action by the turbulent fantasies of a story continually melting into poetry. The spirit of Paolo Grilli brought me near to the fire of Aman's troubled passions; the women I had loved were embodied in Esther: Incoronata with her dedication, Arrichetta with her beauty, Nerina with her regal bearing, and Cousin Dolores (in her wreath of orange blossom) with her desperate courage. And James Murri's rarefied mockery helped me to understand that in that universe starry with emblems and privileges, ruled by the golden rod of the demi-god, it is the impious one who submerges himself in the end – submerges himself in sacrilege so as to bring death from it. In Aman stretched out on the Queen's bed so that the eunuchs could pierce him, I saw the nemesis that guilt brings on itself: that of Capaneus and Argante; and I saw how, by virtue of the funereal quadrangle bounding our horizon, justice would resolve the war on the side against evil, like a divine judgement.

Pompeo Pompei had called me a fakir in my Milan period, but my exercises in those days were mere trifles compared with these present ones; in which Téolo, Pannuzzo and Valente all took part up to a point, at least for the evening reading: Téolo sitting beside me on my bed, and Pannuzzo and the submarine-man Valente standing unobtrusively in the narrow space in front of the little window – Valente, I think, only out of group affection. Valente was a native of Castellabate del Cilento and had been rescued with one or two others from a submarine that had sunk to the bottom of the Otranto channel – delayed assistance had arrived after seventy-two hours. All bones and sinew, he spoke little; but no one picked a quarrel with him because of something disquieting in his russet eyes. With Pannuzzo, whom he protected against the tyranny of his clients, he even shared a cigarette stub.

The conditions of the *Lager* towards the end of winter were bleak indeed. Through the action of some spy – bribed, perhaps, by a tin of sauerkraut – the clandestine radio was discovered and with it went the basic element for calculating one's resistance: which in fact was deteriorating rapidly. But those who died were replaced by others, brought along from areas taken over by advancing armies. Many had already collaborated with the Germans, but they did not say so, and they also knew various other things which they kept to themselves, wanting to blend in with the crowd as if they had shared their destiny from the beginning. Every day clouds of Allied planes passed overhead making implacably for Bremen, Hamburg or Berlin, and various frightened remarks of the guards let it be understood that ours was one of the safest places. Meanwhile, after the confiscation of the radio and the subsequent grotesque threats meted out all round, the Germans – imagining who knows what signalling system to enemy planes – deprived us of electric light during the night which gave rise to episodes grotesque in their wretchedness: for the many sick who could not find their way to the latrines and for the many who were continually woken up as a result of this. There usually followed furious quarrels that condemned the whole hut to sleeplessness, for the din soon became infernal. To get round the darkness problem, and after endless referenda, vote-countings and ballots, it was agreed that each man should sacrifice a tiny quota of his weekly ration of fat so as to make night-lights. But after three attempts the experiment fell through: there was always some hungry person to put out the little flame at dead of night and to gulp down the night-light, so that we were plunged again into darkness amid the muffled beating of hearts and the earth's vibrations as distant explosions tore cities apart.

The final contrivance of the '*crucchi*' (as we described the Germans of the *Lager* in a word of uncertain etymology) was that of leaving us without matches – perhaps still motivated by some fear that we were signalling to enemy planes; so that finally there was not a single matchbox in the whole of Siltau. Every evening thirty delegates from thirty huts came to a certain place at a certain hour to get fire with a single wax taper for the thousands of people who would not otherwise have been able to smoke or cook on the patent Valente burners. Many were already limping on legs swollen with hunger; a malady which generally afflicted the tall of stature to whom fate granted the same rations as to the small. Many were harbouring that tuberculosis which was soon to kill them; but they refused to give way: some of them sincerely bound to a duty that was hardly known or understood; others believing themselves tied by their oath to the King, although the House of Savoy, in its usual way, paid not the slightest attention to those who were wearing themselves out on its behalf (nor did it show, later, that it had even been aware of them!). But as for me, I was so distrustful of human nature in general and in particular that I remained pitiless towards others, just as I was drugged into a total indifference towards myself. I suffered the same hardships as all the others; indeed, I had freely accepted them, almost chosen them, out of humility and expiation. But it had not been given to me to modify my character and still less to restrain my thoughts. I felt that the communal ordeal had no meaning for me, and that it was on the point of reaching its term.

It was on some grim evening about that time, when we were at the very limit of our deprivation, that we saw Pannuzzo arriving at our private area by the window with something voluminous concealed beneath his vast jacket. As soon as he felt he was safe he knelt down and cautiously extracted handfuls of mushrooms from his bosom, and piled them up on the floor under the stupefied gaze of Téolo, Valente and myself. He smiled in answer to our questions and revealed that he had found them all precisely beneath the watch-tower at the far end of the *Lager*, in a corner to which no one went so no one had noticed their existence.

'Under the tower? But what do you mean?' asked Téolo. 'The fatigue patrols pass it every day by the dozen to draw their rations!'

'Yes,' he admitted, 'but the mushrooms were a little further on, towards the main stretch of barbed wire, right up against the tower. No one's noticed them.'

'D'you mean you got them from the other side of the warning-wire, Pannuzzo? Under the sentry's eyes? He must have been asleep not to have seen you! Don't you realise he could have shot you?'

He looked at us with a confused and aggrieved expression. What we were saying did not seem even to penetrate his mind, much less convince him. He tried to explain that the sentry could not have seen him in the concealed spot where he was, and other absurdities. He apologised for having run the risk of death – he certainly had not realised he was doing so, or else (which seemed to me strangely possible) he somehow knew that he would come out of it unscathed. We did not know what type the mushrooms were and they could easily have been poisonous – but this did not so much as occur to Pannuzzo. So, trusting in his trust and his angelic innocence, the four of us ate those mushrooms (which were excellent) together; together to live or die in the best possible way. All they gave us was the deepest sleep we had had for months.

I awoke in the morning even before Pannuzzo got down to brush his jacket, and found the idea for a new work, perhaps a full-length book or play. If Esther were a dazzling heroine like Brandimarte or Erminia, then the immense figure of Jesus breathing in the Gospels should be raised up and explained on the level of poetry. Pannuzzo's humility, and the simple gesture with which he had placed the mushrooms on the floor and stayed kneeling in front of us, showing and offering them with a look that seemed to ask forgiveness for his very devotion – all this was like the blooms on a tree of revealed sweetness whose seed had been sown two thousand years before on the shores of the Lake of Genasareth. I had never meant to meditate on the figure of Christ; and every time it imposed itself on me I had put off receiving his message till some other time. Perhaps the time had now come. I pulled myself up in the darkness and shook Téolo's curtain above me. But he was not asleep.

'Listen,' I whispered. 'Perhaps I've had an idea. Supposing I wrote a book that was different from all the other books? Supposing I wrote about Jesus as the greatest of all poets? Supposing I could show that this is what it means to be the Son of God?'

He didn't answer for a while. Then:

'Go to sleep,' he said slowly. 'Go to sleep, it's still night. We're already atoning for our sins in this place. It's important not to commit any more!'

Above us the distant drone of the plane-formations going to mow down the cities of the Triangle made the small window-panes vibrate imperceptibly. I buried myself in sleep. And it was now the glass of the skylight that shook. There were a few slow sighs and a deep throbbing organ-like snoring from a few, but interrupted now and again and then starting up again as though in a series of nightmares. They were being afflicted by endless intimate memories, desires and loves churning around in the depths of their hearts; as was happening also in mine because I partook of their troubles without wanting to, but I knew them so well. The rhythm of solitude and companionship did not stop. I heard Téolo's quiet breathing above me; and that of the other two, my family. Perhaps I would be able to detach myself from the world only when I had left this one.

The psychosis of hunger far outstripped its physiological reality and drove the prisoners to various forms of strange behaviour. For instance, they had built with great ingenuity a huge quantity of scales of every size on which it was possible to measure everything down to half a gram. They had originally been constructed as a black market outfit; but later they served to measure out our infinitesimal rations: margarine, sugar, salt. And people even went so far as to weigh cigarettes when it was a matter of exchanging them: just as usurers used to do with florins. As for the method of eating their rations, there were those who ate them up immediately, those who nibbled at them taking at least ten bites, and those who put their bread on their blanket and looked at it for at least half a day saying that this gave them security. In default of real meals, the prisoners enjoyed imaginary ones to the utmost. A thriving literature of cookery flourished in the *Lager* to the comfort of the more fastidious palates, and one saw pitifully muffled-up figures running from one hut to another in search of new recipes to add to their own well-filled scribbling-blocks. Then they would read out menus of gargantuan meals and everyone else would listen as if hypnotised. So there was nothing very extraordinary in us four operating in a contrary way. With Téolo's help we established theologically that the pain and gnawing of the stomach could not act as fateful portents of illness or death, but were more like ordinary neuralgia or the spasms of a common wound. Pannuzzo, and then Valente too, humbly accepted this thesis, and once we had quickly eaten up our communal meal not a word was said in that connection by any of the four of us until next day. On the other hand the monastic rule of fasting showed its powerful logic in that no one in the hut ever spoke of women; and perhaps, for many, this final chastisement was not entirely undeserved.

As spring approached the rhythm of the air-raids on Germany became terrifying. In clear sunsets we saw high up above us the swarms of flying fortresses that had shed their bombs over the region and were returning to the coast in hundreds, in waves, having lost their formation while in action. But seen all together like that, and shining brightly so high up in a sun that had already withdrawn from the earth, they seemed more terrible and invincible than ever. One followed in one's mind the flock of airmen returning to their comfortable shelters; and it meant nothing that they had risked their lives and that many of the men flying up there were wounded or dying. They were the masters of space and that was worth any kind of anguish. Then the camp turned its eyes back on to its own inertia and the night brooded over the heavy breathing in the cattle-shed.

At the end of March the Fascist Republic of Salò conveyed a van-load of biscuits to us. Shortly afterwards it obtained permission for Northern Italian families subject to Mussolini's regime to send food parcels to their relations. So half the camp was cared for, and the persistent malevolence of history regarding the South left all the rest, from Cassino downwards, fasting. However, the Germans then distributed request cards to every prisoner. Immediately the firm of Quero, Fabbricatore and Mozzillo sprang up again – it bought up the cards of those who had no one to send them to and gave cut-throat percentages in return. This business was not run without endless intrigues, arguments, brawls and betrayals; but we, being associated with Téolo, the only Northerner among us, placed our cards at his disposal and got ourselves back on our feet: only just in time, I believe, especially as regards Pannuzzo who was the youngest and in the worst condition. As for me, I was beginning to suffer from fevers that later grew more intense and turned out to be malaria of illustrious Greek origins. While these things were going on, my work on the Gospel, inspired by Pannuzzo's virtue, took shape.

It was a work unquestionably weak in its scientific and logical context, yet strong indeed from the point of view of love. It is impossible for me now to reconstruct what I felt and saw in it; and how I thought I could avoid the innumerable shoals which in the eyes of a punctilious and cultured academy would surely have sunk such a doubtful thesis. But I certainly buried myself in it with all the power of my mind; and if I was unable to give the work the depth it deserved, I certainly drew extraordinary strength from it which made me impregnable to every pressure and blow from without, and allowed me hours of peace and oblivion such as I had not known since the happy days of childhood.

Before the arrival of June with its shattering events in Europe, and July, so crucial in Germany, I had elaborated the greater part of the work and was already embarking on the final section – the death, resurrection and reappearance of Jesus to the women and the apostles. But here my fancy, unchecked by any critical impediment (which I would have found restrictive and out of the question) and resting only on the bare lines of the Evangelists, took flight around a theme so fascinating that it became the focal point of the book instead of leading in to the conclusion. And if that work had not been destroyed as a result of subsequent events, together with the story of Esther and my notes on the thoughts they both produced, I would certainly have chosen to put the finishing touches only to this last part: the unspoken drama of Pilate's wife when confronted with the passion and death of the Redeemer.

That woman was a patrician and a Roman confined for a time to a sun-drenched province, like the wife of a modern diplomat posted to some undesirable embassy, and she formed part of that world that had its new-style poet in Catullus and was rich in feelings and scruples adverse to the ancient republican roughness. And in the fantastic novel that I went on weaving in my mind I believe I almost caught her character; and thence the intimate reactions and events that were to flow from it. The figure of Jesus was known to her through the many stories and almost the legend that surrounded his name; and throughout his cruel trial before Pilate, the Nazarene must have appeared to her unique; magnetic in his silence and resignation, and giving rise to disturbing and indescribable emotions.

Though it is not documented, it is reasonable to suppose (following St Matthew's Gospel) that his wife's opinions played some part in Pilate's hesitations when those of the Temple were a crowd of seditious fanatics in the eyes of the presiding judge and the Other a politically harmless man. She must have anxiously followed the doings of the Just Man to whom the crowd insisted on preferring the assassin Barabbas; she must have heard from the servants about the scourging, the mockery, the crown of thorns. The blind and evil forces that struck the messenger of universal love would have been nameless and infernal symbols in her mind, hands without a body, scourges brandished by Evil against Good. And in the same way she would have conceived the Son of Man to be greater than anyone else not so much for his august bearing as for the greatness irradiating from his mantle, as white as that whiteness of soul whose only counterpart is the flaming sorrow at the foot of the Cross, the cry of purple as Masaccio intuited it.

When the Passion was over and Jesus was dead there was the man from Arimathea to take him down from the Cross and send him to a humble tomb. But on the third day it was empty. From this point starts the prodigious story of apparitions and revelations which would grow from century to century and flower into the huge tree of Christian tradition. But the last certain act of the Passion remains the placing of Jesus in that tomb. After that we leave history and enter the domain of faith.

But it was perhaps beyond faith and within poetry that I then searched for the Man of Sorrows, dragged from the tomb not by a divine act but by human passions and emotions. It was mankind and mankind alone that could claim the remains even of God, inasmuch as he had made himself Man and to mankind alone the Poet belonged: if this was what being the Son of God meant. To whom, then, should be assigned not only the idea but the power of moving away the stone from the tomb – so as to receive from it the most holy remains and transfer them almost into one's own heart? From the point of view of the Roman prefect's wife, Jesus' disciples were simply a group of workmen and fishermen who had denied him and left him alone to torture and death. The service rendered to the Man brought down from the Cross was – in its methods and in the persons involved – the final residue of a bewilderment and fear that would later disperse them for ever. For this reason I saw her staying up late, making provisions; through her agency other devoted women whose names are not preserved by Time though they are noted in the march of the universal spirit, through her agency they reopen the unhonoured tomb, take out the martyr, give Him oils, as Magdalen did, and new bandages; then leaving the winding-sheet stained with blood and water, they carry him to her because, as she was the only one to defend him, she now wants to be the sole guardian and repository of the desecrated body of the Man who had understood Love, had flayed hypocrisy, had exalted charity, and had forgiven the men who knew not what they did.

These were the thoughts by which I was totally penetrated and profoundly moved, and I communicated their dangers to a thoroughly upset and almost panic-stricken Téolo who let me talk on and opposed me only with the unbelieving look in his eyes; and throughout all this period the Anglo-American forces were entering Rome and landing in France. The Russians were occupying Vienna, and in Germany they were preparing that *coup d'état* which culminated in the attempt on Hitler's life on July the 20th.

The ferocious reaction following that deed – which in the Reich cost the lives of around two thousand important people including members of the Stauffenberg and von Hasselt families – produced in the *Lager* a new wave of punishments and restrictions that made our conditions very much worse. The dispatch of parcels from Italy was suspended, and inspections multiplied (in which the Germans confiscated whole heaps of our possessions). Once again fear took possession of the camp as persistent rumours circulated that we were to be eliminated before the Nazi surrender. Furthermore, at this time Mussolini dissolved the old Royalist armies by official act of his government of Salò so that we reverted to civilian status and were placed under the rigours of German law – and this prescribed work for any and everyone who found himself within the Reich. This greatly benefited the other ranks who, working as prisoners, were already subject to slave labour and by becoming ordinary labourers they were made equal with everyone else. But in German eyes all possibility of the officers refusing work collapsed. So the struggle became bitter between the two theses though in the end it was the facts that had to be reckoned with.

Once hope was lost that the war would end at least during those months, once supplies had been cut off and restrictions set up, the chances in favour of resistance diminished; many men decided to leave the *Lager* and go over to manual work in factories or on farms. But in September after Paris had surrendered and the Allied armies were heading towards the Rhine, the numbers in Siltau reached alarming proportions owing to those who poured in from the newly evacuated areas, and those who had gone out to work in these same areas and now flocked back to the camps. As confusion reached a peak so did people's needs. A cigarette cost a thousand times its normal price. The prisoners had to smoke tea-leaves, lime-leaves, any leaves, even potato peelings; then came the bark of trees; after which those frantic men resorted to the sawdust from their palliasses, a delicacy that was dubbed 'the lung-splitter'. Many declared consumptives, to whom smoking was lethal and nourishment indispensable, nevertheless bartered a portion of bread in exchange for tobacco.

This was the period of my greatest concentration; but following a system already applied on many other occasions, I allotted myself some exacting and painstaking manual task to alternate with my mental work when reflection on some point had not come to fruition; and this time, strange though it may seem, I devoted myself to washing my two sheets; a thing held to be impossible in our conditions, and it took me nearly a week.

For the cleaning (if so it may be called) of the *Lager* and ourselves the only provision was the fortnightly disinfection of our clothes *en masse* in the gas chambers. The latter, which have played a large part in post-war literature for the last twenty years, were installed in all the camps for the purpose of exterminating insects and providing essential safeguards against contagious typhus; and it was only after the war that we heard they had been used against human lives. But there was no facility at all for doing one's laundry.

To begin with water was scarce in the camp and measured out by a hand-pump, a mess-tin at a time, after interminable queuing. Then there was the scarcity of soap. Finally there was no line and it was forbidden to go near the barbed wire. Could one dry the laundry by holding it out to the wind in one's hands? Or by laying it on the ground to get dirty again? Or by draping it over the dormitory to the indignation of the others and where it would get covered with smoke from the stove? Or by leaving it on the roof for the wind to blow away or someone to try to steal? Under these conditions, and with a cunning and dexterity far greater than were deployed by Casanova when escaping from the Piombi, I washed those sheets – extremely rare articles, incidentally, and not used by anyone. When they were dry I made the bed next to the window, and the whole block, composed of six huts, came to admire the marvel – as when there is an international exhibition and the whole city comes to revere a masterpiece.

Lying between those fragrant sheets I overcame the daily attack of fever that lasted from six in the evening till around midnight – although this was during the coming-and-going to and from the exhibition; then the fever abated and I suffered from a crippling headache till about two. Then I fell asleep and slept peacefully until early afternoon. The return of the fever was heralded by a sense of blissful torpor similar to what I had experienced at Lwow with those drunken bouts of coffee on an empty stomach. It was during those rapturous hours that I had my sublime fantasies about the divinity as incarnate in poetry; but it seems that sometimes I became delirious, and Téolo had to get me into the infirmary which was always in an appalling condition and lacking medicines (beginning with quinine), but perhaps slightly more airy and restful. Autumn progressed. When it became plain that the war was going on and that we would have to endure another winter, the *Lager* fell into a frozen and sinister silence. Once again nothing was to be heard in the hut but the heavy breathing of those who lay motionless, blankets over their faces, desperately conjuring up ghosts. But it also happened that as the situation came to the climax and needs became more pressing – especially as regards clearing the rubble and burying the dead in the cities pulverized by the air offensives – the Germans resorted to force. They sent off a whole company, complete with baggage, on the pretext of transferring it, but in fact handed it over to forced labour. The exhausted and divided prisoners were no more able to react than ants, and when I returned from the infirmary I found none of my friends left. Téolo, Pannuzzo and Valente had disappeared; others were occupying our four-tiered bunk; and no one could tell me anything about them.

That night I slept on the ground with the ghost of Boris Draguliub as sole companion. The bases of our beds were made of fir slats, and most of them were lacking as they had been used for firewood. So the prisoners slept on four or five slats instead of fifteen, each man intent on defending his own and stealing everyone else's. Places left empty were immediately stripped, and this had happened to mine. An examination of conscience was simple this time: my imprisonment was due to an effort at humility and a debt of honour. But I now knew that it was impossible to force one's nature; that I had not really been prepared to accept the communal attitude and had even rejected it. Though convinced of my good faith in making the attempt, I was equally convinced that I had failed. The price paid for an experience of this kind mattered nothing to me, but it suited me to be free again now and to separate my fate uncompromisingly from that of everyone else.

I took less than no notice of all the various arguments; I did not feel bound by oath to King Vittorio or to anyone else; the casuistries of international law were for me merely laughable – the Hague, Geneva, the Red Cross; the laws 'prevailing' for the republicans of Salò, for the king's men, for the Nazis; the 'status' of the prisoner, the internee, the officer, the civilian, the worker. I could not hold out in the *Lager* for another winter, protected from the bombardments raging over the whole of Germany. I did not believe at all in our elimination at the last minute. And the argument that henceforth kept all the others clinging to that kind of rock, bleak indeed but safe, was the absolute imminence of the German collapse. The Allies were pressing on the Rhine; Finland had obtained a separate peace; Florence had fallen and Bologna was about to do so. Hitler's fate was sealed and his days numbered. But what was there left for me to do in a camp whose life and motivations I knew so well? My friends had gone; my book was finished. The tension of my mind would never have been assuaged in the repetition of useless days; with bandaged eyes in the midst of the vast tragedy that was about to reach its climax, a moment such as had not been seen for centuries: a whole proud powerful nation being brought to account amid unutterable events and majestic conflagrations. As a lonely traveller in a land that was not my own, I preferred to take my chance in the open and pay the price of consciousness; I wanted to know and understand.

So one morning towards the end of November 1944 I presented myself to the German sergeant in charge of recruitment. There was a small squad ready to depart and he merely added my name to the other four. An hour later, after the shower and disinfectant, and with the first horse steak I had eaten for fourteen months as provision for the journey, I withdrew from those particular tribulations.

THE GEESE

I looked without much curiosity at my four companions with whom chance had decreed that I should share an extraordinary experience and the risks that could bring it to an end at any moment: a second lieutenant of the *bersaglieri*, of coarse appearance and with a marked Apulian accent; a fellow-countryman of his of the same rank, but flaccid and sleepy; a lieutenant of athletic build, but whose completely shaven head together with the blackish complexion of the declared consumptive gave him the look of an escaped convict; and finally a lean and quarrelsome captain, the only one who took any care of his appearance insofar as this was possible in the circumstances. They were dazed by the open air, and their miserable aspect and frightened awkward movements made me realise that my own were certainly the same.

The journey lasted half a day with two or three changes of train. The coming and going on those little provincial stations, where normal people seemed to be busy with everyday affairs, was utterlv astonishing to us after the length of time we had been cut off from such things; it all seemed like a play on a stage. The Germans deliberately pretended not to see us; but the suffering written on our faces must have made a mark on their uneasy consciences now that catastrophe was becoming evident. At one of our halts we happened to have a front-row view of two departing SS soldiers being seen off by their families. Those powerfully built young men belonged to a distinct class and were certainly sincere in their fanaticism. Their mothers and fiancées – respectable women from solid families – were talking gravely with them as befitted the solemn occasion. But our silent group left its mark on those farewells. Twice the eyes of one of those soldiers met mine; and I felt neither aggression nor conviction in them, but only a dark determination.

None of us knew German, and at the many control points all explanations were given by the man accompanying us, an old soldier who had lost a forearm and was in charge of the documents: new aspects of a specious freedom for the deaf and dumb. The refinements of the German mechanism produced its phagocytic effects by the use of both material and psychological elements, exactly as it had operated when dispatching our army to the barbed wire without the help of guards – knowing that owing to our absurd desire for repatriation we would go there. This time we were kept under guard by our ignorance of the language which curtailed any possible contacts; we knew nothing of where we were being sent; nor with what obligations, and still less, what rights; nor on whom we would effectively depend. Our ignorance of German laws in general, and wartime ones in particular, had handed us over from one imprisonment to another; but it surprised me that as soon as he saw the two SS men surrounded by their families, our one-armed soldier did his best to get out of their view; and by his frightened manner rather than by his few inarticulate words, he intimated that those were people you had to keep away from.

We arrived at dead of night in a place whose nature we could not identify. We crossed a wide clearing smelling of the country and entered a brand new house fragrant with fresh wood. It had six places, and as once again I was the senior man two of them were put at my disposal. The dark sky was resplendent with stars, and high up in the midst of them Orion's belt was shining with a brightness I had never in my life seen before. While I was preparing my bunk I saw a spider escaping, black and hairy and as big as a nut. But though I took it as an evil omen, I fell asleep in this knowledge without the slightest sense of bitterness; like someone who has already willingly offered himself to destiny.

In the *Lager* I had always opened my eyes the moment dawn touched our little window, so now again I awoke while the others were still asleep and it took me some time to realise where I was. My heart plunged into an unexpected void in my inexplicable homesickness for the furtive sound of Pannuzzo's brush over the indelible stain on his threadbare jacket. And the value of a period that at the time had seemed static and useless suddenly swelled within me, human warmth and depth that all Croesus' gold could not have brought back or reproduced. We had not really known ourselves, just as we do not recognise emotions which, nonetheless, will form the basis of our lives for years to come; and in the concentration of captivity there had been a priceless and indefinable aroma whose last trace I breathed in that early morning blueness. But I shook myself: because after all, the present time was of the same quality and rarity and measure; each drop of it being worth the one that had just passed.

On going out into the pristine and mysterious splendour of the dawn, I took my first breath of our new world. Our hut was on the least used side of a vast clearing where I saw great piles of timber geometrically placed. On one side I saw the outline of an antiquated workshop. Further on and situated exactly between two piles of planks was a medium-sized two-storey house; with a doll's-house window, already lit by a brighter light than the dawn's, set in the sloping roof. Behind me, on the further side of an old mossy wall on to which our hut backed, there was the sound of running water, and the tall grass bore witness to the peace of the place. From the direction of the house there came the occasional clucking of hens and one or two streaks of already switched-on lights: an orderly scene waiting to spring to life and re-echo with sound.

The first person to appear on it was a servant-girl – such a ritual entry as to confirm the stage-set illusion. She was about eighteen years old with fair hair and a large bright apron, and she exhaled health and wholesome eroticism from every pore. She was the first woman I had been near for fourteen months and I gazed at her as at an object of great curiosity.

She curtsied to me, pointed to the house, and with other gestures of universal validity was unquestionably inviting me to come and get something to eat. As I followed her I breathed in the damp smell of wood put out to season; our footsteps made no sound on the grass; and as for the house, it seemed to be coming towards me in the still bright morning. The noise of the running water behind the wall was hardly more than a murmur; Orion's brilliant lights had vanished, but not their magical aftermath which still seemed to vibrate on that enchanted portion of the world. As in childhood the first day of a new life seemed to be suspended in time: a shining drop quivering at the tip of a leaf; poised yet not falling.

When the small side-door for which we were making opened, and I saw the cheerful light from the lamps and heard the rumbling of the stove and the frying of the *Speck* that was being prepared for us – all in the warm glow of a traditional German kitchen; and when the mistress of this little world came forward to greet me – so conventional in her ritual part of organiser and dispenser (as the girl had been in her role of servant) – and with many small gestures and rudimentary French displayed a courtesy I had not seen for nearly two years, then the enchantment of that morning came to a climax and at the same time broke. That day was Sunday, and we were left to find our way about and make ourselves at home: we arose from the depths and I truly believe that our lungs swelled out in our painful effort to return to the surface.

The disposition of the mind has a bewitching effect on our thoughts and even our sensations, just as the incidence of light modifies the tone of colours and the key of a musical work transfers its melody. My four new companions clearly did not share my ideas, but then I was not tied to them by any previous links and they were inspired by bitter rancour towards the Germans. All four believed they themselves were somehow to blame for accepting manual labour, so they talked on a level of open-minded superficiality, always ending on a laugh, which was their only way to play down the facts and diminish their personal bitterness. Finding ourselves immediately separated in our work, we realised that the Kurt sawmill had no other function in our regard except to provide us with our lodging; just as the women of that family, though obliged like all German women to do almost military work, had also to provide us with our food. So it was that the *bersagliere* from Apulia had to cart sacks at a farm every day (and very heavy they were, he said); his fellow-countryman, Gifuni, was employed in the stables of a brewery where he had to look after huge horses of the kind that can still be seen in the streets of Munich or even London; the herculean lieutenant, whom I knew to be a Roman and the son of a man in the legal profession, was coupled with me at the goods station to see to the loading of coal and other raw materials. As for the punctilious captain who in civil life was a provincial functionary of Chieti – we had some trouble in finding out his new job which was that of a cleaner in the local fruit market, though he never neglected his habitual care in his dress. At night they recounted the events of the day and made heavy mockery of everything, which did not prevent each trying to fix himself up on his own account, developing relationships and hatching thoughts that the others did not know; though before all this process came to a head there remained an apparent unity between us.

But that poised and motionless moment in that isolated little place was an extraordinary anachronism in the drama that was shortly to consume the whole of Germany. The Allies were marking time in the Rhineland; the Russians were waiting for the winter to end before striking their last blow on the Eastern front; while in the country itself the ferocious Nazi reaction to the attempt on Hitler's life plunged everyone into a deep fear that took the place of enthusiasm and ruled everything with a rod of iron. Of course the war was pouring relentlessly down from the sky; but it had not yet penetrated remote country places which in the Reich are like the dust of the Milky Way. Berg was a secluded village about ten kilometres away from one of the great bridges over the Elbe, and it had hardly even been aware of the war. Depopulated by conscription, it had (as was customary) the old, the wounded and the unfit at its disposal, together with an excessive number of women and a group of forced-labour prisoners from France and the Ukraine who had been there for nearly four years, were simple soldiers and by now rather boring. So that the Italian officers, who had obviously been preceded by a good deal of gossip in that quiet and withdrawn atmosphere, were observed with intense curiosity.

And with equal curiosity did I observe the Germans, indeed with delight, feeling concealed beneath my workman's clothes like a periscope-watcher in the hull of a submarine. In 1912 (the year I began my seclusion at my boarding-school) Italy had been bound to the Triple Alliance by the political pact with Austria and Germany, which she then broke by intervention on the side of the French and British. At that time Italy was by and large pervaded by pro-German sentiments among the two cultivated classes. The monks themselves had close ties with the Berlin court – prodigal as it was of bequests and suggestions to the abbey – and had decorated the crypt with that angular stylisation of Byzantine motifs which, with a somewhat debatable magnificence thrown in, goes under the name of the Bayreuth school.

Encouraged by the enthusiasm of the learned and particularly the philosophers, Germany wanted to retain the compelling good-tempered and largely romantic image outlined by Madame de Staël more than a hundred years earlier – despite the not insignificant novelties that could be read into Bismarck's actions and the Wagnerian postures of Kaiser Wilhelm. Thus little weight was given to vague rumours concerning the self-styled archaeologists, geologists or naturalists with professorial beards who straddled half the world on a mission of wisdom as ambassadors of German *Kultur*; and who were often later reckoned to be special agents if not downright spies. Public applause for the scientific accuracy of everything that bore the German imprint kept the masses silent. Precision compasses and Faber pencils camouflaged the Krupp factories. The universities, Hegel and Beethoven did the rest.

In Gian Luigi's household family tradition maintained an attitude of deference, if not of expiation, towards the Baroness von Egloffstein who had been insulted by the Sanseveros. So out of disrespect towards my elders I always made a point of showing an overall scepticism about the Teutons (condemned also by Mario, I added to myself!) and sought to disclaim any satisfaction over the Niebelung blood that might flow in my veins. These were distant memories and lacked any connection with Hitler's Germans as I had seen them in Greece or in the *Lager*; nor had I attempted to establish a connection – it was as though they were two different races. But no sooner did I cross the threshold of that hut in Berg than I felt the thread of a forgotten thought and secret commentary coming into motion, unwinding and weaving together again in the complex texture of my mind.

Just as I had gone down to Calabria to take possession of my Uncle Gian Michele's inheritance and had found a loved and familiar face there, so on that early morning in Berg – with the long grass on one side and stacks of wood on the other – I had felt a natural inevitability about settling down in that peaceful setting. All its aspects harmonised within me and were immediately familiar and understood. The servant-girl's curtsy to a prisoner-of-war doing forced labour (but in whom she nevertheless did not fail to recognise a 'Herr Hauptmann') was all part of the meticulous care with which the timber had been stacked for seasoning, part of the respect for the trees in those remote woods, part of the fairy-story house, the gleaming pans used for our food, and the mathematical precision of the slices of bread that accompanied it. In the space of a single moment it seemed to make up for all the confused anarchy I had suffered over the past three years. The French spoken by the mistress of the house (whom henceforth I called 'Madame') was the sole means of entering into contact with her and the others. In my heart I regretted not knowing German, which would have done so much to crown our concord. I remembered Paolo Grilli and James Murri and how they used to use this language long ago when, with Faustian cries, they lost themselves in the musical works of the great geniuses born on this German soil.

Whereas I spent my first two weeks in that country loading coal with the strength of my bare arms – utterly exhausting work though enabling me to savour a totally different life: that of the labourer whose attention is focused on the mass of manual work he has in front of him, and who measures his capacity and apportions his movements according to a technique born of necessity. The play of the muscles then becomes automatic, but the outcome is all the more efficient as the effort is properly organised. To gain a fraction of a second in time or a few centimetres in space means that you emerge victorious at the end of the day from an ordeal that would otherwise leave you prostrate. It was a sportsman's technique, but applied by us to a vital need. And it pleased me to create a vigorous harmony in my physical being, in the rhythm of my arms and legs, in the swinging of my chest as I wielded fork or shovel, so that I could congratulate myself each time I made the coal fly a little further or land in the place I had intended. When I had passed the crisis point well known to all athletes and realised I was the master of my material, my limbs seemed possessed by fantastic energy and capable of anything. Returning home along the street and across the main square of the village, I walked quickly and self-confidently under the furtive eyes of the people; with a studied nonchalance that certainly bespoke some kind of defiance on my part.

In a village of general kindliness and an ingrained sense of social values, it was impossible for the blatant injustice and inhumanity of our situation to pass unnoticed. The Ukrainians and few Frenchmen who, as prisoners, were already doing work of this kind had been peasants and labourers in civilian life, so were physically adapted to manual work and knew all about it. But as always happens in small centres, the people of Berg held professional men in high esteem and they knew that we were officers and had academic degrees; moreover, our evident malnutrition had done nothing to help our somewhat frail physiques as men of the pen rather than the spade. Only two of us had remotely rustic complexions, Penne, the *bersagliere*, and the herculean Magaldi, my Roman associate in the coal-yard; but even he was clearly a man of education and good breeding despite his convict's appearance. Moreover, the Army – that constant object of worship in Germany – had given us as officers an ineradicable halo. Here, where a sergeant was in charge of a barracks, the captain was really a 'Hauptmann' or 'head man', following the etymology of the word. Not to mention that when my documents had been checked there had been that small matter of the 'von' (as with the Fascist boss in Milan, that time!) – a monosyllable highly revered in Germany; so much so that one of the Ukrainians had mysteriously whispered to me: 'You! Baron!'

So the exhausting toil of carting sacks, of cleaning out stables or shovelling away like a machine not only had an effect on our arms but also on the consciences of others. In the early days Magaldi and I used to be working in the freight-yard for ten hours on end, in intense cold, and having – just the two of us – to unload thirty-five tons of coal wholesale then reload them in retail. I don't know why Magaldi threw himself so desperately into that back-breaking work – perhaps because he wanted to show his contempt for work he had accepted to his disgrace, or so he thought; but as for me, I endured it with clenched teeth. Neither of us knew that this frantic work was in no way dictated by law, and that as workers we were entitled to refuse one sort of work and opt for another more suitable one. So it must have been instinct that drove me on. When at the end of the day Magaldi wanted to go straight back home, avoiding the eyes and comments of the people, I decided to walk straight through the middle of the main square, covered in black dust, my eyes red and swollen, and my trusty shovel on my shoulder. I told him that it was salutary for the local populations to see us, and it was for them and not for us to feel ashamed. And indeed that is what happened, helped by fear and the existing circumstances. Once the Germans realised the situation, it was they who found a way of pulling us out of our slough of despond from which we would certainly not have been able to pull ourselves; but I think it came to an end for this reason, the last move in the game, but not the least important one for that: apart from the fact that the time of reckoning was at hand and many of them thought it a good idea to make friends with us pending X hour, it must be remembered that as we were Italians the feminine element of Berg was establishing its romantic claims – and about this it is pointless to speak either ill or well.

I had been lucky enough to salvage my few manuscripts from the *Lager* – the one about Pilate's wife and the one about Esther. So no one was better able to understand why it was women who freed us from our slavery; and were even ready to take us, resurrected, to the warmth of their hearts.

So while we were being subjected to the devilish gymnastics prescribed by the Todt organisation, the women of Berg were devoting a whole mass of observations, reflections and gossip to our case. They laid the gunpowder, as it were, and all that was needed for it to burst into flame was for my team-mate Magaldi, together with the administrator Gifuni, to dare to go to the local cinema. This happened at the end of our second week. First the girl at the box-office and then the usherette – both slim and lithe – established a relationship, and after the show was over both were in nocturnal dialogue with our two among the timber stacks, seeking those assurances and investigations that the situation demanded. As for Penne the *bersagliere*, he had not set his sights so high, but wishing (in deference to my rank) to save me the morning chore of breakfast, had entered into a very explicit relationship with the servant-girl who, I forgot to say, was called Kate. Nor did the mistress of the Kurt household seem to object to the situation.

This woman answered to the provocative name of Lore; she was about thirty and while not endowed with any particular attractions was healthy and solid with a glowing complexion and rich brown hair. Her eyes were of a variable grey and slightly squinting, her manner a bit laboured and mechanical – but this was a result of shyness. The Kurts were in a flourishing economic and social position; they owned many woods and a sawmill and rivalled the Krauss family, owners of the brewery where neighed the horses groomed by Gifuni; and Lore was reasonably cultured having studied at the Ilmenau in Luneburg, hence her fragmentary knowledge of French. But, as she told me later, she had brought out and dusted her old exercise-books on that first morning, and by degrees relearnt the words and idioms of that enemy language that disturbed her. At the time of our arrival Herr Kurt was away in hospital, or so it was said; and his wife was devoting herself to her only child, a boy of five, whom she idolised. During the two weeks that she saw us crossing the square every evening with our shovels on our shoulders, Madame Lore must have taken steps which were subsequently discussed and approved of by her husband when he reappeared; for shortly afterwards the *bersagliere* Penne, returning one morning with breakfast, informed Magaldi and myself that the coal-age was over and the wood-age was about to begin: and this at the sawmill of the benevolent Kurt family. We were about half-way through December.

The sanhedrin of our little hut came to the conclusion that

Lieutenant Magaldi, my team-mate with the unprepossessing, almost disquieting appearance, had benefited from an attention directed to me as senior Captain and 'baron'. Those Germans knew full well that the war was lost, and that before long they would have to make some kind of accommodation; so that Herr Kurt, approving his wife's initiative, brought the most senior in rank amongst us to work on the premises, thus hoping to put me under an obligation so that I would act as protector when the time came. Suppositions confirmed by the fact that Magaldi was forthwith sent off to the woods, in a temperature below zero, to load '*die grossen Baüme*', while I was left under cover assigned to the light machinery.

So the characters peopling this new stage were: the secretary of the firm, a poor relation, still young, her face horribly burned by the incendiary bombs which killed countless civilians in Germany. This was the last word in Anglo-Saxon hypocrisy, for this type of weapon was not considered unlawful inasmuch as it could not strictly speaking be called 'gas'. All the incendiaries could do was produce a heat capable of melting iron and they roasted people in their shelters like ants.

Then there was Karl, the foreman and a Prussian, a man of few words and stiff as a ramrod. He had been a prisoner of the French in the '14–'18 war and knew what it was all about. He had certainly received his orders in our regard.

Stephen: who worked on the big eight-blade saw. He was said to be a Cossack officer, but he denied this, though he was the undisputed leader of the other five Ukrainians who worked with us. One of these, Kolya, had belonged to the Siltau 'administrative services' when all those Russian prisoners had died. He filled in one or two details of that episode whose import could perhaps be better appreciated in retrospect.

Finally there was Herr Kurt, a weak-looking man with a greyish puffy face and bovine eyes and unquestionably suffering from some deep-seated illness. Those eyes, behind the heavy circle of black spectacles, looked like dead oysters. Yet even in that degree of cold and in deep snow, Herr Kurt got up at five in the morning to keep an eye on the workers as they took up their posts. Then he disappeared – I think so as to get back to bed until nine. German-style punctuality was not belied even by a second at the sawmill: at half-past five there was a siren blast and immediately all the machines started throbbing. When the siren blew for break the men stopped their movements in mid-air, put down their tools or whatever they were holding on the nearest surface, and off they went. Work always started again to the sound of the siren, whereupon the men would pick things up where they had put them down and complete the second half of the interrupted movement. And so it went on for nine hours, with two breaks.

Ten minutes after the mutilated secretary had entered us in the register and a small truck had borne Magaldi off into the cold woods, Karl accompanied me unceremoniously but not unkindly to a bench at one side; this was fitted up with a small saw to break into pieces fit for the stove all the bark left over from the main cutting operation. He showed me the very simple mechanism of this tool which I could carry on with perfect ease; he watched me sawing half a dozen or so pieces, gave a brief nod, then took no further notice of me for a week. During which time I worked with such unbelievable regularity, being deeply absorbed in the general overhaul of my thoughts, that I cut up a formidable quantity of wood. In the evening the two lieutenants and Magaldi disappeared, one of them after Kate, one after the usherette at the cinema, and the third after the box-office girl whom he had nicknamed Kitten. So I was left alone with Captain Ceci who was not at all talkative after the humiliations of sweeping the market. Our mutual silence in the warmth of the hut was pleasant to both of us and established an imponderable friendship between us.

I found Captain Ceci's little personal drama moving. Cavaliere Ceci, as he was known in civil life, was provincial secretary in Chieti, dignified in his ways but frail in constitution, which was perhaps why the Germans had allotted him a broom; seeing he was not strong they had been humane in their fashion. But the cavaliere was neither old nor displeasing to look at and must have suffered a thousand deaths among the housewives of all classes who were buying their vegetables all around him; and imagining that they were thinking and feeling what he himself was thinking and feeling (which time would show not to be the case), he suffered torments. He found his situation especially intolerable in front of the two lieutenants; he suffered less with me, his senior in the same rank, especially as I was tolerant and detached. But how to live down the episode of the pump?

On that second Sunday, while we were standing around in the main street waiting to go to the cinema, the cavaliere was summoned imperiously by the foreman of the market. And to our astonishment a few moments later an archaic but gleaming hand-pump appeared, rich with red and green varnish and martial brasses and pulled at the trot not by horses, as it should have been, but by four of the market sweepers and among them Ceci dressed in his Sunday best. The job was to clear out a drain that had suddenly overflowed. The whole village was at their windows, proud of their pump and of their emergency service; but an ineffaceable blot had fallen on the life of Cavaliere Ceci. So he passed those silent hours mending and ironing his clothes in whose faultlessness and finish reposed what remained of his dignity, as formerly with Pannuzzo's clients. As for me, I was completing my work on Pilate's wife; he never asked me about it, nor did I tell him what it was that kept me so busy.

But though it was an instrument of torture for Ceci, that venerable pump had aroused old memories in me; of the happy time I spent playing with Checchina in the house in via della Solitaria, after we had metaphorically scaled the Family Tree. Our toys at that time were in fact German: little carriages, little trains, all kinds of tiny objects that imitated the real ones, and they were bright and varnished with the same reds and greens and gleaming with the same brasses as adorned the Berg hand-pump. Added to all these metal toys we also had painted cards from which to cut out highly-coloured little houses, cocks with handsome combs, trees with rich foliage and romantic entanglements of roots; a complete German village just like the one we were now experiencing. And now our real village (like the one in our games) was enlivened by teams of little yellow goslings waddling around in the grass and under the reddish piles of timber; and when pools of water like blue eyes appeared in the meadow from time to time, sometimes covering large parts of it, pairs of geese could be seen, looking as though they were carved in marble, real Hanoverian *Gänse*, as large and bad-tempered as swans.

This Germany from which even the memory of the *Lager* seemed to be banished and whose only knowledge of the war was the passing of very high planes, with its harmless cottages of wood and clay, and inhabited by meticulous and thrifty people – this Germany easily took me into its humanity; and my condition as a worker, however odd this may appear, completed my sense of sweetness and peace. 'Slavery' as I had experienced it in the freight-yard faded further and further away in my daily relationships with all the others engaged in the same work as myself – mostly Germans who were unfit for military service owing to being too old or too young. They were poor people, no more no less, doing what it was their life work to do, like the labourers in Licudi; the circumstances were exceptional only for us, and only we saw them in a bad light. And if the people of Licudi had laughed and sung together with the women while carrying those weights in the depths of the olive grove, the methodical and conscientious Germans affirmed the value, the dignity and even the beauty of work by humbly bending to its laws: the happiness or unhappiness of their state thus depending only on the spirit they were able to bring to it. A lesson beyond nationality, rank and uniform that I needed to learn; a rhythm in which I could take part.

So while contemplating with genuine pride the piles of wood I had so neatly cut for the Kurt stoves, I felt sorry for the self I had been in those days in Milan when I had let myself nearly die of hunger through not having – I would not say the courage, but even the faintest idea of presenting myself as apprentice in that first shop. To have learnt to put trust in my own two arms multiplied my possibilities of freedom in the future; and submission was enlivened by the revival of the innocent subterfuges of the schoolroom – the older Germans with their good-tempered sense of humour being the ones to indicate with a wink when I could get away with something. I recalled the little work-site at Licudi; now I would have been able to understand their most simple thoughts and judge much better who should work for me.

It was Herr Kurt who provided the only blot in this eclogue. As in all natural and simple societies, the mere fact of his obvious physical disabilities set him apart, let alone the fact that he was boss. So when he withdrew after his formal appearance early in the morning, not to be seen again until closing time, we all breathed more freely in our work huts. As from that first Monday, he had always come along with feigned friendliness to the corner where I worked and bestowed a sort of half-smile of welcome on me. It was only natural that for the next ten minutes I should wonder why on earth Madame Lore had married him. But as I had stopped fetching my breakfast and hence no longer had any direct contact with her, I think she looked on the tenuous thread of her husband's abortive greeting as a way of maintaining a friendship that she did not want to relinquish.

The backwards and forwards movement of my saw, which gave a well-turned bow as it came towards me and then flew back with surprising lightness, fitted in very well with the yes and no of my eternal reflections. I recalled the woes that had arisen from the people who had wanted to make use of me, Mavì, Catherine and, more recently, Toia at Reggio Emilia. But this time I was encountering greater loyalty, because Madame Lore wanted to make advance payment on what she was not at all sure of receiving afterwards. True, Magaldi was still in the heart of the forest deploying his splendid muscles in the felling of trees – like a ram knocking down a wall with its horns – but even so it had been she who had removed us from the coal and the *Dreck*; and she also had to reckon with public opinion as well as the Nazi work bureau.

So as I was unable to make her understand that wanting to put me under an obligation only complicated things, and that I would certainly help her in any circumstances out of sheer courtesy, I distracted myself with thoughts of Denise Digne and generalisations about the incommunicability of lives; and so, lost in my thoughts, I reached record heights in the amount of bark I cut for the stove. So the future unfolded itself, like the whole of history, from its own womb. Because when my output was seen to be excessive and had completely overflowed the corner assigned to it, I was ordered to carry it from the sawmill to the attic in the Kurt house. Work that obliged me to traverse the whole building from the kitchen to the roof and remain for a good quarter of an hour each journey so as to stack the logs in an orderly fashion. Inevitably I met Madame Lore innumerable times, and she did not fail to give me smiles considerably wider than those of her husband; to which I civilly responded. Politenesses, however, that did not prevent the women of the house from availing themselves of my services once the wood had been unloaded; with the best will in the world, and where Kate was concerned with the usual curtsy, they gave me buckets, baskets and even refuse bins to deal with in the area behind the house: and this put me in touch with the poultry-yard, and more specifically with the respectable pair of geese of the Kurt stock.

Far away in the distance, and hardly more than two white specks, were the geese of the Krauss stock; so that it was borne in on me that these gentlefolk kept their pair of *Gänse* rather as Renaissance princes kept their peacocks. Our two were of a superior breed, mighty and solitary in that green meadow that stretched as far as a distant stream from which the water fancifully ebbed and flowed in a multitude of varied and shimmering pools; it was here that our geese were really happy, but only when they were alone together and there were no interlopers; indeed, you only had to look in that direction to provoke angry reactions from the gander who would throw a hoarse hiss from his throat, open his fearsome beak and spread his wings as if to fly at you. On the advice of the Ukrainian Kolya, who had preceded me in these household services, the only way of inducing the gander to relative respect for people's calves was to show him the stick. Whereas all I wanted was to love those easily offended bipeds. Squatting beside the gentle eye-blue lakes that had formed themselves out of nothingness, those geese held my spirit suspended in the distant expanse of sky extending over that huge body of land from Ostend to the China Sea, inviting me to endless flights in space. They set a seal on that watery, airy and vegetable landscape, as once Geniacolo's green boat had set armorial bearings on the sea of Licudi.

Oscillating as I was between Georgics and Bucolics, the hut in the evening rather went against my mood as it degenerated from facetious humour to increasingly doubtful farce. Recently in Italy (and following a very ancient evil) there had been some confusion between love, jests and licentiousness, a confusion from which Mussolini himself had not been exempt, as he too was ending up among skirts; while first the Fascist squad leaders, then the Fascist bosses, with the four chiefs at their head, had regarded it almost of political merit and completely inseparable from soldierly and revolutionary behaviour to be (or appear to be) assiduous womanisers and diligent frequenters of brothels. The *bersagliere* Penne and Gifuni the administrator, who had been welcomed as latin lovers in that first fervour, were now accepting readily all the rest – supplemented by other more positive reasons. But though the Nazi laws were extremely severe regarding German women who had relationships with prisoners, they did not take account of Italians who were looked on as free workers and civil collaborators. So the only available and valid male element was concentrated in them, that is to say, in us, given that all the local men were old or ill like Herr Kurt. This love-making without risk was a great relief after the infliction of so much abstinence, moreover it promised a support for the future, and could be endowed with the flame of romance.

Against all his expectations even Captain Ceci was captured almost by force between the cabbages and the turnips in his market, and by a very young girl. As he was as scrupulous as he was dignified, the poor man touched heaven with one part of himself while with the other he suffered agonies when thinking of his wife; and being already a mature man, this passion burnt like fire and was a foretaste of the pains that would afflict him later. As for Magaldi, far from exhausting his energies in the woods, and while still looking on the Kitten as his 'little pillow' in time of war, he found himself in great demand; to the point of being involved in sensational episodes.

'When my woman,' he told us with seeming boastfulness not unmixed with a certain uneasiness, 'realised that her jealous neighbour had put a chain on the door and that I couldn't get out until the morning in full sight of all the other tenants, she asked me quite seriously whether I'd jump from the third floor into the canal to save her reputation and get away by swimming through the ice. Finally as I was passing between two rows of neighbours making impolite remarks, she unfortunately saw her own daughter in the crowd, just back from her night-shift.'

The mother and daughter involved in this incident were Dutch, evacuated to Berg heaven knows how, while their husband and father had continued to fight with the Allied fleet ever since Dunkirk. They disappeared shortly afterwards, overwhelmed by the shame of it; and only Captain Ceci had consideration for that other man who for four years had been risking his life at sea and thinking of his women (like the Greek Spiropulos!). The small group of French prisoners seemed not to want to have to do with these episodes. They were simple soldiers and had no respect for us, seeing that we had accepted labourers' work. In Madame Lore's smiles I seemed to detect (and perhaps in more senses than one) the reflection of all the gossip that must have been circulating. But having been educated by monks, I had the trace of their system for ever in my veins and a leaning towards a certain spiritual narcosis. My long imprisonment had led me to get over that crisis point beyond which the suffering of chastity is transmitted into freedom and mental clarity. Having paid a lot for it, and without wanting to, I had gained a very rare value: a better one than I could have gained in my youth and in the passionate renunciations of those days; and why barter it now for almost no reason, when that very clarity showed me what was demanded of us and why?

On Christmas Eve, when the waters seemed to have been stilled, Madame Kurt forewarned us of her coming and then set foot in our hut for the first time, accompanied by her son and Kate and laden with cakes and good things such as we had not seen for two years. The branch of mistletoe and the Christmas tree were not lacking. Madame made a little speech and seemed not a little moved. As I was the most senior, it was for me to answer, while the others stood to attention and for a few minutes recovered their ranks and, I believe, their memory. Then Madame Lore withdrew and I was held by the others to be responsible for her act of courtesy.

Before the end of the year, when I was emptying rubbish in the freezing cold behind the Kurt house, I thought I observed something odd in the attitude of the pair of geese in the distance. I went over, always armed with my stick, and noticed that the gander not only did not hiss or turn round on me, but was squatting beside his companion and clucking plaintively while she lay absolutely still. So I approached near enough to look at her properly; she was lying on her side, her eyes half-shut, her claws frozen and numb. I put out my hand to touch her and the gander let me do so. Then I decided to pick her up – though a residue of fear and her great weight and a certain reverence made me walk back towards the house very slowly.

Of all the many episodes I have relived in my memory, this is certainly one of the strangest: the rigours of winter, a deserted meadow, an enemy country, and myself walking almost on tiptoe holding in my arms the rigid, heavy yet gentle mass of that curious creature, while the other followed after me step by step, wiggling his behind and muttering to himself. Yet at that moment I was moved by the most diverse and long-distant emotions, not to say passions: affection, pleasure, almost inexplicable pride. When Madame Lore saw me coming she waited anxiously while, for no reason at all, I openly blushed as though I were holding a girl in my arms. Perhaps it was then that for the first time since my arrival she woke up from the fixed idea into which her fears had thrown her for the past months – thus removing her from reality. I had the impression that at last she saw me.

It was Kate who took charge of the poor benumbed goose. I left them to it, and meanwhile the gander, providing an example to all us males of self-control and devotion, waited anxiously in the door-way without moving a muscle.

January had hardly begun when the bubble of that impossible equilibrium burst. The Russian offensive reached the Vistula; millions of Germans abandoned Pomerania, East Prussia and Silesia. The *dies irae* was at hand for stricken Germany, the day of reckoning that Stalin had solemnly promised Hitler when he let him know that he would want a settling of accounts for every soldier who had perished in places like Siltau down to the last man – and the day came with the thunder of enemy armies, if it was not the gallop of the horses of the Apocalypse that made the whole earth tremble. From Bucharest to Lwow, which had already fallen, the front groaned and gave way; Warsaw and Budapest, after epic outbursts of heroism and ferocity, were on the point of collapse, as well as Tannenberg, the former glory of the Reich. Sorrow fell on the little village of Berg which up till now had remained untouched. The refugees from the East flowed back beyond the bridges of the Elbe towards the interior of the country in their disorderly and almost macabre tide, and brought the stench of spectral and muddy defeat which rose over the terrified countryside like Goya's *Giant*.

Those amorphous masses of fugitives whispered fearsome stories of the Russians and the hail of iron hard on their heels – in open disagreement with Goebbels' speeches who even in such extremity continued to guarantee unquestionable victory. But Hitler's obstinacy, razing the whole country to the ground in its effort not to surrender, was surely based on the possibility of perfecting the atomic weapon and hence resolving the war with one fell blow and *in extremis*. The Germans were said to have been after the atomic bomb since 1940 when they had 'heavy water' in hand in Norway; and the whole story of the Second World War (including Mussolini's intervention) will only be explained when it becomes possible (perhaps never) to learn the true story of the bomb; of the game played by the belligerents' secret services; of the part really played by the scientists' scruples (the Germans long before the Americans) in accelerating or delaying the perfection of a weapon which meant that the world would be in the Führer's hands. They were terrible stakes that were being played at that time, perhaps among a few unknown brains. But the Allies must have been certain that Hitler had been deluded. Slowly they strangled him and punished him by making use of his own illusion. And every inch of German ground was marked out for its share in the reprisals.

With the solid common sense of country-folk, the people of Berg carefully collected every piece of information, together with the other news that now began to arrive from the Rhine Front, and without going too far they extracted from it all the pith necessary to prepare themselves for the disasters soon to come. With the onslaught of the fugitives, there began to flow in almost Asiatic types with strange attire and customs, in long processions of biblical carts dragged in every conceivable way and loaded with every sort of utensil – as if for a departure viewed as final. But given the length and danger of a trek like this, numbers of them got scattered or fortuitously grouped themselves together; so that more and more unusable and abandoned vehicles were to be seen at the edge of the roads; then oxen were slaughtered and horses left to die. Everyone did what they could to alleviate the horrors of this exodus or at any rate to help with its various stages; the country was transformed into one huge camping-ground of tents, straw and hay. But the milling crowds did not pass unobserved by the enemy fighters, and these did not distinguish (or did not want to distinguish) between military and civilian targets but dived down to machine-gun them, and for the first time blood was spilt even in Berg.

Meanwhile the German women – including those who had so far been hesitant – came over to our side; not only to ours, but also to that of the French, because by now the Nazi racial laws were just a joke. As for the Russians they were too much feared for anyone to try to get near them, and in any case doing so would not have mitigated their hatred or diverted their vengeance. As the days passed they assumed attitudes of open defiance. In the sawmill Stephen pushed the tree-trunks against the eight-blade saw at maximum speed in an effort to break it. And when he succeeded in doing so, one of those steel serpents flew through the air and cut off his arm. The mocking smile that I caught on his face while they were carrying him away was terrifying.

For some time Lore Kurt had been living in a state of great anxiety and this episode threw her into a frenzy. There were already good reasons for her fears because the sawmill had been working flat out for the war effort and was obviously approved of by the Nazis; and the fact that Herr Kurt was a sick and almost disabled man gave his wife no safeguard for the moment of crisis nor yet was it a defence against the opposition of foreigners; Berg was so small that nothing could be expected from the authorities, and it was impossible to disguise oneself or escape. But if Lore feared for her husband, herself and her possessions, what made her totally irrational was the thought of her little son being exposed to so many dangers. She had been appalled by the machine-gunnings happening so near; she saw nothing but threats from land and sky; she was convinced that the refugees who had lost their own children would steal hers, or that he would get lost in that throng of tormented people, or that the Russians led by Stephen would pick on him to wreak their vengeance; and in her despair she turned to the only point of protection and support she felt she saw – in other words, to me.

I could understand Lore's way of thinking; it had been plain to me from the first. Having married – heaven knows why – a man like Herr Kurt, she had knowingly (there could be no doubt of this) forsworn love in exchange for a position of authority in which, like so many other women, she could fulfil herself and lavish all her affection on the child. All this was normal, as it was normal that her thoughts and repressed longings should have settled down in a life governed entirely by habit. But once this methodical existence had been shattered by circumstances, and in view of her dissatisfaction in such an unsuitable marriage, tumultuous impulses had come flocking back into her mind, and perfectly natural ones given that she was frustrated though still in the full vigour of her thirty years.

Up till Christmas Day she had still retained a relative control over herself however much the dissolute spectacle provided by the other Berg women must have affected her. If the second-lieutenant *bersagliere* Penne had contented himself with the servant-girl Kate, and, moving up proportionately, the Roman lieutenant Magaldi with the cash-desk girl at the cinema, the rule (however absurd it was to want to apply it to this case!) laid down that the first lady of the village should have a certain right over the most senior in rank among us. Without at that time seeing more in me than a kind of hostage, she was prepared for a holocaust for the sake of her own safety and that of her dear ones, without even wanting to examine whether it displeased her or not; she wanted to prove – to herself rather than to anyone else – that it was the circumstances that were obliging her to acquire at such cost what she would not otherwise have been able to obtain from an unknown officer, and an enemy at that. The great drama of Tosca and Count Scarpia, which had moved half the world to tears, was there at hand to prove the thesis true. But the only authentic thing I found in her was a great fear and a certain pardonable hypocrisy, and moreover I knew something that she did not suspect: that I would be able to do little or nothing to help her, so that if I accepted her sacrifice – whether it was real or false – I would be deceiving her. This was where matters stood that morning when I took her the unfortunate goose in my arms.

Can a single drop of pity cast into the ocean of the soul bring about its total change? It was this that I had given or asked from Denise Digne, and she had refused it – perhaps instinctively knowing that this single drop would have undermined her memories and her rancour, both of which she needed for survival at that time. For Lore, who had always lived among the trees and animals of the country, it meant much more to see me with a *Gans* in my arms than if she had seen me rescuing a man, for this would have been no more than the duty of a good citizen, in other words nothing. So this episode, by causing her to divest of its discouraging positivism the relationship she had dreamed up between us, upset her moral quietude through weakening her alibis. And she did not realise how in my eyes the only real obstacle to going out to meet her with an open heart had thus broken down: the obstacle being her desire to pay me for it.

As for Herr Kurt, at the first signs of the breakthrough on the Eastern Front he removed me from the handsaw and assigned me to gardening work around the house: a sinecure which meant that we were always tripping over each other, he with a multiplication of painful smiles which moved even me to compassion. To tell the truth, I did not see that Herr Kurt, as nature had made him, could be considered responsible for anything. Then the child, Martin, was always round my feet – to the joy of Lore who felt safer at those moments; he was a pretty boy though he had a slight squint like his mother. In a very short time I had established a better understanding with him than with any other German, though the mother had made great strides in brushing up her French. Halfway through January, after the first machine-gun attack on Berg, I again fell victim to malaria – unexpectedly as it was not the season for it. I remained alone in the hut during the hours of work. Lore came to visit me, bringing me various delicacies to eat and fruit-juice for my thirst. And in my warmth and inactivity and feverish elation I began to respond to her.

With the advance of February the confusion in Berg became alarming. There was one crisis after another; either water was lacking, or electricity, or essential supplies, so that work was in a constant state of suspension even when the foreigners, from whom nothing was now expected, would have liked to be getting on with it. We had developed the habit of spending several hours a day in the high meadows outside the village, where the approach of spring and the mild weather renewed the whole idyll of nature once we were beside the quiet river. There, stretched out on the grass, listening to distant explosions and the confused murmur from the camps, we watched the Allied formations passing, bright in the sun, and no larger than an ant making its careful journey along a stem – it was like those romantic prints where you see the tender greens of the countryside between the squadrons drawn up for battle, and the smoke from the bursts of fire is indistinguishable from the clouds. Sometimes an enemy fighter would unexpectedly plunge down to earth level, shave the railway lines, swerve, and then straighten up after the surprise attack, and finally disappear, before the crack of their gunfire had melted into space. There were curls of smoke over there; why should it not come from a peasant burning his stubble?

As Herr Kurt found walking painful he took refuge in the cellars of the sawmill while I took Martin on my shoulders and carried him off at a trot, followed by Lore. Her slow approach towards me in those anxious hours, and her scruples which I divined more and more clearly as she felt herself led not by reason but affection, governed my own emotions. German morality, though fairly open with regard to unmarried and independent women, is strict where married women are concerned, especially if the husband is present. But if it was difficult for Lore to surrender herself, it was also preferable for me not to be hurried. It was hard to violate the abstinence that I had forcibly observed for two years. I understood better the reluctance of virgins before their senses have really been awakened, and with many of them the awakening does not happen for quite a while after contact with a man; the weight of a man can be disturbing and even irritating to them, and they need an impulse of the heart to help them endure it. And this was how I felt too, with the additional aid of Lore's doubts – the doubts that made her pause and that chimed in so well with my own slow liberation, for though she aroused me, she did not provoke me. So we quietly followed the path of Spring; the *adagio* eased off into the *pianissimo*: over which there hovered the *a solo*.

But the boys brought up on baseball in the colleges of Kansas or Ohio, encased for the duration in their airmen's jackets so as to hit a target merely called 'the objective' by their powerful bosses, were now directing their inexorable formations against us, and what could they know about these evanescent thoughts?

(*From fragments of my diary: Berg, December 1944.*)

We had only just come out of the *Lager* and still carried around with us the smell of prison, hunger and hate; and in the streets everyone turned their eyes away from us; or we felt cold looks on our backs when we had gone by. But once we met three Ukrainian women, and someone who knew us told them briefly who we were. Then all together they looked at us with their six brown eyes as mild as a young heifer's. And for the first time our disarmed souls were suddenly mirrored in those eyes and found rest in them. As the green meadow finds rest in the calm eyes of a flock of sheep.

Berg, March 1945.

Now at the very end of winter, while the whole of Germany is streaming with blood, and the nights are torn by explosions, and the days by the groan of sirens, and the sun over the countryside is extinguished by the constant nightmare of danger and the endless news of death; and while nevertheless the people here go on with their work (or seem to) and their daily habits in an orderly way, impassively, almost absently, I fell in with two women on the road when I was returning late one night – one of them old and dressed in black, the other certainly her daughter, and both weeping bitterly.

It was a shrill mechanical weeping alternating between the two of them, like the groaning of a pulley or the howling of an animal (as indeed I had heard it once before in Greece). And as I followed them, other people who were coming towards them glanced at them for a moment and then quickly looked away, as if preferring not to have seen them. And they continued to walk on, the one supporting the other and repeating those piercing lamentations.

And everything all around seemed motionless and listening. The dark ground, the cold water, the dry wood. All the harsh land of Germany, from which, however, and for the first time, I was seeing tears flow.

The old Latvian never speaks; he moves slowly and stiffly; he seldom even looks up, and when he does it is furtively. He seems to want to avoid everyone, and not to want to be seen. He has lost his possessions, his country, and even the flower that was his daughter. He has seen appalling massacres. And nothing is left to him but fear. I have been working two days with him, with no word being said. Finally, to test him, I said I would like to visit him at his house. He looked at me dumbfounded, as if such human contact seemed impossible to him or as if it could only present a danger. So I added: 'Later on, in the summer.' He gave a brief contemptuous smile. Then he put down his axe, took two pieces of wood he had just chopped and laid them on the ground in the shape of a cross. 'In the summer,' he said, giving a furtive glance around, 'you and I and all of us will be dead.' I asked him why. 'Millions,' he said, 'millions are dead.' Then he picked up his axe and went on cutting wood.

*

'*Schweine!*' This word, whispered over and over again by a nearby shadow, came back like a moth into the small area of light that was my consciousness, then was taken back again into the shadow. I could also hear a faint sound of running water, rather as on our first morning when we went our way silently across the grass in the glory of the dawn. Certainly my eyes were shut, but I could sense a faint light beyond my eyelids, though this soon became clouded with dark forms which in their turn suddenly became an unbearable scarlet. I thought I was asleep and just about to wake up. But the voice of that shadow changed its word now, and said quietly and firmly as if it had found something: '*Frakture.*' Appalling pain stabbed me at some point on my face and I opened my eyes.

The face bending intently over me was a good-natured one but marked by deep dark lines. Glancing beyond the small white form of the nurse, my eyes fell on a disgusting confusion of dirty buckets, soiled and blood-stained clothes, shapeless objects under sinister shafts of light. The doctor was holding a pair of forceps high above me, then he lowered them and that atrocious pain broke out again, affecting every portion of my body: a fraction of a second and then darkness again. I learnt afterwards that this operation carried out by an old dentist assisted by an inexperienced girl lasted at least an hour. This emergency 'surgeon', who had been operating for fourteen hours already, had no vestige of anaesthetic left and was doing his best simply to keep people alive. So the spasm brought me back to the light of day only to plunge me back again into darkness. But image after image passing in my mind with the swiftness of a dream – which suppresses all intermediary ideas to concentrate on a few that seem without connection – found me in the noonday sun after I had taken Lore home, standing with a group of French and looking up towards the sky; then the terrified expression of someone who put a handkerchief over my face; then clusters of trees passing by; then a nun crossing herself, solicitous but recollected in God. All this must have covered quite a few hours. I knew that the *Schweine*, swine, referred to the Allies who in a few seconds had torn Berg to pieces and killed or maimed a third of its inhabitants. And I knew I was not dead: a matter which seemed to me of total indifference; as if neither pleasure nor pain had ever existed within me and thus I did not know anything about them.

So this was how things were when another voice (and I felt its breath on my ear as it spoke) said: '*Eine schöne Spritze!*' thus promising me sleep in the paradise of morphine.

From then, and for an undetermined period, I had to rouse myself, only for a second or two that first time but long enough to realise there was snow outside the window – the last snow of that year, I think. The stillness, the silence, the torpor of the narcotic and the shock prefigured for me the blissful contemplative and perpetual peace of paradise. Then I went to sleep again perhaps for two or three days, and when I woke up properly it was deep in the middle of the night.

My mind was clear and rested like that of someone waking from serene sleep. The suspension of thought, which had lasted possibly for a week, must have benefited the depths of my organism more than the trauma and the haemorrhage had harmed it. The elusive nervous current active in our every tiny particle was flowing out within an essentially whole entity. I felt that the crisis was over and that my vital forces had returned. I tried clenching my fist, and as it readily responded I moved up my fingers to an exploration of my face and head. I found them swathed in a mass of gauze which left only my eyes and a corner of my mouth free. I contracted the muscles of my legs and they were there, both of them. I tried to move to one side; a violent pain rose from my abdomen; but I realised I could overcome it. Slowly I dragged myself to a sitting position.

The ward was small, tidy and dimly lit. I could hear someone breathing regularly. Based on my experience with my bandage in Poland, I decided to verify these first favourable discoveries about my condition with a supplementary experiment. As I fought down the pain and in so doing recognised fresh energies, I moved inch by inch into successive positions until I finally found myself on my feet clinging to the bedstead.

I took a brief rest so as to concentrate all my powers now in my legs, and passing from one small bed to the next I managed to do the whole circuit of the little room. None of those sleeping figures moved, and when I was able to recuperate between my sheets again, no one heard the lively eulogy that I dedicated to myself for the happy outcome of my test, nor the self-congratulatory speech I made for having saved my skin.

The action carried out over Berg had no military justification whatsoever but belonged to the final solution with which to punish Germany: a thing rendered possible by Hitler's persisting obstinacy when he had no effective defences with which to back it up. The Allied air fleet, with clear skies and from a comfortable height and without in those last days encountering either anti-aircraft fire or fighter planes, was stripping the oak of the Reich leaf by leaf and with it all that remained of old Europe; a kindness defined by a linguist of the High Command as 'carpet-bombing'. Berg had forty-eight thousand-pound bombs dropped on its small surface. The Kurts' house was unharmed, but the sawmill had a direct hit on its machinery and was a headless body; our hut disappeared together with the administrative second-lieutenant Gifuni, the only one of us in it at that moment; the *bersagliere* Penne had got out in time. As for Ceci, he left three fingers of his left hand at his devastated market, while Magaldi had the huge tree-trunks to thank just for once because the 'carpet' did not reach that far this time.

As for me, I had been talking that morning with some of the French and was the only survivor of a group of seven – we had been thrown into the air from the crater of a bomb which must have burst underneath us after penetrating the earth obliquely for the usual four yards. A leafy but indiscreet tree ripped off all my clothes and a good deal of skin but served to soften my fall. A fractured jaw, a massacre of teeth, a mournful series of wrenches and minor gashes and the abdominal injury following the headlong fall – these were my rewards for sawing the Kurt wood. I reached hospital (thanks to Lore, as I found out later) with no covering other than mud and blood, and they put me among the desperate cases who – as happens in such crises – are the last to be attended to. That was when I saw the nun piously indicating heaven with her eyes. In that first moment she could not identify me; and the *schöne Spritze* with which she assured me an immediate paradise, pending the final one, was an impersonal act of kindness. Later on the nun was more directly attentive to me, thereby sweetening my lot – perhaps someone had told her about the 'von'. When I began to groan without even realising it owing to the intolerable pain in my back and face, she hurried to me with her benevolent little phial and sent me back to the limbo of my fathers. Some emotions are highly complex. She was transferring her own mental anaesthesia to the physiological one she was bestowing on me. She was neither old nor displeasing to look at. Just a little masculine and brusque.

So next morning the nun found me sitting up, my eyes open and my hands which had not even a scratch spread out on the coverlet. The expression on her face was heartfelt but undefinable; perhaps she had thought it more salutary for me to abandon this vale of tears rather than remain in it. But the imperceptible hesitation vanished when she realised (as she must have) that it was the Lord's will that I should not die; and, indeed, that I should have been put in her care in those crucial moments to be the object of her prayers and, moreover, to be saved by them. So she devoted herself to washing my hands and only left them when she had made them shine like those of a duchess.

Shortly afterwards Lore Kurt arrived, having been notified heaven knows how of my return to consciousness. As soon as I was pointed out to her as the man she was looking for, she made a gesture of despair and sat down beside me with tears in her eyes while producing presents that were perfectly useless, given my condition. Then she started to recount a whole string of painful details – very rapidly in view of the limitations of her French – while I looked at her through the gaps in my gauze headgear. As I could not answer her with my voice, we got hold of some paper and pursued our conversation in this way, I asking questions, she answering partly aloud and partly in writing, a scene that was repeated in the days following. But after one of Madame Kurt's visits the nun, who had watched everything, unexpectedly pounced on our sheets of paper still scattered over the bed and quickly read them; so she knew French. After this intervention which luckily did not provide her with any dangerous information, she seemed to relapse into an unswerving subjection to the decisions of heaven, and did not feel any kind of obligation to justify her indiscretion.

The ward had six beds, but as the days dragged by there remained only a soldier of the much-feared SS who, however, was in a coma for a long time and died without ever coming to, though his eyes were wide open as if deep in thought; and an old sea-captain of the river traffic. A large piece of shrapnel had carried off one of his feet, but he did not know this and thought the foot was there inside the bandages, and kept on asking for news of it, even from me. Shortly afterwards Captain Ceci came to visit me; he was a patient in the same hospital, had his arm in a sling and looked to me under great strain; and indeed he had suffered considerably in the early days through not knowing what had become of his young love – but fortunately she was safe.

Whereas Magaldi's 'Kitten' had been flung arms-first on to a sausage-slicing machine at the pork butcher's – where she happened to be at the time of the raid – and was horribly mutilated. I wrote a note to the nun in French begging that Ceci might be with me at the moment when my bandages were removed. And I read the sympathy and compassion in his eyes. I then looked in the mirror and did not recognise myself, but though I was resigned to remaining disfigured for the rest of my life, nature's unexpected resources, added to many operations and much cruel pain, finally enabled me to regain a fairly reasonable appearance.

At the beginning of March the crowd of fugitives swarming along the road beside the hospital were machine-gunned at low level and reduced to a furrow of blood. Though I could still hardly stand I saw myself without further ado accompanied to the door by the Emergency Service men; and in the indescribable tumult of the stretchers with their tragic burdens not even the nun could spare me more than a glance, for which I am still grateful to her after all these years. Berg itself was over a mile away; and with Captain

Ceci supporting me, and avoiding the hazards of the main road with all the people and the heart-rending cries, we made our way over the fields and the low walls and ditches dividing them, and reached the village after four hours. Ceci was immediately abducted by his beloved who took him off to her house; while Lore, after a seemingly agitated scene with Herr Kurt, gave me Kate's little room in the upper regions of the house – Kate having fled elsewhere: Kate whom I saw in that dawn light on our first morning.

The room overlooked the already archaic grass square, now reduced to a sort of lunar surface with its arid craters, and here I once again pondered the human condition in all its inexplicable complexity. Having left for the war to fight beside the Germans, I was now a prisoner in their country; and having here been made a slave owing to my coolness towards Nazism, I had also been ill-treated by the Anglo-Americans who pounded everyone indiscriminately in their hatred of Nazism; nor would this even protect me from that final extermination to which Himmler's secret orders had vowed us – or so persistent rumour had it; and certainly not from other unforeseen occurrences, given the hostile attitudes of Stephen's companions who haunted Lore's nights.

Lying on Kate's little bed I contemplated the ceiling, and its fanciful corners fitting into the edges of the roofing. The room was very pretty, and had I not known that girl's habits I would have though it the sweet refuge of a child, as Ariadne is described in the *Epithalamion* of Catullus 'in her mother's bosom, in her little bed redolent of her chastity'. It was strange that my chastity should be there instead, now no longer defended by intention but by my lack of blood and the protests of bones, joints, tendons and muscles every time the smallest demand was made on them. And Madame Lore, on her side, interfered with my indolence no less than eight or ten times a day, as if afraid that her talisman might fly off through the window. When I looked at myself in the little mirror that had formerly belonged to Kate, I asked myself how far a woman's constancy can go when she has some purpose in mind. The shaving inflicted by the dentist on the centre of my skull now looked like a discouraging greyish area crossed by the dark slash of the wound; my eyes were dull and swollen; my face puffy and divided between Tiepolo-like yellows and greens (though he used them magisterially for tufa or fabric). It was unbearable to look at my chin, lips and jaw. But Lore Kurt, who now saw me as a soldier of the Reich on account of these wounds, seemed to find in them a new stimulus to devotion. So the Cardinal of Este was wrong when he called Ariosto's stories 'nonsense', including the one about the spell cast by Alcina on Ruggiero which caused him to see that terrifying witch as a gorgeous woman.

Meanwhile, with only a fifth of its houses still habitable, the village had lost every trace of tranquillity. The Germans (who listened attentively to Radio London and knew that the Allies were pressing in great strength along the Rhine from Wesel to Coblenz and had already occupied Cologne) were always frenetically babbling together and articulating at least twice in every ten words 'Invasion, invasion . . .' They were living in constant fear of enemy parachute troops, as the Central Command persisted in ordering resistance to the bitter end. So on the one hand they put up anti-tank defences, following the instructions of the mayor, and on the other they called this individual a half-wit and a criminal. A desperate effort was made by the German armies on the Eastern Front to fall under the occupation of the Anglo-Americans rather than the Russians. But the treaties signed between these parties made a mockery of even that last hope. As they were almost on the frontier of the two presumed zones of influence – the Elbe – the inhabitants of Berg lived, so to speak, with a map, a watch and a compass in their hands. Lore's anxiety became a fever; perhaps she was now convinced that I would do everything for her that I could; however, she must have feared that in view of my condition I might be transferred elsewhere; or else in the frenzy of those days, and confronted by my listless spirit and helpless limbs, she was really moved by love. This is what Herr Kurt must have finally thought because he never came up to the attic; he acted secretly and prompted by the unexceptionable motive of procuring me the attention I needed. Such authority as still existed in Berg served to provide me with an obligatory travel permit to the hospital of the main town of the district, Uelzen, a few hours' journey by train. Lieutenant Magaldi was detailed to accompany me. This move took Lore by surprise and there was nothing she could do to counter it.

The first time I saw Magaldi again he had seemed to me gloomy and disturbed. He had had to dig in the debris of the hut to recover Second-Lieutenant Gifuni – literally chopped into pieces by the myriads of planks that had been trajected from all around by the force of the explosion and gone hurtling through the air like whips.

But it was the ghastly amputation suffered by his little cashier of the cinema that really overwhelmed him. Having been detailed to accompany me, he was unable to refuse – not so much the Germans as me – and presented himself, grim and silent. I would willingly have released him if I could. We had hardly any baggage as all our belongings had been destroyed, including my story of Esther and Pilate's wife. But he had found a sheaf of my papers in the remains of a drawer, fragments of a diary I had begun at Bay, and these I took with me.

The Kurts' two geese were safe: they had been recovered from the bottom of a bomb crater, no more than slightly dazed. As I was leaving – this, too, was at the crack of dawn – I caught sight of them over in the distance in the shining eye of a tiny pool, alone and at peace.

The journey from Berg to Uelzen should have taken less than two hours, but this time lasted five. The train stopped continually under cover of the woods to escape enemy reconnaissance planes, and as soon as the sun rose I noticed how oddly its rays fell through the many bullet-holes in the train's roof – enemy action on previous journeys. I had plenty of time to study Magaldi, and I was forced to the conclusion that he had sustained a psychological shock of some intensity; he was incapable of overcoming his obsessive fear; and on his dark face his pallor looked almost blue and moved me to pity. Uelzen station, a macabre skeleton of twisted and foul-smelling ironwork, could hardly have consoled him.

The hospital was rather far away for my faltering powers, and when we got there we were greeted by the usual spectacle of crowds of people and feverish work certainly inadequate to their needs. A group of surgeons were in grim confabulation at one side; one of them, a small nervous man, came over to me of his own accord, looked briefly at the wound, consulted in undertones with another who had followed him, and with no further explanation handed me a paper referring me to a specialist. Those gentlemen did not concern themselves with people still standing on their own feet. So off we went again.

It was past midday when we arrived in front of the elegant residence of the person in question. The hot city seemed deserted: it was the moment of rest for lunch which even war does not refuse. We sat on some steps like beggars and ate our rations, Magaldi morosely chewing his bread. By now his silence was an overt reproach to me – who was dragging him through an unknown country where no one would even have looked for us had we disappeared. So I decided to try to get through that door alone, though I assessed pretty accurately how difficult this would be now that I was reduced to the level of a beggar. And it would surely have been shut in my face had I not pushed aside the terrified receptionist and crossed the threshold by force. Our raised voices brought into the hall a man with a severe and obviously ill-disposed expression. Suddenly Kolya's words flashed through my mind: 'You! Baron!' So I took two steps towards this man and said in French, without defiance but without humility either: 'I am the captain of cavalry Baron of Sansevero, Italian, and prisoner-of-war. I have been referred to Doctor Aesckloni.'

The doctor, for it was he, jumped as though pulled back by a violent tug at the reins; straightened himself, made that bow peculiar to Germans who just bend their heads with a jerk, and pointed to a door at the side. It was a washroom for visiting ladies. He picked up a pair of tweezers – also looking as if it served for women – and lightly pulled aside the edge of the wound in my jaw that I had kept uncovered for several days. And suddenly his eyes lit up; the interest of the doctor and the zeal of the surgeon had sprung to life. Nothing would have made this man forgo the exaltation of the scalpel, the only exaltation capable of arousing those dedicated to it. A complex and dangerous commitment that can become a vice like drugs.

A telephone call to the clinic, a few excited words of explanation to his family, a little girl crying because her birthday party had been spoilt, and ten minutes by car through the devastated streets empty in the sun. What followed lasted almost two hours. Aesckloni refused the famous gold sovereign that I hurriedly ripped out of my jacket. He assured me that my survival was due entirely to chance because, clinically speaking, I should have already been eliminated by septicemia; he consoled me with the assertion that there were no immediate dangers but that the operation would have to be completed later and, to my mute question, merely extended his arms with a shrug of the shoulders. Half of Uelzen was burnt out and all that could be done was to send me back to Berg. He got the necessary papers ready and made off. It was three in the afternoon. We had been on the move for ten hours; I had walked enough and endured a cruel operation. In front of the clinic there was an open space with trees from which one could see a part of the city that spread out into the country. We threw ourselves down on the grass and I immediately fell asleep.

In accompanying me to the hospital Magaldi had hoped that they would take me in and he would be able to go back home. Terror prevented him from understanding that we were equally unsafe wherever we were; and, like all frightened animals, he thought that the best refuge was the one most familiar to him. He must have been grappling with conflicting possibilities while I slept (as in Shakespeare's sonnets) and the temptation must have seized him to leave me there alone, if not (still following the poet) to pour a phial of poison in my ear. However, he was still beside me when I woke at sunset, but he had made up his mind.

'Captain,' he said to me point blank – his wide staring eyes were the first thing I saw as I opened mine – 'you certainly won't want to go back to that station!'

Now that the effect of the anaesthetic had worn off, my freshly bandaged wound was giving me acute pain. The sun was gently sinking behind a landscape of surviving villas surrounded by their gardens. Magaldi's extreme agitation showed that during my sleep he had had to force his will almost to breaking-point; there was no opposing his nervous charge; so I looked at him without saying anything.

'In the clinic I studied a map of the city,' he went on. 'The first train for Berg leaves tonight at ten – exactly when the raids start. You've already seen what the station's like; you know we'll never get away from there. But if we walk to the first little station after Uelzen in the direction of Berg, and wait for the train there, then we'll be all right. So let's get going!'

As it was a walk of ten or twelve kilometres he was asking me to make a superhuman effort; but I felt sorry for him, because if I put him in the position of abandoning me then he would have to bear the shame of it for the rest of his life: for man has a treacherous nature and it can betray him when he least thinks it will, at the moment of our crises. But if Peter denied his Master, all the more could Magaldi deny the cultivated man and Roman citizen that he was, especially when he was groping like a slave along an enemy road.

'Let's go wherever you want,' I said, heaving myself up.

We arrived at the little station he had in mind at nine that night –

I in a state of total extenuation. I collapsed on a bench as if dead. But after some vague interval of time I felt myself being roughly pushed while hoarse voices shouted imperious orders. I was blinded by a strong torch directed straight into my eyes. We finally found ourselves in the station-master's office and kept at bay by the machine-guns of two men whom we recognised as belonging to the dreaded SS.

Luckily the explanations were not long as the doctors' papers seemed to possess sovereign powers. Magaldi's disquieting looks had been noticed by someone who had forthwith supposed us to be Allied parachutists. The two disappointed SS men got ready to search us, and I would have readily given them my pathetic gold sovereign (by now a family heirloom), but Magaldi who perhaps had considerably more – though he had never said so – passed over his knapsack to the German's outstretched hand with the words:

'*Achtung! Loese!*' – meaning to convey that it was infested with lice.

So the men dropped his knapsack with disgust while the station-master quickly showed us the door. We were back in Berg by three in the morning, twenty-two hours after our departure, and I regained my attic where Lore whispered words to me which she must have flattered herself that I was in a position to understand. But I had saved my life by stating that I was a member of the cavalry and a baron, and I had safeguarded my poor possessions by appearing to be a verminous beggar, and this surely was enough for one day without adding in love at the end.

The alarming flow of refugees from the East had been diminishing for some time and now almost completely stopped – a portent of what was happening on the Western Front. The Allies had crossed the Rhine some time ago and were slowly penetrating into the heart of Germany and the country was awaiting its doom. The railway ceased functioning in early April. On the half-destroyed and isolated Berg there fell one of those perfect calms whose significance may easily be divined. The fresh green leaves made their voice heard in the crystalline air, and the stream that encircled our small stretch of ground added its own solitary one.

My operation at Uelzen not only brought back my fever, but owing to the enormous effort expended that day, drained away all the energies I had managed to build up in the hospital near Berg and afterwards. The effect of this was to deflect Madame Kurt's attentions, because as I hardly answered her when she came to visit me or showed myself as half-asleep with exhaustion if I heard her coming, she had to resign herself to walking about on tiptoe and then leaving me alone for hours on end. I was grateful to her for her devotion, yet did not feel the slightest possibility of responding to it while all my instinctive energies were concentrated on saving my life. Meanwhile I found incredible peace and calm in my mind, freed as it was from any duty towards others and even towards the limbs it inhabited. It was in my mind and imagination that I found my equipoise and my delight now that I was liberated from needs, commitments, aims and from matter itself; my solitary and unquiet spirit (as already in the distant past I had always liked to think of it) rediscovered its buoyancy and happiness in conditions which to others would have seemed provisional and uncertain in the extreme.

The destruction of the hut had dissolved our already somewhat loose community. With Gifuni's death his fellow-countryman *bersagliere* Penne had gone off elsewhere. Magaldi's panic went so far as to make him look ridiculous to the Germans who, when it came to courage, had plenty and to spare. He put his things in a wheelbarrow – of the kind used by the local people to transport anything from potatoes to babies – and took to the woods he knew so well.

Captain Ceci was the only one I still saw and together we wrote a report on the death of our comrade, adding a sketch of the place where he was buried so that he could be found should his relatives inquire. The grave was simple enough, just a mound of earth and an uncarved stone, and it lay outside Berg at the top of a gentle slope going down to the great river, the Elbe, winding along with its huge loops between humps of hills dense with trees; and it seemed almost possible to descry a river of calm air up in the heavens following the water down below – the two clarities vying with each other in brightness above and within an endless landscape of unmatched dignity and loveliness. If once I had chosen to die beneath the burning sunsets of the Roman sky, now there was another place where it would be sweet to end my days; a soil to which I could entrust myself without fear so that it would make me part of its gentle womb. But I was sure that I still had a long time to live; I asked myself why; and found I was convinced that the third-time-lucky would let me off for a while.

Soon I was again spending the day at the far end of the clearing, cheered by the gentle swaying of the trees and the tinkling of the stream, and enjoying the love-affair that the two rescued geese made no attempt to hide from my benevolent eye. With the advance of spring the river water often rose to cover the meadow; and that prudent gander displayed his excellent memory by letting me pull the odd blade of grass a few paces away from him while he preened himself like a king in that fresh greenish water. At the same time even Herr Kurt laid down his arms.

The old scruples that had tormented me long ago in Ferrara regarding Marsi in the days of Mavì, now came again but more strongly – because now the force of things was entirely in my favour and not, as in those days, largely against me. In the early days my sheer physical prostration had served to postpone things; at the same time I could reassure Madame Kurt by showing her how deeply I felt my obligation in honour to protect and defend her. She would also naturally have supposed that I had ties in Italy which were soon to be reforged; and she also believed me to be a convinced Catholic (a somewhat broad interpretation) and as a former pupil of monks at least bound by the ten commandments (which was true). But from her point of view some new episode was needed to give her reassurance – and indeed it is true that an action speaks louder than words.

We were out together one day, assuming that little Martin was with his father, when an attack at low range was made against Berg exactly like that previous one that had caused such havoc. The people fled without looking where they were going and we ourselves were swept along in the midst of the tumult and with the heavy thunder of the guns getting louder and closer every moment. Then suddenly we saw Herr Kurt running with all the others, but he was alone, and when Lore desperately signalled to him he answered back that he did not know where Martin was. So the child must have been in the house or in the meadow. Madame ran back to the village. The road was empty now and her solitary figure must have been only too visible from the air. The enemy planes coming against us were almost exactly over Berg as we entered it – for in defiance of reason and through an invincible instinct I had not been able to leave her alone at that moment. Within the village walls the roar of the engines was deafening, and as I ran blindly I expected flames and explosions to break out at every instant. But the excruciating noise diminished and the bombs struck further on, in the woods. Lore leant against the wall, gasping. I caressed her and I believe I kissed her, but lightly and as an encouragement. Afterwards she avoided any form of direct invitation on my part almost as if she had resigned herself to my decision, whereas I now felt attracted by her. So what had finally decided the outcome and saved Herr Kurt's marriage from shipwreck was precisely Herr Kurt's own weakness.

Warned by an instinct lurking somewhere in the depths of his torpor (and having avoided me in the attic, be it remembered, as if awaiting what was to come) he seemed still in some doubt as to the relationship when I started my convalescence in the meadow. For while I lay there watching the geese, he would sometimes join me, sketch his characteristic abortive smile, and though keeping himself apart, seem in some way to want to join in our heterogeneous company. But as he did not know a word of French and I only a very little German (not easy to study in those times of stress) no conversation was possible between us. With the result that that man's thoughts were as incommunicable to me as those of a strange exotic animal, and (I must admit) did not tempt my capacities to understand any more than those of the gander. But as I was incapable of depriving anyone of his rights without feeling that I myself was diminished by doing so, I raised my eyes to Herr Kurt with nothing but respect, like someone who knows he is touching a painful area. I had no idea what his relationship with Lore could be, what she had told him or was telling him, what she was forcing him to believe or submit to. In the early days my inclination for her had been clouded by the mere thought that she shared a bed with him; but now I was worrying about what went on in this poor man's mind: a man unlucky from birth, threatened with desertion by his wife, his property destroyed, and his very life in the balance.

The gander's rock-like fidelity was a solemn warning to us all, like the face of Nature itself. It gripped me and humiliated me, and Herr Kurt seemed to understand.

After the first ten days of April the skies were emptied of Allied reconnaissance planes which formerly had been ceaselessly patrolling them. The radio transmitted only censored news – though Goebbels and Hitler himself continued to dictate that Berlin must be defended to the bitter end in spite of the fact that the irrepressible Russian armies were already almost there. Every day the Western Front was gaining more and more territory this side of the Rhine. That Berg would come under fire was certain, as it lay on the main route to one of the important bridges over the Elbe. The calmness and orderliness of those people thrown back on their own resources and foresight was exemplary. They had heard how the Allies behaved in the places they took over. With or without authorisation the people of Berg removed the stupid anti-tank defences, put up by the Nazi mayor – they felt that creating a point of resistance would inevitably bring about the final destruction of what remained of their village. The shops distributed their supplies house by house. Everyone killed their animals, learnt how to cure them, and buried their potatoes against future hunger. They hid their silver, their precious objects, their furs, and I was begged by Lore to keep her jewels in my knapsack – I must admit that the jewels made me smile, for they were those unfashionable trinkets handed down from one generation to the next to which a sentimental and even a money value are attributed, both largely non-existent. Finally, they camouflaged their cars and tractors in the woods; while they stowed guns, tools and equipment of all kinds in chimney-stacks. or hayricks When a vast red halo rose on the horizon which was recognised as the burning of Luneburg, and when the roar of the cannon was heard, little Berg was fearlessly prepared for its ordeal, and I was ready for mine.

The village was attacked at midday. The wise decision of its inhabitants to surrender without giving battle was overruled when half an infantry company appeared unexpectedly towards ten o'clock in the morning and formed a thin line with a few machine-guns placed in ditches in the fields. What is more, they planted a small cannon just at the back of the Kurt house where a silent group of women and children had taken refuge because it was a little bigger than the other houses. As their chosen place had thus become an obvious target, I advised them to leave it. Herr Kurt – the only German civilian present – seemed willing to hand over the command of the operation to me as being more expert in military matters, and we moved while the first enemy cannon-fire decapitated the little church tower not far away from the sawmill.

The riverbank seemed to me a fairly safe refuge from these shots (from tank guns, I thought), though this meant crossing about a kilometre of open space directly behind the German emplacements. The American shells were diving into the deep rich soil with a dull thud, but often they did not explode or hurl splinters of stone into the air. So I thought it was a risk worth taking. Having issued brief instructions through Lore to my little band of women and children, I saw my plan executed in a way I would not have obtained from Italian recruits after a week of hard sweat. The little group took cover with me behind a mound of earth protected from the firing; then I made a dash to the next cover, and one by one the others did the same. As soon as our little platoon was again assembled we repeated our military operation to the next cover; meanwhile no voice was raised nor question asked. Herr Kurt was the least prepared for this exercise, but he went through with it, if awkwardly. I myself carried little Martin pickaback — a first instalment on my debt.

At one point during our run we passed close to a German machine-gun manned by three soldiers who were awaiting the attack so calmly that it could have been a routine military exercise. They exchanged a few words in undertones with the women, without showing any surprise at what they were doing or who was leading them, though they saw he was a foreigner. Once again the inscrutable orbital movement of things was leading an Italian officer to guide a group of German women and children into shelter from the cannon of the free world. A point in favour of Democritus who, as Dante said, 'Explains the world by Chance!' When we finally arrived at our goal, Berg looked like a distant stage whose doings we would be able to watch. It was only then that a girl of about thirteen revealed a splinter wound in her shoulder which was forthwith bandaged up with strips of clothing and without her uttering a word of complaint.

The cannonade on Berg lasted seven hours, or until sunset. We saw the shells striking the village, stones and tiles flying in all directions, rising columns of smoke and dust. The women and children watched intently but without visible agitation; they exchanged remarks about where the shells had fallen, anxious only to identify the places that had been struck. It was their own houses that were at stake and yet I heard no complaints or imprecations. When one of them thought that it was her house that had been ripped in two she consulted with the others, and if they nodded she said nothing but withdrew into herself. The small lonely German cannon persistently returned its fire from the Kurt house which was for us of prime importance – but it was not hit. As evening came the guns fell silent. We saw the mines gleaming under Berg's little bridges; then it was night. In the belief that the Allies had occupied the village, we made our way towards it. The German emplacements were empty; but shortly before we reached the house there leapt from the shadows a small tank marked with a swastika, and coming against it there appeared another one, bigger. The two of them exchanged numerous shells and machine-gun volleys that whistled past us. Leaping like a hare, and still with little Martin on my back, I threw myself into the Kurt cellar and the others followed. But as it turned out, the Americans had not entered the village. Instead, throughout the night while we lay listening, they continued sending over tearing volleys of grenades about every half an hour.

Once again I was surprised by the silence, reserve and acceptance of their fate with which the community faced this ordeal in their own lacerated village. The women did not pray as they would have done in Italy. And Lore, who from the moment of joining the group – and as its 'first lady' – had busied herself with comforting all the others, continued to do so and to treat them as her guests because they were in her cellar. Having recently been affectionate towards me, she was now deferential as I was the provisional leader of her people; and as I was sharing their fate I believed I was also sharing their thoughts, their very human, simple and moving thoughts. At a given moment we heard the crackling of flames: the nearby brewery was on fire, and we could hear the fierce neighing of the horses trapped inside it. Herr Kurt and I went out to look, for if the fire spread to the sawmill there would be little hope of saving his house. But this time he showed the same character as his people; he lifted his hand to measure the direction of the wind, and once he was satisfied that it was blowing in a favourable direction he did not even go out again to reassure himself. And indeed it was the buildings beyond the brewery that the fire burnt out as it moved away from us.

Shortly after dawn, when silence had fallen, I went out to see what was happening. A ridiculous and unexpected procession was moving off to offer surrender with a small white sheet; the people were dressed in black as if for a funeral, and the idiotic Nazi mayor was at their head. A quarter of an hour later the procession returned – still more comic if this was possible, because behind the mayor, their feet scrunching over the debris, there marched two American tank-men, the first I had seen, grotesquely encased in battle attire and their helmets covered in netting and brushwood. In addition, their guns were almost resting on the mayor's back – the caricature of an allegory portraying the immense pointlessness of war. And the climax of that labyrinth of absurdities occurred when Lore, having run to the roof to spread out a white cloth, appeared before me with a gleaming tray for the purpose of toasting heaven knows what: given that my liberation, and the end of the Nazi regime, and the fact that her life and that of her family was safe, all nevertheless represented the defeat of Germany and the beginning of untold sorrows. However, we all drank, and she not only drank but wept.

However, this joy-cum-sadness was short-lived because hardly had two hours passed than news came heralding fresh disasters. The two Americans who had been seen marching behind the mayor had soon been overtaken by a rapid little van in which they had disappeared. So that though Berg had been abandoned by the Germans it was not yet in the hands of those others. A swarm of Polish, Ukrainian, French and even Italian ex-prisoners – increasingly swollen by a nebulous band of civilians of all races as well as fugitives from a nearby prison – made an indiscriminate assault on everyone and everything. The uproar was infernal. Lore looked at me in despair; everyone sought their own hiding-places while we brought out Herr Kurt's fowling-piece. The rioters were certainly equipped with fury though not with actual firearms, so we were able to put up some resistance. Not that this was necessary in the event: because when I was sitting outside the door with the gun on my knees, a group of these people approached and made signs and shouts indicative of congratulation and praise; they thought I had captured the house and made off at once – out of respect (as they thought) for my participation in the looting. However, these pleasantries were interrupted by shells arriving from various directions. Americans and Germans were both now firing on our poor village which was viewed as a no-man's-land; and this put a brake on the sacking. But a final wandering band discovered a store of schnapps in a surviving cellar, and savage howls of delight accompanied those madmen as they ran over the neighbouring fields where they had gone to celebrate. Thus the revellers' last victims were our two romantic geese (and truly mourned they were). I found their severed heads torn off and left on the grass – together in death as, in their exemplary way, they had been in life.

As evening fell the shell-bursts diminished in intensity and then completely stopped. We all dined together for the first time, Herr Kurt, Lore, the child and I, as if we were alone in the world. The night was damp and airless. In the distance the sky was still glowing. The stream whispered quietly. Our words were few, our looks dark, our thoughts irrecoverable. Up in my attic again, I lay down and thought – then heard Lore coming quietly up the stairs. I did not move, and she sat down at the foot of the little bed which had formerly been Kate's, silent against the pale light of the window. I knew what was going on in her mind, all the vague, nostalgic, anxious imaginings; similar to my own, except that to mine were added all the things I personally had been through: the tormenting themes of an obligation to an image of the good outside all rules but nonetheless absolute – hence a devotion in freedom; and of a stirring of inevitable reasons which I did not doubt in my inner self and yet were inexplicable – hence a secret within truth. The silence was so perfect that we might have been on a desert island in the middle of the sea. From downstairs I thought I heard Martin's breathing in his sleep; and Herr Kurt's intent listening. Thus he on his side certainly heard our stillness, the sweetness and I think the goodbye. Finally Lore stood up, and in that movement I saw her eyes momentarily gleam in the darkness. We parted without having exchanged a word.

I fell asleep – submerged by great dark waves like the ones that had engulfed the men of Licudi in that storm. Then I heard echoing sounds and loud voices. These, together with the daylight, woke me up, and dashing to the window I saw a patrol in front of the house with arms at the ready. They were German soldiers who as soon as they saw me shouted in their usual raucous voices for me to come down.

On the stairs I met Lore who seized hold of my arm; she was followed by a terrified Herr Kurt. The agitated exchange with the sergeant in charge of the group was brief enough, but by Lore's feverish replies I realised I was in grave danger: she pointed out my wounds and then her child – who had arrived on the scene in pyjamas and his eyes heavy with sleep. I gathered that a detachment of the Wehrmacht had descended on Berg, no doubt at the request of its inhabitants, and had shot a number of the people guilty of yesterday's looting. The sergeant seemed to be thinking; but as he did not like the way Lore addressed a few halting words to me, he briskly turned to her husband with a direct question – so my life lay in Herr Kurt's hands. He shook his head and said something that made his wife's face light up.

Then the German signed to me to go in front of him to a truck in which there were already others, both soldiers and civilians. So although I had escaped reprisal, I saw myself forced to follow the retreat of an army in agony. Without even having time to fetch my haversack I was driven off, watching Lore and Herr Kurt and the child in a group in the doorway.

And as they disappeared from my sight – the symbol of a family that for a time had been my own, despite the doubts and disorders involved – so did that world of birds and flowers and grass. It had to make its exit from my life, like so many other apparent things. Only to return now, like a ghost in my memory.

TEARS

'But what good soul could have informed the sergeant of my existence in Kate's room?' I kept asking myself as the truck jolted over the cobbles and, in clouds of dust, transplanted me for the nth time into the unknown. But I was rendered speechless by the thought that if the looters, when they saw me with my gun in the doorway, had assumed I was one of them, then the same assumption made by some intimidated citizen could explain everything. But it seemed grotesque that the recent upheavals should have ended like this, cauterised by that inexplicable smile of mine which produced itself so readily and was really not called for, when – to use Demetrio's phrase – it once more fell to me to be 'heavily called upon'. A few more hours and the return of the Americans would have sorted out my long adventure in the becalmed river of time; whereas the demoniacal finale was dragging me right back into the middle of the furnace. The invincible Russian armies had been pressing on Berlin for months and were now fighting in the suburbs; and whatever the loss, the Germans were not to yield a single stone of the capital save at the price of blood. An upheaval of earthquake dimensions, where a human life counted no more than a speck of dust in a storm. My truck, and all the others in the convoy, were going straight into the lion's den.

Jolting along with me between cases of arms and kit of every kind were an old deaf Lithuanian and a Russian without a leg. The five German soldiers – who I took to be participants in Berg's summary justice – showed not the slightest animosity towards us; from a personal point of view their predicament was identical to ours, except that broadly speaking their destiny was more uncertain. For them, too, it was a matter of living through the final paroxysm, the Caudine Forks of a tight spot in which every hour counted; but if they possessed arms they were also under an obligation to use them. We only had to survive, whereas they could look forward to the concentration camp which swung from one side to the other like a pendulum with the rhythm of things. So we just had to show a certain submissiveness so as not to annoy them, so that they would not act cruelly simply out of resentment or so as to prevent us ever going home – given that in their opinion we were unjustly free whereas they might truly never see their homes again.

From the height of our truck – which, as it belonged to the army, was to some extent a solid rock in the turbid sea of humanity ebbing and flowing all around us – our stupefied eyes surveyed that immeasurable dissolution. Berg is about 130 kilometres from Berlin as the crow flies; but to cover the twenty kilometres that separated us from Wittenberg, our first port of call, it took the whole of that day, April 18, the day on which (as I learnt afterwards) the Russians established their strangle-hold over the capital. Those days, and especially the 20th, which was Hitler's birthday, were fatal ones for Germany, for in a good-wishes action bearing this time the stamp of British humour the Allies sent over thousands of aircraft to sow death on the already defeated country – twelve thousand on a single day, it was said. The formations came over in waves, alternating with the clouds in a wind-blown blue sky. The streets were flanked by the charred ghosts of houses, and the groans of the wounded were drowned in the thunder of the oncoming wave. The German people, its structures torn to shreds and its links with its leaders severed, was writhing beneath an apocalyptical scourge and sweating blood like a body under torture. It was a horrible punishment for the horrible crime that had incurred it. This was the melting-pot of the two barbarisms that now faced each other, and the mind could not really conceive of them or encompass them in any way whatsoever.

The soldiers roughly pushed off the many people who tried to climb on to our truck or even cling to it. It seemed absurd that three precious places coveted by their own people should be sacrificed to transport three useless prisoners. Only one person was permitted to join us – a woman of good standing who could stammer a few words in English. That night when we halted at the Wittenberg bridge – it was impossible to cross owing to the hordes of fugitives – it was through her that I established contact with the commander of our convoy: an elderly officer who came up and spoke to her. He threw me a rapid glance then asked me to give my word of honour that I would not try to escape. This was absurd, because he had no means of preventing me had I decided to do so, and the other two prisoners – the Lithuanian and the Russian – were only following him because he was carrying them in the direction of their country. But by asking me to give my 'word of honour' he was trying at the eleventh hour to bring back a chivalrous usage that was two centuries out of date, and in a Germany that had thrown off every kind of rule, law or convention so as to replace them all with the law of Brennus – which is anti-law. But on some strange whim I decided at that moment to press on to the bitter end, whatever the price. So I ceremoniously gave him my word of honour for which he seemed grateful. We would spend that evening together.

The speed with which things changed around us meant that we had to be constantly re-examining facts and people, and as our very life depended on these, the soundness or otherwise of an immediate judgement was decisive for what would inevitably befall us in the logic of events. Like a tightrope-walker who is slightly shifting his balance every fraction of a second, or a mountain-climber on a cliff-face who has to decide not only his route but the exact amount of support his foothold will give him, so I sailed on that ocean, putting my trust in Providence, yes, but also in my own wits. A dangerous yet fascinating game. So I scrutinised at some length the German woman and the captain with both of whom my destiny had become involved and on whom it might in part depend.

The woman was elderly and certainly related to high-ranking German officers – which had won her her place on the truck – and though her face was authoritarian it was not hard. Her clothing, though now torn into shreds, suggested that it had originally been that of a woman who had dressed suitably for the day, had gone out as was her custom, and through who knows what misadventures had ended up alone on the main road. Her fatigue seemed almost unbearable and yet she managed to say a few low words, and if her dusty eyelids seemed in danger of becoming moist with tears, she quickly pulled herself together. When I told her not my name, but my rank and regiment, she must have derived from them some hope of understanding, a glimmer of the world she had belonged to but which was now sinking headlong together with the whole outfit of the ideas belonging to it. As for the German captain, he was not to be envied. When darkness fell he found that six of his nine transport trucks had disappeared, and that he was also short of a number of soldiers, including the one who had come to the Kurts' to take me. Presumably men with homes and families on this side of the Elbe had no desire to cross to the other side, so had vanished into thin air leaving bag and baggage. The other soldiers had set up their bivouac a little apart, in sight of the deaf Lithuanian and the Russian. The latter, who was of powerful constitution, remained calm and silent and seemed not to worry about his disablement – and anyway I had noticed that he manipulated his crutch with enormous flair.

After the storms and stresses of that hellish day the night seemed calm. Once cries had been soothed, an appalling weariness enfolded the multitudes in sleep. The darkness was reddened by distant fires and now and again penetrated by shots which, however, hardly made a hole in the silence. I sat opposite the German woman on a case of biscuits. The captain stood between us. Made equal to each other by a common danger, and perhaps destined for the same lightning death, we were separated by rules and conventions that were all the more paradoxical because, of the three of us, I was certainly the freest.

The captain was silent. I guessed he was certainly over fifty. His hair was almost white; a tall thin man with a distinguished bearing, a lean face yet slightly softened by a reddish rather than a brownish tinge, pale questioning eyes, delicate hands. He obviously belonged to the reserve and perhaps had been called up only very late and for territorial service. Up till now he had said no more to me than those few German phrases asking me for my word of honour. But after he had thought a while he suddenly came to a decision. Unexpectedly addressing me in accurate Italian, he said:

'I know the islands of Procida and Ischia. I've lived quite a time in Positano.'

'Are you concerned with art?'

'Yes,' he replied. 'My name is Rolphe and I'm a painter.'

'In that case,' I ventured, 'I think we can complete our introductions.'

And I stood up and gave my name. He bent his neck forward with a jerk exactly as Doctor Aesckloni had done, and held out his hand which I shook by the fingers; then he turned to the woman and introduced me to her in German, at the same time telling me her name: Frau Haendel. When I sat down again the captain did so too. With all the solemnity peculiar to their race the two of them then settled down to give me an explanatory lecture.

'All this,' Rolphe began after a pause and with a sweep of the arm that seemed to take in the whole immensity of the darkness, 'all this is meaningless compared with the real German people. I love Italy and I understand Italy, but – quite apart from individual people – there have been appalling mutual misunderstandings. I was in the '14 war; Germany was misjudged then as she will be again now – a mistake that was and will be the cause of infinite subsequent evils. This land is the body of Europe. At the moment it's being torn to pieces. But it's the suicide of Europe.'

'Does the Signora understand Italian?' I asked with a slight bow in her direction.

'A little I understand,' Frau Haendel answered, finding her words with difficulty. 'I often in Venice.'

'In a few days, perhaps tomorrow,' went on Captain Rolphe, not allowing himself to be diverted by my trivial interruption, 'the Anglo-Americans will reach the Elbe; then the Russians will arrive, and what will they be able to do but fight each other? We're expecting this encounter any moment now. If we had been understood by the rest of Europe, today the continent would be a mighty body, and not a heap of ruins from the Pyrenees to the Oder. Those who were with us, those who have been against us, and we ourselves, all ruins, nothing but ruins. How is it believable?'

'It's strictly unbelievable, Signor Rolphe,' I admitted, thereby demilitarising him at a stroke. 'But you know very well that in politics, and still more in war, only facts count.'

Rolphe threw me a dissatisfied look. It would have been useless to point out to him all the countless 'unbelievable' things that the Germans had poured down on us since 1940 – among which, for instance, that Captain Sansevero had been put to hard labour. But as his generalisations tended towards acquittal, it was important to bring him back to the particular.

'That's why,' I said, 'it is up to us to look at the facts. Do you think it serves any purpose to take that deaf Lithuanian and crippled Russian to the other side of the Elbe?'

'Those are my orders,' Rolphe answered without conviction. 'Justified by the excess of prisoners in the undefended areas.'

I had not mentioned myself who was standing before him as a living refutation of what he was saying. I had to suppose that he had another reason and it was not opportune to go against him: but this was not why I did not want to press him, but rather out of compassion perhaps touched with a slight contempt.

'Just the wheels-within-wheels of things!' I was able to say in conclusion, 'from which mankind to this day has never been able to free itself. That's what war has been; that's what the whole of history has been, which unfolds and develops and makes judgements solely within itself – or so it seems to me.'

Frau Haendel obviously failed to follow this over-complicated dialogue; but as Rolphe said nothing, she said nothing either and did not ask for a translation of my remarks. We wrapped ourselves up in our blankets. And with my head resting on the haversack of one of the deserters – the captain seemed to have passed both it and its contents on to me – I fell asleep.

But I doubt if the captain slept at all. He was already up and away before dawn in an effort to reassemble his convoy. An almost incessant rumbling could be heard from the pale sky and from not far away I recognised the tearing sound of American shells. The tumultuous tide of fugitives had unexpectedly disappeared. Having escaped from the Berlin area under attack by thousands of Flying Fortresses, they had then come up against the cannon, so one could guess that they were now swarming and stumbling through the woods and over the hills sloping down to the river. The bridge had now been cleared, and over it there streamed the detachments going back for the hopeless last-ditch defence of Berlin, following Hitler's orders. Though these troops were still fairly numerous, they were a rather haphazard collection and even included civilians, or boys of hardly more than sixteen who were already utterly exhausted, and yet were singing. It was the *Volkssturm* of the Nazis' final hour. Enemy fighters dived to machine-gun the bridge a number of times, but it was adequately defended and the flow of soldiers continued, slow but regular. Rolphe was standing meditatively on the bonnet of his staff car. Frau Haendel was anxiously watching. Our soldiers said nothing; but it was an untrustworthy silence because the moral collapse of the German comes suddenly; and it is here that lies his personal inferiority to the Englishman, whose so-called phlegm is no more than an unlimited tenacity.

That halt lasted five hours. In Rolphe's truck there was all the stuff I could have needed, and I packed the haversack that had become mine with all the deftness and common sense that my *Lager* experience had given me. Frau Haendel then helped me put a fresh dressing on my wounds which I had neglected for two days and they were hurting badly. She wanted to lend me the little mirror she carried in her bag. Her kindness was extraordinary in view of the discomfort and palpitating fears she was enduring. I promised I would visit her in Germany after the war to thank her, or would receive her as a welcome guest in Italy – formalities which served, I think, to prove to ourselves that we still stood for something. The thunder of the cannon had got much nearer when we left, and the sun was already high and burning. Up to this moment Rolphe had ostentatiously avoided looking in my direction. He had put me on parole and perhaps he wanted me to break it so as to despise me and be one up on me for the thoughts I had expressed. Whereas I wanted his misplaced verbiage to turn against himself with a woman of his own country and rank as witness and judge. While mulling over these inconsistent motivations and imprecise impulses of my mind, I watched the great silent whirlpools of the Elbe swirling below me. There were other prisoners in Rolphe's truck but all of them, like the Lithuanian and Russian, from the East. In looking at the Elbe, which at this point was about a mile wide, I was able to evaluate the insuperable barrier lying between me and freedom. This bridge was already mined and I had no idea where the others were; I assumed they had already been destroyed or were very far away; and in such circumstances a stretch of road more or less could be the price of life.

We avoided Wittenberg which was enveloped in an ashen-grey pall of smoke, and I lost not only my sense of direction but any desire to concern myself with it – so absorbed was I in the details of a catastrophe so atrocious as to leave one stunned to the point of insensitivity: devastated factories, gutted hangars, contorted metal-work smelling of decay and unburied bodies. Poor Frau Haendel was so appalled that she kept her handkerchief pressed to her nose and mouth. In an area that might have been Rathenow we were obliged to halt again. It was then that Rolphe threw me a quick glance and I in my turn looked back at him. Once again, as with the Greek guerrilla disguised as a workman in the doorway at the Krano Command, the obstinate Sansevero put into that look all he had staked in his game of dice with existence, a game always lost yet never lost: the truth that (whatever I myself had said to the contrary) there exists a world completely different from the one governed by 'the force of facts'.

At a sign from the commander the soldiers leapt down from the truck, followed by the prisoners. Rolphe was standing stiff as a ramrod in front of an officer clothed in a cloak from top to toe, in spite of the heat. This man was obviously a General, and he was giving orders. The soldiers forthwith disengaged their small field-shovels from their packs and formed into a squad. Rolphe came up to me.

'Captain,' he said, 'we have a fatigue here until nightfall and won't be moving off till tomorrow. I have your word of honour: you'll keep Frau Haendel company until we get back tonight.'

And off he went in the wake of the General. But I saw them stopping less than a hundred yards away; and I saw the soldiers begin digging, while a horrible stench drifted towards us. Frau Haendel blenched. I quickly concocted two masks from my supplies of gauze, one for her and one for me. Then I signed to her to keep calm as we would only be a short distance away, and I set off towards the group of men rhythmically digging, their faces covered with dirt and sweat; and the poor woman went and ensconced herself in the cab of the truck so as not to see. But Rolphe barred my way.

'You're an enemy officer and a prisoner,' he said. 'There's no reason of any kind why you should take part in this work.'

His voice was shaking with anger and a sense of shame that I should so much as see the atrocities that had taken place. I found the indiscriminate bombing of a defeated Germany a horrible act of barbarism – that was true; but not that every individual German should be confronted with the shame of having abused his power over others. I was certain that Rolphe, as he knew Italian so well, would at some point have been in charge of an Italian prison camp. It was a bit late in the day to snatch from my hands a spade I wanted to use in a work of mercy – that of burying the dead who, after all, were men – when in the past just such an implement had been thrust upon me as if I were a slave. So I pushed him aside and took my place beside the others. He could not produce an answer; his face was so white he looked as if he was going to faint; and he moved away. We pursued that labour of love and sorrow until darkness fell; and whenever any small decision was to be made, the Germans looked to me and followed me, though no word was spoken.

Again that evening I shared my rations with the captain and Frau Haendel. New orders had arrived, and Rolphe's detachment had been joined by others which were to be used as a single unit in the final defence of the capital. And in fact we were not far from Berlin, perhaps to the north of Potsdam, in woodland that seemed to cover a wide area. Scattered lights could be seen between the trees on all sides and there was the noise of running water. The sky glowed now here, now there, or suddenly became clear again. There was the dull roar of high planes going to do their work in unknown directions. As a perpetual background to the darkness was the distant throb of the cannon. Exhaustion numbed my limbs; or perhaps it was the tangible and crushing force of the unknown that was weighing us down.

Wrapped in a cheap blanket, Frau Haendel looked like a seated clay figure roughly hewn by a sculptor of the grotesque school. She had had to remove her own shoes and pull on a pair of military boots, perfectly new but unlaced owing to her swollen legs which protruded above them together with her torn stockings. Nevertheless she had imperviously retained her small hat, that object by which – according to Francis Carco who has gone deeply into the subject – a woman's extravagance may be judged. There was some lace around her neck, but though it was dirty and crumpled it was still adorned with an old-fashioned brooch. Behind her pince-nez (one glass of which was broken) her short-sighted eyes were peering vacantly at the biscuit she should have been dipping in her soup; she had placed her bowl on her knee without realising she was letting it spill, and neither Rolphe nor I wanted to tell her so because we did not want to add to her confusion. The old lady's white plump hands were trembling in the half-darkness; she seemed at that moment weaker than a babe in arms. And then she was tormented by her memories.

Rolphe was a little way off, absorbed and rigid. His uniform clinging to his lankness made him look like one of Callot's nervous etchings in which colour and joy are alike inconceivable. That morning he had had to make an enormous effort not to give in entirely, a thing he especially dreaded doing in front of me who stood before him with searching eyes and as the symbol of that judgement from which he needed to defend himself – together with all the rest of his country. His pig-headedness in wanting to keep me in his power had roots in deep-seated complexes of his own, because I do not believe he had clear ideas or precise motives stemming from the ghastly realities around us. Perhaps he remembered Hitler's angry injunction after the 1943 armistice: 'Every

German soldier is arbiter over the life of every Italian soldier!' – or perhaps he nursed some ancient bitterness compounded of desire and contempt and resulting from what he had gained or lost in those Italian trips of his. But he certainly wanted to convince me of the crime that was being perpetrated against Germany; yet at the same time it was intolerable to him that the witness should look right down into the wound: torture, perhaps; and perhaps also punishment. And yet I suspected that in the depths of his confusion he was simply suffering from fear; not physical fear but moral fear; and that in the tragic solitude of his German soul and in the annihilation of his country, his need of me was greater even than the old lady's. I belonged to the world that condemned them both and from which they would be excluded. I was perhaps his last contact with what he both loved and hated; with what he wanted to punish, and by which, deep down, he sought to be exculpated. But he must have understood that, together with the rest of his country, he had to resolve a problem within himself that concerned the human conscience in particular and the whole of history under the eyes of God. That was why I said nothing and he found my silence intolerable.

He put down his mess-tin from which he had eaten practically nothing and started to hold forth in the manner described a year or two later by Vercors in a small book that had its moment of fame: the endless soliloquy of the German at grips with his demons. England had her full share of the invective. And so did we.

'You call yourselves masters of life; yet in five hundred years you haven't even provided cemeteries for your southern regions! Is that why, here, everything has to become a cemetery?' There was anger in his eyes and at the same time supplication. 'The Russian prisoners? And what did Caesar do? The Jews? Haven't they shouted for two thousand years that they are the Chosen People? Why do they think it odd that another people should call itself Chosen, after them and instead of them and for much better reasons?'

I got up and put his bowl back in his hands.

'My dear Captain,' I said, encouraging him to pick up his spoon, 'this is a tragedy not only for you or Germany but for all men. We're all victims of the disaster. But I'd like to say to you what Nausicaa said to Ulysses: "You suffer these things because you're a man; so endure them like a man!" '

This classical quotation falling anachronistically into a wood full of people who did not even know whether they would live through the next day, had a calming effect on Rolphe who once more started to gulp down his soup – but with a trembling hand and spilling it on his jacket in his turn. I thought with tenderness of Pannuzzo and his famous jacket drenched with grease – perhaps due to some circumstance similar to this one. Where was poor dear Pannuzzo, with his angelic goodness, on this cannibalistic night? Frau Haendel made me repeat word for word Nausicaa's magic phrase that had so soothed Rolphe. When she had finally grasped its meaning she made an instinctive gesture as if looking for a pencil. This admirable woman had not lost the typically German habit of noting things down.

We stayed in that area for another two days, though gradually moving to the western borders of the capital. The Russians were already shelling Berlin and fighting in its eastern suburbs and were soon to start an invasion also from the south. The detachments into which Rolphe's column had been incorporated now looked like a real army corps and was establishing positions round the forest of Grünenwald. The prisoners still following the troops as auxiliaries were submitted to the killing work of digging or reinforcing the labyrinth of fortifications concealed in every fold of the ground; but as Rolphe had omitted to hand in my name I took part in his and his men's activities without anyone giving me orders, though I agreed to do my share of their work only if I so wished. And it sometimes happened that if he was absent the soldiers again took their cue from me. Though I had been attached to the Germans ever since my Athens period, there was no logical reason why I should not be recognised as an officer of the Allied army; but so much water had flowed under the bridges since then that only the desperate peculiarity of the situation could have so bizarrely restored me to my rank. As for Frau Haendel, who had a house in the centre of the capital and was living under the delusion that she would be able to get to it, she was kept almost hidden by Rolphe owing to her important relations: so there was this sixty-year-old lady in the firing-line, a pathetic symbol of that ultimate Germany that was about to be wiped out.

On the evening of the twenty-second we were again called on to perform the heart-rending task of freeing bodies from ruins caused by the incessant bombardments; the last one had lasted a horrific eighteen hours and had almost levelled the area to the ground. A half-destroyed hangar served as assembly-point; and the orderly spirit of that uncrushable people had not failed even on this occasion, with the addition of some subtle and absurd talent for the macabre, or perhaps it was insensitiveness on the part of the agent or the man behind the scenes – similar to the insensitiveness that transfixes a butterfly with a pin so as to classify it, or places a marriage-bed and a bier side by side in a shop, the prices and measurements of both duly displayed.

How and where in that cataclysm had the authorities requisitioned so many coffins? From the massive magnificent carved ones enthroned in the foreground of that extraordinary array, to the less grandiose ones, the ordinary ones, the simple ones and the very poor ones. And when the commercial range had been exhausted it was supplemented by the private product made by the local carpenter, with whatever means lay to hand and in any sort of wood: even rough planks or packing cases. There followed blankets, tent material, furniture-covering and finally sacks – all methodically laid out on the bleak cement floor and with concern not to waste space.

On the other side were the bodies: a ghastly jumble over which the searchers lavished endless patience, like a surgeon dissecting a wound with grim punctiliousness, or like a philosopher when he lays bare evil in the clarity of his thought. The people intent on identifying the bodies passed over that frightful area, whispering and pointing. I could make out torn bits of flesh lying in the abandoned shamelessness of death; young girls, old men, a tiny baby; ghostly discolourments, horrendous fragments, frozen eyes. And while on one side the industrious ant-like line was slowly reducing the funereal pile, on the other new teams came in to refill it; between the doleful wail of the sirens, the thundering explosions coming from the sky, and the shattering ever-advancing shells; until slowly that multitude of shadows faded away; the carved coffins, the ordinary ones, the poor ones; then the packing cases and all the make-shift wrappings; the vast mass of misery disappeared into the mouth of death. It was during those very hours that within the city itself the German lion and the Russian bear were clasping each other in a ghastly embrace and tearing each other to pieces. Through the tunnels of the underground railway, trains bristling with men and arms came up behind the Soviet advance troops and destroyed themselves so as to destroy everything and everyone else. Similarly loads of explosives in the sewers were let off beneath ground already trodden by the enemy and burst out in flaming gas and putrid slime. Meanwhile the exasperated Kirghiz, Tartars, Kalmuks and Siberians, under Rokosovsky, Koniev and Zhukov, were converging towards the legendary Bunker of the Chancellory. There Hitler's demon, or his genius, was about to be consumed in a crackle of sulphur, leaving nothing behind but the echo of a final, epic malediction.

That very night our corps set off again to penetrate the Grünenwald which was threatened by the endless fire obliterating the capital. But in the few hours that the march lasted everything was scattered and swallowed up by the human lava pressing in on us from all sides. It became impossible to recognise the places or roads of a nightmare journey during which we fought desperately backwards and forwards like a wave within an imprisoning and ever-narrowing circle; finally it was like the tunny-nets when the fishermen bring them under the hull before the frenzied and bloody massacre. Perhaps one contingent of the men met the Russian advance-guard coming from the south, fought with them over an obscure strip of land with the fury of a wild beast who knows he is condemned, killed and then died. Rolphe's trucks did not reach that far, they lost contact and got separated; dawn found us once more alone, two trucks, five soldiers, Frau Haendel, Rolphe, myself and the Russian prisoner. It was our last halt and, for me, the culmination of the tragedy.

This time, too, we were in a gloomy suburb; devastated factories, burnt-out houses, clouds of fetid dust, and sudden silences into which, like jets of flame, there burst cries, explosions and the dull roar of falling buildings. Over in the direction of the city a funereal vapour rose from the horizon and darkened the sky. The growl of the Russian cannon never stopped – similar now to the hoarse incessant roar of the sea crashing on the rocks in a storm. Ragged bands of men came and encircled us as though scenting prey, then withdrew at the sight of arms and let out menacing shouts. Defenceless soldiers ran away from us, heedless of Rolphe's somewhat petulant orders. The five who still remained seemed to be thinking. It was then that that obsessive drone started again, grew louder, came nearer, and seemed to shake the whole arc of the sky. And we, too, shuddered as we saw squadron after squadron coming over, myriads of bombers, flying low, gleaming in the light, the tight formation testifying to a sole invincible determination; and our condemnation.

'*Mein Gott!*' exclaimed Frau Haendel softly, while beads of sweat (I saw them) broke out on her forehead. Her eyes were blank; she was not thinking of herself but of her family whom she would never see again. I took her arm and she automatically followed me. The soldiers had already disappeared into the ditches. Rolphe remained standing.

'Rolphe,' I shouted, 'lie down!'

Almost simultaneously the ground rocked. A terrifying shower of stones and rubble leapt up in front of us, as if the earth had let loose a spectre from hell. The dust was blinding. Then stones, slag, splinters hailed down. The stench of TNT cut one's breath. Frau Haendel was stretched out beside me and her hand clutching mine pulled me down.

'Frau Haendel!' I called breathlessly, trying to turn her over for she was lying on her face. But when I touched her I felt the blood running between my fingers. I let her fall back and she stayed still.

Then through the smoky hell of that gehenna I made out various vanishing shadows – they were our five soldiers who now viewed the war as over. Rolphe was still at his post, but now on his knees. He did not seem to be wounded, but he contorted his face every now and again and the thick coat of dust overlaying it made it look like a grotesque mask.

It was then that a shot rang out just near me. And it was only then that Rolphe doubled up. A man was running away with a strange rolling motion of the body. It was the Russian limping off with the aid of a German rifle. He had got his own back on the imprudent captain who had signed his own death warrant by taking this enemy into his truck.

I tried to lift Rolphe's body up but the bullet had got him through the throat. So I was alone now. And the formidable quake of the bombardment as it sank deeper and deeper into the unhappy earth seemed like the breathing of a monster inimical to every living thing and prepared to stop only at annihilation.

Terrified shadows came and went; slow groans penetrated my stunned senses like painful needles. My faceless weeping woman, my little statue, had found her way here from the house of my soul destroyed at Licudi; the woman who had been stolen from her dead and stolen from me, the woman who beat her head and struck her breast with her cold clay arms: tears of horror and desolation still intact across the breadth of the centuries. And hearing her weep in my absolute defencelessness as I lay on the open ground, I put my hands over my eyes for a moment and then fell into a faint for many hours; or perhaps I fell asleep.

That was a very long day! I had walked for many hours, guiding myself by instinct towards the West and with every step getting nearer freedom. I did not feel my life was seriously imperilled; I had brushed with death so recently in Berg, and then again this very morning, so I did not think it would visit me again for a while. My mind was in a fog because I was not unable, but unwilling, to organise my thoughts and was continually distracting myself from myself by concentrating on the details of the road: the rubble, the rags, the gleaming splinters of metal. And I never looked around and about but closed my eyes and my nostrils and my skin to any stimulus likely to arouse perception. All I wanted was to press on. Later I would stop; later I would remember, and think.

I had been unable to find Rolphe's map in our shattered and overturned truck, and I could not find it on his person either. I had laid out his and Signora Haendel's bodies before leaving. Both were already cold. I laid them behind the truck and covered them with canvas on which I placed his military cap. There was nothing else I could do. I did not want to bury them because in that case they would never be found. I knew I was about a hundred kilometres from the Elbe and I wanted to reach its banks before the Russians. It was not impossible that the Russians would come into armed conflict with the armies who had previously been their allies, and if that happened, and I was behind their lines, as an Italian I would again be seen as an enemy and again receive the pounding from which I had just escaped. I was not thinking only of Italy at this stage but of establishing any kind of life outside that appalling graveyard of thoughts (worse even than the graveyard of flesh) by which I was surrounded. My jaw was hurting terribly as a result of those heavy days – the only sensation that I could not ignore; the rhythmic throbbing of the blood at that tender point beat more or less in time with my footsteps; and I noticed I was saying with every beat, giving it a kind of musical lilt, that line from Dante: 'I saw our madding little threshing floor.'

As evening fell I stopped out of sheer exhaustion. I was in a kind of wasteland that had once been a residential area. The houses had been destroyed with scientific precision, but this was some time ago because the ruins were old and cold. Each house had its large green wilderness around it; and each had had a direct hit so that the roof had fallen straight in on its shattered foundations – making a kind of instant funeral monument for those within. The trees had suffered less; or perhaps the greens of spring had covered over their wounds; at any rate only a few, those killed at a stroke, raised absolutely bare limbs into the air. I climbed through a window and made free of the wreckage; I laid down my blanket, and with my head pillowed on my haversack watched the stars appearing in a portion of the sky. And I tried to imagine the thoughts of a man who knew himself to be the only person alive in the world, the only survivor. From the East came the incessant growling of the Russian cannon. Perhaps I was in a fold of the countryside, because the noise seemed slightly muffled. Or had I travelled further than I thought? How far, I wondered . . . Rats creeping across the rubble looked at me with luminous eyes; but perhaps my eyes shone in the night too; they kept their distance; and finally everything fused into a single darkness.

During my days with Rolphe everything in the trucks had been at my disposal, so I had carefully foraged through the luggage and equipment knowing that my subsequent survival depended on them. My shoes were not new, like poor Frau Haendel's, but they were strong, and I had given them a coat of reddish aniline to disguise them. And in all other ways I carefully avoided any sign of belonging – not only to the German army but to any group or nation whatsoever. I had come across some anonymous civilian clothes earlier in a bombed house, and with Frau Haendel's help had sewn my identity card into them so as to have it available if it were really necessary. Naturally I rejected any idea of carrying arms. I tore away the outer part of my haversack and only had the lining, and here I concealed what food I could; I bound my blanket tight around my waist so that it would not be seen; and I put conspicuous bandages over my wounds to hide my face. The smallest possession could become an object to be coveted; the slightest mark of distinction could arouse a hostile emotion. As it was I was strong, provided for, and determined; but I looked like a castaway belonging to nowhere, a tramp at the end of his tether. This could help me to get through.

But there were many unknown elements, and these were serious. In coming from Wittenberg to Potsdam we had travelled in a south-easterly direction; but as the crow flies the Elbe was nearer if I went west; but I had no idea of what bridges lay ahead of me. So crossing the river would be the final problem, but meanwhile it would take at least five or six days' walking even to get there, without a map or road-signs. The food was enough, if I apportioned it carefully and made full use of my experience as a prisoner. But what about my wound? My jaw was hurting badly; and perhaps a fragment of bone, buried at the edge of the fracture, was working its way to the surface; this would mean an abscess, very painful near the trigeminal nerve, and probably producing a fever. That is what I was afraid of. So as I walked I spared myself every superfluous movement: walking yet saving one's strength with every step is an art not very well known. In the evening I made a thorough check on shoes and laces, because any flaw could bring me to a halt. Over this I profited from Binutti's instructions at Ferrara. At every crossroads and bifurcation I gave deep thought to the new direction to be taken. Sometimes some surviving little road-sign helped, but almost always I had to trust to my own intuition and the sun. When I stopped for the night I dossed down in such a way that I could keep an eye in all directions, and like a bandit kept an escape route always clear. I took off none of my clothes or belongings so as always to be ready for a getaway. Then I settled myself for sleep, though always on the alert mentally, and I think sleep came. All these precautions will make people smile today. But no one will ever know the number of people who disappeared or were murdered in that no-man's-land during those lawless weeks. The Anglo-Americans were already on the left bank of the Elbe, but by the Yalta agreement the Russians were given the honour of reaching the other bank, an area choked with ruins, abandoned by the final remains of the Wehrmacht, and teeming with disbanded troops, deserters, fugitives and robbers. Endless armed brigands roamed the countryside, ransacking villages and taking all remaining supplies; with savage fury they destroyed factories, broke up machinery and set fire to stocks. Total strangers would suddenly group themselves together for violence then separate again, like storm-clouds that gather and then part and fade away. Myriads of people, each with a soul, a past, an aim and an ambition of his own, would join forces for a while then disperse in as many directions as they had come from. A strange abyss where the circles of hell were all jumbled up together, and also perhaps those of heaven; a mass of memories, passions and greeds, irresistible in its fury and taking no account whatsoever of life.

Like a huntsman in a thicket with an eye alert for the slightest incident, I made my way by laps of about a quarter of a mile at a time. I decided against using the road, the haunt of restless hordes and sometimes of demented cars whence issued shouts or even shots; and nor did I go through the woods where a man-to-man encounter could be fatal and where fear could produce worse things than malice. So I kept to that neutral area that is neither too frequented nor too deserted, the area fairly near the road, where one could be seen, yes, but by an eye that sees more than one thing at a time and has to make a choice among the things that claim its attention. And as stillness is nature's best defence, I lay down at moments when I thought I could be seen as no sight was so common in those days as that of some utterly exhausted wanderer. If anyone spoke to me I showed my wounds, pretending I could not answer or could not hear.

I must admit that this game afforded me a certain amount of entertainment – first and foremost, strangely enough, because it had the real tang of a game although the stake was life itself. In that immense disarray I felt I was carrying intact within myself laws, rules and measure. With all my strength and will I was engaged in creating a strong if fragile system in which a delicate balance of perception, cunning, readiness and energy would get the better of the brute force all around me and of the impassible adversities of space and time. This masterpiece to which I was committed even involved my pride, the more so as none of the things I was trying to overcome resembled me, so that the value of their opposite was put to the test. The creature patiently formed by the monks at my school so as to extract (perhaps) a cardinal's purple, was now challenged to extract himself from a dehumanised jungle where all was revolt, blindness, things; he had to tame it with the quiet intensity of his mind. I thought of James Cook, master of the oceans, yet who fell beneath a savage's club. And here Caesar was of help to me, not swathed in his red emperor's mantle and declaiming on the stage of history, but plunging headlong from the mole of Alexandria, naked; but as a sword is naked.

At night endless camp-fires appeared among the trees lining the roads. Under the impulsion of darkness and in the need for sleep, all those varied and diverse people – dangerous to others yet frightened for themselves – instinctively slowed down the tension and by silent agreement laid aside the conflict of wills. To the first group others would immediately be added, until in the end there was a vast encampment, yet hardly a whisper rose from it. As fifteen million foreigners had been brought in convoy to Germany and endless refugees had poured in from the East, the majority of these dispersed wanderers spoke unknown languages; but most of them would have said nothing even if they could. Each one kept himself to himself, though he studied those beside whom he would have to spend the night. So as not to lie on the damp ground they preferred to throw a plank over the ditch at the edge of the road – hence their resting-place was sometimes over the trickle of a stream. Each slept closely flanked by two others, and each was disguised as I was disguised; and the man beside me, who was communicating to me part of his animal warmth, was perhaps another me, or was perhaps my very opposite: a man of learning, a fanatic, a simpleton, a murderer. Words were few; but the secrets they hid were fascinating. There the encounter of lives was pure and unsullied, stripped of all spurious attraction; and perhaps there for the first and only time did I merge perfectly with men.

Four more days and four more nights passed in this way; and on the morning of the fifth day – after two hours' walking – I stopped in a meadow very like the one in which the Kurt geese had lived their happy days of love and together found death; except that the water of the blue pools lying in the fresh green grass came up from the network of streams and canals below Genthin, beyond the Brandenburg lakes. My abscess had flared up during the night, and the sedatives I had salvaged from the German truck were quite inadequate to relieve the excruciating pain – a pain that was hit as if by a hammer-blow with every step I took, so that it invaded my mind and made thought impossible. In that meadow I had seen one of those groups of refugees from the East who had appeared beyond the Elbe back in February in their flight before the Russian advance troops. I recognised this particular group by its antiquated horse-carriage. It is impossible to say by what vicissitudes these people, who had nearly reached the Rhine, should have now turned back to be threatened yet again by the Soviet advance troops. There were five of them, survivors of an entire village that had been put on the trek for four months. When I went up to them they seemed incapable of reaction and hardly moved: a couple of old people, a younger man, still strong though his face was marked with terrible bruises, and two little girls of about eight and ten. The smaller of the two girls was lying on the grass and she just stared at me fixedly, her white bloodless little face bearing witness to the sufferings she had endured. The look she gave me was totally without hope, and heavy with that condemnation of things that can always be seen in the eyes of the dying.

I tried to comfort the oldest of the group in my rudimentary German, and he told me that their carriage had been robbed of its horse and its contents. That unfortunate refugee, perhaps from the Mark region of the Oder, must have seen in my attitude some promise of assistance, and he in his turn tried to help me. He had just come back along the road I was going to take but knew nothing about bridges, he said, for he and his little group had ferried across the Elbe at some point; there were great stretches of empty country in front of me and many streams and small rivers, he said. Then he proceeded to draw a map on the ground with twigs and straws – only slightly more sketchy than the ones used by the first navigators to conquer the world. Meanwhile the little girl never took her eyes off me; she had the huddled look of someone who has always lain on a very narrow bed; and her head was resting in the other child's lap. The throbbing in my jaw was getting worse and worse and the pain becoming almost unbearable.

From what I gathered, the Elbe was about thirty kilometres away, but across country. I did not know that during those days Berlin was being fought for street by street, nor that the Russians would join up with the Americans somewhat later and considerably more to the south. I imagined that they had passed beyond the capital and that their advance patrols were already near the river, and I thought I had a narrow but decisive margin of time at my disposal. Free of pain, I could if necessary do those thirty kilometres in a single forced march, and in that case I would have no further need of my supplies – which would be equally useless to me if I failed. Like that shipwrecked lieutenant of the Alpini, who had to make a choice between a final sprint or death, I had to come to a decision and quickly; and I thought I was acting according to reason. But now I know that it was the look in the child's eyes that decided me, for that look swept away the differences between our conditions and asserted a value that I would not be able to recognise later – but which was nevertheless the only true one.

I took the blanket from around my waist and spread it out on the ground, signing to the children that it was for them. Then I took out my packets of food, one after another, and put them down – with the same dumb-show towards the children. Finally my groping hands reached the medicaments, and I brought them out too. The elder child sprang to life in the belief that the other could now be helped; but I knew that the little one was at death's door and that not even a major operation could save her. But a gentle light came into her eyes too, as if she, like me, knew it was only a game, but a game it would be fun to play, with a pretending doctor and a pretending bed and pretending medicines of pebbles or bits of chalk; so at least she would not die without a smile.

The others looked at me without a word – like country people looking at a conjuror setting up his props, unable to guess at the surprises in store. But when I showed my wound to the old man, and gave him my penknife – after passing it a number of times through a flame – he understood. Perhaps he had had some experience in these things or else my abscess had reached the exactly right point; but at any rate he lanced it with a single stroke, and yet, in that harsh cut, I felt myself liberated. Then the two of us, God knows how, made another dressing, after which I fell into a deep sleep, the first really relaxed sleep I had had for some time, for I knew I was being watched over by others, and anyway had nothing more that needed to be guarded. At midday I awoke, ready for my undertaking. But I would have preferred not to wake up just then, because from the silence of the others and the way they were grouped I knew that the little girl had died; I saw her pathetically huddled up on my blanket, with my medicaments arranged around her by her sister as funeral offerings, and my packets of food next to her hands: exactly as the age-old inhabitants of Licudi had done things for their dead thousands of years before.

I made the sign of the cross (which I had not made for years), not only for myself but for the others; and they made it too. We bade each other goodbye with a gesture of the hand, each one of them to me, and I to each one of them individually. Then I went off towards the uncertainties of dusk, and in the quiet glimmer of the night I no longer thought of the Elbe, or the Russians, or Italy, but only of the little girl lying in the middle of that meadow, and I would have liked to go back and be with those poor lost people who were keeping watch over her.

I walked for many hours. It was a misty night, but perhaps high up above there was the moon casting a faint but even light through those low vapours and making all shapes look mysterious in the deep silence. As my refugee had warned me, I saw little but the outline of some distant cottage but no sign of life. I often heard the sound of running water and the floods were up in some of the fields I crossed. At first I had carefully chosen my way, knowing that if my shoes got soaking wet it would be a great nuisance; but now I could not pick and choose because everything depended on my being able to hold out those ten or twelve hours. So I forced my pace, intent only on not losing my sense of direction which was difficult in that ghostly gloom, and trying to drown my thoughts so as to concentrate on the continual questions that arose from the necessity of choice. Every strip of ground I covered was a small victory contributing to the total victory; at every doubtful point I paused for a moment; tested my muscles; stroked my wound which was hurting again, but from the sharp pain of the cut, so as to ease this away; concentrated on 'sensing' whether to go to the right or the left; then set off again. On some stretches I think I almost fell asleep and found myself on that interminable walk over the Krano mountains, and had a sensation of safety because of having that little shepherd to guide me; and into that dream there entered the other pilgrimage to the All-powerful Virgin of Licudi, which also had merged me with the common people. Then I shivered with cold, and when the darkness cleared a little I thought it was the dawn – until I realised it was only a thinning-out of the mist letting in more light. I now dimly made out a large stretch of deserted countryside in front of me, with, in the distance, a sort of thick homogeneous wall, as if a cloud were resting on the ground. I told myself it was a river, but when I got there down the slope I found I was in a marshy wood; yet water was flowing near, wide and dark; and through the rolling mist I discerned a dark low-lying shape. I realised I was on the bank of an obviously impassable waterway, and the shape was that of a barge at anchor.

Between the Oder and the Elbe there is a network of canals cutting across rivers, lakes and pools, and navigable for hundreds of kilometres; and that captain without a foot in the hospital at Berg had been wounded on the quays of Dessau. This barge, like those on the Rhine, served as a house for the river-men who plied the small coasting-trade; I would have to take the risk; but I had not even had time to shout when a huge dog leapt at me out of the blue and bit my thigh. I reeled back, tripped and fell. I now thought he would make for my throat, but I suddenly saw him rearing up on his hind legs, barking furiously, but unable to reach me because of a restraining hand on his collar. A man with a lantern had appeared from the boat, and now looked me over. '*Gefangen Offizier! Verwundet!*' I said, still lying on the ground. He had a think, then quietened the dog and went back to the boat, where I heard him talking in undertones with a woman. At last he came ashore again, helped me to get up and took me on board. Blood was pouring from my bite. A worried-looking young woman was in the cabin, but she put down her baby and helped me to bandage myself as well as possible, while the man looked on, frowning.

Owing to the behaviour of ex-prisoners throughout the country, not much could be expected from these Germans, torn as they were between hate and fear. These two had hidden themselves in a lonely place among impassable marshes, and it just happened that I had chanced on them.

'The Russians are coming!' I said, summing up in a phrase my position and intentions. And the woman immediately muttered some sentences to him, pointing to the baby. So they intended to cross the Elbe for the same reason as me. It was lucky for both of us; the man had a young wife and a boat, both very dangerous possessions in a region teeming with outlaws. He had found someone to help him, and someone in such poor condition that though he could perhaps use me he had no cause to fear me. So my misfortunes were still my best defence. I would get across because on the practical level I was worth almost nothing.

He weighed anchor almost immediately. He knew that waterway network like the back of his hand, and though keeping well away from the banks, he halted now and then in some inlet, so as to listen, or turned aside over shallower waters so that I heard the scraping of the keel on the river-bed. With dawn the mist grew thicker and it was impossible to make out the mysterious thread by which he got his orientations. I realised that a third person had been absolutely indispensable for him, for he depended on poles and grapnels for his progress much more than his modest engine. Once the sun was high he again got under cover in a thick growth of reeds and gave me to understand we would wait there till nightfall.

To say I was utterly drained would be an understatement. It was five days since I had eaten anything hot. My leg had been stiff since the dog's bite (he was now stretched out on the prow without seeming to remember anything about it) yet I had had to use it for hours on end in steering the boat. In those very hours Berlin had fallen and Hitler was dead, having called down a hundred thousand devils on the West and impervious behind his last ditch. But we were not aware that that dark shadow had withdrawn from the earth, hidden as we were in our marsh, our huntsman's paradise, the innocent retreat of frogs and dragon-flies. There was a chorus of croaking when finally we weighed anchor beneath a delicate crescent moon. And it was under the discreet eyes of the moon, in a landscape of uncertain light and romantic shadows, and in the silence of a deep peace undisturbed by men, that I crossed the Elbe that night.

'What is a wise man?' I found myself asking myself while enjoying the last rays of benevolent sunshine lingering on my bunk. The bunk was enclosed within a low alcove scooped out of the wall, and the setting sun cast its rays on a crowded array of brightly coloured holy pictures fixed to the back wall which was also adorned with all sorts of fanciful paper decorations; and the curtains around the alcove were a real feast of colour. Two memories crept almost imperceptibly into my mind: the way Téolo used piously to pull his curtains when he said his prayers, and the last rays of the setting sun on Marchese Lerici's penthouse window.

'What does "knowing" mean?' I asked next, as I looked obliquely through the small deep-set window from which I could see the heaped remains of the pillaging that had been going on for the last two weeks: a slow fire in the square burning at its own sweet will but now reduced to a single scab of dried filth. Every now and then someone came and stirred the mass of decay with a pitchfork, and a nauseous cloud of black smoke was let loose.

'A philosopher?' I asked myself, going on with my soliloquy. 'A down-at-heel old man who talks to you about good and evil and perhaps about God. But he doesn't even know what a child is really, if he's never had one, never brought one up, never loved one or lost one.'

'An intellectual?' Even my Rolphe looked on himself as that, and the others would have accepted his judgement. Yet he hadn't managed to find the key to anything and was as tangled up in his arguments as a fly in a spider's web; incapable of standing up to the spectacle of death, or of saving himself from what he so dreaded. And what does an intellectual's knowledge imply? Knowing the names of things but not knowing the things themselves? Of course he knows what it means to 'flee on foot'. But if he hasn't walked for six days, with fifteen hours at a stretch on the sixth, and hasn't felt at his back the people on whom his very life may depend, then he understands the concept behind those words but nothing at all of the reality. And how about hunger? – especially if he always insists on having his egg mayonnaise, like Omobono. And what about wounds – if the only blood he has shed is from his nose at school? Thus some did the living and others did the theorising. The two currents evolved separately and hardly ever merged. For obvious reasons a judge knew nothing about murder; and one half of the world contended with the other half, wanting to enclose within words the absolute force of facts.

Tecla came in, the boatman's wife, holding her baby in one arm and bringing me a bowl of soup with the other. Eight days had passed. The Russians and the Americans had not wanted to fight each other after all and, by all accounts, had met at Torgau with mutual congratulations and thereafter had withdrawn to their respective banks. Patrols passed swiftly from one side of the river to the other rejoicing in their victory – even though there were a few dead in the process. Perhaps the war really was over. In view of the fact that many people had reasons for crossing from one side to the other, Tecla's husband had found a couple of partners – not Germans, but strong this time – and an excellent machine-gun from the army, and in association with a Russian lieutenant on the opposite bank, was tacking back and forth across the Elbe. It was dangerous work, but he must have made a lot of money. In theory Tecla had been entrusted to me; but facts, incontrovertible facts, arranged it that I depended absolutely on her.

That heap of muck on the mud of the square! Sometimes there was such a mountain of fresh rejects that the fire reached as high as a first floor, and I had the unbreathable smoke all around me for a couple of days as it slowly decomposed and fell in and burnt down to a height only two feet from the ground. Then from the filthy mess there emerged a little iron bedstead which would not burn and had stayed there at the bottom for weeks – revealed by the low tide and then again submerged, to appear again thirty or forty hours later, each time blacker and more eroded, a symbolic relic of that enormous shipwreck. It was a child's bedstead over which who knew how many times a text-book mother had bent to kiss her good little son goodnight? Where was the little boy now, and the mother, and the school satchel? And whoever thought of saying good morning or good night to anybody now?

Situated a little to the north of the point where the Ohre joins the Elbe, and far from any centres of habitation, this strange human conglomeration where my march towards the West had ended up was managed in conformity with the strictest piratical traditions. A row of sheds outside a large walled factory housed a mass of about five hundred men of all races vowed to robbery and plunder; while a resolute band of two or three hundred women occupied the enclosure – a paradoxical gynaeceum whose one gate they guarded even more fiercely than the Amazons of old. It was Tecla who had obtained me my place within the walls, using a ferry-crossing or two as bargaining stakes, though I think it was my obvious weakness that really won the day. My cubby-hole had previously been occupied by a Serbian girl, and she it was who had left me all those decorations, the holy pictures and the little paper curtains. I was the only male element in the stronghold; and when she left the Serbian girl paid her respects with a hint of piety, as if I had become part of her little shrine; and all under Tecla's neutral but vigilant eye.

With the relaxation of the tension that had sustained me over the last period I barely had the strength even to lie down. The unknowable power (to which Demetrio denied the name of Chance) had measured out its doses of trials and aids with such judicious parsimony that it deserved a round of applause. When things in the *Lager* were at their worst, then the devout Téolo's parcels had arrived; when loading the coal was at its worst, Herr Kurt had come to my rescue with that merry saw; at the worse than worst moment, after Berg had been smashed to pieces, Lore's bowls of soup up in Kate's little room had given me just enough strength to survive the final saraband; and even at that I would not have got by without the deserters' belongings found in the truck; without the refugee-become-surgeon; and – the most recent incarnation of Providence –

without Tecla. I was certain now that she was setting me up for some further ordeal. No one in that place seemed to be interested in looking for contacts with regular organisations, whatever they might be, and Tecla's husband less than anyone, for he depended on that conglomeration of bandits – excellent clients for him; the worst possible neighbours for me.

According to the Latin learnt at my school, 'I pondered within myself' – and pondered the same thoughts, I believe, as an early nineteenth-century explorer, wounded in a savannah and looked after for a while by a Congolese tribe. My people here were nearly all Slavs or from the Balkans and they, too, lived by hunting, for every morning they set off over the countryside and every evening came back with what they had plundered. News reached the encampment immediately from any point on the horizon, and the flight of the vultures started. They had carts and sleighs at their disposal; they ganged up together for particular raids and then dispersed again; they tore one another to pieces for the division of the loot; they filled their lair for a while with mattresses, carpets, linen, poultry, which all immediately rotted in the general filth. After a few days a thick sediment of mud, frills, feathers, skins, broken china, bones and human excrement covered the floor of the huts. If one group decided to move off, then its successor cleaned things up with pitchforks and the whole lot ended up on the smouldering heap in the middle of the square, while the new inhabitants started to behave exactly like their predecessors.

Those people had a way of stealing an ox or a horse, and slaughtering it, though without the slightest possibility of conserving what they would not be able to eat yet not wanting to give it away. Sometimes Tecla brought me a piece of roast meat, but so burnt that it was impossible to eat, so I cut it up into tiny pieces with a penknife and swallowed it like pills. Once from my little window I saw six or seven people skinning a pig of over 200 pounds, eating a tenth part of it and throwing away the rest. As for the supplies of food for the regiment of women, this just happened according to nature: though the men were excluded in a draconian way from the enclosure, they nevertheless came with their offerings as if to a sanctuary. Of course they had a few women with them in the horde, but very few, for the women preferred to be together, even if they had come from a penitentiary, a rehabilitation camp, or forced labour. And there were women of every quality and condition:

women still decked in a remnant of fur; Ukrainian viragos who were stronger than a man; consumptives in the last stages lying inert on their bunks; mothers with children; disguised collaborators; the impure of every origin. They could be heard quarrelling, crying, swearing; yet mine was not the only niche decorated with pictures of saints; indeed, the female chaos was as moving as the male chaos was repulsive. Some of the women, still young, who had been through tragic experiences, affected arrogance and aggression and sang coarse songs; but prayers could be heard too; and many of them were just silent and kept themselves apart: so much so that I thought they must be like me.

Conversations with Tecla were necessarily of a basic character and consisted of signs rather than words. She was perhaps about twenty-five; a flat, unemotional type, though there was a rather animal-like intensity in her pale eyes. I did not understand her thoughts although I lived for the most part entirely by her help. The baby she was always carrying was pretty, and sometimes she let me hold him for a short while – and in so doing displayed unlimited trust. I enjoyed playing with that baby as he crawled around on my blanket; and when his charming little ways made me forget the train of my thoughts I managed to persuade myself that there was nothing better in the world that I could do.

Often other women came to put their heads round the opening to my cubby-hole, and they looked at me with a thousand different expressions, then went away gossiping and laughing. They seemed to enjoy looking on me as the protégé and perhaps even the mascot of their strange brigade. Sometimes Tecla brought someone in purposely to visit me – doing so with a hint of ceremonial, perhaps feeling that she should do the honours of who knows what ancestral cult. It is possible that such things have happened in other places and at other times, as matriarchy is as old as the world. My favourite among these visitors were two Jewesses of the cultured classes who knew a little English. They kept me informed of events.

The war in Europe was certainly finished; but it seemed as though nothing had taken its place, as though confusion and uncertainty were still reigning; the vast dust-cloud of collapse, deafness and blindness following on a measureless deflagration. Without it seeming so, the moralists of the Pentagon left things so that a further decreed punishment should be played out on Germany: the punishment of leaving her defenceless at the mercy of millions of foreigners who had formerly suffered slavery there. The occupying troops touched nothing of German possessions, contenting themselves with machine-gunning the radiators of agricultural tractors, cars and other machines, perhaps out of a simple dislike of their trade-marks. But they let everything be looted and destroyed by the foreigners. In this way, too, they had their pretext for rounding them up, when this was necessary; but for the time being the combing of the country areas was proceeding very slowly. Here and there they put up road-blocks to halt the wandering bands and take them in convoy to assembly centres; but they did not keep guard over them and any who wanted to could easily escape and go back to robbery. The troops carried out various manhunts: against the SS who, as they were branded under their armpits, could hardly evade identification; against Nazi criminals; and against individual enemies. The Germans of the defeated and disbanded armies were all just trying to get back to their homes, separately, usually through the woods. This was happening all over the Reich, and as many were armed their rancour against their victors made them dangerous. The two Jewesses advised me to wait in patience until the Allies decided to clean up our encampment. We only had to wait for them, without trying to seek them out. I held Tecla's baby in my arms, trying to hold him in exactly the same position and attitude as I had usually seen his mother adopt; and he played with my chin with his little hands. That contact was of an indescribable sweetness and was almost enough to compensate for my misfortunes and even my wounds.

'This morning,' one of the two women said, 'Leitz was sacked. The people had received orders to evacuate the village within two hours as it was requisitioned for troops in transit. So the Germans had their suitcases prepared, but these were all left in a row on their doorsteps because they were bundled on to the lorries without being allowed to take luggage. But our people from here got there before the troops arrived. Leitz is fairly big; our people couldn't carry off thirty or forty cottages, farms and houses full of stuff. Even the suitcases were a bit much. So they threw everything out of the windows: thousands of plates, glasses, lamps, furniture, pictures. And all the ripped-open mattresses shed their feathers as they fell so that it was like walking in a snowstorm. Hilda told me all about it; she was there.'

This woman had the pure type of Jewish beauty – a perfectly

oval face, an ivory complexion and heavy very black hair. The other, the one who had been at Leitz, had a pair of lively green eyes and a sardonic turn to her lips which, when she laughed, revealed teeth that seemed to want to bite. Her extraordinary overcoat, hanging in folds around her, emphasised her astonishing thinness, and her nerves were as taut as a hungry cat's; she was rocking backwards and forwards on her chair with an expression of savage bliss on her face.

I listened without saying much. I did not ask them about their previous lives nor how they had landed up on the same bank as myself; and I did not want to know what they had been before; just as we do not ask the dust of ruins what sand and what sea it came from, now that what it first went to build has been swept away in the flux of time. From below I could hear the looters quarrelling over the division of their booty; and the crackling of the fire which was very high again now. Again the little iron bedstead had been submerged: a strange root – but perhaps only of my thoughts.

Tecla came to fetch her baby. I was left alone with my two Jewesses who now fell silent. Once the brief animation of their story had died down, their faces seemed to me completely empty: inert remains, worn away to nothingness. For centuries the wailing wall in Jerusalem has been maintained, a grey blind wall, a final barrier where you could only stop, all thoughts drowned, all hope abandoned. Where all you could do was wail, then as now.

Standing in the very place where Magaldi and I had sat like beggars about three months before, I tried to take in what had happened to that quiet residential area in the suburbs of Uelzen where Doctor Aesckloni had lived.

Only half of his villa remained, though this included the door which was still in good condition, and closed. In the half that had been destroyed I could just make out the ladies' cloakroom where the surgeon had made his preliminary examination – it was recognisable by a few surviving tiles. The other houses scattered among the trees had undergone the same fate. A dust-laden silence weighed heavily over the place, and the summer sun beat down oppressively on that wilderness. In the distance I could still just hear the jeep that had brought me as far as the square, put me down, and then moved off again too soon.

The women had bade me farewell with cries and protests while I was helped down the steps by Tecla of whose animal warmth, so strong and close, I was very much aware; I had thanked her and kissed the baby – still in her arms as if he were part of her body. The pirates' encampment had been evacuated. Gigantic bulldozers manned by Negroes had razed everything to the ground – huts, furniture (such as it was), rubble. The spectral iron bedstead had gone down like a piece of straw and now lay buried deep in the earth.

The door of Aesckloni's house opened unexpectedly and a man came out. I called to him sharply. At that time it was difficult to establish who was in authority. He looked at me uncertainly for a moment but then gave way.

'Unfortunately Doctor Aesckloni is dead,' he said in English after he had read my papers. 'Unknown people attacked and set fire to the house. The doctor had his little girl with him and was hit in the forehead while protecting her. It could have happened because of the doctor's political background. There's been a lot of trouble.'

He had mastered the use of that invaluable word 'trouble' whose significance only the English understand, as it can refer to bloodshed and rebellion as much as to a broken tea-cup.

'And what about the clinic?' I asked.

'It's out of commission at the moment. I am Doctor Gann, Aesckloni's first assistant. I myself am working at a military hospital. That's where you should go, but I can't come with you. All our cars have been destroyed or requisitioned.'

'Does anyone still live in the house?'

'The widow,' Gann replied with deliberate impassivity. 'And a British officer who, it appears, is very demanding at night.'

Another month dragged by while I went from one hospital to another, from one camp to another. The July heat beat relentlessly down on the ruins marked with crosses in coal or chalk. The immense body of Germany lay with its face in the dust. Yet another month, and the atomic bomb was to wipe out Hiroshima. The High Command gave no consideration to the place accorded to charity in St Paul's first epistle to the Corinthians; and they intended to solve the measureless enigma of the war by listening to the lawyers' harangues at Nuremberg.

On the eve of repatriation at the beginning of August I nearly tripped over Captain Ceci in the assembly camp of Garmisch.

'Thanks be to God!' he said. 'I've been thinking so much about you!'

Ceci was fine, with a good colour on his dry skin and an almost new uniform resplendent with his epaulettes, the ribbons of his campaigns and the *croix de guerre*. Many things had happened at Berg which he would rather not have told me and I would rather not have heard. *Bersagliere* Penne had landed up in prison owing to obscure dealings between him, Kate and a couple of Americans who had appeared on the scene. Magaldi, who had graduated at Harvard, found himself promoted overnight to the position of right-hand-man of the American Command and with quite considerable power in his hands. That university freemasonry! He had shown himself merciless towards the Germans, Ceci said.

'And what about Herr Kurt?'

'They say he's in a concentration camp for Nazis. He would have got out of it if Magaldi hadn't denounced him. And then,' Ceci went on, very reluctantly now, 'his wife had to pay the price too. She had to follow him, dragging the boy after her. I didn't like it at all. I didn't like it for your sake. And finally,' he concluded, taking a smart leather wallet from an inner pocket and tipping a coin into his hand, 'and finally, here's your gold sovereign. I knew it was in your jacket so I salvaged it for you. I'm so delighted to be able to give it back to you at last!'

I had arrived at Garmisch from a camp at Harburg, together with three thousand other officers who had been assembled in the former barracks of the tank corps, one of the only buildings left standing in an urban conglomeration that had been razed to the ground for over four kilometres. The Allies intended making use of it later. There was also a large factory still standing, together with its fine surrounding wall. They said it had been built with British capital. When the British airmen, for once on foot, arrived at that nightmare scene they demonstrated their characteristic phlegm by saying in mild astonishment: 'We didn't realise we'd achieved results like this!' The Harburg camp was among the first to be evacuated because serious fighting broke out between the foreigners installed there and the German soldiers who had got back to their homes round about – there were not only many wounded but even a few dead. The German railways had of course been devastated as if by an earthquake, but with quiet determination and a tremendous effort the Germans got a part of them sufficiently operative to transport back to their frontiers those millions of invaders who were laying waste to the little of Germany that remained. So by means of a maze of railway tracks that wandered capriciously for hundreds of miles to cover a distance a fifth of that length as the crow flies, we slowly made our way towards our homeland. To many the endlessness of the journey was a crowning frustration and they were a prey to anxieties of every kind. But for me those days seemed like a safe shore that was leading me back to a life I would understand better; and I would have liked them to have lasted longer so as to savour them to the full and prepare myself better for what lay ahead.

I now realised that it was true, and I had already heard Paolo Grilli say it in his flat in Rome: mankind had persistently blamed the Evil One for what was really the preserve of human nature; only human nature was capable of defiling creation, of denying it and blaspheming against it instead of singing its praises. And it was pride – in virtue of a potency derived from the Creator himself – it was pride to usurp his powers, to overstep the limitations of the species, and replace the solemn rhythms of common living, of things, plants, animals, souls, with a violent game of lawless tyrannies and undisciplined impulses from which only perversity and unhappiness could spring. Animals were harassed and their species extinguished in the process; all growing things were exploited or uprooted; the earth itself was treated with contempt. Would not Eternity – compared with which the millennia were but infinitesimal fractions – would not Eternity wipe us out as some kind of vicious deviation from its changeless order? Then the rivers would invade the plains and give back their ancestral homes to the myriads of insects and reptiles and amphibians; the mountains would again be covered with woods to regulate the falling of the rain; and the circulation of the air, brought back to normal by the free interplay of the currents, would revivify the earth. Then the myriad of events that take place between birth and death, having recovered their balance in the equipoise of the whole, would pursue their course without even a suspicion of Evil.

And yet (as Descartes's syllogism reminded me), no awareness, no history. For both the inescapable price lay in our human drama. The fortune of a Vanderbilt was not enough to pay for my night outside Berlin, and my wounds were a minimal diminishment for all I had learnt and understood through their agency. When Nerina died I felt I had exhausted my capacity for suffering, burnt out my share of punishment here below; that was why I was still alive when Arrichetta, too, had to leave me; that was why I wandered about for years thinking that the world could offer me no other kind of love. But so far I had only looked at myself; and now I realised that what I had expected from dedication could come from renouncement; that where affection had not succeeded in binding me, suffering had succeeded; and that what had not been identified or sanctified in one single name had countless names. Denise, Demetrio, Albertina, just as much as Zagara and Niko; Pannuzzo, Téolo, Theodora; and Spiropulos; and all the others, all the others. I had felt a catch in my throat when I saw the silent group of the Kurts standing on the doorstep of their (and my) home and watched them fading into the distance, and also when Frau Haendel's blood had trickled through my fingers; nor could I forget Rolphe's ravaged face and his white hair rising over that grotesque mask of dust. All these, together with the dead child in the meadow, and Aesckloni who had died with his little daughter in his arms, and Tecla, just recently, instinctive and warm like a servant in an inn – all these had been my brothers and my sisters. That account which had been closed at least ten times where individuals were concerned, had now been boundlessly reopened to include anyone, everyone, in a circle as large as mankind. And as for Evil, I was going back to render my account to Uncle Gedeone. I felt that even if I stood as a miserable beggar before a closed door, the fact that I had said no to it was enough to conquer it entirely. I knew that (as the ancient Poet saw it) the Divinity who rules the world had assented to my infinitesimal but bold refusal. He had sustained me in the interests of what he had reposed in me and entrusted to me. And he was leading me back so that I could bear witness to it.

On our way we met troop-trains of disarmed Germans coming down from North Italy – so full that the men were crouching on the engines. And they were finding their country torn to shreds by the same acts of violence as they had used on the countries of others. And when we had passed the Brenner, and civilians and workmen mixed with us, we in our turn heard their stories; and when we saw the gaping wounds in our lovely cities and knew how blood had been spilt without law or pity, by all, against all, from the Fosse Ardeatine in Rome to the piazza Loreto in Milan, I was overcome with shame.

There were countless women gathered all along the railway lines. They were shouting the names of their men, showing their photographs, and asking, asking. Others were scrutinising our faces, one by one. Or else they were lost and silent, not seeing.

And tears, blessed tears, gushed forth without pause, passed on from one group to the next, the matchless rosary prayed in hope. And I answered them in my heart, as in my childhood, when I answered one praise in the litany by another.

THE BUTTERFLIES

The fires of the war had left in the air a bright dust, slow to be extinguished and to fall, which still deceived the gaze and the imagination, a mineral ash good for fertilising new grass in due course, but itself destined to vanish. Between the last months of 1945 and the following spring Rome was a dazzle of will-o'-the-wisps, a coloured rain of particles, an ephemeral magic produced with mere dross. And the self-centred and majestic city, heavy with its splendour and its marbles, was beautiful, vibrating and echoing in its whirling phosphorescence, confetti glittering in a night of inspiration in a stone labyrinth.

The capital had suffered only slightly, though injuries to its appearance were taken seriously; and one peculiarity of those who had lived through the cinematic - and eventually filmed - times of the 'Open City' was the gloomy story they told of it to those who came out of the war. But then everybody was too obsessed by their own affairs to have ears for those of others. Italy freed itself from the past through the soliloquies of millions of individuals who all recited together. And since in story-telling the truth is distorted, a little for convenience and a lot because of the play of the imagination, these millions of stories whelmed the facts in an impenetrable fog, utterly unsuited to any act of collective conscience, which therefore never took place.

That vast prattling, and the city swarming with refugees, survivors and adventurers, frothed like yeast in numberless groups, in wine shops, in studios, on steps, under gates, in cafés, in offices. Italy had lost the war, it was true, and with it nearly a century of effort, but for whoever had survived the storm, his personal war had not been lost; and one saw therefore not discouragement, but optimism and the resolution to seize opportunities. When the play was acted, the history, as has been said, was all farce. Wild passions, first held in by fear and then loosed in the final fury, seemed attenuated by the pleasant pause. The simple delight in finding tobacco, coffee, white bread, salame and cakes of soap, neutralised evil humours. The politicians, swaying in the breeze like spiders, looked for their first reliable supports for new webs.

The anti-fascists and political exiles imposed a certain tension as they descended upon the country which, since it had been ruined by the other lot, they imagined now belonged to them. In fact they hadn't saved it; and it did little good to say 'we told you so' all the time. They went around looking ill with liver complaints, and not attending the banquets where the speeches upset the digestions of the healthiest. The heavy battalion of bores (with the regime, responsible for our sea of troubles) which had sucked the country dry for a good twenty years, now camouflaged itself completely; none of its members who had once been so authoritative came to the fore, and they all scattered to different regions. Great generals and officials, magistrates, prefects, councillors, directors of all kinds and degrees, were silent and hid like bedbugs–except that you couldn't even smell them. For an expertly calculated interval, the people were left to speak for themselves, it being known perfectly well that it would be their fate sooner or later to hand the seats of power back to their primordial occupants. The law of specific gravity, unalterable for individuals after a social earthquake as for particles in a solution, would soon show itself to the advantage of the well-to-do.

In such a volatile atmosphere formalities were derided, starting with those of dress, and one saw people decked out in the oddest styles, men with studiedly careless wartime coats, women hardly recognisable at a distance for the coloured scarves in their hair. Those who had not been to the war suffered in their threadbare suits, marked like deserters. For a short while, long enough for the colourful dust to be reabsorbed into the earth, the solemn minds from universities and academies were replaced by those not trained with books at all (which anyway could be had for nothing on the stalls in Campo dei Fiori) who settled to prepare the coming of Any Man, the hero of the immediate future. The national vices of pomposity and bombast became laughable; everyone used the familiar form of address the first time they met and drank cheerfully from the same jug. Cars were rare. Houses were perishingly cold. The streets were crammed with people looking for real or psychological warmth.

If there were innumerable displaced men, there were more scattered and therefore single women. A busy cloud of bees, and sometimes of wasps, searching relentlessly for a new hive, fluttered and murmured from the furthest corners of the city up to the ceilings even of ministries. If instinct enables couples to find each other in the dark immensity of the oceans, inexplicable magnetic forces passed through the walls and spaces of the capital to arrange meetings. The flood of humanity, swept beyond its accustomed sphere by the conflict, naturally tended to resettle itself. Like called to like with invisible antennae, and came together. The first layer of the social structure, which consists of couples, formed the base of the whole edifice, after clearing the ground of the ruins that remained. Occasional ties were dissolved, for the pressure of circumstances imposed the definite and the secure. Love affairs at the point of decay and at the point of fruition filled the city with whispers, tears, promises and lies. Behind this enticing veil the cast-iron desire of women to re-establish households started putting the country back on its feet.

The foreigners, our victors, who still held almost all power through their network of command, the Anglo-Saxon industrialists, the bankers and privileged managers of currencies and of trade, the Swiss who at last succeeded in getting a look at the remains of a tragedy of which they had heard only the awful rumours, stared in astonishment at the euphoria of the defeated crowned with roses, rich in all the good things of life, alive with hope and free from the slightest regret. That irrepressible Italian life, which is to the lives of other peoples what flying is to walking, reasserted itself with a kind of ironical challenge. The English, strangled by their moral seriousness, mortified by the countless obligations of an unnerving triumph, brooded indignantly, and Rome smiled at them. The weaker spirits found themselves unable to practise much austerity, and there was vast collusion between the victors and the vanquished. Finally, what of the people?

Bureaucracy was hardly getting under way again, criminal law had some slight authority but civil law none whatsoever; and so the three classic enemies of the Italian, I mean the administrations of city, province and state, left people in peace to concentrate on returning to normality. There was great relief among the multitude dedicated, between the pleasures of eating and drinking, to sorting out on the pavement the debris of the general shipwreck. It was the *finale d'orchestra* or a Roman sunset; there was much delighted sarcasm; and it was found that everything spoiled or dishonoured or stolen, while waiting for new walls, new peace, new owners, could be accounted for by the same reference to so-called historic moments.

How different from musings on the highest terrace of the Hotel Colonna in wistaria time! This was *andante*, *fugue*, *cantabile* and *cabaletta* in a full symphony directed by some fleeting spirit then fluttering in the zenith. The river of humanity along the Corso swelled. From hundreds of wine shops and restaurants the soliloquies were taken up. The immeasurable reality which had overwhelmed those millions of existences broke up into infinitesimal splinters luminous with minute but piercing reflections in each one. There was as it were a pause in the music before the emergence of the main theme; and the probable protagonists of a scene already in preparation used low words and gentle looks and gestures, kept their plans secret and hid their weapons.

Bunched around their fat Margutta, a nasty piece of work, the artists of the moment swarm like coloured fish in tropical water. At every other table would be sitting a sly and eager American magnate ready to fly examples of the marvellous reborn Italian to Miami or Honolulu in his private aeroplane. The lodgings of the elect were usually wretched, serving at once as studio, living quarters for oneself and one's friends, and as a deposit for dubious merchandise. Few works of art were produced; nor were they all acclaimed as masterpieces, as later became normal, the more so since almost no one found it convenient to have a past. But they showed themselves as new men, replacing the New Man invented by Margherita Sarfatti who was so old he was the first to die. These painters and sculptors were for the most part provincials or immigrants, their women circus riders, their speeches Catherine wheels from Calabrian festivities. Among partisans, among petty politicians, among swindlers, among the unknown, they enlivened the Roman nights.

Such was Rome at that time, an immense auditorium of dead stone were millions of the newly born played with ephemeral Bengal lights.

'Why were you not born Greek, Giuliano, in the good days of the Sicilian expedition more than two thousand years ago? You'd have missed nothing, not a siege, in order to prove everyone wrong. Under the Terror you'd have been with the nobility, but only at the guillotine. Now you run down the Savoys, but it'd be the same if they were Wittelsbach or Comneno. You say the aristocracy are no good any more. The leftists give you stomach-ache. The middle classes are timid and treacherous. The common people are hopeless till they transform themselves into one or other of the above, at which point they get worse. In June you'll vote, perhaps, and for the republic too, but what'll it mean to you? Less than nothing, I reckon.'

Swathed in the folds of a blue cavalry cloak, though one cut for a dragoon nearly two metres tall, Memé Arquà challenged me with his eyes while still somehow seeming nervous of my answer. The room was freezing. There was nothing for one's comfort, no cushions, no carpets, no lamps. There being no curtains, we could see the secluded, haughty trees of villa Savoia, and suffered the icy light of the white December sky.

Michelino had not changed much in the sixteen years since I had left him in the regiment in the old days of Padua and the horse called Ursano. Then he had been a sublieutenant like me, an easygoing yet troubled exile, and there had been superficial familiarity between us. I found him again after something-or-other he had been doing in the Resistance; he was on the personal secretariat of the premier, Parri; physically hardly changed, exactly the same in his manner, intellectually restless but eager. So he at thirty-seven and I at forty-two found ourselves before the *tabula rasa* of a future to be entirely remade. This was so habitual for me that it made me feel positively secure, but it seemed to make him more anxious.

'Any form of politics might work,' I answered without raising my voice, 'but only in time and with the right people. How will a republic get on in a country given so tenaciously to privacy? And communism, in the classic land of civilised individualism? A republican and communist Italy will perpetuate old uncertainties and produce new ones. And if you say I like nothing – in a rough sea, which of the waves around you would *you* choose?'

Arquà shifted on the uncomfortable mock-rococo chair, trying not to lose warmth.

'One can't discuss these things messing up politics and imagination. You only throw doubts in my path, you're no help at all.'

Coming up to the referendum, the republicans and monarchists made their polemics more savage every day, perhaps thus to disguise the unspeakable ills suffered by the country. The Savoys themselves were beyond help; with pitiable ideas, shabby administration, vulgar habits and dubious faith, they were so far from representing any notion of regality that the cardinal error of the monarchists was not to ditch them. If they had done so the monarchy might have been saved, for the majority of Italians appreciated it if not politically then for its romance and pageantry. But it was impossible with a royal family which had shown none of the looked-for courage or abnegation or honour. But wouldn't it be a new leap in the dark to alter our institutions, which were essentially abstract, on account of circumstances which though they were disappointing were only of the moment?

'Italy,' I went on, making him shudder, for he suffered physiologically from others' mistrust, 'Italy, Memé, loves muddled ideas. Catholicism is not only a creed, it's an attitude to life, a way of understanding life. The monarchy is less an institution than the synthesis of an ideal grandeur; with the aristocracy, it represents dimly recollected glories. Appearances notwithstanding, the Italians are all Catholics to the marrow and have been monarchists with all their hearts for centuries; and the two went hand in hand splendidly till 1860. Then things went badly wrong. Those Piedmontese kings didn't understand that Rome too was worth a mass; but the Neapolitan Bourbons understood it, and did better giving up their kingdom then than these are doing losing theirs now.'

'I've warmed up,' Memé said kindly, 'you can have the cloak now.'

'Mussolini tried to put the country together again, and the people shouted: "*Duce*, you're all of us!" He was a socialist and he espoused first the king and then the pope – the devil and the holy water! – but behind him, despite their black shirts, the people remained monarchists and Catholics all through those twenty years. During the war they scrapped the regime, but looking to the pope for help and with hopes of the king. Is this pure imagination?'

Instead of replying, Memé shut his eyes and pulled the cloak up over his nose.

'The clergy, by arrangement exempt from military service, after five years spent piously invoking peace, having mourned the destruction of fascism now look to the republic to destroy the king. What can they say, seeing their arch-enemies the communists desiring the same thing? Such a republic will give rise to governments not dreamed of in the *Metamorphoses*. Have we got to slit our throats for this?'

'Sansevero, Sansevero!' shouted Arquà, wriggling as if icy drops were trickling down his neck. 'You must start all over again. I beg you to read and to reflect upon Chuang Tzu. You must humbly place your talents at the service of the Good Cause.'

He was, among other things, a student of Chinese. Bizarre sheets of paper covered with minutely coloured characters were pinned here and there to the walls of his room. Memé pretended to attribute magical powers of these sheets, and in passing would sketch a bow in front of one of them.

I kept the rest to myself. The only united, coherent group of the aristocracy were the two thousand Roman nobility faithful to the papacy. It was evident that none of them had put forward a new name to replace the discredited Savoys. The monarchy therefore even as an insitution was condemned by the Vatican. The monsignors were looking to the distant future, certainly far beyond our lifetimes.

'Memé,' I concluded, 'in the *Stube* in Poland it wasn't as cold as it is here. Let's go to via della Croce to hear what the others have to say and have a glass of white wine.'

Having an American mother, and being quite unlike Paolo Grilli, Arquà based his behaviour on the beginning of the constitution of the United States - which he likened to the Book of Genesis - and put his flat in via Panama at the disposal of every shipwrecked sailor who floated alongside. This had an instant effect in a city swarming with people without lodgings and without money, and after only a month he could hardly defend his little room and his Chinese scripts from the friendliness of his guests. Outstanding among these were the lieutenant of the cuirassiers, Max, a noble Roman of mighty physique and the owner of the blue cloak which served everybody on occasion as heater, dressing-gown or bed-cover; Tommy, a Romanian Jew who had already hidden more than a year in the Vatican while waiting to settle in South Africa; the paratrooper Belgarbo, of perfect health and primitive intellect, and his sluggish but Junoesque model. Three flights down, below ground level, through Tommy's intercession groups of Slavs followed each other by turn, with whom he kept us on polite terms. A woman of uncertain status kept an eye on everything and, by organising an early-morning collection, offered a daily meal which truth to tell was more or less symbolic but which had a certain style. In recompense the kitchen was always presided over by naval telegraphists from the ministry, and they perhaps found things to eat.

In Rome I had to attend the appropriate clinic for repeated operations on my fractured jaw so painful it was hard at times to find the courage to submit myself to the implements, and in an atmosphere made macabre by others worse disfigured and tormented than myself. Sometimes luxuries such as cigarettes or condensed milk would arrive from the prime minister's office.

'How did you manage to find me in this hell-hole, Memé?'

'One of the doctors happened to mention "that cavalry captain".'

I accepted Arquà's offerings because the war, without really touching my inheritance, had still managed to leave me temporarily penniless. Licudi was still in military hands. My Calabrian bailiffs all too faithfully paid the land's profits into the bank only for the devaluation to wipe out four years' work for them and savings for me.

The woods of Acerenza were safe because they were so remote, and must remain so. In the house in via Panama I shared a room with a Lombard count left over from the struggles of the partisans, thin and quiet, commissioned for the time being to sell at any price a farm near Rome Memé owned but had never seen.

It was a fairly large house which had been despoiled during the German occupation, and here at the beginning of the war Arquà's American mother had died on her own. The same happened to my mother Annina who died in a remote village in the Abruzzo in the winter of 1943. I was in Greece at the time, and Memé was tied up in clandestine activities in Milan or Bologna. It seemed he had not actually fought as a guerrilla. I imagined that though longing for the fight he had been stuck in some backwater by chance circumstance, regretting it bitterly then and regretting it still now. So I never spoke to him of my war; he never referred to his; and nor did I speak of Checchina who had joined a nunnery and whom I had not seen for five years.

Fleeing from the marble floor and polar cold of the great salon, we finished the evening in the little eating-houses between piazza di Spagna and the Corso. There we concluded our conversation.

'The Italians, Memé, to prove to themselves that they're free, to convince themselves that everything's different, that the regime and the war and their innumerable ills never existed, will vote for the lay republic which will be the antithesis of their nature. Then they'll take fright at the reds and go back to the priests, in their hearts always mourning, not the king, but kings. Every one of them when he pulls the bedclothes over his chin to sleep, imagines himself received at the Quirinale, but not with republican honours, which would never be good enough. A president doesn't present you with a gold watch symbolic of your loyal service to the crown. Every housewife dreams of riding beside the queen in a carriage, honoured the length of the Corso and applauded from the palaces of the princes of Rome. How can you fantasise about the ceremonial top hat of a man elected for seven years? You want plumes, helmets, trumpets. The republic will only have dark suits, and parish priests ringing bells.

The painter Guttuso, in his shirt-sleeves even in that cold, and the writer Levi in a velvet jacket (two celebrities of the moment) appeared together on the threshold of the Re degli Amici amidst the admiration of the peasants who had come to see them. Levi, catching himself in a mirror, restrained his glances. Memé shook his head compassionately.

'I don't know what to think of you. You know the people well enough to know they won't change. Why not forgive them?'

'Penitents should be forgiven, though certainly not by us. And if in Rome this evening you find me ten penitents, I'll go round with a stepladder and a bucket of glue sticking up republican posters for you!'

'The bible and Charlot in one go!' exclaimed Arquà, getting up in disgust. 'Comrade waiter, the bill!'

Bringing me home the previous August, the German troop-train, bit by bit relieved of the soldiers who had arrived in their villages, and filled instead with civilians, almost all of them smugglers, broke down outside the city walls, towards Casoria. There were no carnations strewn for this homecoming. All the way from the goods-station it was a painful march through the dust, over the sleepers and stones, though all the others were delighted to be avoiding the customs. At the station, a silent, passive crowd on the pavements stared at me expressionlessly. It was impossible to get any means of transport and, as years before, I trudged the long way to the Riviera di Chiaia. The town of my youth appeared to me yet again a torpid, hostile chaos, supine in the sweltering summer.

My uncle welcomed me white with emotion, his head trembling slightly as happens to the old. I found him emaciated and wretched. He had not abandoned Naples throughout those ghastly times, taking to his own heart the city's distresses and fears, and still more the barbarous dishonour later inflicted on it. The 'conduct of the war' led the Allied air forces to devastate savagely the city where the Axis had had least support. Hitler being loathed at Cologne and Mussolini at Naples condemned those two cities to ceaseless bombardments intended to terrify people into rebellion. But if over a hundred air raids, ordered so stupidly, were a crime against the leaderless and ragged people of Naples, worse followed in the outrage of degrading the capital of a once famous kingdom to the level of a tropical colony. The victors never hesitated to provide for their junior officers' comfort by establishing their mess in the finest rooms at the front of the royal palace, among the statues of the kings. The troops of all armies bought and sold the local women at crossroads where clinics for venereal disease were opened. Profiteers monopolised the sale of supplies to the army and then loudly proclaimed the dishonesty of the 'natives' (who bought from them out of hunger what was sold to them as bribery and for outrageous gains). All this gave the lie to the reasons for which it was claimed the war had been fought, and renewed that contempt for man which was said to have been avenged.

My uncle listened to my slow telling of all that happened to me in those years, his eyes lowered so as not to see the scars which grieved him far more than me. At the end he shook his head and still said nothing. The hazy and yet certain pledge which had somehow been transmitted from his life and had spread into mine was that we should weld our bond of affection more strongly still – this was the only truth between us, the only truth for us – and we left each other somewhat comforted.

I went down to Paola, getting there as evening fell. For five years I had not see Gian Michele's house; nor did I know how Incoronata had arranged things after taking the furniture and library from Licudi there. Her husband came to meet me, with the biggest of the children, a handsome boy who looked like his mother. When I went into the little courtyard with the well it seemed more cramped than ever. I found the bailiffs with their families gathered to welcome me. They stood in two rows on either side in their country clothes, with their haversacks, their sandals, their walking-sticks. And Incoronata, before I crossed the threshold, came out in front of me and with a gesture that shook my very soul bent and kissed the earth. I embraced her lightly, as the clergy embrace each other, hardly bringing my cheek near hers on one side and then on the other. Then I shook hands with everyone else, while they humbly rejoiced, thanking the Lord for having preserved me, and wishing me well for the future. And with these simple ways, with their dignity, with their good will, they cancelled the evil of many years and many offences. Honoured in honouring me, they gave me back my self-respect, and received me back to my home among them.

I stayed down there nearly two months, reading and finding my old thoughts again. With almost superstitious devotion, Incoronata had protected and gathered in Gian Michele's house every slightest object, things which I now understood I had unjustly neglected. Though the ground-floor rooms around the courtyard were not large and were sometimes damp, she and her family had used only those, leaving the rooms above empty all that time. When the evacuation of the cities made lodgings in the country invaluable, with the help of the old notary she had recourse to every imaginable stratagem to protect me from having the place requisitioned. Her sacrifices and those of her family, undergone for affection's sake only, told me that none had understood so well as they the violence suffered by Licudi, by the house of Houses and by me. In her mercy the 'bare-footed fisher-woman' rooted me again where I belonged, as my uncle Gian Michele had already wordlessly offered my roots their earth again. Between the walls where I had thought once more to live through his affliction and join it to mine in an act perhaps of liberation, her loyalty had risen to the level of his wisdom and conferred the message to me.

Because of her nervous constitution, after five years and three childbirths Incoronata was still lean and lively. The children, all boys, had her velvety but brilliant eyes, her blackest of black hair framing their bright faces, and her happy nature. With their father, who always had the smallest in his arms, they gambolled like puppies. As I had at the Lily, I passed my days watching from the study window the clouds coursing over the impoverished land. I faced a future as unknown as it had been then, and now burdened with memories; but breathing the goodness of these people and that place I nearly abandoned myself to a mild, drowsy peace.

Towards October, before going back to Rome for treatment, I went to stay in the big farm by the river among the plantations of cedar. That still, calm countryside had expelled the war from its vast breast as a healthy organism neutralises poisons. Italians, Germans, English and Americans had passed by, and all had been offered oil, wine and oranges. Not a drop of blood had been shed.

'How did things go here that eighth of September in 1943?' I asked the women as they worked, sunk in their thoughts.

'It was the day of Our Lady. The sergeant kept ringing up headquarters but nobody answered. The soldiers, poor lads, set off on foot along the railway tracks to get back to their homes, God knows how. They came by in hundreds. They'd walked for weeks. They stopped, dead with exhaustion, and asked for water. We did what we could.'

'And the Germans?'

'They weren't here long. They said they'd been cut off by the Salerno landing, but they wanted to get away through the mountains. We pitied them, they were far from their families, and among enemies. They asked where they should burn their vehicles so as not to damage anything, and we chose the place on the bank of the river. If you want to see, the remains are still there. We all said goodbye. Nothing happened.'

'What about the English and Americans?'

The women laughed. 'They only wanted wine. The Germans on the other hand only wanted fried potatoes, one plate after another, you know?'

There had been no saboteurs, no partisans - words that meant nothing in a place where a man was only a man. I knew what it felt like, I too had tried to save myself, in France, in Greece, and later. With antlike activity they had made use of the equipment three armies had abandoned or half-destroyed or given them, the tools, tents, tins, utensils, clothes. No one had touched the weapons which had been put in the coastguard's store-room. The old bailiff had the keys of the stores and gave them to me. The wisdom of that people had returned all warlike things to usefulness and kindness. This was what it came down to, this was what had been achieved in the silent sunlight and noble green of the citrus orchards.

It was a sacrifice to leave the Garden of the Hesperides for hospital wards and consultants' waiting-rooms. More than any other body of professional men in Italy, the doctors and dentists value their time highly and that of others not at all. The treasury has never calculated the millions of working hours wasted by clients (who are only waiting to spend money and undergo pain) so that the 'professor' can make a hundred per cent profit. Arquà rescued me from some of these torturers, but he had to use no less a name than that of the prime minister. After Parri had fallen, he got himself into an Allied office with vague duties of liaising with our authorities. To be getting along with, he found me a ministry job too. And thus we reached 1946. After Hiroshima the time came to lament, to try to make historical judgements, and to forget.

In Italy the partisan movement was a very mixed bag. Those who, rather than surrender in 1943, took to the hills, were for the most part from the armed forces. They were, therefore, of all social classes and all political views; and in time they were joined by stragglers of every kind, many of them politically very ignorant.

There were also those who wanted to fight the Germans because they remembered the Risorgimento and the war of 1915 - the romantic tradition first encouraged and then denied by Mussolini. These were passions which in the context of an elementary nationalism justified anything a patriot did. The confusion between Germans and Nazis was easily made. Then it was easy too, seeing Hitler the arch-enemy of the Soviets, to ally oneself to the red flag. The first partisan groups were therefore made up of both anti-fascists who till then had barely tolerated uniforms and respected soldierly codes of conduct, and monarchists and career officers most punctilious about their military honour and the oaths of loyalty they had sworn. After that, circumstances decided what happened.

First there was that Italian individualism which, if it doesn't choose the service of power, easily turns to anarchy. Then the regime's repressiveness infected spirits with the virus of civil war so quick to spread among us. These things, added to the atrocious German reprisals, were moulded together by the logic of events and gave the movement a sort of unity, at least by contrast with the forces against it. It was when all was nearly over that the survivors among the first and more genuine elements were joined by a sea of late arrivals. And in the transformation from war to politics the extreme left triumphed. Certainly it was no good fortune for anybody to find themselves in Italy in the days of the so-called liberation. To the open sores of hatred, ferocity and suffering, were added the devastations of the Allied occupation, infamous episodes like the outrages of the Moroccan troops against the women of Ciociaria. By a sort of political revenge, there were days of hideous bloodshed, particularly in Emilia. Numberless individual loathings and private grievances were released; there was revenge and the pleasure in revenge. That it was not a case of revolutionary fervour is plain because the populace was turning against itself. Men who had served the fallen regime were killed, but so were peasants, artisans and workers. That these actions were neither predicted nor planned is clear from what happened in piazzale Loreto – at least, one hopes that the vile crime of the mockery of the dead bodies of Mussolini and his lover was not ordered by the leaders. But like the Roman slum-dwellers with the ashes of Clement VII and the Parisian mob with the tombs of their kings in St Denis, the man in the street in May 1945 was as frenzied as the dog that bites the stone that hits it. The bloody week that year, like the September of two years before, was a tragedy of the people. Later others, pursuing their own ends, came and worked out the 'data' with which they 'technically' replaced the 'facts'.

Because of the bad relations between the United States and Stalinist Russia, and with the menace of Soviet armies in Prague and Vienna, a strong Communist Party appeared to be indispensable even for a people like the Italians, anti-Marxist *par excellence*. And then it was essential to argue that the war had been lost by fascism not by Italy – an ambiguity which the Allies were happy to fall for to keep us in their sphere of influence. The partisan struggle, despite having been confined to the north and having had minimal effect on the general situation, served both these ends at once. It could be used to obtain better conditions of peace, and to obtain for the left a share of power. In the swamp of our numberless disasters, the first painful stirrings of the Tripartito were seen.

With every group having a hand in it, everybody establishing their own fief and above all trying to obstruct other people's enterprises, little got beyond the stage of programmes, projects, debates, plans. Everything was left to get by on its own, or better still left to time. The ministry I had got into turned out to be communist. That party, full of its successes, then enjoyed considerable credit and influence. In the confusion of the moment its massive ideology, by being the most outspoken, passed for the most advanced. (Worse still when now, though a hundred years old in Europe, it's dusted off and comes back from the ends of the earth as the latest thing!) A lot of intellectuals and artists were fellow-travellers. That brilliance, that passion, the exploits of those leaders and followers, were sacrosanct. It was impossible to feel free in a political atmosphere like that.

Deep down, I didn't think I was at much risk. The concentration camp had taught me once and for all to discern the falsification or equivocation in the chaotic frenzies of the mob, to discern the weakness or passion when not indeed simple fantasy and the need for illusions. Convinced of a small number of clear rules I had proved during the war, I wasn't afraid of getting mixed up now, nor did I hesitate to estrange myself. But in any case, as a grateful ex-pupil of the monks, I strengthened myself with a short series of 'spiritual exercises' in the museum of villa Borghese.

It was one of the first galleries to reopen after the war. Indeed they gathered there many works which had been moved from their normal places to be hidden or spirited away or just stolen. Apart from this kind of interest, the muses were neglected during the Second World War. There was no Kipling for the English and no D'Annunzio for us, as there had been the first time. Nor were there the music or the hymns. The free-flowing waters of the other war, like 'Goodbye Piccadilly', 'Deutschland über Alles', 'Il Piave', turned to muddy swamps in this one. The Germans, who were winning at least for the first two years, achieved nothing better than 'Lili Marlene', a nostalgic return. Our Alpine troops produced only a lament, 'Il Ponte di Perati'. The arts declined. We were deaf to Apollo's lyre. The idlers in the grounds of the villa never went in to look at the masterpieces there, and dust settled on the marbles.

Following a method I adopted when young, I looked at only one work of art each time, often the same one several days running. Memé Arquà pretended to be superstitious about Chinese scripts. I had to recognise my own purity of soul; I was just like the simple women who ask their saints questions and confide in them. In the same way as I had looked at Rubens and Goya in Paris, I sought in art the laws of the tumult I had emerged from, and signs of what was to come. My mind fastened on three symbols: the 'Dafne', the 'Danae' and the 'Narciso'.

'The Nymph,' I said to myself as I looked at Bernini's group, 'is not fleeing from a robber or an impudent satyr. It's the most splendid incarnation in all creation who's approaching to persuade her to join in nuptuals which will make her immortal. The lord of the sun, the fulcrum of the world, has chosen her for his wife. She escapes and in the chase begs to be saved. But from what? From being raised to divinity? Her prayer is fulfilled. How? She declines from being a woman into being a cold, sappy, motionless plant. What sense is there in this?'

Outside, on the usual park bench beside the perpetual vagabond immersed in his memories, looking at the rags of cloud and the spaces of clear sky, I brought to mind again the still face of the God. He shows no amazement, no disdain, no sorrow. When that shadow has vanished from between his arms, he will continue on his course without turning back, and nor will the rays of light from his crown be diminished. Though master of fate, Jove still is subject to it. 'But,' I continued anxiously, 'any superior being turning with passion to a creature his inferior, will he not see her flee from him and change herself between his arms into a sexless, sterile plant? Years ago at those workers' dances in tents on the outskirts of Milan, why could you never find a sweetheart?'

In the Caravaggesque 'Narciso' it was perhaps possible to find, if not the answer, at least a possible solution. In the cavernous dark of the mirroring water, the passionate young man sinks his gaze to his own image, which with equal passion looks up at him from the depths. Can there only be affinity, harmony and rest therefore when the mind is reflected in its own being? When there's that concentration before the leap into the black water of memory, silence and oblivion? Was this the only melancholy flower that he could pick on earth? There's a thin line of white, a mere sign, that separates the water from the other shadow, and which in us divides the true from the ghostly, the corporeal from the abstract – the fluctuations of memories, in time.

Lastly, the 'Danae'. The marvellous body shone, bathed in voluptuousness, bent upon its own pleasure. From the invisible lover, the divine seed approached her breast. There was an almost fearful conception without union, as if the creator did not want to know how his power was propagated, but trusted to empty air as those plants do which trust their fertilisation to the blindly wandering winds. Here was the mystery of art, revelation scattered in space and time, absorbed by men at first because they liked it without understanding its power or what fruition it would bring. I thought how the works of the mind, and the solitude, loftiness and silence of the spirit regenerated the world in their recondite ways, fell like invisible, fertile rain. It was not necessary to be known or understood; it was enough to know, and to think.

Before presenting myself at the ministry – which I had passed earlier, seeing its vastness and ugliness – I stayed musing another half-hour in the museum. It took nothing less than the immaculate loveliness of the lady Paolina to console me for the rest of the dreary day. As beautiful as Leopardi's 'shadowy goddess asleep', she would not have survived her awakening. Like Michelangelo's 'Night', she asked nothing but to be 'made of stone', keeping all reasonings and inspirations in her stillness. After all that had happened I was seduced by this kind of hermeticism.

The next morning, shuffling wearily up staircase C or D of our ministry with the others, I didn't mind when the doorkeeper's bleary glance slid over me as over any 'temporary clerk, equivalent to the eleventh grade'.

The new Babel – part of those coloured ashes with which Rome was covered – found me therefore set apart but not indifferent. As many years before when, with a walk-on part at the S. Carlo theatre, I had made myself keep in tune with the chorus, now I kept my good humour amid the catastrophic disorder, and tried to be of use to something, perhaps something purely abstract, that deserved at least one's honest efforts.

The Ministry of Post-War Assistance, set up who knows how, badly placed, burdened with the most heterogeneous duties, going by its name should have sorted out all the consequences of defeat that all of us together have not put right in thirty years. Swarms of officials from suppressed or redundant organisations, most of them temporary like myself, had been sent there for party political reasons, out of favouritism, by chance, above all because they were hungry. There were as many survivors, partisans, ringleaders and young hopefuls as you could wish for, and they suffered no less from want than those beggars who sat all day on the stairs or in the lobbies of the ministry. If the ancient Roman populace asked for bread and circuses, these demanded bread and justice, and quickly too.

My total ignorance of administration worried me, and in the first days when I was left sitting on a chair I tried to teach myself something from manuals. I saw that, in the world of bureaucracy, not to be given a desk was not to exist. But I had, after all, asked for a job, and they fixed me up with the task of 'studying the creation of a library' in our ministry. Of course, they told me, there were no funds for this project, so mine was a purely theoretical venture which should take five or six weeks, the right length of time, they believed, for me to 'orient myself'. But by the next day I found I had 'planned' the job. I had programmed interviews with the heads of public libraries, contacts with the directors of the libraries of the houses of parliament and the other ministries, meetings with experts. I had planned a fast technical training course to equip one for such an undertaking - which presents difficulties right from the start, simply in disposing books in a library.

Vittorio Emanuele III recounts in his memoirs that in the distant times of the Giolitti governments, that statesman, speaking of the clerks of his day, whom we cannot suppose were worse than those of our own, had whispered to him: 'If they worked only two hours a day they'd find a way of halving it.' The king comments: 'Why then didn't he ask them for those two hours of work, and not halve it?' To which I answer as I read: 'And why, your majesty, do you ask the reader this question forty years too late when you didn't ask Giolitti, to whom you had entrusted the government, at the time?' And in fact my visits to libraries and my 'contacts' became mere pastimes for my mornings. I put in a couple of hours at my desk in the afternoons. In the first week the project was more than finished, complete with schemes and proposals. However, I was innocent enough to advise the head of my section that there were several libraries which had belonged to fascist organisations now suppressed, libraries which had been abandoned but which could be saved without difficulty or expense. I saw him become thoughtful. It was rumoured of him that he had been a double-agent in Ovra, the regime's political police. He told me the under-secretary should know of this excellent idea, and after the usual delays I was sent in to him.

I found myself before a man with a threadbare collar and dirty cuffs, buried by heaps of papers which had waited weeks for his approval, but which he had no time to sign, let alone assess. Indeed he received me pen in hand, and scribbled while he listened. I knew the poor fellow had spent twelve years in a political prison, and who knows how many of them in solitary confinement, and I recognised the signs of the prisoner who will always bear the scars of his chains. By a morbid reflex, persecution had made him afraid of the human gaze, as can happen on occasion with horses. So out of charity I stood behind his armchair, pretending a form of humility, and used my forefinger to indicate the chief points on the pages of my proposal. In the end he stopped signing and in a shaky voice said: 'From what I hear, you could go far. This library project will certainly go ahead, and you may expect to be given further undertakings.'

It was clear what my superior had in mind. Having the information on the fascist libraries that might be saved, he intended to go ahead without witnesses. If, in our dealings with the victor, we had made a spectacular distinction between Italy and regime, for the internal administration the relics of the abhorred fascism constituted a land of plenty. Even the most useful organisations had been suppressed – those for sport and for young people for instance – simply because they had been established by Mussolini; and they represented an enormous patrimony, all of which had been paid for with public money. But if the lictor's *fasces* was in the cement of the gateway, those who held themselves to be the victors over the dictatorship considered them at best *res nullius* and otherwise as the spoils of war. This was to be the fate of the libraries I had improvidently unearthed (I who had learned nothing from the destruction of Licudi!). As a strange recompense, I found myself transferred to a new and rather distinguished office, with a distinctly pretentious desk. Here I was directly subordinate to the under-secretary of state's personal secretary. I was put in charge of the papers 'pertaining to survivors from prison' – and all day therefore I was in contact with others.

I found that one of the privileges of an official of a certain grade is that they do not have to receive anybody. They had a screen – always a mark of high rank – so that going into their offices it was not at first easy to find them. Not only did they hide thus from their colleagues' eyes, but they made a point of not being there in the morning when the ministry was full of people, but only later, when almost secretly they carried out their duties till night. It was the principle of non-responsibility, which by means of numberless controls and signatures permeated the whole administration and reduced all the tumult of life to greyness and documents. It became tacitly necessary to be impersonal and disinterested so as not to suffer from remorse. (Therefore the most efficient modern organisation is the bank which with its calculations and numbers ignores thought and passion.) But even in the administration – for reasons a long way from loyalty to a mandate, or devotion to the public good, or personal integrity – traces of inconvenient scruples survived. And the simplest way of avoiding any personal conflict, of not letting oneself be swayed by kindness or pity or even by hurry, was to avoid all physical contact with reality, with the public. I found working there the most wretched misfortune.

In those carefully segregated corridors the nemesis of protocol was that the stacks of dossiers, divorced from any real life, were desperately boring, and this of course produced neglect and idleness. Perhaps Giolitti foresaw the fatal results and therefore did not ask the employees in public administration for those two hours, and King Vittorio, absorbed in numismatics, in forty years never worked it out. I understood how this amorphous world left the way to the top open to a handful of cynics and careerists (like Toia and, perhaps, my superior). They were steel blades slicing through dough. Their falcons' eyes were fixed on power, and most people didn't contest them much. I now understood through and through my Uncle Gedeone's sad life, a man of sensibility, of hard work, of integrity, in a solitude greater than that which for many years I had believed to be my own destiny.

I had to deal with all manner of people who came to suggest ideas, ask questions, complain of injustices and always, when it came down to it, ask for money. Often I wanted to be like those snakes at the zoo who go on digesting or sleeping peacefully while the visitors bang with their knuckles on the glass; often I wished I were deaf. My reactions couldn't be contained, they overlapped with each other. But each new arrival, once the prolixity of his predecessor had let him in to me, confronted me armed with a thousand shortcomings in the administration, threatening it and me with the Court of Accounts or the Council of State. Or he came to tell me a world of lies according to which he was a veteran, or he had been persecuted, or discriminated against, or he was a second-class citizen. Or I was tactfully allowed to understand that I might be put in contact with people of a liberal disposition who while minding their own business would not forget my interests either. It was a sorry panorama of a world which in penury and chaos was looking for alibis to justify its faults. I'd seen so much of this before, that in almost everyone I recognised a human type I had suffered from in Reggio or in Germany; I could imagine them in those military uniforms or in the rags and tatters of prisoners as I identified the braggart, the tyrant, the coward. Sometimes I was so mortified that I pretended to grant their requests just to get them out of my sight, and so several took their leave with hopes that were later disappointed.

But those were not the greatest evils, for a lot of true unhappiness – often I'm sure not even openly confessed – came bringing its cold breath of indifference and the abuse of power. Then I felt more directly responsible. It was hateful to be believed arbiter of impossible interventions, to read in so many eyes a faith already betrayed in advance, though not by me. The help one could offer was a drop in the ocean. All my own fortune wouldn't have satisfied the needs I confronted in a morning there. If St Martin is the symbol of saintly charity for giving only half his cloak, and pious charities give away more of other people's money than their own, one could expect little of the brutalised and ailing administration; nor truly did I need to shame myself by passing money to a widow and her children across my ministerial desk. But the uneasiness lingered, an ambiguous mixture of my possibilities, my duties, my limitations – mine and those of others and of circumstance. I had to square my conscience afresh every half-hour. I had to judge my activities as they clashed with those of my ministry. I saw great efforts producing minimal good. I often confused others, I nearly always confused myself.

The minister and almost everybody else were in the Communist Party, and it occurred to nobody that I was not in it too. But among so many other uncertainties this worried me not at all. Such a welter of requests, pressures and recommendations came from the party that in the turmoil one could keep one's own straight way without it being much noticed. In the evenings I escaped with Arquà to the freer atmosphere of the cafés and bars of piazza Navona and Trastevere, not infrequently meeting again those I had seen in the morning disguised as victims, but now transformed in the small hours into seasoned captains of industry with flashy cars and lovers. This soothed my pangs of remorse.

The political struggle – which we assessed half from what Max the cuirassier told us, half from my morning observations – reached its climax. The old king had fled to Egypt and intended to abdicate, deluding himself perhaps that this would save the throne for his son

Umberto, who was even more worthless, and trusting possibly those obscure promises the Allies had made him, and which had prompted, one supposed, his flight to the south in 1943 and cost the country the collapse of that September. In the Marguttian studios there were furious arguments mixed up with much drinking and with poetry readings - readings of the work of Lee Màsters for example. The newspapers printed macabre photographs and hammered away at the grotesque Nuremberg Trials, where the Russian judge sitting to try the Nazis represented the country that in the graves of Katin had butchered eight thousand Polish officers; not to mention the carnage of Dresden, perpetrated by the Allied air force, when the war was practically over, against about three hundred thousand civilians who had taken refuge in woods where they were exterminated like insects. But Brenno's sword kept its weight. Arquà loved these polemics, preferably in a Chinese restaurant whose proprietor, one-time secretary to the embassy and a well-read Confucian, kept us occupied for hours, partly because of the difficulty he had in pronouncing Italian, which he spoke from the throat like a deafmute, partly because he embellished his learned arguments with all possible ceremony.

'The war,' I said, haunted by the shades of those who all day had tormented and relieved me, distressed me, even threatened me, 'the war is a tree of evil that bears only poisoned fruit. On the banknotes we've got now under the occupation it's printed that one of man's basic freedoms is to be free of fear. But the atomic bomb has established a regime of terror for nobody knows how many years to come. With a threat like that hanging over us, what meaning have the Nuremberg Trials? And Goering's dead body, one more dead body, what does that do to make good the past or give us finer hopes for the future?'

'Come off it Sansevero! Are you telling us it would've been better not to drop the atomic bomb but to have sacrificed another million soldiers to occupy Japan? Fighting those fellows, who reckoned on their pilots killing themselves for their country, and then maybe after that all the rest? This is no joke!'

'Why occupy Japan in such a hurry? A naval blockade would have reduced the country after a few months. The war in the Pacific had been won. If I've got a quarrel with you, and in order to be the one who finishes it I draw a knife on you - what would Lincoln have said to that? It's true kings are no use any more. But what good is a president from the world of commerce not that of culture, a Truman who first trades in neckties and then decides the fate of the world, us included?'

The ex-employee of the embassy interrupted with his gasping voice. 'There is no call to disturb men's souls. It was always the error of all dictators to make their peoples rave after illusions. I am sure the cultured gentleman with whom I am speaking will allow that beneath every political weakness there lies a spiritual deficiency.'

The moths fluttered around the exotic lanterns, reminding me of the anxieties and complaints of the morning, that murky tangle of causes and effects, mistakes and troubles.

'Certainly, Secretary! Indeed, I think we're saying the same thing. Since Florence Nightingale took her mission to the Crimea, from Clara Barton to Edith Cavell, the Red Cross spent a hundred years trying to "humanise" war. And now the nation that has been the standard-bearer in the long march towards liberty, with the atomic bomb outdoes in one stroke all possible war crimes and sets civilisation back those hundred years at least. Hospitals, women, children, the old, journalists, diplomatic corps, all in the mushroom cloud in a second. This put them on the same level as Hitler!'

'Sansevero,' shouted Memé, still swigging the shorts to which he was so attached, 'you stink of your communist ministry a mile off. Wait and see, you'll be wearing the red star on your chest, where since you're a poet you ought to be wearing Annunziata's chain.'

We started laughing. The Confucian cook's speech defects reminded me by an odd association of the under-secretary of state's gaze, humiliated by his fear, unable to bear one looking into his face. The burned moths fell one after another. We turned out the light to save them. But the silence between us was unexpectedly serious.

The cuirassier Max had got a stove from the barracks at the Quirinale. The paratrooper Belgarbo managed to acquire fuel for it from the English headquarters. This had taken some of the chill off the drawing-room in via Panama; but it made free lodging in Arquà's house ever more desirable, and it increased our density coefficient, which was already an average of more than three to a room. Two new interesting personalities had joined our community and took part in our evening discussions and our silences and our music. The music came from a record-player, it's true, but was always conducted gesture by gesture by Memé, using a baton which, he said, had belonged to Toscanini. He was particularly proud of his interpretations of Schumann, whose violins threw him into raptures. He drank plenty, and towards four in the morning appeared happy. In the split of the 'party of action' he had followed Parria and La Malfa. He never doubted a shining future for Italy, a tomorrow very different from that seen and lamented by Petrarch and Leopardi. He was connected with the foundation of a controversial newspaper in which he wanted to get me involved.

To go back to our newcomers, they were two German women. We had no notion of their origins, but they were dazzling. Memé met them under the portico of the Esedra at the very moment when they realised they could not pay for the ham rolls they had just eaten. It had been easy to convince them that they should join us. Now they sprawled comfortably on the pair of big divans in the drawing-room, enjoying the quartets or trios so well presented by Arquà. The others, all men, because the model Yvonne would promptly withdraw with Belgarbo, sat on cushions or chairs or in soldierly style bivouacked on the floor. There lay the noble Roman lieutenant Max – but strategically placed so he could delight in the beautiful knees and somewhat more of Herthe. Like all those who take the passion for horses too far, Max always smelled vaguely of stables. Full-blooded even to excess, with bristling black moustaches and hairy hands, thick-set and very heavy in spite of his great height, it was hard to conceive of him without armour and above all without a helmet. But nature as we all know favours the conjunction of opposites, and he was inexorably attracted by the tender Herthe. She was a slender and lazy blonde who wore diaphanous dresses hemmed with the most perilous black lace at the neck and at the border of her petticoat. Nor did she seem to deny Max's unspoken longings. Her slow turning on the divan let the fascinated cuirassier glimpse a voluptuousness he had hardly imagined before and that can only have been meted out with calculation.

Herthe's companion Fritze, thought to be a sculptress from Helmstedt in Saxony, maintained a different and more hermetic attitude. She was twenty-two, with a beautifully strong yet fine figure, stylish and provocative. Even the way she dressed, which seemed audacious to audacious eyes, seemed demure when modestly regarded. Sometimes her sensitive face thrilled with delight, sometimes it was sad. She had moist, shining romantic eyes. Her teeth were perfect, but too strong, rather like her precise, hard nails on her delicate hands. Her talk was so soft you could have thought it innocent. At once she drowned us with a deluge of stories of her art, which had been interrupted by the war, and the joy of having got out of gloomy Germany to start again in magnificent Rome. Herthe and Fritze had mysteriously managed to cross the frontier without passports, the former even bringing a lot of suitcases, furs, jewels, though no money. None of us wanted to enquire. I sensed something elusive in Fritze, but I didn't dislike it. I imagined things were hanging over her that she was trying to forget, things which had left their mark on her. She shrewdly worked out that I had known, during that forced march from Potsdam to Elba, a territory and a time like those she had emerged from; and perhaps she was troubled by the idea of being questioned, though she wouldn't have been afraid.

For me, to cross the German border had been to have an oppression lifted off me. The incalculable suffering of Germany didn't compensate for the suffering she'd inflicted on the rest of Europe, but added to it. I left the defeated country shutting my eyes not to see the calamities and dishonours I felt were partly mine. As when thinking of Denise Digne, for me the symbol of France in those days, now faced with Fritze's disheartened, wounded vivacity I couldn't suppress my pity mixed with an indistinct feeling of obligation. The beautiful Herthe had probably been the lover of a high-ranking Nazi, and she had lost that situation; but she was at her ease bathed in Max's admiring gaze. But Fritze avoided my eyes. When the record-player stopped, she chattered and laughed, not to fill the silence between her and others but that between her and me. In my mind I was far away, I smelled the TNT, I felt Haendel's hand pulling me down, I saw the little girl on the swamp down there. The paratrooper Belgarbo was sure that to appear in a box for a first night with Fritze would be sensational. I wondered what she had borne and what, in a sense, one owed her.

The dawn was shining through the shutters when we went to bed. The Lombard count who had fought as a partisan hinted to me, as he did every evening, his insurmountable difficulties in selling our host's farm, which justified his chronic presence in the house. The only money coming in at the time was Memé's and my very meagre pay. But Incoronata had sent us her husband, who with remarkable loyalty and skill managed to provide us, from Paola and perhaps also from Licudi, with sacks of flour, demijohns of oil, jars of sardines and slabs of *pecorino* cheese, enough to keep us and the naval telegraphists in the kitchen from dying of hunger. A trusted farmer of Arquà's managed much the same from Pordenone. So the future, although uncertain, was not desperate, and I meditated on it with the bedclothes up to my nose, as at Siltau.

Once again, what meaning did life have? During the day, the petitioners in my office; in the evening, the eccentric companionship of

Arquà; and now Fritze. At the ministry, where all Italy's bad luck gathered, on occasion a shade that had passed from my life would return. I found the name Magaldi in a list of veterans who after coming home had died of tuberculosis. His fear, then his hatred of the Germans, had come from agony of mind when he could already feel the pain in his chest. In the list of those shot by the so-called republicans in 1944 in Piedmont was Lieutenant-Colonel Gualtiero di Michelis, my rival for Mavì in Ferrara twelve years before. (And her image had come to my mind with a sweetness perhaps not known before!) Paola Grilli was dead among those interned at Ponza. Gian Giacomo Jacono had died of pneumonia and neglect immediately after Rome fell. I had caught sight of Toia at an official ceremony, among the others holding high office, but the woman sitting beside him was not Albertina.

If that had all long been cold within me I would have felt nothing. But each time I was shaken, assailed by memory. I gazed into the past. I tried to push into the future. It was like looking down a well and seeing the sky above. I was starting life all over again for the hundredth time, as civilisation has had to do over the centuries, though at least in my soul I hadn't failed as civilisation had when it came to the trial of the war. I'd understood from my uncle that though the ties of affection are delusory, the ties of duty sometimes hold. It was odd that when I saw nothing but obligations in front of me I should find peace. The Lombard count asked me courteously to turn out the light. I apologised, did as he had asked, and heard him sigh as he rolled over in his bed.

My career proceeded in ways I hadn't hoped for. The new duties I was given by the under-secretary made me more or less a head of a section, except that my pay was rigorously kept down to that eleventh grade I've mentioned. I had to guarantee the concession of an enormous number of vehicles ceded by the Americans to our government as aid, and to be assigned for laughable prices to the most deserving. One can imagine, what with escorts wiped out, and supplies which had cost no one a penny and therefore were most casually defended, how many people got busy to lay hands on them, starting with semi-legal methods and going right down to thieving. Among the squads of aspiring applicants I at once recognised the shirkers, weaklings and petty politicians; but I based the dossiers on the information given me by the *carabinieri*, though it was monotonously similar even on the most disparate people. I used to shake my head when handing over the forms, and that left them in doubt only for a second. Two ideas come to me from that river of humanity I saw when doing that job. For the first, I've found this in a notebook of the time:

Rome, March 1946

An ex-partisan, talking about the Germans after they left Rome, told me about Kesserling's command hiding in the caves of Soratte. The last soldiers couldn't escape, they were hounded from crag to crag, and when they'd almost reached the summit of the mountain they were shot and left there. I suggested to the German Red Cross agent that the bodies should be searched for, and they were found. This man's bearing was so uneasy and cautious, it was as if he suspected a trap or couldn't work out my motives. Like the woman who asked me to save her vineyard above the fortress at Krano, he humiliated me by judging me capable only of malice and the abuse of power.

The other spark of light - and it was that for me - was when I came across a sergeant of my division I had left in Greece and had heard nothing of subsequently. Major Oliviero had abandoned himself to the Germans in the time it takes to say a Hail Mary, and had returned home to enjoy his fesi. But the men from Krano and most of those from neighbouring positions retired into the hills, mixing with the Greek population, peasants and workmen, and coming back to Italy when it was all over without much difficulty, thanks to Zagara. There was a good number of cases of disorder of the sentimental kind, and even of bigamy, but no blood was shed.

That spring, whenever Herthe accepted an invitation for an evening with the cuirassier - and this happened more and more often - Fritze asked me to keep her company. She found Max repellent, and said she preferred me to the others because I wasn't insistent. I didn't want to tell her that this was because, though I liked her vivacity, her girlish laughter, her high spirits, I didn't find her attractive. There was always that hidden something in her that seemed to block or turn aside certain feelings. But I had to acknowledge I was fascinated, and it was not from simple human pity.

In the middling sort of restaurants either not yet discovered or already being neglected, bohemian places, countrified places, Fritze delighted in the Italian food; she praised it to the skies; she simpered a bit; she fascinated the waiters; she filled the cook with pride, so he came out from his stoves to steal a glance at her. Then she'd openly give part of her delicious main course to her pedigree miniature poodle; she'd fling herself into consoling the dog for its woes, telling it these were only trifles; but I saw only her beautifully kept nails that looked so sharp, so ready to wound, and her teeth that were somehow too strong . . . Her relations with Herthe were hardly explained by their common misfortunes, so utterly unlike were they, as Fritze's blatent boredom with Max's courtship of Herthe made plain.

Slowly we became friends. Late at night, at home, she'd always tell me what she'd done that day or planned for tomorrow. She hardly spoke about jobs, still less about sculpture. As Herthe had solved the problem of board and lodging with Max, so had she done with me. I didn't regard this as an abuse of our friendship. I willingly took her on her terms; she willingly took me on mine. True, sometimes when silence fell she may have been waiting for something other than my usual conversation; sometimes she was reserved, as if inviting enquiry or confidences. But I had no wish for her to unburden herself of a secret that was becoming ever more transparent; I didn't want to lose what I liked in her, and complicate everything else. I was sure that if we told each other everything about ourselves, shadows would fall between us.

At the end of April in villa Borghese, not without premeditation, I stood her in front of the 'Apollo' and the 'Dafne'. All at once she was sad, she bowed her elegant head.

'She's running from him,' she said, though I'd asked her nothing, 'because of his violence and cruelty towards her. But if a man could at the same time be as tender and sweet as a woman . . . then, with him . . . one could!'

Now she seemed desolate, almost in tears; her beautiful shadowy eyes were full of shame and supplication. I took her hand and felt her pulse beating, and her hard nails. There was no one there, and she offered me her face to kiss. When I kissed her in the presence of the dusty masterpiece, her lips which looked so alive and red were motionless and dead. We came out arm in arm. The doorkeeper admired us and envied me.

Our feelings and our thoughts are so intimately entwined that this episode had consequences even at the ministry where, what with the exacerbated political passions of the coming institutional referendum, the pressure upon me to join the party of the minister, the undersecretary and the whole band became blatant. The Propaganda Agent, a button-holing imitation of Carlo Pieri in the days of the Levi bookshop, often dropped in with some execrable witticism, and at least twice a week tormented me at greater length. This strange personage, paid so much a month as a party official, made me laugh as he preached the Word inspired by prophets and apostles but without recourse to handbooks of economics. But it would have been impolitic to spill on to him the bad humour with which Fritze had filled me. Instead I joked with him that Monsignor Montini, at that time head of the Vatican's administration, would we well able to run the Communist Party, and Togliatti likewise could run the Vatican. These two were interchangeable because the Italian Leninists, though they thought they'd broken with the church by denying it and not going to mass, still in their families, in their habits, in their thoughts, were perfect Catholics, and this meant more than their party membership cards. He pretended to laugh, and undoubtedly reported back.

As for Fritze, I found myself unable not to have faith in her. If previous experiences - particularly during the horrors of the first Russian occupation - had given her a horror of men one could understand her relations with Herthe, as an accidental aberration, and anyway it was so common as to be banal. On the other hand I disliked and was chilled by the German simplicity with which she kept going back to that delicate subject, asking me to rehabilitate her to normal contacts, to reassure and heal her as was in part already happening. From the clinical point of view her proposal, which was far from rare in such cases, was far from enticing. But she considered me capable of the sacrifice. It wasn't a great sacrifice, she added laughing.

'Giuliano, we're the best possible bedfellows. How often have men taken women knowing well that they'll feel nothing, that they're only doing it out of laziness or for money? Why shouldn't it be like that for us? And if it works out well, later why shouldn't we love each other?'

When there was nobody in the house, Fritze came to me, and her fondling, the way she hugged me and breathed on my neck, the way she pressed my hands to her breast, provoked some very confused feelings in me. I'd come out of the troubles of the war with my nerves a bit worn. She offered me nothing for its own sake, she was following a cure, she was inuring herself; but sometimes she came up with tricks so graceful and spontaneous that my reluctance gave way to resignation. It was an unusual game, not without charm, played loyally and with good intentions. I'd looked for a way of life without prejudice and falsification, and to have refused would've been at least as contemptible as to accept. But Arquà, in whom I'd confided without

Fritze being offended, said he was enchanted by what he called in English this *exciting experience*.

'A woman gives herself to you body and soul in order to return to the world. She thinks you're a miracle-worker! This is more than love!'

During the war Memé had separated from his wife, a temperamental brunette I had heard. But that event had not caused him to lose enthusiasm and faith in the rest of humanity.

'You're not married,' he went on, 'therefore with women you must give yourself in instalments. And giving and taking between people is played on a big stage. You take from someone in Peking and you give to someone else in Madagascar. You just have to be honest when you draw up the account.'

On 2 June the referendum broke upon us. The monarchist propaganda hadn't amounted to much more than portraits of well-combed princelings, so the women could exclaim, 'Poor fellows! They'd lose the throne!' The left, on the other hand, ever funereal, had recalled scenes of bloodshed and gone in for stirring slogans. The squares were full of anxious whisperings. Millions of telephone and telegraph and radio messages crossed each other, everyone tenaciously listening only to himself. The nation was busy in every cell of its being, like an organism reacting to a crisis. The votes – indicated on the forms, with involuntary irony, by the illiterate's cross – for everybody meant years of hope and suffering and thought. But I never felt a judgement was being passed; it was more like the confluence of incalculable streams of events. The Italians didn't get rid of the Savoys because it was necessary or was a good idea (nor were they signing an unknown project for a republic). But there was a feeling that a sensational gesture would free us from the nightmare of the past. There was no liberation. The new dispensation was much like the old, which it aped in the very halls of the Quirinale. The most useless of the old forms were kept. But I think I saw the driving force of history in that action in which illusion brought to bear the same weight as reason.

The Propaganda Agent didn't fail to ask me how I'd voted, fixing me with his policeman's eyes.

'Weren't you sure the monarchy would be defeated?' I asked. 'It's chivalrous to be on the losing side!'

He grinned, but I knew they thought me unreliable. Even if I'd joined the party, they'd have used me but never trusted me because of my uncancellable background. They believed in natural selection, but only in order to call it degeneration. They were willing to introduce me to the comrades as one who had seen the light, though they wouldn't have let me leave the party without branding me as a traitor. I hadn't voted, and I watched the embraces of the victors as wearily as I listened to the lamentations of the losers. Umberto II, 'the May King', packed his bags and absolved his subjects from an oath of loyalty nobody could recollect, still surrounded by the same councillors who had served his father so outstandingly. Almost immediately after, I found myself removed from my post and entrusted with a special mission to Eboli. There was a camp there for foreign refugees, who were given to all manner of mischief, and it was hoped to displace them in favour of local homeless people. Towards the end of the war, Eboli had been heavily bombarded, by mistake it seemed.

The cuirassier Max, when the whirlwind at the Quirinale had died down, and his detachment, helmets and all, had been appointed to the service of the republic, suggested to Herthe that they go to a small flat in Parioli. The partisan Lombard count unlike Giuliano set off for the North to the profitable property he had inherited, without completing the sale of Arquà's farm. Fritze then asked me if she could share my room. My transfer to Eboli settled this delicate question, because while I was leaving Herthe went to stay with Max.

'When you come back,' Fritze said, smiling with a good grace, 'you won't be able to run away from me any more. I'll think things over, and you think too. I shan't write. There's nothing between us that one could write down.'

'Blessed be the memory of Janaro Mammola, and the concept "house" according to Licudi,' I said to myself, finishing the building of a little stove after the plan patented at Siltau by the submariner Valente. At Eboli if I had wanted I could have had a bed in the repulsive refugee camp. Instead, I repaired the roof and did up the one remaining room of a ruined house; I added a table, a camp bed, a sink, two chairs, and my lodging was ready. I had a good view out over the countryside. In the midday brilliance, if I drew the newly revarnished shutters and half closed my eyes, with beating heart I could make a prodigious leap in time and imagine myself in the sergeant's room in the barracks at Ferrara.

Seeing how things were at the ministry, it wasn't hard to imagine that my exile from Rome could last some years. The transformation of the refugee camp into a model quarter of the town would anyway be a slow undertaking; but for our ministry, which hadn't got the money for a library, it was impossible. I therefore could study the plans indefinitely; the more so as the personnel office, having sent me down there, would be happy never to hear from me.

The refugee camp, based on a previous American complex of the time of the Salerno landing, was then from the logistical point of view the only part of the unhappy town in good working order. It was on the plain at the foot of the low hill where old Eboli stands; it had asphalt roads, electricity, plumbing, good masonry huts. The people were discouragingly like those I recalled from Germany on the Ohre, and had hoped never to encounter again, a wretched motley crowd of survivors from numberless shipwrecks. They were hardened by chaos, we perhaps by habit, and there was more repugnance than pity. Above all they were clothed, fed and lodged rather better than the astonished locals crouching forgotten among their ruins. Eighty per cent of the houses in Eboli had fallen or were uninhabitable.

Open to the west over the burnt plain, and dominating it from the ramifying slopes of Picentini, Eboli was in sunlight till the last rays of evening, and the arid heat among the ruins was aggravated by the abandoned silence. First involuntary accomplice, then inevitable victim, Garibaldi hadn't realised that to conquer these regions for Piedmont was to put them in foreign hands yet again. Below my window the flat, impoverished land lay, without houses, swept by dust, as far as the blinding line of the sea.

The mayor, to whom I had turned since my first day, had shown surprise, almost dismay. Like his people, he hadn't recovered from the trauma of that terrible day that had cancelled out his land's slow centuries. The people of Southern Italy, in the unfathomed depth of their customs, can be wounded as it is impossible for others to conceive. After five hundred years, down in Otranto they still recall the bloody axe that executed their martyrs. In memories of the ferocious repression carried out by Cardinal Ruffo under the yellow flag of the Holy Church, Crotone and Altamura in their silence keep the secrets of the overthrow of the Bourbons and a different destiny for Italy. 'Christ stopped at Eboli,' Levi said, later a senator on the strength of this discovery. There's an equivocation here, because he meant that further south there were no Christians. His Christ came from Milan, therefore, not from Galilee. But Eboli still had the wretchedness of the South its name had been used to signify, still bore its witness, like the sacred blood clotted in a dusty reliquary, that its testimony should not be lost.

The American lieutenant who commanded the camp, a sort of cowboy, had thought only of establishing himself a harem among his charges. The locals deprecated this, it's true, but they were always picking up the crumbs under the table of the affluent. They made a fuss if the Balkans, inveterate plunderers, took the hens from their threshing-floors or the water melons from their orchards. So too several wives protested at husbands involved in amorous intrigue with amenable Slav girls, and husbands protested at wives' escapades. But the sun in its slow arc towards evening undid the resentments and anxieties in the demolished streets. There were lights here and there among the huts at the foot of the hill, but the city lay in darkness like a sleeper who can't feel himself breathing and so is afraid he isn't breathing any more.

From the Salerno office of the ministry - which as is usual in Italy was less torpid than the head office - engineers, surveyors and bookkeepers descended on Eboli. So that week by week, a sheet of paper at a time, in the tropical heat that lasted all through September, among the mosquitoes, in the solitude much like that of some fortress in Messenia, the project for the Model Quarter began to cohere almost miraculously, like the shredded newspaper that a conjurer makes appear whole. The drawings, calculations, technical reports and estimates reawakened the mayor's interest and even nurtured faint hopes in me. I tried to imagine the Plan realised on the dusty lowland, looking like the watercolours in the office, bathed in green and planted geometrically with trees. There would be squads of houses with little loggias and roofs based on local designs. Inside, there would be model families, like the Plan said, not these hoarsely yelling refugees, greasy and filthy as goatherds, the dregs of Europe that the Allies insisted on keeping there like not very domestic animals, whose only connection with the human race was the use made of them by the lieutenant from Arizona or Texas or wherever he came from.

To pretend to help the people of Eboli, whose ancestral life had been abjured in thirty seconds to the shame of Vanvitelli, the Romanesque architecture and the princes of Angri, may have been bad of the administration or it may have been good. Illusions can serve as reality; sometimes they're even better. In the questions the people of Eboli asked when I turned over the pages of the Plan, in their wonder, I recognised the good-natured respect of the people of Licudi faced with the House of Houses. They smiled and shook their heads. As the girls then had asked, 'Don Giuli, what'll happen here?' they pressed their lips together and muttered, 'Who knows who'll be able to have these beautiful houses! How marvellous it would be!' Then they went back to their wretched hovels; and the night, lit only by the reddish lights of the camp, indifferent and sad as the lights of a barracks, brought back the silence over the dead land.

If I was unhappy, or didn't want to cook, or felt like company, I went to the tavern, which was undamaged, being slightly outside the town, one of those places where you still heard horses on the uneven ground where the remains of lorries hid the squalid corners. Early in the day there were a few workmen and carters; in the evening there were two or three taciturn drinkers, one of them, the drunkard Casillo, in the last stages. The taverns in the South aren't just local colour. The authentic people, living on sardines, croquettes and vegetables, find their real food in wine, that wine as dark as a well, that leaves a ruddy foam clotting on the rim of the glass. This isn't the drinking of the rich, that embitters rather than exalts. Nor is it the foggy melancholy that turns to vice in the North. Under the Southern sun to contemplate the tart country wine like a magnetic block in its glass is to concentrate one's thoughts and, I believe, to exalt the mind. Like oil given by a god, wine is sacred in its fashion. The obscure and discordant humours of the earth produce a medicine for our sorrows, an impulse for delight, and later, with its decline, a living stillness at the heart which is a secret held in common between the supernatural and the human. But for the sad labourer Casillo, drinking was a rite. He'd lost everything the day of the bombardment; he seemed the most negligible creature; but with his devotion to death he rose up on the town's rubble and entered the arcanum of a sacrament. Sometimes I imagined he saw his own blood in his glass of ordinary wine, and that when he drank it he was destroying himself.

It was in the same tavern that I met don Alfonso Aromatico, a big landowner from Ogliastro, they said, though he was going the way of Casillo. Aromatico would stop at the petrol pump, come in because of the heat for a drop of wine, and would sometimes have to be carried home late at night to his farm at the foot of the hills looking towards Agropoli at the margin of the Salerno plain. Don Alfonso traded widely in war-surplus, and he had two lorries from our ministry which had certainly not been assigned to him. He kept urging me to visit him.

The disorder of his farm shouldn't have surprised me. As often in the South, and reminiscent of the brigands of the old days, his complex of workshops was enclosed by a wall and guarded by ferocious dogs. It was full of the most extraordinary things which no one would ever bring to such a remote part of the world, but which on occasion an army might abandon there. In the chaos one could see a primitive order which had subsequently been lost. The house was packed with heterogeneous people. We escaped to the beach a few kilometres further down, with Aromatico's two daughters who, tormented by the pandemonium, gave themselves the most unsuitable, heavy work to do.

One of them was fourteen, the other seventeen. Agatina, the older, was a great beauty; while Giannetta, though less striking, seemed very intense and very intelligent. Aromatico was of good Salernitan origin. He had been for a time a mining engineer in the Belgian Congo, and perhaps there had discovered his propensity to drink. When he became a widower during the war, he rapidly fell into his old vice. The girls were at a Roman boarding-school, but they had to come home for the summer holidays, and I could imagine their thoughts. At that time, fishing with a mask and a harpoon gun, which before had been unknown, was becoming popular. They had the equipment and they let me try. Swimming silently in the cool, deep water, I discovered the quiet sea bed, and being weightless I lost myself in contemplation. Their two shadows followed me and guided me. My heart became confused; I felt that only then was I freeing myself from the foul mud of the war. Afterwards, on the beach, they shook their hair in the sun. When Agatina came towards me, in an old black bathing-dress that perhaps had been her mother's, I wished she were naked, but only so she would shine the more.

Going back to Eboli, I realised that, at least for a few hours, I'd forgotten Rome. And yet Memé never left me short of letters, and each time he let slip the name of Fritze. Not without reason my ministry, where I had been appointed through his good offices, had got rid of me, and thus, as I realised later, killed two birds with one stone. The sister office in which Arquà worked was the High Commission for Internal Affairs, and these affairs were numberless, comprising our own and those of all the foreigners stationed in the country. Therefore the removal of the refugees from Eboli fell under the jurisdiction of that commission where Arquà acted as a fifth coloumn, and trust was placed in the friendship between us. Not only this. Even if it had been the intention of the high commission to hand over the camp for the purpose of implementing the Plan, would they actually have given it to us? My communist under-secretary was more than suspected of intending to use the assignation of lodgings for his own political ends, and was not well regarded by the Allies. But the Machiavellian trick of sending an aristocratic Sansevero to unravel that tangled skein, a man not even in the party, reassured no one. The usual mess of equivocations and hidden motives was added to 'our splendid disorganisation', by which the Germans had been first amazed and then amused in Greece. The one thing that was given no weight was the wretchedness at Eboli.

My other correspondence was with my uncle. 'I'm worried about Checchina,' he wrote to me. 'I can't get her to leave the convent and come to live with me. She would never go to your brother.'

Ferrante and his young wife, against all expectations, had in more than ten years produced no children. He was extremely rich, having inherited from his father-in-law, and lived in a three-storey villa in the Ludovisi quarter, with all the furniture and the collections which had been Gian Luigi's. I hadn't seen him again; nor had he looked for me.

'Your brother,' my uncle went on, 'has no heirs. He thinks of nobody, he passes his life without friends, without pleasure in anything. That's just how it is.'

I had visited Checchina coming down from Rome. The nunnery was near Sora, and was signed by five vast black crosses roughly set up. She received me on her feet in an utterly empty hall. She had lost a lot of weight, and looked just like her aunt Francesca used to; she even had the same name. From the fronds of the family tree, climbed with her when she was a little girl, a voice not my own read from the yellow discs, 'Sister Teresa' (or Francesca . . .)

'Bless you!' she said. But in the cadence I recognised more the exclamation than the greeting. Her head was covered, her once laughing eyes were still and downcast.

According to my uncle, in those troubled times, and soon after the death of Annina, she had met a Canadian officer who was later killed in the battle of Cassino. But she didn't speak to me of this. She told me their story, of how when the front reached their village in the Abruzzi she and other fugitives were lost for weeks in the hills. She told me of our mother's death. 'At the last,' she said, 'of all of us she only named you.' I held her hands, which were cold and trembled slightly. Since she was tiny she had always come to me when her hands were cold, and had put them between mine to warm them. But now she didn't look at me. Her still, low eyes followed her other grief in the emptiness.

I could understand her. I remembered Lore's silence sitting on my bed in Kate's room that last evening; the women of Berg and little Martin riding on my shoulders under fire; the generous animal warmth of Tecla. As Arquà had said, the give and take in this world was not limited to a few people or one time, but included all one's life. I had done for others what another had done for Checchina, helped and comforted and loved her, for splendid days never to be renounced, forever to be relived in imagination.

After that I often went back to the hill of Ogliastro, without asking myself too many questions. I thought of Fritze, of Checchina, of Giannetta and Agatina. These last two, and maybe the younger more than her sister, seemed to have undergone something during the Allied occupation that they wouldn't mention and were trying to forget. On occasion I believed I caught ambiguous notions behind the gestures or glances of the guests at the chaotic farmstead. Meeting Aromatico again sitting with Casillo, I felt he might be sinking into dissolution for similar reasons.

But whereas once I had lived apart, had observed from a distance, my instinct now was always to be involved, starting with my under-secretary who was afraid to meet the eyes of others, and coming up to Casillo. If anything, my difficulty now was in opening and dividing myself up, each time giving part of myself for what I took of other people. Particularly, Agatina's beauty seemed to ask more than a part of me. 'If you really wanted to be a missionary,' Memé ironically informed me in the deathly cold of the drawing-room in Rome, 'you should once in a while consider a plain woman too.'

He made me think. But the last of my symbols from villa Borghese, Paolina, told me that the original strength in her mother, the lady Letizia, had divided itself in two parts, between Napoleon's genius and her, Paolina's, loveliness. These were strengths of equal worth.

The cicadas stopped singing. The country became tawny, the sea receded and darkened. Summer declined into autumn as one music fades into another.

In the middle of March 1947, the Plan for Eboli being finalised in its smallest details, since the Roman office showed no signs of life I returned to the capital without anybody's permission. My superior took off his glasses and looked at me as if I'd come back from the dead. Then he weighed the fat bundle of papers I'd inflicted on him and sighed.

'The hitch is, my dear Sansevero, that our ministry is about to be suppressed. The plan is that the dossiers and acts hitherto within our competence will be distributed, according to subject, among other branches of the administration. This splendid project – for your work on which you're to be officially commended – will go to the Ministry of the Interior, or perhaps of Public Works. But to tell you the truth, the real question is where *we* are to go. One hopes they're not going to throw one thousand five hundred people out on the street from one day to the next. You too had better look for one or two enemies you could suddenly be helpful to!'

This time I'd been hit, and I admitted it. In the corridors, those afraid of being sacked formed tumultuous groups. But I was thinking of those down in Eboli, of the mayor who'd come to believe in the project, of Casillo who'd be dead the sooner. Having on the telephone obtained the permission of the Mother Superior of the boarding-school, giving out I was a relative, I went off towards Monte Mario to find Agatina. It was no good pretending I hadn't come to Rome for this.

There were several other visitors in the small, tidy hall furnished almost like a chapel. In the centre of each whispering family was the schoolgirl, in her hour of vivacity and delight – the star twice over, for her relations, who admired and hugged her, and for herself because she'd been called from her companions as if elected to a special ceremony or prize. I recalled the Lily, where no one ever came to see us, where there wasn't even a hall where we could have been visited; I had intuited then in my childhood bitterness what now I knew I had lost. Perhaps for this reason, I found this small world extraordinary, with its images of the saints and its flowers.

After what felt like a long wait, Agatina appeared. She was already the most senior in the school, and helped the nuns look after the smaller girls. She embraced me, calling me uncle. My age and her youth made this relationship convincing to the others, who smiled benevolently. She shone in her dark dress with a red ribbon which indicated her authority in the school. Her hair shone, and smelled sweetly of youth. She recounted the thousand charming trifles of her day, constantly naming her favourite nun, whom then she presented to me. I was led through the school to the terrace, from which there were excellent views over the countryside. I admired everything, and assured the nun this was the best school I'd ever seen. She assented, sighing; then she joined her hands and cried out: '*Hélas! Mais nous ne voyons pas le Vatican*!'

Agatina laughed. We went in again, passing through a dormitory. Amid all that whiteness, those veils, that lace, I felt awkward; it seemed to me I brought with me a stink of man, like a wolf in a pen of lambs. I took the train without seeing my Roman friends. But before finally abandoning Eboli I paid a last visit to Giannetta Aromatico.

I wondered what the girl's life could be like in that ruinous house in the country, open to all comers like a harbour. What were the evenings like, when she was left alone with her drunken father? I could guess why the nuns had agreed to have Agatina for another year, though she was really too old. Since I'd torn my heart away from Arrichetta, I'd had only fleeting encounters with women (I included Madame Lore among these) but now I had two in my thoughts, and however different they were I imagined them in the same way. I didn't forget Fritze's sad face that day in the museum. Sometimes it seemed that Agatina's shining purity would dispel that other image, and sometimes not.

At the hill of Ogliastro, Giannetta met me barefoot at the gateway, with a wicker basket of eggs in her arms.

'I know you've been to see Agatina,' she called. Then she put on her clogs and we climbed the steep outside stairway of the barn. Inadvertently I held on to the handrail; but it fell away from the wall and hurtled down with a ghastly crash.

'I should have warned you!' Giannetta shouted, excessively amused. 'You can't touch anything here, don't you see?'

We went on up the hill. Giannetta was nothing like as beautiful as Agatina, but she was free and easy, she was lively, and certainly she was more amusing. She had been brought up in a region as remote as a colony, among the rough, the brutish, the maliciously mocking; but there was something ambiguous in the carelessness of her clothes, not that she dressed like a peasant. She moved with no restraint, hanging on to a branch, jumping a wall, throwing herself on the grass. She was like fruit partly still green and partly overripe, as people are sometimes when they have been badly treated.

'What did you do here during the war?'

'For heaven's sake don't make me think of it! When the front passed over us, Daddy was in Salerno and we were left for three weeks in the countryside. Do you see that cave? Agatina and I were there for eight days with almost nothing to eat.'

'Who else was there?'

'A lot of shits!' She threw herself down on the turf and ate a blade of grass. 'We had to run like mad! But luckily there were quite a lot of other women. But all the same there was trouble. When Daddy got back he hardly recognised us!'

'And Agatina?'

'Oh, oh,' she began to chirp and twitter, looking at me fixedly. 'I don't know. But when the Allies arrived she had an English captain stuck to her twenty-four hours out of twenty-four. Agatina's very demure, you've seen, but the nuns have done that. But the captain was a force to be reckoned with!'

I returned to Rome without warning Arquà, and holed up in one of the little hotels used by actors near the Argentina. It wasn't far from palazzo Grilli, which had been divided up among small businesses; the doors were open, the courtyard was clogged with cars being repaired. For three days I didn't leave my room. They said Petrarch had stayed in the place, and the plumbing I believe hadn't been improved since. There were no bells or telephones, people just thudded on the door. The first to turn up was Fritze, wearing a hat fit for an opening-night and menacing me amiably with her glove.

'You're a monster! But someone saw you at your office, so I found you! Don't say a word. You've got to come back to us. Memé's waiting for you.'

Fritze's vivacity, though it was only partly the real thing, overcame me. Rome was marvellous in the spring afternoons, and we passed happy hours while she screeched and laughed, on foot or in taxis or buses. Or we went into a cinema and came out at once, having seen a boat or a chase, or having heard a cry, cavernous echoing voices, shots. Or we drank sweet wine in a carters' wine shop and then perched on stools in a smart café and ate ice cream. She told me all she had done and planned: her ceramics were at that very moment being baked; she had done drawings for a fashion-house; she had done a screen-test; she had applied to be an interpreter for an aviation company. But every now and then I caught her fearful, shadowy, riveted look. She didn't want to see my months of silence as a refusal; she didn't want to lose the possibility she'd nurtured with so much care and true feeling. So she attacked once more with her caresses and her girlish laugh. She was determined to avail herself of my weary apathy after the failure of the Eboli undertaking, which she knew about, and my silence in which she could imagine the shades of Checchina earlier and Agatina now.

At dusk we were at the house in via Panama, in the bedroom that had been mine before. There was nobody else in the flat, and while Fritze had a shower, coming and going each time with a garment the less, I noticed how she'd transformed the dull dormitory I'd shared with the partisan count into a charming room; she seemed to have given new life to the lights, the curtains, the mirrors; her ideas and her bits and pieces had imbued everything with zest and imagination. And I, at my age, with my face somewhat reorganised by plastic surgery, what could I expect of love?

When she was in my arms, the illusion that a beautiful woman knows how to cast round us seemed overwhelming. She was splendid in her flawless nakedness (she always left some last obstacle to remove) and her modern hairstyle lent the whole a charming ironic touch; so did her painted nails and her rosy knees and elbows which seemed almost like regal decorations. But when I responded to her, and held her to me, and waited for the growing fervour to resolve itself, I found instead that an invisible veil of inertia and silence was drawn between us. This didn't come from me, with my pity of love and my desire; but I felt her shrink away and become cold. She panted, with her strong clenched teeth displayed; the light in her distracted eyes was hard. She delayed briefly, then her face was as if extinguished, she rolled over, covered herself with the sheet, and said nothing more.

In the evening I found myself alone with Arquà who, with the help of a bottle of real gin, was well up to brilliantly conducting the record-player's Brahms variation on a theme by Haydn.

'Giuliano, it's marvellous that your red ministry is falling to pieces. The friends of the glorius CLN, now that the constitution is to be promulgated, will start the real political fight. We've decided everything to do with our newspaper, and you're in it. We must achieve power to show this dirty Rome why the war was fought, who caused it, and what can be made of having lost it.'

I promised Memé everything he wanted. They'd already criticised me enough for not making the inexhaustible series of facts and impulses cohere in a 'single faith'. Later Fritze came and joined us, recomposed and apparently tranquil. She looked at me in a way which was not unfriendly, and actually smiled.

Shortly before, the terms of Peace for Italy had been laid down in Paris. Not only did we not have to pay for our defeat, but we could count on considerable help in getting back on our feet. Deep down, I was convinced we'd taken the worst possible course, that it would turn out that for a plate of lentils the country had bartered away any honourable position it might have had in the new order of nations, denying itself a voice for a good twenty years.

Circumstances dictated that the new newspaper, of vaguely liberal orientation but basically concerned with the South, had its headquarters in Naples; and there I prepared to return, whatever confused feelings it aroused in me, only for my Uncle Gedeone's sake.

The ministry was dissolved, along with the three-party coalition. Through the windows came a tremendous, ceaseless uproar, reminiscent of our last days in Athens. The city was invaded by, and overflowed with, an almost sadistic delight in change and revenge. The provisional president Enrico de Nicola, a monarchist through and through who should have known how to find a style suitable to the republic, was about to be replaced by the graceless bourgeois dynasties. With all my colleagues, I had the extraordinary surprise of learning that our Ministry of Post-War Assistance had in fact never been formally constituted. The employees had been paid from funds allocated, indeed, for assistance, so the books balanced; but the ministry died without having been born. Therefore, from the administrative point of view, none of the equipment or furnishings in the offices existed, since nothing had been paid for with money that appeared in the accounts. A lot of stuff vanished, consequently, without anyone objecting. It was a miniature 8 September that mocked the tragic one of 1943.

Before going back to Naples (for good, as I thought) I went to Sora to see Checchina. This time I'd asked my brother to take an interest, so that when we had listened to what she felt we could come to a decision. He replied with a few lines, writing all over the top of a tatty piece of paper without leaving a millimetre to spare, but leaving nine-tenths of the sheet blank. We met at Sora at the end of October. The gloomy damp of the woods and hills was cold. I hadn't seen Ferrante for about ten years, and he seemed extraordinarily dried out and wooden. He clearly took time and trouble over his punctilious dress. He showed no sign of wishing to embrace me, he didn't hold out his hand or ask me about anything. He asked me how I was, but without conviction; instead of answering, I said, 'You look well.' I let him go before me into the parlour. Checchina was on her feet waiting for us and said, 'Bless you!'

Through her uncle, Checchina had asked us for an endowment so she could enter the nunnery for ever. The money left to Annina, and therefore, after Gian Luigi's death, to her, had depreciated during the inflation to a hundredth part of what there had been, and was hopelessly inadequate. The tree of war, still bearing evil fruit, had ruined the economical, and awarded at their expense gigantic prizes to those who had spent their way out of debt. What had happened to the five years' labour of the bailiffs at Paola, and had happened to me, happened equally to half Italy in its relations with the other half. Never had I felt as I felt then that money truly is nothing; it was only her dream and her renunciation that wrung my heart.

'Checchina,' I begged her, feeling the cold of the parlour on the nape of my neck and in my very soul, 'Checchina, come and live with us, with our uncle and with me. He's old and alone. He brought us up one after the other. If you want to make an offering to God, do it by helping this poor man who needs your help. This is charity. What are you staying here to undergo, leaving us alone down there?'

'Giugiu, I've decided. If you'll be kind enough to give me an endowment, I'll stay here. I haven't yet taken the veil. I'm at the nunnery only provisionally. You must both understand me. And you, Giugiu, must forgive me.'

I knew how she loved me. She had known in what state I had come back from the war. Still she'd kept herself distant and closed, but I felt how her striken spirit withdrew to force herself to lose me, and with me everything else.

We embraced. Her nunnery smell of new material, of chapel, of flowers, lingered in my nostrils. Her wasted youth was like the air in a worm-eaten chest. My brother said almost nothing. Nor did he discuss the clauses of the agreement with the Mother Superior. He agreed to assume half the financial responsibility, with a motion of the lips that could have been assent or distaste.

He was of our blood, the blood that was passionate in our two sisters, and tumultuous in me as it had been in Gian Luigi's veins. The Propaganda Agent, himself an everything manqué, would have been horrified to know I asked myself where in Ferrante a value – Value itself indeed – might be encapsulated, and that I was sure it was there, even if it had not germinated.

THE SAINTS

On New Year's Eve in 1948, two people were talking in low voices, almost alone in the wide square that from San Martino overlooks old Naples and the Vesuvian coast.

There were still two hours to go till the year ended. For days the city had crackled with fireworks, and since morning the banging had mounted hour by hour; but now the dark city waited and collected itself. At their shoulders, the enormous bulk of the castle of Sant'Elmo lost itself in the blackness. Only the great marble escutcheons, with the glorious bearings of Carlo V, glimmered elusively on the *tufa*.

'Once a year, Giugiu,' they had told me when I was a child, 'only once a year, Time himself comes near to earth and touches it with the tip of one wing exactly at midnight. It's like setting a pendulum going. Time, with one little push each year, keeps the world going. Very soon he'll be here.'

In Gian Luigi's collection many years before there had towered above the other pieces a massive porcelain composition showing Time tearing off the wings of Love. Both the bearded old man and the riotous child were half-naked, and of an unnatural whiteness. Love writhed, he twisted his little mouth; while the Other, holding him fast between his knees, got on with brutally plucking his feathers. It was much admired by connoisseurs, though I didn't like it. But my Uncle Gedeone didn't go to rhetoric for his analogies.

'Here the people have lived and suffered for three thousand years,' he slowly went on, looking steadily down. 'Everywhere, those who live must suffer; but we look inward to our souls more than most, I should say. Therefore the injustices I've seen in these times have oppressed me. But in the worst times here in Naples I've also seen something which gave me hope for mankind all over again. Now it has passed. And it's right I should go back to placing my hope in God alone.'

There must have been electricity in the air, for down in the dark valley strange lights shimmered. The mist around the foothills of Vesuvius dimmed the countless lights of the shore into a glittering milky way.

'Yes, now it's different,' my uncle continued. 'After all that passion, we're to be treated like earth, planted with seed none of us recognises. This bunch of rascals fighting for power weren't here during the bombardment in 1942. Do you know how I'd punish the Germans for what they did to Europe? I'd forbid them for a generation to come here as tourists. Do you know what I'd demand of a political candidate? The truth about his five years of war. We've got a Defence Minister who never did military service! And now by way of propaganda I see the saints carried through the streets. They didn't appear then, it wasn't Paradise here then.'

My uncle said this so tiredly that it was just a melancholy comment with no irony. But the faint light that still shone in the gloom seemed softened where it fell on his weary face, not because he had carried the burden of a day or a month, but that of a lifetime. He had wanted to see the New Year's fires up there, and I knew why. We'd been fourteen months together; and it had been granted that I should not desert him at the end. He seemed content, as if he'd desired exactly this. I watched the life dying in him like one watching a small flame waver and shrink, begging it to flare up again, knowing it cannot last. At the same time I felt I was garnering up his life in me, I was comforted and strengthened; and he knew he was pouring his life into me and that not a drop was being lost. The Tree was between us, or we were in it; and one branch perished only because all the sap was being concentrated in those remaining.

'What has this city meant to mankind?' my uncle's voice pursued. 'What have we been, here? And you, among us? You seem to have always lived alone and far off. But you were right to do for all of us what only one can do. Your mother Annina, who lived so gaily, and who forgot so easily, at the end spoke only of you, as Checchina told you. But why, do you imagine?'

From the darkness a hollow rumbling arose, like an underground stream making the earth quiver. Here and there blue, violet and red flashes of light sprang up. There were bangs, Bengal lanterns momentarily showed tiny living figures on loggias. Seaward, the fog had thickened; beyond the cold lights of the port, the curve of the gulf was motionless.

'What has this city meant to mankind?' The voice already re-echoed from the wings offstage in my memory, each repetition more intense than the last. 'The land of song!' the foreigners said as they disembarked enchanted on the shining shore between hills and sea. 'The mandolins, where are the mandolins?' asked the ageing ladies already fluttering their tickets for Positano, Capri or Ravello. 'The illustrious homeland of Campanella and of Vico!' declared the luminaries come to pay homage to don Benedetto Croce. 'Swindlers!' ticked Interpol's tele-typewriters. The archaeologists headed for Pompeii and Ercolano, the vulcanologists for Vesuvius. The naturalists were after the lizards on Capri. There was the cult of the dead, the blood and the treasure of San Gennaro, the traces of eight dynasties and of three or four cities one above another. There were the dishonour, the slums and the cooking! It seemed Naples had everything and yet we did without everything. It was illustrious and famished, poetic and sad. But then in the city's breast a smouldering fire exploded uselessly, a myriad passions exhausted in the imagination were thrown up, occult pleasures, shames, stifled rebellions, super-abundant illusions. The distant rolling was now audibly that of drums coming in from the outer spheres towards the black, still heart of the city. Dimly I could make out maybe the obelisk of the Gesù, between Santa Chiara and Port 'Alba, maybe the off-white façade of the cathedral. In dribs and drabs poor people were gathering, climbing the ramp of Sant 'Antonio or coming up the little lanes behind the fort. None of them spoke. Too poor to buy fireworks of their own, these sad philosophers came with their buried thoughts to watch those of others.

'This isn't a city to be governed by a mayor,' my uncle went on. 'Only three or four of its kings have just succeeded – Alfonso d'Aragona, shall we say, or Carlo III, and while things were going well Gioacchino too. Philosophers and churchmen have had something to say to Naples on occasion – Father Rocco for instance. Now engineers, technicians, professional people and industrialists are laying siege to her. You're right to fight against them. You know as I know that the agony of the Bourbons deserved a poet.'

For over a year since my return to Naples I'd served and fought on the newspaper where Arquà had posted me as a sort of outlying sentry. After the strangest obstructions, infinite hesitations, possibilities that appeared, vanished, came back with the heedless zigzagging of the Roman butterflies, the paper had got under way in Naples rather than Rome, and with hopes and orientation completely different from those at first conceived. I alone of those present at the start had stayed the course, I who had never cared about the reasons and the ambitions but who had been sure I could always make myself useful. But the mysterious driving force of my life, which bound me in duty to my Uncle Gedeone, also called for a new attitude towards my ancient homeland. Youthful grief was no longer an adequate response to what the people had suffered. The political battle unleashed in Naples then was a sort of rash, daunting to look at, perhaps not very serious, but indicative of a disease spread throughout the bloodstream. The attempts to gain power over the municipality, for reasons ranging from pure speculation to a hybrid romanticism, but always having an effect on the populace; the odd figures acting out the drama; the feeling of struggling in a flickeringly illuminated darkness – all this dispersed my old glooms for the first time. Every morning at daybreak in the Riviera di Chiaia, empty at that hour, palazzo di Lerici waited for me, and each time I gave it, so to speak, an account of myself.

'We never left the city.' The voice of my uncle came to me at last through the growing thunder and lightning. 'From the most distant times, through tumults, in the plague three hundred years ago, from Africa with San Luigi, from Holland with Farnese, from Lisbon, from Morea, we've brought back here all we've done, as you've brought what you've done back to me.'

They were not the hands of an earthly clock which told the last moments of the year. The burning breath of the city panted from the outer edges to the glittering, exploding centre. Splashes of light were flung high and far, deafening flashes shook the old masonry, the decay of the land troubled with its wisdom oozed out heavily as shouts and cries. The crackle of the lesser explosions lay below the roar of the greater. The remnants of the year were falling like hail down there, exultation in freedom, mockery of regrets, a challenge, even revenge, against oppression and unacceptable law. A pungent cloud rose over the burning landscape.

Then the mysterious stone breast of Naples breathed less violently, the cloud lay so thick one could barely distinguish the last ruddy, tired flares. The enchanted wing of Time had touched the enchanted places so they would live another infinitesimal fraction of their infinite history, called by men a year.

'I don't expect to see it again,' said my uncle.

Natale Caramiello's gang, who had set themselves to conquer the local administration, were an excrescence of the body politic and thoroughly dangerous. Caramiello had been a trader in cattle and corn, and came from Fratta. Already in the fascist period he was gaining power in the Agricultural Confederation, expanding from pastures to mills, and finishing up with almost a monopoly in *pasta*. The Allies had succeeded in saving him from immediate reprisal by interning him in the camp at Padula for ten months as a supporter of the fascist regime. But when things were quiet, in an exhausted country without public authorities, Caramiello's ship was powerful enough for him to feel himself the natural admiral of the fleet.

His most loyal councillor was don Ciro Mellonio, a scrap-iron king from Mercato, a haulage contractor, a builder of trawlers and coasters trading between Genoa and Trapani. The third was Peppe Semmola, a swindler from Resina who had gone into property speculation and the building trade. Caramiello's capital, Mellonio's transport and Semmola's network of clients were formidable when united, and they vaunted from all corners of the city. But what they really wanted was to control the municipality, because then with Semmola's building yards they could exploit their power over the planning regulations and distribution of building licences for the bombed-out quarters of the city.

I didn't deny the gang had certain values. Brought up in the poverty of the streets, and victorious in the end against a world that from the start had to them seemed utterly fraudulent, they applied the lessons they'd learned from the pangs of hunger and the kicks of the bosses. They didn't believe they were doing wrong, and they were to be preferred in charge of the city to outsiders even greedier and with no right to be there. And then they were ready - indeed, they were anxious - to distribute benefits to their clients, friends and relatives immediately, in that utterly Italian way long since consecrated by the papal courts. They weren't intellectuals, they had no notion of what their country meant or what its place in the world might be; but their country had vomited them up after years of sorrow. Their disorder and trickery were at least genuine, and they cleared the air after all the allies and parties and their formulae had been seen to be the old masks of despotism.

That is what the gang thought; and the vast swarming city agreed with them. Naples was up to its neck in debt, and depended for its daily bread on the encampments of stalls overflowing from Ponte di Casanova and from Cippo di Forcella down by Toledo as far as the affluent centre. Attacked from the air for thirty months, a shameful barracks for twenty more, at least now the city was free to get on with its inimitable talent for surviving. Caramiello, Mellonio and Semmola represented the exodus of all that was not Neapolitan, and the city's moral revenge and determination to live only by its own laws. They had to be opposed, but in my heart of hearts I admired and even envied them.

We managed to avoid a confrontation between Caramiello's gang and our newspaper with the somewhat rusty name *Free Vesuvius.* The editor, Filippo Mestica, a wily old expert who'd been wrecked and got afloat again more than once, couldn't at that time negotiate because of other entanglements. As for his past, Mestica spoke rather weakly of a long sojourn in Central America. To his most trusted associates, he'd say, 'It's enough for me if one copy comes off the press each morning. I'll know the right person to get to read it.' He had no interest in anything that wouldn't profit him, either openly or covertly. An editorial, a couple of more or less poisonous articles, and a few facts about the public or private life of the city, constituted his income. The rest was just window-dressing, all he needed was passable decoration. Being the one survivor of the original group led by Arquà, I commanded wide authority, and when Mestica was worming money out of Rome I took his place. My real reason for staying with the paper was his indifference to what I did when it didn't involve him – and this held good for six pages out of eight. Late at night, when the last workmen slipped away into the damp darkness, I looked at the press, quiet now, like a mighty forehead, closed, wrinkled, thinking. I knew that when the blood raced through that mind it had the power to overthrow a state. Where was that strength? The paper had begun with liberal hopes; but then, through a series of influences, private interests, deviations of all kinds, it had ended as a muddle dominated by Mestica and a businessman from Genoa. They employed the impoverished, first welcoming them, then tolerating them, always exploiting them. All the splendid plant was the result of adroit wheeling and dealing. Everything was paid for by the chaotic political groups who gave blindly what they'd extracted from others who paid blindly.

To set Mestica against Caramiello was difficult. He couldn't support him; but by keeping quiet he left the door open for unforeseen eventualities. I knew that the chess players of government, serving their own interests as ever, were perpetuating the play of equivocations by exaggerating the trio's lack of political weight; they called their supporters apolitical, or corrupt, or subverted and rebellious. I'd have liked to stop the trio making the boorish mistakes that gave their opponents a reason for cutting off the money. This hypocrisy was stretching its tentacles over the mean shanty-town of booths selling soap or cosmetics or overcoats. It was bad enough that Italy was doing virtually nothing to help the men coming home after the war, forcing them to fight all over again for any indemnity. It was disgraceful that in the North, where recovery was well under way – in the North which had been responsible for fascism, which was born at Predappio and multiplied with the *panettone* a few paces from Milan cathedral – they should mock the city in all Italy that had been most indifferent to fascism, but which had suffered most because of it. In the shadows, the press thought silently.

When Gian Luigi's house was cleared out years before, my brother Ferrante had overlooked a lot of things. But Gedeone had found in the archive our father's extensive work on the planning regulations for Naples based on practical experience in the slum clearance after the cholera epidemic of 1884. Others had finished these researches; and he had studied them during the war when he had been responsible for clearing the shelters and church charities of Naples. He spent three solitary years moving things and people on an immense chessboard, getting nothing for his work but the knowledge that he had done it.

'This is the right moment to heal the sores of Naples,' he said when I went over these things with him. 'The state must make vast compensation for what the city has undergone. The greater part of the old quarter is ruined, and for good or ill the bombardments have begun what the administration would never have been up to. If someone of good sense draws up and implements a plan of reappraisal, and then of clearance and repairs, it should be possible both materially and financially. No one has ever done a scholarly census of the old city. You'd find that three-quarters of it belongs to the church charities, to the state and the corporations. A law could be passed to co-ordinate these forces. You must push for this, in your newspaper.'

This would all go against Caramiello, for when he was in power, Semmola, with his close links with the most wretched sectors of the population, would not have satisfied anyone but them, even at the expense of such famous landowners as Castelo Angioino, when there was all that public money to spend. What was more, it was impossible philosophically to say he was wrong. Don Benedetto Croce seemed to think this way too, who in the heart of old Naples behaved exactly like a Trappist, as sure of his thought as the other of heaven. But maybe like all our other philosophers before, he didn't want to change the city, and so confirmed it as it was, saying it was perfect like that.

Therefore I decided to undertake a secret guerrilla action, and printed a few pages for the neighbourhood, with a folkloreish look to them but with some political substance. At first I presented the stuff so well disguised that Mestica suspected nothing.

For this job I recruited the poorest journalists and got them to explore the hidden recesses of Naples. The plan for my publication was to follow local history, from ancient times to the present day, by charting the growth of the city, which over the centuries had spread from the small hill occupied by the Greeks as far as the viceregal quarter of Toledo, to the Bourbon quarter of Vomero, and to the Murattian Riviera di Chiaia. This seemingly topographical survey gave me the chance to discuss problems of the quality of urban life, and to propose some ideas based on Gian Luigi's and my uncle's researches. The circulation of *Free Vesuvius* went up.

Professional journalism is almost never able to give in its reports that excitement which distinguishes a partisan camp from an army camp. My impoverished men, longing for successful careers, ferreted out and interviewed vintners, ragamuffins, women who lived like nuns and never went out, usurers, cripples, police informers. They uncovered the sacred and forbidden places of the most abstract, recondite and spiritual city of Europe. These legion figures of unfathomable appearance made me shiver when I realised how far popular beliefs were from what I had thought modern life to be, how anachronistic and how recondite. At least a hundred thousand Neapolitans were devoted to the transcendental cult of the dead. The walls of the nunneries concealed fine ladies a hundred years old, who had lived in seclusion, silence and stillness for three-quarters of a century amid the tumult of the poor quarters. Hospices ruled by unflinching sisters followed medieval and barbarous regimes. Some public services, like the slaughterhouse and the morgue, looked like paintings by Spadaro or Goya. Mastriani re-emerged alive from the stinking caverns of Sant 'Antonio Abate, from the ruins of Granili invaded by a plague of beggars. But the purity of the popular chorus endured intact. From the hill where with my uncle I had passed New Year's Eve, I heard it come ringing up, and the yellowish mass of houses seemed transparent, delicately balanced on the light.

My paths, and the paths of journalism with which mine were entwined, brought me inevitably into some contact with the cut-throat Mestica kept for his own clandestine purposes. He had smarmed-down hair, spectacles, and long thin moustaches. He took infinite care of the extremely long nail of his little finger – and the people who go in for that sort of refinement are generally mellifluous, vain, of lower-class background, and capable of cruelty. Every now and then he received sibylline telephone calls from, or made them to, crooks who seemed much distressed by being involved in some scandal or by being about to be denounced. Our newspaper could either make their predicament worse or present them in a kindly light. Here lay the services rendered by our man. The accused even turned up at our offices. After they left, Mestica, aware of this almost by telepathy, appealed for a report. Everything always took place in the same room, and I was sure he had it bugged.

This fellow was cautious with me and, no doubt following instructions, never acted on information that might have come to him from our work. I likewise pretended to ignore his work, and kept my weekly local publication distinct from the daily paper. But it seemed I was becoming important in sectors I'd never thought of impressing. A small delegation, which had little to say for itself but that I judged came from Peppe Semmola, arrived to see me. They asked me, with the exaggerated humility of popular leaders who in fact carry a lot of clout, to intervene in what they said was a rather delicate matter.

'Look at the company I find you in!' It was Arquà, gesticulating gaily, in a Tyrolean hat and a smart yellow silk scarf, incongruous against the ruinous background of the Old Market. This lamentable area from the wharves to the Bianchini barracks was clogged with the rubbish that clung to the homeless. It seemed at once corrupt and prison-like.

Beyond the church of the Carmine towards Borgo Loreto lay the kingdom of the swindlers. Infamous throughout the world, this most original of corporations is composed of charlatans, gypsies, psychologists and cheats of all kinds. But they only practise their art outside their own country, and usually far away. The Neapolitan swindlers were selling calico to the Indians before the missionaries got there. They've penetrated the Arctic Circle, the Australian desert and the Chinese interior. The technique is to acquire on credit from one of the established bosses stuff that would be cheap on any market from Mexico City to Copenhagen, and then sell it in the countryside or in that very city for twenty times its value, pretending the goods were stolen or smuggled, and dressed as a sailor, or in a Tunisian fez, or in Turkish or Japanese clothes. These men venture everywhere, without knowing the languages; they're brilliant mimics, as shrewd as mediums, and endlessly resourceful. No frontier stops them, no police force can control them. They've been seen in England, the country of the most meticulous law and order, charged in court on fifteen or twenty counts but then somehow going free. They pass on their mystery from gifted master to pupil. Their morals are incomprehensible, for they're excellent fathers of families, and capable of extraordinary feats of endurance, of initiative and ingenuity.

Gennaro Sperino, who had been one of the most brilliant, was hunted for years as a murderer; and when he was killed on the Cordigliera in Chile, nobody knows how or by whom, his Neapolitan comrades hastened to honour him as he deserved. The body had already crossed half America and then the ocean, at great expense, when the cost was increased again by the piracy of the captain who threatened for reasons of hygiene to pitch the dead man into the equatorial seas. However, a large sum of money immediately raised by the corporation induced this sensitive sea-wolf to close both his eyes and his nostrils. But the worst obstacles arose at disembarkation. The neighbourhood called for a solemn funeral in the historic church of the Carmine. The clergy refused admittance to one who had undoubtedly died without repenting his sins, and whose soul was black with the very crime that had removed him from the world. The prefecture and the police were alarmed, for the poor of Naples can react unexpectedly and dangerously. What was more, the entire criminal class, and not only its local representatives, felt their honour was at stake.

'Many years ago,' I told Memé, who was bewitched by the menacing throng in the poorest alleys of Lavinaio and Porta Nolana, 'for no good reason a stray shot, possibly fired by a policeman, killed a boy.' (This was one of Gian Luigi's memories.) 'They laid him naked on a table and bore him aloft through the streets, so for ten days the cavalry were stationed in the squares, here in Naples!'

'When?'

'Under Umberto I. Ciro Esposito on the other hand died in the early thirties. For half his life he'd been head of the city's rubbish-collection service, and in charge of the public gardens. He was undisputed master of the squares and streets, the government relied on him far more than on the prefect. He protected the people from the fascism they ignored, and yet he kept them docile for the regime. When he died, the dustmen, who are the nerve-centre of the lower echelon of society, wanted his funeral held in the Palatine Chapel of San Francesco di Paola, which as its name implies is reserved for the funerals of royalty. The House of the Princes of Piedmont (which was ruling at the time), the prefecture, the police headquarters, and the *carabinieri* could think of no better plan than to lock themselves into their respective offices and barracks. The citizenry locked themselves into their houses. From the head of the procession as it descended from piazza Carita towards San Ferdinando not a living soul could be seen. It was three in the afternoon. Ciro Esposito had his funeral lying on the king's bier. The dustmen withdrew in good order and life went back to normal.'

'And how do you come to be involved in all this now?'

'There's going to be a meeting here of the Mafia from Sicily, our Camorra from Naples, thugs from Genoa and Milan. Yesterday at police headquarters it was established that there would be no intervention by the forces of law and order. No one will be stopped or questioned, let alone arrested, whatever warrants for his arrest have been issued. The whole Mercato area is to be a free zone. And these fellows have guaranteed perfect order for the three days of the agreement. There remains the curia . . .'

'And who spoke for them?'

'Peppe Semmola. That's the point. "This isn't a city to be governed by a mayor," my uncle says. And there are no more kings. We talk of liberty - but ours, or theirs? I'll end up opposing Caramiello, going against these people, against myself. At Licudi I did what people wanted, always against myself!'

The priests of the Carmine listened to me with all the correct compunction; and because from all sides others were applying the same pressure, and the cardinal archbishop said nothing, they decided simply to abandon the church. They retired to the monastery and held no communication with the sacristy for three days. In sight of the Madonna Bruna, who's the chief focus of popular veneration, with no priests, no monstrance, no church candles, Gennaro Sperini's coffin lay raised high like a lonely castle for so long that it became covered with dust. And there was a church festival as odd as those that our seventeenth-century artists painted on canvases big as houses, among crying children, nursing mothers, feasts, and at night in the shadows ceaseless cries of succour for the imperilled spirit of the departed. Memé and I stayed a while in a peaceful corner. As we were leaving, someone who worked under me at the newspaper approached me.

'Your Excellency,' he said. (It was the first time for years I had heard that word, in the old days often used by Neapolitans when addressing the aristocracy, then abolished for them and recently readopted for the bigwigs of the republic.) 'Your Excellency, we're most grateful to you, and especially Signor Semmola wishes to express his thanks. I have explained to him who you are. I am a nephew of Marcariello.'

'And who is Marcariello?'

'You knew him for so long and you don't remember him?' said the other with an indulgent smile. 'He was honoured because you always addressed him by name. My uncle Marcariello's good soul went by the same of Giustino.'

The quarter of the Sanità was in my view the most unusual. It was separated from the city by the ravine of Foria; once it had been at the foot of the walls, now it hung there with tumultuous thoroughfares and winding streets with fantastic names: I Cristallini, I Vergini, La Stella. Swarming, impoverished, colourless, with its vast but crumbling buildings, it still had a genius both for festivities and for usury; it had its myths of the catacombs and the trade in reject furniture; it had its talent for theatre and its memories of crime. Its metaphysics shone on the stage of San Ferdinando, consecrated to the Devils of the Shepherds' Song, and on the courts where perverted justice was auctioned off, breathed from the charnel houses of the Fontanelle on to the Hospital for the Incurable, and set themselves against the cathedral and to the glory of San Vincenzo above the blood of San Gennaro.

Reverence for the Saint and communion with the Hereafter as practised in that part of Naples, hardly tolerated by the clergy, dismissed by a lot of people as mere superannuated folklore, appealed to me, particularly when contrasted with the new-found pride of science in this civilisation of machines. One saw this feeling for the transcendent in the many mortuary chapels set aside for souls in purgatory. There would be a tiny cave in the thickness of the wall, with six or seven small papier-mâché figures, their bodies appearing in a tangle of candle-flames, their eyes on heaven. For a people immersed in circumstance and resigned acceptance, hell was inconceivable and was hardly ever spoken of. The expiation of sin could be long, and could start on this earth; but forgiveness was assured. No deity could be so cruel as to burden the finite with the infinite, to punish slight, brief offences with eternal retribution. So the devout help the penitent with prayer; beseeching for him and with him, they cut short the time of his punishment; their desires follow him towards heaven. What more natural than that he, when he is among the blest, should remember those that helped him? The saints are moral heroes, they rise above temptations and therefore are severe with earthly sinners. We will find more indulgence, and perhaps more attention, with the wholly and merely human soul of one whose frailty did not avoid guilt. There will be a more immediate contact with the eternal; the spirit that was helped towards beatitude will help us in turn.

This principle of brotherly recommendation, this establishing a bridgehead in the Beyond (like the people of Licudi with relatives already established in the New World) struck me as being very far from foolish fantasy; it was a marvellously devised relation between the transient and the immanent. The last stage was the cult of a dead body chosen for the purpose from among the dead in the holy ground of San Pietro ad Aram, in the catacombs of San Gaudioso, or from among the countless, heaped, abandoned corpses in the caves of the Fontanelle.

It was profoundly pious to substitute one of these derelict dead for the impersonal and abstract Spirit of Purgatory. They named him, called him a citizen of their ancient homeland, paid him filial and familial homage. With him they made a balanced pact between sense and dream, between their terrestrial souls and his incorporeal soul made equal outside space and time in a loving vow.

The greatest thinkers and poets have seen life as a dream or only the projection of an idea. The people of Naples thought likewise, and fixed their eyes forward at the Eternal. The ancient Messapi put their dead to guard the walls of Manduria, but here they brought them into their houses, they took them back into their hearts. It was not superstition, I think, but a moral action which collectively asserted a civilisation, what the Neapolitan Vico understood as the insuperable limits of birth, marriage and the grave. 'Who is laying on his hands, beware of laying hands on humanity.'

The miracle of the city's patron saint came down through prattling, curiosity, argument, scepticism, simple wonder; but it remained the synthesis and symbol of the cult, redemption from death brought back into the circle of life, the bringing to life again of the blood shed in martyrdom. The blood of San Gennaro, black lichen more than a thousand years old, shone like a ruby for the faithful. Those who prayed to him called themselves his 'relatives' and that weeping in the packed chapel was for the whole human family, the whole race of the dead and the living and the yet unborn. The city was holy ground, and I recognised the voice of its regeneration.

I reflected, as I watched the usual *déclassé* mandolin players in a restaurant full of uninterested people, that they went on performing simply for themselves and for their daily bread. By contrast with the Naples down in the gorges of Capodimonte, there was the other Naples of Posillipo and Vesuvius, which threatened the picture-postcard paradise. The domesticated volcano, bordered with white villas up as far as the lava, cast a shadow over the gulf as enigmatic as Pulcinella's familiar, mocking mask, black and white, with the white the more mysterious. But I didn't feel Neapolitan improvidence was either an inclination to joy or a hiding to forget a threat. 'What has this city been in the world?' my uncle had asked. It had been human life itself, the daughter and matrix of death; not nothingness but the infinite.

In the silence of the night, I went back to the newspaper, to the press, with its nightlights red and green like signals, and its cylinders dark. It was a hopeless dream that one might influence the ministries by mere journalism since the famous days of De Zerbi, Scarfoglio and Sarao. With its gloom and dirt it had been the bilges of the profession; there at night generous thoughts had entangled themselves with base. Sunlight and greenery are unimaginable there. The sickly smell of ink hangs over the alley. The place is blocked by the gigantic rolls of paper for the presses. Black trucks wait there till at two in the morning they hurtle towards the railway station howling like whipped dogs.

In nearly a hundred years even the better local papers have never achieved a decent circulation. The figures they release, which are always false, and anyway represent the entire South, are laughable for such a big area. In the city, about one person in ten glances at a daily paper, if only to look at the deaths column. Any political cause ambitious of success must diffuse itself through other channels. Mestica pretended to ignore this, and would delude the stupid or the timid by giving them 'one copy only' of *Free Vesuvius* and not even printing the other supposed two hundred thousand copies. But Natale Caramiello and his gang understood the situation perfectly, and knowing their opponents understood it too, overwhelmed the city with demonstrations, which had a far more direct effect.

There were only two formidable political forces in Naples, the Catholics on one side and the extreme left on the other. So the gang, seeing that at the referendum Naples had voted for the king, adopted monarchism, which was going begging. Caramiello arrogantly declared himself for the king. Vast gilded crowns and crosses were set up in the squares, where they glittered nostalgically at night. First the crown was lit up, then the king's name around it, lastly only the cross flamed as if to display the good exile's martyrdom.

They set up platforms at the nerve-centres of the city, among the small traders, stallholders with and without licences, who would never have allowed the other parties such liberties, but who indeed helped and defended them, even if they went on making their sweetmeats right up till the rally started. The work of decoration was contracted out to the *maestri* of festivals in the Carmine, the Borghi and the Torretta; and because they used the same trappings in religious ceremonies, the whole Caramiello bandwaggon took on a sanctified appearance. The Catholic party, with the Peregrinatio Virginis, with processions restoring the patron saints to their original places after the war, had enjoyed a certain popular success at the expense of the communists. But now it seemed as if the echoes of those holy displays hung around the decorations on the platforms where Caramiello and his friends spoke. Their pictures on the myriad leaflets dropped from helicopters every Sunday over all the gardens and meeting-places had an almost religious dignity and reserve.

Everyone knew that don Natale was not exactly a model of virtue; but since people had always allowed the court a certain licence, his monarchism saved him. Everyone knew too that the swindler Semmola got most of his money from this mistress, who was at the head of a certain gang at Bagnoli, but here Edoardo de Filippo's *Filumena Marturano* gave absolution. As for don Ciro Mellonio, the sage of Mercato, there could only be good spoken of a man with nine children, all boys and all legitimate. In September 1943 he had opened his storehouses and rescued thousands of the poor from hunger. And since the trio spoke for a movement which was against those who had abandoned Naples in her worst hours, they were invincible. The king showed no sign of wanting to come anywhere near; but for three-quarters of the people, kings had always been merely immanent, from Ruggero the Norman to Francesco II, with the Savoys thrown in for good measure. But what really tipped the scales was that aura of regality and a last whiff of incense. For poaching on holy land, Caramiello was attacked as vehemently by the clergy as by the left. The people were boisterously anti-Marxist, so they had to choose between their actual rulers, half of them priests, and the trio, afflicted as they were but at least with attractively colourful plumage.

After the feast of San Giuseppe which with its gay festival of birds marks the beginning of spring in Naples, the election campaign opened officially. Mestica supported the right-wing Catholics and tried to squeeze what he could out of the situation. Caramiello's opponents poured out money on our newspaper, most of which Mestica pocketed. I was given a free hand to fight the gang as I saw fit, which gave me no happiness at all.

'The days are past,' my uncle said, 'in which a generous king appointed an enlightened minister to set the city to rights. These days everything comes to grief, between the building co-operatives and the manipulated companies and the ponderous administration. But it's possible to work towards ends that are still far distant, so long as nobody realises what we're doing. I don't think we can stop Semmola, or stop him committing numberless abuses and wrongs. But we might diminish his success. That's all we can hope for, and it must suffice us.'

If it had just been a matter of don Ciro Mellonio, I'd have let things ride. I had a notion he read my local sheet, certainly finding more in it than his fellows. I could see in him a paternalistic but efficient mayor, much better than the kind the Propaganda Agent admired. 'Man must be demolished so he can be rebuilt!' he cried; but he wouldn't have liked it if the others had pulled him down to rebuild him from scratch, as was surely necessary. But beside Mellonio stood Caramiello, who needed only a wooden leg to be the perfect pirate, and Semmola with enough vitality to be dangerous when harnessed to so much ignorance. He and his group were in permanent festivities, banquets where the diners were proud to come out with their fancy silk shirts spattered with sauce to show how delectable the *ragù* had been. I believed him capable of establishing stallholders in the courtyard of San Francesco di Paola, which would have been no bad thing, and of staging Caramiello's funeral in the Palatine Chapel, which would not have been beyond what is reasonable. But I could also see him out of mere caprice inciting the poorest quarters to sack the shops. To put Naples into the hands of its homeless beggars would be unjust to the cautious and thoughtful middle class, the wise professionals, the dignified 'fallen gentlemen'.

What a curious battle! It was easy to show, in the pages of *Free Vesuvius* or any paper, that the gang hadn't the foggiest notion of what a king was or might be, or what monarchy might lead to. Likewise, that it was ridiculous for them to stand up stained with stew in piazza del Plebiscito and catechise the crowd in front of the statues of eight founders of dynasties, any one of whom should have been able to hiss and boo them even though remaining stone. Our newspaper sold maybe ten copies in the ravine of the Sanità; but Semmola dished out ten million lire for the festival of San Vincenzo. The prefect feared for public order, and forbade the processions to come out of the Valle and into Foria; but Semmola simply threatened rebellion.

On the day and at the hour given, San Vincenzo came forth, to a multitude of faces pale in the blinding aceteline lights, to glorious silk hangings on the balconies, to enormous heaps of water melons, stalls of oysters glistening like precious marble, monuments of fruit, masses of boiled octopus the colour of coral, and to immobile watchers and thinkers, like Casillo in front of his glass of wine as dark as his musings. The saint was surrounded by clouds of incense and the plumes of the *carabinieri*, by silver candelabra and by garlands of flowers, followed by lights which climbed and flew and exploded at last on the lantern of the cupola. The saint! His gaze and his smile never altered, his eyes were enraptured, his open arms trembled slightly with the uneven going. He knew, he saw, he gave out superhuman virtue from his rosy lips that almost spoke!

Clearly, the election was lost.

For some while my uncle had suffered from asthma. Coming up the stairs, I smelt the acrid powders he burned and painfully inhaled. But that spring of 1949 his strength gave out, and he reached the stage when almost everything was wrong with him. Taken up with the newspaper and the election – which he wouldn't have me abandon – I was unable to care for him as was necessary. So Checchina left the nunnery at Sora for a time and came to stay with us. Just as her aunt Francesca, whose name she bore, went to Paola to Gian Michele's deathbed, she came to the modest house in the Riviera di Chiaia, and performed the offices that fell to her or to me to perform for him in death even if in life he had gone without. Checchina brought her nun's silence and austerity to the house. For long periods no voice was heard. If our uncle called in his week sufferer's voice, it was heard all over the house.

Seeing him approaching death, I would have spoken to my uncle of other things; but he spoke of it.

'Many people worry about death,' he said, 'and think and talk of little else. They give instructions to those who'll survive them, as if they wanted to go on playing a part in the world after their exit from it. But death is extraneous to us and none of our concern. Our business is life, while we've got it, and, alas, the deaths of others; but others will concern themselves with out death. The poorest of men, who has always served others, will on that occasion himself be served.'

My uncle smiled tiredly, his eyes humorous, patient, remembering. How many funerals he must have attended in his official capacity! Funerals of prefects, generals, aldermen, magistrates . . . And the next day, in the newspapers: 'The authorities were represented at the sad ceremony, among them the *commendatore* of San Maurizio and Lazzaro, don Gedeone Sansevero, lawyer of the state, etc., etc.' How many had gone before him from the warm dazzle of day into the shadows, 'that were no concern of theirs!'

He went on feebly. 'Almost all us think ourselves indispensable. "If I wasn't around, how could things proceed?" they say. The majority don't realise that life would get by far better without them. Death keeps thinning the wood to let in light and air. Death sorts out what life entangled. Human selfishness, or perhaps human need, pretends otherwise, but many hopes are founded on the deaths of others. When somebody dies,' my uncle concluded, still with that shrewd light in his half-closed eyes, 'a lot of people sigh with relief because they won't have to put up with him any more. If he was a great man, before whom they felt oppressed or humiliated, their relief is immense; and this justifies the solemnity of funerals. It's a way of sweeping someone out of the door.'

'And what about widows and orphans?' I asked. 'And what about good people!'

'I know you want to treat me gently. But if it wasn't for you and Checchina, in this vast city where I've spent so many years few would grieve for me. People buy a newspaper to see who's died, but from curiosity, not from affection. Widows and orphans will grieve, yes, while they're short of love and short of money. But if they can get those things again . . .! No, death's too natural for life to suffer from it. If we give someone a meaning, and that meaning becomes part of our soul, and that person dies, then part or almost all of our soul dies with her. Perhaps it happened once to me, long ago; so I started to die then. Gian Michele was the same, and Checchina now, and you. But you won't let go what the others were, and we last ones have been!'

The light softened in the bedroom. Over the wash-basin stood a small moulded looking-glass with hand-painted flowers, myosotis or daisies or I don't know what. The bed was black wrought-iron, with four glittering brass apples on the bedposts. The one at the right-hand side, at the head, was hollow to hold holy water.

'I haven't made a will,' my uncle concluded. 'Do what you all please with what you find.'

He pretended to doze so as not to notice my agitation. The saint was here too, but in him.

As the day of the vote approached, Caramiello resorted to modern techniques. His pearl-grey Maserati, recognised by everyone, raced at ninety kilometres an hour past the respectful eyes of the traffic police, who had only to pick up the thousand-lire notes tossed out by way of atonement for his excessive speed by the man about to be mayor. With unheard-of audacity, Caramiello had promised the electorate that this year the blood of San Gennaro would flow with no delay as a sign of approval of the city's conduct, and to augur well for the new council. And when the saint's day came, his blood flowed almost before the ministering priest's hand had touched the casket; and the king's beggars outdid themselves in orgiastic demonstrations of exultation. It was then that Peppe Semmola, catapulted by now well beyond the limits of the credible, had the genius to involve the heavens in the voting, and set up relica altars to don Natale, don Ciro and himself.

The scouts working for the newspaper and for my local sheet told me of this, and I went to see. At strategic points around the city the trio had set up their shrines in those modest houses half underground which are common in Naples. The decorators had richly arrayed them with the materials of religious festivals - blue brocade with gold fringes, brilliant crimson with silver fringes, tassels, plumes, crowns. There were palms everywhere. The enclosed air was rich with exotic odours (this was an old fascist trick Caramiello had not forgotten!) Record-players drugged one with soft, evocative music. In every shrine, by way of an effigy, a life-size photograph of Mellonio, Caramiello or Semmola, touched up with pastel colours, stood in the glittering circle of the lamps. Semmola was wearing a silk shirt (the *ragù* shirt) and smiling with all thirty-two teeth. Caramiello had had himself taken wearing dark glasses, as if to suggest the nightlong vigils he kept for the good of the populace. Being the best of the bunch, don Ciro was the least photogenic.

The stroke of genius, which from their lowly election campaign raised these *condottieri* to the skies and associated their smiles with that of San Vincenzo, was a lightning success. Like saints, they became mediators and intercessors, which in earthly language meant they were capable of innumerable semi-miracles, they would give a helping hand here or pass on a recommendation there. Filippo Mestica seemed plunged in reflection. But he had to counter-attack. With a spectacular publicity campaign, and a lot of money forked out by politicians, he launched his 'Songs on the Sea'.

It was a memorable evening, though it started with fears that, though the city was mad keen for songs, we'd be condemned for being on the enemy's side. But minute by minute, even three hours before the start, we saw it turn into an overwhelming triumph. Mestica's idea was an old one, dusted off for the occasion. Forty years before, as my uncle recollected, Tamagno had sung from a boat quite a way out from the bank, and it was said that legendary and most moving voice rose to the hills above Mergellina. What's more, we had the use of loudspeakers.

Enormous grandstands were built on a long stretch of via Caracciolo, but they were inadequate for the tide of humanity – informed of the event not by the newspapers, no doubt, but by the mysterious antennae of Naples – which flowed out from the gorge of Chiaia right along the shore. Semmola's altars were venerated and meetings applauded, I then realised, not because they were really dust thrown in the eyes of innocents. As far as Naples was concerned, this gang was no better or worse than any other, or for that matter the most correct and sober political party. *Free Vesuvius*'s articles in favour of candidates from Rome were superfluous. So was the spate of papier-mâché monarchist crowns and lights the city was starred with. Naples had already decided, had enthusiastically taken an idea to heart, and for a short time, from inspiration or fancy, would stick to it. Just as the Eternal will on occasion allow locusts to devour the harvest or fires the forest, so it was ordained that Caramiello should govern. But this stopped no one hastening to enjoy the songs organised by his opponents; for the songs belonged to everybody, like the miracle of San Gennaro (though it had been appropriated that year for a splendid vulgarised masquerade!)

So the crowd forgot all political candidates, and for hours seemed to hold its breath almost so time stopped, and lost itself in the music and its thoughts and the night. From the pontoons anchored in the evening bay, fountains of notes were flung up as if in all the colours of the rainbow. When, at the end, Toti dal Monte sang 'Solé mio' with her nightingale's voice, far higher than any male singer could reach, and the notes rose and then broke up, I could feel the multitude shiver. For them, as for me, losing and winning were the same in that heaven where the music leaped up in white cataracts.

Next day Mestica appeared cautious and reserved. This was easy to understand, for he had not only charged everything to the ruling party but had then, in agreement with the builders and decorators of the grandstands and pontoons, charged the listeners too, even those seated on the public street, which he had barricaded off with railings borrowed from the municipality. He thus made a colossal profit. More important still, however, were the good relations he established with the decorators, who were supporters of Semmola and had built his shrines.

In early May, a week before the election, my uncle died. He struggled painfully through the afternoon and the first half of the night. As dawn drew nearer he became more quiet, and he fell asleep in that special moment night-walkers know, when a shiver at the back of the neck tells them the first light of day is breaking. The doctor put down Gedeone's wrist, stepped back and bowed his head. Checchina took down the crucifix on the wall and put it between our uncle's hands. Then we stayed alone there till daylight began to filter through the shutters.

His face was fine and smooth, the lines and the white hairs streaked with light. There was still a faint smile lingering on his lips, as if for something he had kindly pitied here on earth, that only he knew about. Then his face set like a mask, and I recognised in him the cardinal, Gian Michele, Gian Luigi, and, strangely, even myself. It was as if it was always the same person who died, or as if all the others always died in one of us. It was as if one of us had to go on living for all the others.

Ferrante arrived a few hours later. Even though we didn't announce the death in the press, and fixed the funeral for an unusual hour, there was a large congregation of modest-looking people none of whom I recognised. They kept apart from us and looked at Ferrante and me humbly, rather like we children watched my father and Gian Michele make their stately entrance into the house at Monte di Dio. That same evening Checchina went back to Sora in my brother's car. At the newspaper, nobody knew what had happened; Mestica thought I'd lost a distant relative.

In the last few days, and to the sound of fanfares, columns of lorries loaded with *pasta* in special packets bearing the royal coat of arms gave out provisions to the needy. In the trio's sanctuaries, in the respectful shuffling and whispering, the funereal scent of tuber-roses, reminiscent of a crypt where a dead man is laid for people's last farewells, surprised the passers-by.

The left, yet again desperate at losing a country they were sure should have fallen into their hands like a ripe pear, but which stubbornly disproved all their theories, dragooned the famous into their service. Actors, singers and pettifogging professors, dedicated to the new (a good hundred years old, this new idea, as Christ's is two thousand years old) raged furiously, harried by anxiety and by the joyous stirrings of spring.

'Where were the saints when tons of bombs were falling here?' they shouted. 'Where were those who now cart the saints around?'

'Where was all this agit-prop?' demanded Semmola and Caramiello. 'Who'd ever heard such a Turkish word in Naples anyway?'

'Where were Caramiello and Semmola?' prated those in power, pretending to forget don Ciro Mellonio. 'One of them was dividing with the other leaders the spoils they'd stolen from the state, the other was starving the citizenry by profiteering on the black market.'

'Where was Mestica?' I went on in my thoughts, 'and where were a hundred thousand others now raving about their rights?' I thought of the silent spirit of my Uncle Gedeone, who had defended the city, who had gone away without scorn or sorrow, smiling at the cruel play of events. 'Nothing is ours,' he had said towards the end. 'Everything you see belonged to the dead, it's all dead men's stuff. You've got the duty to look after it, but you can't take it.' Just so, I thought. But Caramiello and the left and the ruling party were like Pilate's soldiers, they only wanted to divide up what wasn't theirs, things that had belonged to people like my uncle, who'd died without even making a will, knowing that sooner or later everything would be taken by others, and then by still others after them.

The poll was as exciting as the finish of a steeplechase. Caramiello had been going around raising his hand and making the victory sign in imitation of Churchill. He'd also, they said, given out five hundred million lire in cheques for ten thousand each, to be drawn on an anonymous account, but only when he had been elected. And he won by miles, though he had in part to share his victory with don Ciro. Semmola did less well than had been feared. The mysterious genius of Naples this time had launched its swarm of locusts with some reservations.

Four days later, I was in the office. It was late. I heard Mestica calling me in a low voice.

'I want you, and you alone, to receive these people who've just arrived!' he begged me.

I opened the doors of the lift and found myself face to face with Caramiello's dark glasses and the ageing locks of don Mellonio. They had a conversation with Mestica that was brief but no doubt long enough. Next day the editor came into my office looking cheerful.

'Given the results of the election,' he said, 'our paper must review its policy. It's undoubtedly to your credit if the new mayor has realised how we can be of use to the administration. You must share the editorship of *Free Vesuvius* with me.'

I thought things over, sitting at Uncle Gedeone's writing-table, where long ago he had drawn up the deed for Amalia to renounce her inheritance from Carruozzo. From the blinds, a shaft of sunlight fell exactly on my hand, and seemed thus to propose it as something important and different.

I felt time concentrated within me, like a little, hot, invisible flame within the cage of free will. Since 1940, what with the war, then at the ministry, then at the newspaper, I'd obeyed others' rules for nine years, I'd served, and with what loyalty had been possible. When Montaigne left public service, he retired to his tower; and Gedeone had retired to the Beyond.

I had them send my uncle's bed and desk to Paola, with his papers and a few things he'd been fond of. Checchina arranged that everything else went to the poor. On leaving Naples I did not even bother writing to Mestica.

THE RIVER

Just outside the silent streets of Guastalla, the Po, very wide, attended by canals and studded with islands, is crossed by a bridge of boats. Down beyond the poplars and water-meadows, the soft colours of the great river reflect the sky, sometimes serene and drowsy, sometimes racing turbulently. The horizons of the vast plain stretching away towards Mantua and Verona absorb and disperse moment by moment the notions which moment by moment the imagination recomposes. For others, nature may be more splendid elsewhere, in the biblical hills of Calabria, in the magnificent Appenines of the Abbruzzi, along the glittering shores of the South; but I'm most fascinated by the Po valley, so richly worked as to seem a ceaseless meditation. The lukewarm shadows of the clouds gallop away, the greenery trickles with rivulets, the water talks as it flows past the anchored barges, which creak under your feet. Taciturn fishermen watch the bends of the current and watch their lines. Only the Po has seemed to me, not so much a landscape to be loved, but one which itself gave out loving thoughts.

'I don't love him,' said Elisa, looking into the air beyond me, beyond the water I saw reflected and shining in her pupils. 'I don't love him any more.'

With her black hair and her face at once young and old, with her regular features, with the fine oval of her face and the tilt of her throat, she was beautiful. Sometimes the play of her expressions obscured this beauty, at other times, like then, enhanced it.

'He understood nothing about me at all,' she went on, with her soft voice and Po valley accent. 'I went to him never imagining love was like that, but he forced me time and again. I wanted to dedicate myself to others when I was at the hospice, I wanted to be a nun or a lay sister or an assistant, to help others. I did all I could, and for his sake. He didn't realise; nor did I realise how useless it was. When we did both understand these things, he truly fell in love with me at last, and was desperate at losing me, and I still didn't know I wasn't in love with him. I've only understood it now that I'm used to being with you.'

She pronounced the 'you', 'tè', almost childishly, like the 'veh' in the accent of Reggio. While she spoke, I heard too the solemn river murmuring as if flowed beneath the keels of the boats. I could hear three voices - my own, silent in my head; hers, poised and quivering; that of the quicksilver river, which drowned the other two in itself. 'Nothing I have is mine,' the river says. 'All turn to me, they call me father and provider; but not a drop I carry is mine, it all comes to me from the countless ramifications of the valleys. I resolve things in myself, but I'm nothing, or perhaps I'm a destiny.'

'Why have you come here and stayed here, Guiliano?' I ask myself. 'Perhaps you too have a destiny; you own nothing, though you've gathered from others and you carry for others. Where will you arrive? When you flow into the sea at last, you'll be as vast as the sea!'

'I'm lucky,' Elisa's sweet voice went on. 'I was maltreated and hurt till I wanted to die. But then you found me, and showed me how marvellous living in this world can be. Even if you leave me I'll want to live all the same, because what I've had will always be mine. That's enough; I'd live a hundred years, even living with him and serving him without loving him.'

Apart from a single road with traffic bound for Reggio or Suzzara, the houses of Guastalla were silent, their doors and windows shut, gardens hidden, porches empty. In the outskirts, where the houses are poor and you can smell the countryside, stood my house, which was amazingly large, for there space has no value, and one can pay less for rooms six metres high like in Gian Luigi's house than for a new building where you can touch the ceiling by raising your hand. Indeed the old houses with thick, soaking walls, full of freezing fog all winter, are shunned. A family declines and disappears, and no one wants their old villa, which is probably haunted, they'll say with lowered voices. From my living-room I can see, over the thick tree-tops, the line of the river bank with its processions of poplars. The place had been abandoned a long while. There are small ponds as black as ink. At night it is noisy with the croaking of frogs and chirping of crickets.

With what I imagined my last big decision (but how many times had I thought I was making final decisions?) I hadn't chosen one of the four cities where the legions used to break their marches, nor one of the rural communities, the villages and hamlets near Ferrara, Cremona and Salso, going up to the ridge of the Appenines. Now at the halfway mark of my life, I'd chosen Guastalla in which to gather my thoughts and return to the meditations I had known in my youth at the time of the hanging veranda. It lies at the heart of a circle of cities, of works, of memories, and is one of the most intense places on earth.

Elisa was born at Scandiano. She is not tall, but she's very lovely, with shining skin, and eyes that seem brown but then turn to a colourless radiance. If everyone has one age that seems to fit them ('Annina will never be more than eight,' Gian Luigi said with gentle irony) Elisa will always be fifteen. She has that exuberance and energy. She has transports of delight and ephemeral distresses; but she hasn't yet matured, her spirit isn't ready for voluptuousness.

'I was alone and we were so poor! For a long time he respected me, and I accepted him without imagining anything. But the first time, when I realized what he was doing inside me, I was so appalled I had to get up. He never knew what I felt.'

I too had had no understanding of voluptuousness, I now realised, neither with Mavì in Ferrara nor with Caterina in Paris. That was pleasure, simple youthful vigour, an explosion in the blood. But Elisa, who knows nothing of voluptuousness, has given it to me: an entwining and sapping of mind and body.

When Elisa comes into the room I use to work in, she sits in the greenish shadow that falls through the tall window shaded by the trees, and stays still for a while with lowered eyes, her face a gleaming cameo; she seems the shell of a person, or the pod of a beautiful plant. She's poor, and always has been; but poor like a fallen and exiled queen who has abandoned infinite riches but in her mind has them still. What she carries within herself is as limitless as human potential can be, though never given a worthy opportunity. She lives and dreams everything she says, deluding herself constantly; but she seems to stay in a truth that is not to be expressed in words. I know that this is what I've been attempting for years; so what she sees has been formed by me, and reflects her thoughts and satisfies her desires.

Once I visited her house, where she endures her weary, unhappy existence in poverty, disorder and noise. She flees from it, and regains in the white lamplight that falls on my papers the fantastic paradise from which she feels herself driven forth. She gave birth painfully, I know, and the scar on her womb is an offence against purity, a cruel whiplash added to the servitude of the species. When she undresses and gives herself to me, I feel it as the hostile sign of an unforgivable god. She simultaneously takes me to her and pushes me away, because what she has suffered – the shame more than the wound – has made her feel guilty, has wronged and changed her, and I feel it. I am consumed with pity, though with her I can reach oblivion.

What kind of oblivion? One in which no line of the face goes unexamined and no mistaken word unrecognised? Which makes no allowances, and permits not a single falsehood? Which takes you whole, obscure evil and obscure idea of good? Which knows the deceit she lives off and the illusion she wants to offer me, I who have no need of illusions? Which accepts and even explains these things? But still it is oblivion.

'I was a virgin till I was over twenty. I thought that to love all you had to do was hold hands. I was hit, burned, constrained . . . You've taken pity on me, and now, with your compassion, a timorous sense is awakening. Giuliano, you must help me to not need you. Don't hurl me into love. If it touches me it will destroy me.'

'What are you thinking and hoping?' the other voice says. 'You've known everything and left everything. You pass your days in a silent room with green trees and croaking frogs. As a snail leaves its track, you write words on paper that are meant to tell the truth. You believe this to be your duty. But your sweet cheat has only to come to the door for you to realise that the truth lies there. You're already old, and have only now discovered love, now when she cannot love you, and only, perhaps, because you are capable of loving her. How much you must have accepted and forgiven! How much will have to be forgiven you!'

Then Elisa, since there was nobody around, just the water murmuring over the mud, held me to her and slowly kissed me. And I was aware of the motionless fishermen on the curving tributary canals, the palisades of poplars, the sky, the slime, and musing river flowing by.

To compose one work out of all the traces scattered behind me was an old idea of mine. As the years passed and left me only a sad sea of memories, and since I felt that my particular life, like the universal life, had its only meaning in the motions consuming its ends, I imagined the only way of recovering my life would be to give its story.

For if man is the conscience of things, my written synthesis of my inner and outer experience would be like the flower that rounds off the whole process of the tree, from the opening of the seed to the proliferation of the foliage, and not only the tree but all of nature expressed in it.

How I undertook such a desperate venture I cannot say; but I had learned in the college of the Virgo as a boy to be methodical and patient. I am sure that sustained me. That which reflected me became my confession; but I also had to bear witness to the others I'd seen living through good and ill, neglecting nothing, distorting nothing, and for that matter forgiving nothing. Unconditional truth became my dogma. Being brutally frank about myself gave me the courage to be so about others. The overcoming of pride perhaps in its turn augmented it. But there were also kindnesses and affections. I didn't want Uncle Gedeone to die, I didn't want Arrichetta's beauty to fade unseen or Nerina to go unpraised.

I distrusted the idea of an autobiography because, as I'm writing it now, it's a private document and should remain so. But when this genre aspires to literature, it has all the shortcomings and awkwardnesses of melodrama, hoping the orchestra will carry it through, for the stuff of ordinary life is not the stuff of opera. Writing about himself, an author stumbles along with a bit of dreary narrative and a bit of pure fantasy. What good is it to know that in the seventeenth century the doctor Carrano particularly relished the tips of birds' wings? And all about Pontormo's stomach-aches? And Carlo Gozzi's quarrels? And despite Cellini's more passionate pages, who cares about his boasting and his gossip? Those six volumes of Casanova could be reduced to two, and writer and reader would benefit. Not even Alfieri got it right, he's too woodenly theatrical for the pliancy and quickness and brightness of life. Giambattista Vico was the best model, but his lofty tragedy was on the same universal plain as Augustine's *Confessions*, which could be offered to men only when addressed to God.

Looked at differently, all the arts were autobiography, because the artist can draw water only from his own well. Art synthesised the formless mass of the real, and made a mirror and a symbol of it. Novels were composed of fragments of the real integrated with the imagined, pieces of other works, things heard of but not experienced, rather like Raphael's 'School of Athens' in which there's a real portrait of Michelangelo and imaginary ones of Plato and Aristotle. I found that idea cold, and wanted to avoid it. Therefore I couldn't write a novel, even if the magnificent Stendhal had fixed its archetype with almost those same canons. Nor were the grand models of *Werther* or *Ortis* or *Copperfield* any help, where a large measure of autobiography is melted into the romantic flow of time. Nor could I learn much from the mammoth enterprises of Joyce and Proust.

I had studied both of them closely. The Frenchman, whom most people kept on their shelves for snobbish reasons, but read only in part or not at all, seemed to me anything but an historian of himself. And as for synthesis (which should be the hallmark of art) he seemed to have made a pont of avoiding any kind of structure and breaking all the rules of form. Microscopic analysis, but conducted only as the fancy moved him, suffocated a large part of *A la Recherche.* But in his melancholy digging among the ashes, once in a while he turned up a spark or a red hot ember of the most powerful lyricism, which sufficed him. On the other hand, nothing could be much less harmonious than a work composed of countless disproportions, facts and notions drawn out page after page. It was a long, sinuous tape suspended between two abstract points, or an intermittent throbbing in dark water. As for Joyce, there too one finds poetic passages, usually nothing to do with the theme of the book; but I judged the whole remarkable demonstration a failure. For the Irishman, an idea multiplied itself till it became inconceivable. But at that point writing is dead and art implicitly negated. Then there was Constant's *Adolphe* which I admired for its veracity; but he isolated the 'I' in a particular moment of passion, rather than sinking it into that whole where our passions and we ourselves pass as the slightest incidents only. There was the first volume of Nievo's *Confessioni.* Spiritually, I felt him to be a forbear of mine, but he died young, more than a hundred years ago; and I didn't feel I could take his methods from him and use them out of time.

The stuff of life was motionless, but was forever changing in the play of the mind. I intended to use only the real; but to present it so it was transformed, as I used to play with my building-bricks alongside Checchina, bricks precise in form and limited in number, making a building at once real and fantastic which rose from the flat box where before the bricks had been stored in rows, and which amazed Gian Luigi. Thus I saw the world of reason integrated into the world of imagination. It was almost like transposing into writing the feelings and thoughts which had built the House of Houses, where every heavy static stone block had been an idea, where there had been hidden life coursing through the rafters of Acerenza like the hermetic writing on the hearth, where reality had been infused with poetry and only poetry could explain life.

I didn't want to recuperate the past by following its winding thread; I looked at it all together, a mass of facts and notions. I mixed and sorted episodes and places and times, till I had an exemplary story that would gather and represent everything, as the sum represents its factors. From one person I would draw several; from several I would draw one, who was true in every part but who had never existed as a whole. Redeeming things from the trammels of force of circumstance, I could draw out the symbols which life had so often started to clarify, but had finished elsewhere on another occasion. Everything from first childhood awareness onwards was subsumed in this final judgement.

So I made myself concentrate, and evoke, to start with, the essential scenes of my life: the country house at San Sebastiano when I was between boyhood and youth, or the beach at Maronti after Gian Luigi's death. The scenes evoked the figures, with their accustomed personalities and attitudes, even their gestures and words; and threads of life lived elsewhere, or lived by others, were woven in with them.

Finding the responses for this harmony, lighting upon the right resolutions, was a cruel and often frightening business of digging in myself, forcing my mind to produce what I wanted. But slowly I realised that, if left free and quiet, my mind would perform this labour of its own accord, or as if asked by some thought which was not mine but which knew the ends and foresaw the answers. In the end my memory gave prodigiously, and I no longer asked but waited for it to bear its fruit, like a tree that asks nothing of the earth or indeed of itself but receives, transforms and gives in the determined measure and time.

What surprised and fascinated me was the meshing of the real with what had been made out of the real; in the end, I couldn't tell them apart; I couldn't distinguish between what I'd recalled and what I'd constituted, actions I'd witnessed and actions that had been possible and I had imagined fulfilled.

It proved necessary not to work up reality but to tone it down for the real kept changing and expanding. Nothing comes to us without being interpreted and modified by our senses and then our reason; so the only truth we can tell is our very own truth, which resembles us. So instead of making sure everything was accurate, I made events conspire to produce my symbols, my unique world. As I had felt since looking at the Rubens in Paris, and thinking of the conflict between Louis and the Duke of Burgundy, the secret was to distil the essence of culture and reject the forms, fusing universal and personal history as one.

So my book was composed not by an act of will, not with any outward regard, but as if with the invariable rhythm of a pregnancy. It had its conception in a moment of pleasure and illumination. Its gestation had the pain, nausea, uncertainty and dizziness that every mother knows, afraid of giving birth to a cripple, hoping for a god, unable to stop this slow process, or slow it down, or speed it up or alter it. At the end, in the ineffable joy of knowing that the child of my labour was alive and healthy as a baby born to create in its turn other lives, I rested like a mother, knowing my debt was paid.

When I'd drafted the book, I left it for a few months for the sediment to settle, and then I read it more than once. It seemed new, not written by me, and in parts marvellous. But all the things wrong with it seemed to reflect me; I felt I was disfigured or had bits missing, so I had to work on it endlessly till it was well formed throughout, finished in every detail, as a plant needs each smallest leaf to have the right veins.

I worked on every sentence, word by word, comma by comma, as I had worked on the larger scale with the structure of the book, its figures and symbols, attempting the solid style I admired in authors of antiquity. I tried to get every sentence right, as even the smallest patch of skin on our bodies has a unique quality, all dissonance or discolouration being a sign of sickness throughout the whole. I was later able to be impassive whatever was said about the book, because nothing in it had come from outside and all within it had come from an unstoppable impulse. It was the measure of myself as a writer in the same way as my life, judged incomprehensible by so many, had been the measure of myself as a man.

The palace rises unexpectedly above the landslide of the river bed. Behind the sheer walls stand unfinished porticos, vaults which end in nothingness, arches like shoulders braced to take weights which never came. Below, the roofs of Piacenza flicker in the sun, dusty rubble and crumbling brick contrasting with the colossus in hard stone. The green gardens pale with summer waste away in the air of the stagnant waters. There's a deathly emptiness in the noon silence and the blinding August plain.

'Why do the countries of the sun have this breath of death?' asks my other voice. 'From the Pharoahs to the Aztecs, from Spain to Naples to Palermo with its ghastly tombs of the Cappuelini! It's as if the great giver of hope and of life destroyed himself in his own heat. Just as Philip II had built the Escorial, so his half-sister Margherita had built this palace in Piacenza. Here are the infernal stairs of the court of Caserta which Oderisio and I mocked in our thorny childhood.'

Elisa was thoughtful beside me. For decades the palace had been a barracks, a plague house, a refuge, and it had only just been cleared out. The great rooms were squalid, rubble and filth lay on the outer walls, passages had been earthed up, stairs cut off. This wing had only recently been abandoned by refugees and was like the thieves' camp on the Elb in Germany. The old prisoner of Siltau again smelt the unmistakable stench of bed-bugs.

Elisa looked down fearlessly thirty metres from where she had climbed.

'This is what I often used to do. We had a house high up in old Parma beyond the river. From the attic you could get out on to the roof. Below there was a wall that went down four floors. I shouted to him, "If you touch me I'll jump!" '

I got her by the ankle and gently urged her back. Her flawless skin was warm, and felt like satin. But the youthful wax of her face had already been marked, as if by the thumb of a bitter sculptor. Her changing expressions, the colours of her cheeks, her changing eyes, all veil the signs. But in repose, with her Greek profile and her black hair, she looks like Salvator Rosa's 'Vita-Umana', a heavenly figure but dressed in clothes once splendid but now worn out, crowned with flowers now withered, drooping, broken. The seated figure looks like a goddess; but in her face there's the faintest suggestion of the ghastly.

Elisa's and her family's new house has no high places. It stands in a desolate position a little beyond Gualtieri. Gualtieri is depressing, with its porticos in the square the rotten yellowish colour of Maria Teresa's Austria, the colour of Pavia University and the Marchesi Palace, that melancholy pile of bare brickwork. Beyond, the countryside near the river becomes squalid, with its ditches and swamps, its mosquitoes and the reek of the pig farms. Elisa's new house stands in a rectangle of wire with her husband's little factory, part of the speculative fever from Carpi sweeping the province, enterprises that lived on debts and on hopes, but were doomed by the market and the stock exchange. Elisa's youth had been worn out amid brand-new machines, half of them stopped; she had been director, worker, assistant, bookkeeper, maid, a succuba forever lamenting her fate to me, but unable to free herself. I believed there was love there.

I had met her on the tiny antediluvian train that goes from Guastalla towards Reggio, with old-fashioned carriages without compartments where everyone gets to know everyone else. The train runs happily through the thick greenery on either side that almost cuts it off. At each of the lanes that cross the railway line there are warning bells, and the shrilling seems to increase the pleasure of the ride. Given over to this rural railway music, I didn't at first see Elisa; she had already noticed me when I caught her eyes. I found her on the same train on other occasions. I imagined she was looking out for me. Still more time passed, and then I looked out for her.

Trains are the life of that valley. The worker bees swarm from city to city, village to village, here and there. Elisa is twenty-five. Since tragedy first came to her household, each morning she's up too early, and at half-past seven is on the little train going to work at Novellara. She comes back at seven in the evening. At home, she finds duties and torments that go on till after midnight. Come fog, come snow, come sunshine, for seven years she's done this three hundred and sixty days a year.

'My father could have saved himself,' she says softly. 'He was hiding in an empty house next to ours, and the partisans hadn't found him. I was in the courtyard, behind a wall, but a neighbour said, "That's the fascist's daughter." One of them stuck his submachine-gun into my chest and said, "If you don't tell us where he is I'll kill you." Then my father came out. They shoved my mother and me away, we heard the shooting but we saw nothing. They threw everything out of the windows into the courtyard, and set it on fire. I was eighteen. I went to work in the factory at once. Emo was out of work, but as soon as he'd earned enough money we got married.'

Her story is strange. She tells it to me when we go out on Saturday afternoons. She manages to take the time off work, and accepts from me the equivalent of the overtime she would have earned, which she has to hand over to Emo. Each time we go somewhere else, as I did with Mavì and each time Elisa too gives me an echo of the past. But how different she is! Or how different I am, who find the flowing river enough, with its mud flats and springs. I even understand what the saint meant, when he said that everything that is is good.

Her murmuring, regretful story-telling enraptures me. She has the same name as my mother's aunt, Elisa Lareme, who presided over my childhood with her white hair and diamond earrings. In the house at San Sebastiano in a chest of drawers as big as an altar, there were old love letters and flowers almost turned to dust. My great-aunt Elisa seemed at once old and young, silver-haired and blonde, and a timeless voice, that was not hers, spoke of love. And this other sweet, voluptuous Elisa seems timeless too, and writes me love letters that I can believe are the same ones mysteriously resurrected.

When she's in her office she writes to me on accountants' forms, perhaps secretly, like a schoolboy working away at the bench with a penknife. She covers every inch of the paper with her uneasy handwriting, using common expressions, many of them commercial jargon. But there's always *her* imagination, there are *her* words which ring true. She gives me the folded letter, and wants me to read it while she watches me. I'm sure she doesn't love me, so I ought to disregard both what she's written and the look in her eyes, because she's looking at me only to know me better and to keep me more securely. But I'm moved all the same by her real thoughts, by her real anxieties and griefs, at which I guess. And her devotion clutches at my heart, though it's not devotion to me. This is no doubt clear from my face, and it makes her gay and triumphant because she imagines it the result of her sweet deceit and my loving error. She doesn't know how much I can love her, for the very reasons which prevent her from loving me. Nor can I make her understand without destroying the coloured chimera which holds up this impossible love, of which only dust would remain.

I'm forty-eight, roughly twice her age. I've always thought love needed two people, that one-sided love wasn't love. The common phrase 'a good-looking couple' has its good sense, for a body in decline, old and ill, is repugnant beside a beautiful girl glowing with health. I looked at her and me . I knew I didn't want to fulfil myself in this love; I wanted only to support myself on her youth now mine was deserting me; and this fraud was dissolved in her deceitfulness. I couldn't resist the last rays of my own sunlight, or the splendid shining of her sun. 'You're young!' the voice pretended. I feel her in my arms, warm and tender. Her face is still. She's concentrating deep in herself, holding herself to her absurd sacrifice. What suffering, and what a heaven! Hers and mine are very far from each other.

Elisa's husband, after her father's fate, was discriminated against in that communist and sectarian neighbourhood, and in his turn became sectarian. He found her as an innocent girl, and dazzled her with lies. He understood her usefulness, appropriated her, relied on her with all the megalomania of the sufferer from meningitis, and passed in her gentle eyes for a hero and a martyr; and since her family was derelict, he presented himself as a protector, and became a despot. This one-time fascist militiaman was a veteran of anti-submarine warfare; he had been a paratrooper in Africa, a legionary in Spain, a volunteer in Ethiopia; and to the girl tormented by reactionaries calling themselves revolutionaries he seemed a god on earth. Seven exhausting years hadn't stopped her loving the only person who'd had her and had kept her. Elisa's lamentations were the paradox of all such love: what she perpetually deplored she at least thus kept fresh in her mind.

Emo Cavagna is heavily built, short, with reddish, leonine hair. His voice is deep, his solemn face is freckled, his eyes are watery and furtive. He must be around my age, maybe older. He wanted to set himself up in business, but he had no industrial or technical training, and the whole house of cards relied mainly on the valiant efforts Elisa dedicated to it at night, after drudging all day at Novellara. It had been she who had prepared contracts and discussed subventions; she had obtained first discounts and then, later, guarantees and postponements. He had thrown her beauty into hazardous situations which he must have been able to assess. Her inner simplicity had never entered his foul mind. Sent by him with foxy cunning into situations where to save him she had to sacrifice herself, she had done so more than once. She had taken on that guilt, remorse, disgust and the terror that he knew. He not only knew; he drove her innocence to lose itself in these sad entanglements. He went on swearing he loved her, to aggravate her sense of having sinned by betraying him, and thus locked her into a ghastly silence. But it is from there that her tender voice reaches me.

She came to me, as to others before me, on Emo's behalf. From the start he was most obliging; he let me visit the factory, which was blatantly foundering; he reckoned I was suitable; he advised her and set his murky game in motion. Elisa was incapable of prostituting herself if in her heart she gave it that name, so she painted her experience with chimerical colours. Perhaps working up a previous rough draft, she had spoken aloud both parts in a drama, she had acted out a story of falling out of love, and dreamed up a ghostly new love. I know she takes every penny I give her to the bank and to her husband's creditors; I know she kneels before her confessor, who cannot pardon her because she cannot promise not to fall into the same sin again. But I forgive her. And I abandon myself in loving her, in so far as I am still capable of loving.

Later, though the sun is still high and the heat intense, we stand in the big square and look at the monument to Alexander. It's rather like a cloud, nimbus or cumulus or cirrus, that circles around animated by some gay spirit, some beneficent energy. It's life in the form of a horse and rider, a combination of noble deeds with simplicity, for this Caesar rides like a barefoot cowboy. It is perhaps this that I am looking for with Elisa. At Licudi, the fisherwoman Incoronata was in herself all that fabulous countryside since before the Greeks arrived; and here I feel Elisa to be the personification of the glorious valley. The involved doubts, deceits and perhaps perversities in which she lives are those that stirred in the souls of the princes here. The thoughts that knot and unknot in Emo Cavagna's base mind, and also in hers, confirm them children of the renaissance, with that mixture of passion and guilt, those intricate fantasies of grandeur and evil, mankind at its most various.

We pass back over the bridge of boats, where before she told me of her dreamed sacrifices and sins. Her mouth is sweet when she leaves me, soaked in ambiguity and oblivion.

From the vantage point of *Free Vesuvius*, it had been possible to cast indiscreet glances to see how publishing was developing after the Second World War. The old Garibaldian publishers had been at once impresarios and critics of the authors whose risks and glories they shared. Now, writing was sold like any other commodity. The capital invested should be guaranteed, according to the banks, by 'experts'; but since the only experts that could be found were themselves in the field of letters, a contradiction arose. Those genuine writers utterly incapable of turning themselves into clerks were judged by those constrained to do so, either because they hadn't yet got under way themselves and thus were inexperienced, or because they'd already been got rid of and therefore were bitter and jealous. But most of the critics were academics, half of them speaking with the authority of anyone with a well-paid job, half of them lunatic interpreters of contemporary art. Worse still, I had to be ready to stumble among large numbers of men like Omobono.

As if that were not enough, I had to tread a long, thorny path to get a long and complicated book looked at closely, let alone assessed. The publishers were bureaucratised. They were extraordinarily slow in their enquiries, wearisome in their procedures, enigmatic in their conclusions. The publishing houses that appeared most open operated like partisan camps; one risked having one's manuscript plagiarised, misused or even lost. Feeling my way with one of the more reputable, I was received each time by a different person. As for the chairman, he was big-game hunting in Rhodesia, or he was on a cruise to the Bahamas, never at his desk. Needless to say, he never answered his letters, having dispensed with this and most other forms of good manners, like a lot of other boorish people recently risen to somewhat eminent positions they're quite unfitted to occupy.

Not for practical reasons, but for the sake of the ideas in my book itself, I realised I had to arm myself against these intellectual parasites. It needs no repeating that while they are alive authors will never be helped. But when they are out of the way, and it suddenly becomes possible for someone else to reap their success, there will be no lack of rivals eager to claim the spoils. There were three or four showmen in publishing who were competing ferociously to discover new talents – talents among the dead, of course – the discovery being more important than the discovered work. One recent famous case made me keep my eyes open; it was a short and very readable book, that had got nowhere while the author was alive. What sort of discovery was it, if any reader anywhere in the world could see at first glance the book was readable and in good taste? Rather, what poverty, to have to clamber on to the bier as it passed in order to make any sort of appearance at all!

Knowing and understanding the way things worked, and being strangled neither by need nor by longing for success, I was determined not to allow those who wanted to exploit me to indulge in rosy hopes. I came across badly. And since I was new and unexpected in the republic of letters, I was a nuisance. Worse, what I'd written was far from normal; and I had to deal with people earning their daily bread, reluctant therefore to risk money on the unproven when they could live off stuff they were sure they could sell. My work called for knowledge in those who would recognise it, and courage in those who would defend it. After several false starts, I fell back on the Roman precedents of the ancient playwrights and decided to print the book myself.

I worked at Parma, under the wing of the tradition of Bodoni. But it was less the fascinating minutiae of his art which occupied me, and more the endless work of revision and correction. But when at last I had the finished book in my hands, I was sure of what I'd written. I cheered up when I thought that all I'd lived through, even the mistakes, came back to me as experience, reserve, culture, and this I could offer to others. But it was then too that I began to look more critically at the changes, and often the deteriorations, in our culture since my time at the Lily.

Here too, the careless South, and Naples in particular, had been the most faithful guardians. Outside fashionable movements, away from commotions merely concealing mediocre interests, they went on studying the archetypes and reflecting on what endures. The South, neither fascist nor partisan, under Croce's aegis maintained the discipline of the empire of reason. But when the philosopher died the aegis fell. I felt that the real landslide had begun to gather way.

Croce was respected by Mussolini, but after serving briefly in Badoglio's government he retired from a sphere of action which was never his; and slowly the nation came to regard him as the representative of our intellectual life. He was immensely popular with modest Neapolitans. Vast crowds came to his funeral. But though the affection of the common people was sincere, it was disturbing to see others competing for his inheritance. But no one was capable of taking over where he left off, and so the landslide began.

Before becoming an art critic, one ought to undertake appropriate and extensive studies so essential for that most difficult discipline. The academics were so corrupt and divided that it fell to the newspapers to do this job, though they rarely employed anybody who was up to the job. Mestica installed his nephew as drama critic at *Free Vesuvius*; but after writing the most fatuous rubbish he disappeared and never came back to the office. A lot of newspapers hired people to write their arts pages who scribbled ignorantly away and were never contradicted, so effective were the chains of interest that held the cliques together. The publishing houses therefore ran weekly journals in order to defend their books, and surreptitiously kept in their pay a handful of critics on allied or on supposedly neutral papers; but these contrived reviews all sounded alike. Then there were others who fancied themselves as judges of the arts, and set up their own reviews, though they never praised an author who didn't help finance them. The picture was completed by the avant-garde and the fashion for the abstract.

My Uncle Gedeone had found futurism an agreeable joke. But even then Boccioni and Balla had exhausted its possibilities; they then busied themselves strangling it in blind alleys. Marinetti's free writing, upside-down numerals, letters mixed or alternated, only went to show that in literature it was ridiculous and futile to savage syntax or orthography, because a language develops naturally, brings itself up to date, becomes richer or impoverished, along with the civilisation it expresses. Insisting that all the canons of art could be transcended (except goodwill among men, which when it ventured towards the informal tended to disappear altogether) they made an incredible array of sophistications possible. Anyone could produce any daub or scrawl, without draughtsmanship, without grammar, and claim he was misunderstood, not untalented. In three-quarters of the world this nonsense spread like wildfire, though it seemed inconceivable in the name of silent art, with its selectiveness, its filtering, its destiny.

But it was easy enough at the time to establish these uncouth great works. There was a lot of money in the hands of the tasteless and the uncultured. The fake critic and the fake artist allied themselves to pass off the fake work of art on the unwary rich. The arts were marketed with advertising as effective as that used for promoting a football team or a beauty contest. The literary prize was linked with the name of a liquor or brand of woollen product. Those who arranged such prizes, seeing themselves indispensable for fake painters and writers, became arrogant and full of their own importance, even towards serious writers. They forgot that, like all the rest of the world, they ought to be devoted disciples and servants of art, that they should wear those vestments and officiate at those rites and sing praises at that altar; but they should not, after their homily, aspire to judge the presiding saint. But there were countless poetry prizes – as if poetry could be given any prize except Apollo's laurel wreath – and one saw hundreds of versifiers claiming to be poets and being called poets by others who called themselves critics of poetry.

The last contaminated was the cinema, the seventh art and already a hybrid, always apt to fall for any new drug being sold. To the stupefaction of the masses, a swarm of film directors arrogated to themselves the roles of sociologist and philosopher. The carnival grew, and every day some weird trick thrust a new genius into the limelight. Everything was justified by appeals to freedom of thought, or passed off as a break with the past, even revenge on the past, as if the past were an enemy to be destroyed. The avant-garde became merely those who set themselves up to try the rearguard. It was an odd army, in which the part advancing fastest had the duty, not to wipe out the enemy (what enemy?) before them, but the main body of their own force behind them. It was a rough sea into which the little ship of my book was launched, inexperienced but strongly built.

With innocent coquetry, 999 numbered copies had been printed, and I sent them off ten at a time to names who to me were only names. Since my time at the newspaper, I had made a note of anyone in the worlds of writing or current affairs I deduced held to some values. I sent the book to newspaper editors too, whoever they were, to reviewers of literature, to publishers and their helpers, to the heads of cultural organisations, to magazines from the extreme right-wing nostalgic monarchists to the extreme left-wing anarchists, to university professors, to people who cropped up at congresses and meetings. With each copy of the book, I sent a personal letter, in my own handwriting, each one as appropriate to the recipient as I could make it. I sent off 250 copies in this way, and then, without anxiety, but with a certain curiosity, I waited.

The results were not unlike those obtained by the bookseller Pagano when he sent out a red circular to try to get money for *The History of the Fascist Revolution* by his old friend Chiurco. From all those I had imagined representative of the Italian intelligentsia, I received a small number of notes of courteous acknowledgement; but no one took pen in hand and wrote a real letter. It was a sign of the centrifugal tendency in our society demonstrated on 8 September 1943. The old and praiseworthy tradition of writing letters is still held to in England; but here it has been let languish even in commerce, and letters creep through the administration like snails. I didn't expect replies from newspapers, because I knew that no weary journalist pays any attention to any sheet of paper unless he is himself producing it. I knew too well that every day an editorial table heaps up with booklets, bad books, fat books, and that with the combined intellects of Mithridates and Spinoza it would be impossible to deal with the lot. Something of forty pages would often get a mention, because the critic could dispatch it with a quick phrase, ignoring any substance the work might have, so overworked was he, suffering from ophthalmia, goaded by the editor, obsessed with others' petitions, their complaints, their spite, their threats. God was considerate to Saint Thomas allowing him to write his *Summa* when he did. I liked to imagine him being reviewed by the mighty of the Roman press now.

Involved as I was in my love affair with Elisa, sometimes the book's fate slipped from my mind altogether. I was confident of its future well beyond my time, and short-term success didn't interest me. Success is useful to the young and to the disinherited because it offers them money, esteem, love or the illusion of love, a level in society to which before they couldn't aspire. But my dificulty was to keep out of things I had rejected but back into which I forever found myself being led. As far as money goes, I knew it wasn't important, having had it by inheritance from Gian Michele, having had to earn it with the Latin American Trevd Aguine and in Rome, or having had none at all as in Milan. I knew the soul will always find its balance on new fulcrums. I could do without respect, having been a slave in Germany and felt a vibration of the spirit not unlike that of the solitude on Ischia. As for love, I'd known and questioned it in various guises, now I knew it again, and had to prepare myself to abandon it. Therefore fame could only have perhaps satisfied an abstract ambition to overcome others and to be considered superior by them; but over the years I'd learned too much to indulge in such an illusion. I wanted to offer my book, not to get anything for it. At the end of all that tormented accounting, I wanted to give and to share. I imagined people would accept my offering, and at last I'd be regarded as free, a man who had, however late, honoured all his debts.

When, after the initial silence, a few laboured notices came out in obscure weeklies, written by reviewers I'd never heard of, from what I read in their lines and between their lines I realized how absurd my brooding had been. There seemed to be no communication possible between the world of my ideas and the worlds even of those disposed in my favour and ready to praise me. Most people felt the book just about passed muster. One young man treated it as if I'd written it solely in order to beseech his agreement. But most of them just compared me to writers they knew and I didn't, an old system, by which Tom is compared to Dick, Dick to Harry, he to someone else again, and nothing is in fact said about anyone.

Then, unexpectedly, a complicated essay appeared in German in a magazine published in Zurich, written by a woman who, they said, had now gone back to America. I saw in a Catholic review an essay that scrutinised the book most carefully, to which a Marxist journal replied tit-for-tat. A few other reviews appeared here and there, usually at a pretty low level. I had struggled through forty years; it was crass ignorance to imagine me a beginner; it was simplicity itself to ascertain that my experience as an artisan, for instance, dated from a long time back, and fairly clear that one couldn't produce a work of this kind without a lot of preparation. The last paper darts were hurled at my by the famous avant-garde. My ancient name and my respect for grammar were quite enough to cause a few heart attacks in their ranks. Born into the nobililty, they said, he can only have written an out-of-date and class-conscious book – though they denied that one born a peasant was tied to digging all his life. But I kept out of these things, confident that I'd made my offering and need do no more. There were hundreds of prizes and thousands of winners up and down the country; but this never made their writings any better, nor mine, even if it found no readers, any worse. I sent four hundred copies to all the libraries, making sure they were understood to be complimentary copies. Because most of them replied with the usual forms, I knew this time my labours had not been in vain. I was content to withdraw into myself. I felt not oppressed but freed. It is absolutely true that after a short time I nearly forgot the whole thing.

I avoided Emo Cavagna as much as I could, but I often found him around me in the little shops of Guastalla, in the local wine shops or cafés, almost as if he'd known where I was going. I thought Elisa told him. He was unctuously polite, but I could tell he was embarrassed. Vanity mingled with baseness in him, the bold with the vile. He was the kind of adventurer who from the time of D'Annunzio up to the republic of Salò trailed his vices and his bragging all over the place, and then reviled his country for not having recognised his years of service. They were at once shrewd pimps and frightful bores, who in society were like those old servants or peasants in a household, who having exploited their position for a lifetime still reckon much is owed them. Emo had imposed himself successfully on the little offices of the province, taking the lead at rallies, where he wore his old uniform with a lot of ribbons on it; but subventions and contributions couldn't satisfy his incurable megalomania. His office at the factory was kitted out with grand furniture, and dozens of editions of the classics and of illustrated works, all expensive, none yet paid for. He now said how glad he was to see me; then told ambiguous stories designed to produce complicity, which would make us more intimate; then went over his past sacrifices. Then he got on to the trials encountered by anybody who after a lifetime of distresses dares to undertake generous but arduous projects.

'My only solace is art. I'd like to save my library! You're a writer, you'll understand.'

It's the first time he's dispensed with Elisa and made a direct request. I fail to avoid shaking hands with him. He's now tied to me in the game of things.

This is the countryside of fog. In winter the garden is a spectral, quivering transparency. From the white roads stretching around, sometimes restless sounds reach one, but at once they are muffled. The mind is motionless in the dazzling, formless light, more frightening than darkness, till the thick curtain begins to part, there comes a hint of colour, of the pale gold sun. It's like that now, in the room shaded by the trees, empty since I stopped writing, in the useless time that carries its echoes more and more slowly. Nothing is any use to me any more. I have no wish to live, nor do I think of dying. I go back to the bridge of boats and watch the river flow. After the confusions of the past, I drowse on Elisa's breast. But something is hanging over us, something will happen, as always before, so I wait.

Sometimes on a Sunday, with Emo's consent, I can remove Elisa from the squalid, prefabricated house among the stopped machines. Emo, a widower when she first knew him, has a grown-up daughter from his marriage; she's anaemic, idle, perhaps affected by some ambiguous mental illness, for she seems retarded. She plays in the open ground with Elisa's only child, a delicate and intense little boy. Emo's daughter has an odd authority over the boy, almost as if that flaccid bulk fed itself on his sap. The first time I saw Elisa go to her child, take him in her arms and gently hold his hands to her breast, her eye shut, I was filled with pity for all the world, starting with pity for the wretched Emo. It was then that I decided to shut my own eyes and let the warm, heavy waters of the Po bring me the scent of life, as precious and turbid as themselves.

When Elisa talks of people she has known or met, in her sing-song voice there's a perpetual implication of sorrow, of the erotic, of the vague. Her relatives, whom she hardly ever sees, appear to be a tangled undergrowth of distresses and vices. She tells me about them, but only distractedly, without seeming to be deeply involved. When we go about together in the neighbourhood, she's always being greeted by friends who wink at her and pretend not to see me. She always has new people, a tide of relationships flows with her, people from all over the wide valley, from hundreds of villages and ten cities, a grey river of human history between its only constants, pleasure and cruelty. What Emo has done and what Elisa has felt and is capable of giving, is what I understand in the last adventure of this countryside from Piacenza to Bologna when in April 1945 there was that festival of blood-letting, a final exaltation of a voluptuousness that before had never been fulfilled. I see the men's eyes become shadowed at every passing woman; they light up when they see Elisa. When I kiss her, I breathe her sweet warmth: it's the smell of blood that comes through her delicate skin, fused with the smell of honey. I go back to her secret, her way of disturbing me, of confirming me in my silence, melting me in her voluptuousness. She'll be like her father. Her passion goes into a suicidal, almost sadistic devotion. When she's with me she thinks of Emo; or she gives herself to him but hides it from him. Is it he or I who abuses her as if he was plunging a sword into her womb?

'You were in the war,' Elisa says. 'Did you kill anyone?' Her eyes are troubled. To my silent denial, she responds by shaking her head, as if it were incredible to come out of the war without having killed. 'Who knows if my father killed anyone?' she then says. 'Once I went to fetch him, when he was a guard at a prison, where they said horrible things went on inside. I don't know. Emo tells me about battles in Ethiopia. He says blood is more loathesome on negroes' skin. He tells me these stories when I want to go to sleep. Then I don't want to touch him, because I smell something strange. It must be blood. I don't know.'

I look into my thoughts, but I don't recognise them, whether soft, arid or desperate. I read a few passages in my book. It seems the work of another man, who then went on elsewhere. Elisa knows my book. Often she praises me; she tells me Emo has said it's the masterpiece of our time. I've not minded the many things that were said about it, but this comment has hurt me. She has gone on daydreaming, with that accent of hers that gets into the folds of life where sense and memory are hidden, or into the wavy locks of greenery in the river, or the eddies of slime.

This morning we are going to Busseto, with two tough, insolent girls who work in the same company as Elisa in Novellara. In their laughing eyes I read the benevolent consideration they have for the old, whose whims they know and will indulge out of affection, respect, self-interest, fear, but for whom they have banished love.

I don't mind not being young in their malicious eyes; they hardly know what youth is, who spend it like unearned money. I wouldn't go back to the weary, conservative years of my youth. But it's sad that time is unjust to those who have lived adventurously. It's a shame that life doesn't avail itself of what it laboriously brings forth, that youth and age go against each other when each might be exalted in the other, exchanging their love with wisdom and wisdom with love.

The countryside towards Brescello, Roncole and then Busseto is marvellous. It was from the river that the genius Verdi got that wave of melody, his lamentations and glitterings, his cascades of madness, his rustling fronds and funereal tolling bells, his pyres and courts and banners. The colours of the heroic scenes are the colours of the valley: bitter greens, tormented turquoise, chaste rose and the vast greyness of weeping.

The two girls smile not only at me but also at Verdi, for the mind's image of Verdi is as an old man, a solitary and predatory thinker, with his aquiline nose, bristling beard and his head lowered, thinking. They make fun of his worldly taste for honours. Silently derisive, they regard the bed and wardrobe brought back here from the old-fashioned

Milanese inn where he died. Their cruel youth understands only the bloom of its own skin and its clean scent of healthiness. They link arms with me as if I were a decrepit uncle. Elisa keeps herself apart. Perhaps she knows their desires and their needs; perhaps she thinks they'll ask me and I'll consent. Then they'll talk among themselves. I listen to their heartless dissection; they have the insensibility of a child pulling an insect apart or martyring a cat.

We go back towards the Po. The poplars rise from the river bank and curve their single breasts of leaves against the light. The outlines of the hillocks flow into each other like colours on canvas mixing in their oil for the watcher's silent gaze. The three women say nothing. But the *maestro*, old and buried in the flesh, consumed in his insatiable spirit, set forth his grotesque anguish in Falstaff's lament. All those old lies of love from the women of Windsor! 'There is divine punishment for those who have loved women too much' (it is the voice of the chevalier D'Emiddio, but where is it coming from?) 'and the punishment is to love them for ever!' Why did the merry wives take no pity on you? Why were you the laughing-stock?

'You're young,' says Elisa. If she wants to give me back my youth to redeem a ghost from utter abjection, I shall not refuse it from her hands.

I see Verdi die alone in the inn bedroom. Behind his closed eyelids his last image is not of glory but of a girl.

Like the Farnese palace at Piacenza, the Gonzaga palace at Mantua is shut, and will be for who knows how long. Once an official has been employed to do up a public monument he thinks it's his. He helps slow down the bureaucracy, delays the transfer of funds, indulges in controversy about overlapping areas of responsibility. If the work will take twenty years, he'll remove the whole complex from the cultural life of the nation completely. Then, once he becomes fond of the palace, it's as if it was his creation, he wants in all innocence to live in it, in the apartments of the famous princess or the enlightened queen or the illustrious scholar. What a caricature of glory!

Using my old journalist's card from my time on *Free Vesuvius*, I manage to have a servants' door opened for me. They tell me not to get lost, and to keep quiet. How could I go into the labyrinth, second only, in Italy, to the Vatican, when accompanied by the splendid Elisa? The ducal palace is empty, like a maze of caverns worked and smoothed by the sea. In dusty silence and a few rays of sunlight, I explore Isabella's gardens, the kennels of the ferocious Great Danes and mastiffs, the ghostly houses in the shades of the riding-school, the warriors' chambers with starred ceilings. Chambers, stairways, passages, perspectives. Breaths or voices from hidden openings. Elisa seems to be there, seems bound to me; her steps are soundless, her breath like that of a flowering plant. In her voice I hear that other voice which remembers and grieves in this famous sepulchre. Splendour, betrayal, voluptuousness. Verdi again: the damned courtier and the fair victim; the crippled clown and the sadness of the love of the imperfect for an unattainable beauty. And then blood.

In the dwarves' apartment deep in the walls the malign buried spirit hisses. I see the evil little conspiracy, reared in spying and treachery. My imagination is as fertile as when in the college of the Lily I imagined the Consul's retinue. Now I see a crowd of tiny kobolds brandishing plumes and screeching like rats at me, then around Emo who shrinks and becomes one of them . . .

'You know it's now a matter of life and death for Emo's business,' Elisa tells me. 'It's that loan from the usurers at the Piccolo Credito in Ferrara. He'll talk to you about it. Will you help him?'

Her face is furrowed with tears. How can it be that her kisses are exactly those I had from Nene's chaste generosity that years ago closed the chapter of my youth?

The end of autumn has come again when Emo asks me to go to Ferrara with him. I've offered to stand surety for him, but they need my signature so I have to go in person. When we get there, I mechanically read the name of the bank, and I make a vertiginous jump through time, for this was Giunio Marsi's bank twenty-five years ago.

The clerk is old and courteous. When I question him he confirms that it's the same bank, far bigger now than then, with branches in many countries and the headquarters in France. I mention Marsi. He doesn't appear surprised.

'He's one of the most powerful men in international finance,' he replies. 'To all intents and purposes, this bank is his.'

'I'm a journalist,' I say dishonestly. 'I think I interviewed him once, I have a vague recollection of him.'

'It's all public knowledge,' he says. 'The newspapers talked a lot about it. You know, the story of how he collaborated with the Germans in Pétain's time, how his daughter vanished, how he ransacked the world for her and offered enormous rewards. You'll have heard all about it.'

'Yes, in Paris I think.'

'In England, during the war. In London, maybe.'

Emo got out the dossier. The faintest quivers pass beneath his freckles, his leonine hair shivers reflected in the glass table. His stubby hands tremble. The document is signed and sealed. I feel his watery eyes running over me, as if looking beneath my clothes for the limbs she has embraced and that have embraced her, These horrible thoughts pass without touching me. Chance does not exist. An omnipotent hand has brought me here to sign this base deal, as too I feel it binds me to a higher duty in life.

I have come with Elisa into the province of Modena as far as Nonantola. For some while there have been no further echoes from my book. It lies in the four hundred libraries like seeds in tombs which will regerminate perhaps in a hundred years. It's a good sign that society has rejected my work; for society defends itself from the poison of art, absorbs it only slowly and in convenient doses when immunised by distance or time. So I feel it'll last a good long while. It will be disturbing for a few people, with its hidden strengths; they'll try to see it as the past because they don't dare understand it is the future.

'Elisa, I shall have to leave you,' I say gently.

I shall leave Italy for the third time. All here is inanity, all is dispersed; the ancient structures that held together the world of the Cardinal, of Lerici, of Gian Luigi, have disappeared, Now they destroy that beauty, and ignore its value. This explosion is only the death of one type of equilibrium in another greater; the molecules fly apart from one another; they will come to rest at the right time and place for the same game played by the impulse which now drives them apart. I see them already in the blessed light over the river. I have been freed, as is my destiny; I shall be guided where my destiny will come to a close; and this time I hope it with all my heart.

'Emo told me,' says Elisa. Her voice quivers. She has saved him. What better than that now I should go away? 'He's promised I can leave my job at Novellara. I'll be able to be with him in the factory. And I'll be able to look after my little boy.'

Her shining eyes look behind me to the line of the horizon which is reflected in them. The waters of life flow between us as the river flows contentedly through the grass.

In the sacristy of the basilica, the worn-out shrewd old priest who for some time has guided us looks at me for a long time, thinking. Then he opens an armoured coffer and puts a medieval cross into my hands for me to admire. While I'm looking at the splendid enamelling, not thinking of anything in particular, I hear his voice whisper to me: 'Look at the splinters of wood in the joint there. You have in your hands the only surviving fragments of the True Cross.'

I feel myself shudder to my very marrow. Tomorrow I shall leave – but what does this sign mean?

THE JADE BRACELET

Telegraph Hill is one of many lost in the sea of London, hunchbacked hills surrounded by roads like rivers in the hollows of valleys, roads which leave the hills quiet and secluded. But it's one of the few vantage points from which a tract of the city can be seen: not a vast area, perhaps a hundred square miles, a tenth only of the monstrous agglomeration of more than eighty villages, hamlets and small towns that now is called London.

One way, Kitto Road skirted the walls of St Catherine's church and rapidly descended towards Nunhead. The other way, the row of little houses badly balanced on the slope, in one of which I lived, looked out over the immense distance of London, like sheep slanting across a grassy slope. My small windows were square, like those of the Lily, and later at Paola. The view melted away, sketched in white and grey, to Hampstead Hill opposite, to the forest of cranes in Surrey Docks, or the other way to the ash-grey woods of Wimbledon, down, down, till the gaze lost itself in the sky. Foggy forms raised themselves, gusts of the ashen or the roseate blew across, a myriad roofs and chimneys and towers stretched away. Webs of rails, pipelines and cables shone. Patches of greenery floated on the vapours or drowned in the shadows. Where, where, could Penny be? There wasn't much space and there wasn't much light in my small room. But if I switched on the lamp, there was the engine of the ship - where should the ship sail?

'You need a reason,' Jack had said, putting his finger on the nub of the matter like a true man of the people. 'In this country you've got to convince people of the reason why you're looking for this girl. Otherwise no one will help you find her, not even for money.'

The room's walls were hung with maps of all kinds and dimensions and colours, criss-crossed with markings. The largest maps were of all the 1,500 square kilometres of Greater London, seen as if by an eye twenty or thirty thousand metres up, and seeing around the wandering ribbon of the Thames only varied bruise-colours and greens, scraps of white or red or brown. The winding river was azure, a colour that doesn't exist, and so were the waters of Charlton or of William Girling, which, if then you want to see them, are grassy embankments, and resemble miles and miles of prison walls.

There were maps of the postal districts, with the numbers of course in red; maps of monuments, artistically indicated by a peristyle or an obelisk; maps showing theatres, showing railways. Others were maps not generally available, that I had obtained with difficulty, maps of police stations, markets, graveyards, public parks, big companies, banks. They all brought names and things out of the vague bruise-colours and greens, and they all seemed to mirror different realities. How could one recognise the underground routes of seven tube lines, each one deeper than the last, running through the nameless depths? And the red threads of the bus routes were an inextricable tangle disappearing and reappearing where least expected among the streets.

'There's one that goes thirty miles,' Jack had said.

And the railways? There were thirteen main stations and seven hundred lesser ones, and still, judging by other maps, only a quarter of London could be reached by train. The underground too was spread evenly over the whole, and likewise served a quarter only. Other maps showed stadiums, racecourses, tennis courts, golf courses, all in green. Municipal maps, with an eye to reconstruction work, changed a lot of green to the colour of brick. Some maps showed hospitals, others barracks. The oldest mixed up or separated the quarters: the earliest showed just Stepney, but then you got Bethnal Green too, then Poplar too, then all together in Tower Hamlets. So Fulham came with Barons Court or without, was longer and narrower according to the decade. How could one pursue a search in such altering, jellyfish-like plasma?

But where in all this was London? There were workshops, factories, walls, vast depots. There was the constellation of associations and clubs, there were the companies that from the City had governed a third of the world, there was the traffic of goods. A network of hidden powers interlocked, a mysterious sea of millions of presences spread and dissolved as infinite names were resolved into impassive anonymity. There were the rubble and the rubbish of what had been, the emptinesses for what was to come. The wind swept the streets between the closed shops and the ambiguous lights of the pubs. The gloomy tide of asphalt flowed through twenty thousand veins towards the heart of the city, gathering force artery after artery, and flowed out again towards the dark, silent outskirts. Millions of human beings were alone in their cells, as I was alone in mine, thinking.

Jack used to be a long-distance runner, a champion over ten miles; now he was a travelling salesman, selling carpets. The first time he saw that extraordinary exhibition of maps, he pressed his lips together. That wasn't the way to get to grips with real life. Nor was it easy to get hold of him and induce him to come into my flat. He avoided his own flat, below mine, because of his wife Daisy. She, when she saw him ready to go out, shouted loud enough to be heard from the street: 'I hope you never set foot in here again!' Jack would therefore vanish for weeks together. I imagined he was pursuing his business in the provinces. Only later did I get to know his real habits. Sitting on the one, uncomfortable wicker armchair, he was already looking at the way out. Jack was tall, and heavy because of his bones, not because he carried much flesh; his face was dark and unrefined, furrowed by lines; his eyes were bitter and opaque. He looked consumed, worn-out, like anyone exposed too long to dreadful pressures, like the crocodiles that endure the muddy rivers of the tropics. It was the mark of London, that I recognised on men unloading crates in markets, on the drivers of enormous articulated lorries that shook the earth when they passed, on charlatans selling dubious merchandise in the open markets of Petticoat Lane or the Caledonian Road, on the old comics of the popular theatre, as wasted away as the boards of their stages. They were creatures the city consumed insensibly, as the desert wind carries tiny knives of granite which, a fraction of a splinter at a time, destroy the most impervious structures.

In spite of this I would have trusted Jack utterly. Our house, like countless others, was of the dullest design: two small rooms and a kitchen and bathroom on the ground floor, where Jack and his wife lived; two similar rooms above, that were mine; and a horrible little room under the roof where the landlady holed up. Her name was Molly. She got up to her attic despite her sixty-five years by climbing a ladder, which she then hoisted up after her as if she had been on board ship. She was quite unable to provide for herself; she slept through a large part of each day; and we tenants provided the pittance she lived on. Jack had weighed me up as a lifeline for her; and I, though I had to be prudent, thought I had understood him, when he assessed me with his bitter glance. When he accepted me as a tenant of Molly's, he had heard me to be a writer of short stories, called Sansa, and had been satisfied when I paid in advance. To make everything smooth in the household, he had explained my maps by saying I wrote the thrillers the English liked so much. Burning a hole in my pocket, I now had the two very thin pages, without smudges, without mistakes, of the first report of the private detective agency on my behalf looking for the daughter of Mavì and Giunio Marsi, if she was his daughter. Before, I'd undergone the solitude of this wait without really feeling it, but now it lay on me unbearably heavily. I looked in the lined face of the old champion for some human contact, like that I'd known on the march from Berlin to Elba, which went beyond the mind and was Being itself.

'My dear Jack,' I said. He at once realised I wanted his time and attention; he turned his armchair with its shoulder to the doorway and didn't move. 'I'm writing a story for a very demanding publisher, about the search for somebody who has disappeared in London. I'm working on the report of the police officer responsible. You know the way they talk, I want you to tell me if I've got it right. I'll skip the preamble.

' ". . . for the search for the person in question," ' I read from my report, ' "we can confirm the following facts. Miss Penny, of Italian parentage, was born in Paris in 1927. Presumably she took French citizenship. She was sent to an English boarding-school in 1939 and disappeared in 1945. We suppose that she does not wish to be found by her father, who has remarried since his first wife, Miss Penny's mother, died in Marseilles during the German occupation." '

'If she doesn't want to be found,' Jack interrupted, 'your short story is going to be long. In London every year dozens of people disappear, whose names, ages, habits and friends the police know about, whose photograph they've got; but they find only one in twenty.'

'The policeman I've imagined is no fool,' I said. 'Listen to the next bit. "The registers of French immigrants from 1938 have been examined. On 1 July 1939 a Miss Penny, of French citizenship, born in Avignon, 6 May 1927, entered the country. The file also includes a photograph of the girl, then aged twelve, her father's request for a residence permit, and a declaration by the headmistress of the girls' boarding-school Allenswood, in Wimbledon, that she has accepted the girl at the school for the next three years. Unfortunately the school Allenswood no longer exists. The buildings were demolished to make way for London County Council housing." '

'Yes,' said Jack, 'they're brick and glass cages for people with no guts, they're building them all over the place.'

' "Therefore," ' I went on, reading the second sheet of paper, ' "we have visited the appropriate offices and consulted the lists of teachers in private education. For Allenswood, an upper-class girls' school, we have the names of four members of staff whom we are setting about tracing. We enclose copies of the documents and a reproduction of the photograph of Miss Penny. Etc., etc." What do you make of it?'

'Yes, that all sounds reasonable,' Jack said. 'But if her mother's dead and she wants to keep away from her father, why should she be wanted?'

'I'm still working out the plot,' I said. 'But she may only appear to be the Italian's daughter, and it may be the real father who's looking for her.'

Jack folded his long arms and was silent for a moment.

'Then it's very difficult,' he said. 'You can't put appeals in the newspapers, because the girl would think it was a trap set by the Italian father, and would hide herself even better. The police won't want to get involved, because it's a purely private matter. And other people would need a motive that sounded good. But your plot starts well. If I can be of any help, tell me.'

Back to my notebooks, a diary abandoned and taken up years later.

London, 4 January 1953

I can claim to know all the many faces of solitude. But this now is the most complex, the real thing. It's not born out of misfortune. It's innate in this city and its usages, and therefore it's unavoidable.

Let me invoke the spirit of Professor Omobono, so early flown to join the angels! I put down the diary, shut my eyes, see myself again as in a gloomy painting, two shadows talking a foreign language in the half-darkness of the room, a sailor's wretched cabin with its cabbalistic maps pinned to the wall. The poor quarters stretch away down to the canals showing their mud now that the tide in the river has gone down. Who has brought this man from the wide azure Mediterranean to these depths to whisper with a consumptive carpet salesman living on London fog and the carbon dioxide of the slums? And why?

I go back again to scutinising, not one event or another, but all past time together. It's an amorphous mass, always getting heavier, which vibrates to every slightest motion of the present, as if hung at the end of a rope, in proportion to the length of the rope and its own weight. I've come up here answering a call that others would say was affection or desire. Like in the ancient myth, I go forward unwinding the thread of life, almost hoping at every turn that it will come to an end; but it leads me further and further, among presentiments I cannot understand.

Really! What did the object of my search mean to me? Not my search, with the detective agency's help, for Penny (who was she, anyway?) but my deeper search in my own mind. I had to keep making my mind stop and accept things. My mind was forever escaping in order to return later, not knowing where, but certainly not down here. Beyond the circle of streets around the hill, at an unforeseeable point in the forest of houses, men, thoughts, facts, did there exist a single leaf that could be said was mine. Would I resolve myself in that? In that only?

I had been to talk with the detective again. Coming back in the evening through Peckham, I followed the black asphalt river of the road, blacker than the night. I passed boarded-up houses, dirty shop-windows. But somewhere in that sea is a drop of living blood that is the same as mine.

The atlas divides the city into 144 segments. I've walked for miles, high and low, always further east or further north, as if I could impress the great metropolis with a sense of my indefatigable commitment and patience – to get to know the city, but also to be known. Every evening, exhausted, I go over where I've been on the map, street by street; but I've barely covered one of the segments. I thought such a challenge would be picked up, that those millions of walls might help, not hinder me, might bring me to my child rather than hiding her.

Yes, I feel for the diarist Omobono now, and for myself. I see why I came to perch on Telegraph Hill, near Nunhead, the most dramatic of London's cemeteries; why I live next to Molly, who goes for walks, sleeps on a bench, brings back on her clothes that stench that has become hers. I know why I've surrounded myself with these evil maps, which multiply the city to infinity; I know why from up here I am forever looking down over it. I am forcing a confrontation. My furious, proud blood insists I win; I must even fight my great need to die. This is the alternative; it's very simple.

Down there, distance and time seem a tightly tied bundle; it's a countryside from another world, on an inhuman scale. It's strange that men, with centuries of effort, should have composed something that isn't human, that is deaf to love and to death too, like nature herself.

At night the shadows seem to sweat. I hear reverberations, always deeper and deeper, like an organ about to fall silent. I wanted to save Penny from that monstrous bosom, where undoubtedly she was suffering; we would destroy it by forgetting it.

I heard Molly's voice greeting me weakly as she hauled up her ladder. I recognised the unmistakable smell that came from her garret, and that other strange smell too . . .

The fourth V2 that Hitler sent his British cousins exploded two miles south-east of London Bridge, in the fork of the roads for New Cross and Lewisham, which delimited therefore the longer sides of the empty space, while the third side was just demolished walls on blackish grass. A little further on, the first block which had survived the blast, perhaps because it stood at an angle, housed the auctioneers Stoker and Coe.

At least ten or twelve houses remained, which had grown up around an open space held in common, each different, some old enough to date from the days of Marlowe and the Globe. They provided twenty-five or thirty premises which communicated with each other at ground level; and thus Stoker's could spread as they pleased through numberless rooms, and into the dramatic gap left by the bomb. The first time I went I was so amazed as to be almost unnerved. I only understood later that dozens of such places existed, from Putney Bridge, where there was one underground, to Marylebone, from Watford to Bromley, not to mention the more important ones in the centre, some of which were famous.

A seemingly magical power loaded all thirty premises to their ceilings with improbable things for half each week, and for the other half made them disappear. With the impassive regularity of the tide in the Thames, furniture, paintings, carpets, porcelain, weapons and glass, fearlessly mixed up with shoes, biscuits, soap, crates of beer or of hats, came together and three days later always went their ways, when not left heaped in the desolote square the bomb had made.

The weird and unstable matter obeyed only the law of space. It would go as high as was possible, first a fine mahogany chest loaded with a refrigerator, then a sofa with its springs being ruined by the trunks piled on it, trunks bulging with things that one could only guess it. Among these towers, kept there by dead weight alone, the examination of the goods, as far as it went, was conducted by angling along disturbing alleys where crockery rose from the floor, and by peering into wardrobes and finding dozens of saucepans, tools, books, maybe silver even, peering into drawers and finding fans or iron-mongery, the dregs of innumerable lives. A smell of dust and mould came from the bales of linen and the hangings piled as high as a man.

Then there were model ships, stuffed animals, implements I didn't know, suitcases with labels from all over the world; a chaos of things Chinese, Indian, Burmese, Maori, Turkish; cannibals' masks, Redskins' plumes, coins from Central Asia with holes in the middle. There were all the things London threw up from its wounded innards, perhaps in order to forget them.

Like devils by some strange damnation condemned perpetually to make then unmake their hell, a large number of all manner of employees, right down to the slaves tied to heaving rubbish about, performed this Sisyphean task under the evasive but acute gaze of Mr Coe. The senior partner in this enterprise, Mr Stoker, whom everybody seemed eager to avoid anyway, kept himself invisible behind frosted glass in a tiny office.

Closely observed, those who were ruled by the unseen but hissing whiplash of Mr Stoker's authority, and lived under Mr Coe's pallid stare, were a proud bunch of rogues ready for any trickery or theft. But give the superior structure of English society, forms were respected and limits not transgressed. The most precious things, from which most profit might be made, were indeed cunningly buried, disguised, artfully disarranged, so it was difficult to identify them, let alone buy them, if you weren't in the game or hadn't suggested the devils take some share of the profit. But if a resolute, shrewd, stubborn buyer unearthed a rare piece of porcelain hidden under a saucepan, if he broke the evil circle, Mr Coe wearily sold him his article under the hammer as he did for everyone else. And in the instant of silence that followed, the memory of yet another thread in the warp and woof of life at Stoker and Coe was registered.

Within me, a wave as high as a house, a wave with no name because it has thousands of names, rose up and broke and was reabsorbed into the empty sea. By disjoined stairways one could descend into cellars where it was nearly dark and where there was an absurd jumble of things. In the squalid prison of those damp silences, I went back to the wreckage of a piano which, like the iron bed in the thieves' camp in Ohre, stuck out from a clutter of rotten carpets. Ten or twelve keys, the high notes, were all that emerged. I put a finger on a key and produced a poor, false note, like the lament of an old woman who has stayed a virgin all her life and therefore is still a child. Perhaps when Molly went to the cemetery at Nunhead she talked to the dead with a voice like that.

Because my life was a questioning and a testing of others' lives, impalpable affinities bound me to things which had once belonged but had then been abandoned, breaths of echoes of infinite thoughts. Gian Luigi's antiquarian's passion had always seemed to me a weight on him, not a source of new energy. He meant it to be a corollary of the courtly ideal, and satisfied with it his taste for the beautiful, though I felt the beauty had been stripped of its humanity. For myself, I found in an availability that overflowed into paradox a slow fascination that was nostalgia, or regret, or fastidiousness, or love, or all together. I recognised things that reminded me of other things in the house at Monte di Dio, things held to be rare even if not precious in our eyes; and I saw them maltreated, bartered, misprized, worse than the evangelist's clothes (and that notion made me realise how sacred they were in my memory!) This annoyed and mortified me. I saw my sister Cristina's moist eyes behind the mouldering dusty lace; I saw Gian Luigi's renaissance pride in the chipped majolica. I recalled his precepts; I saw him tilt an encrusted painting beneath the light, and with a rag dipped in solvent bring out again a face, a drapery, a cloud. I fought against the little horde of dealers for these things which had in imagination been my family's. I wanted to assess once more the ideas of that time. I wanted to rediscover a delusion or an inspiration, a hint of irony. I wanted to re-examine myself. Slowly I was nearing the age my father was then. Soon we two, burdened with the same length of time, should really be able to judge each other. Perhaps his shade was afraid of the confrontation, as I, waiting for it, was afraid.

Acquiring small things was easy; but difficulties arose when one cast one's eyes on an armchair that wouldn't go up our staircase. But the inexorable Stoker, as soon as the sale was finished, threw the entire contents of the catalogue out into the bomb site; and if one didn't take one's purchase at once, bad weather came, the idly curious and thieves and dustmen came. So I took a storeroom near-by; and as and when I fell for the longing to possess one of these things which for me were the ghosts of things, I heaped them in there.

Not that I thought of making a collection; still less did I imagine these objects in an ambience, like in the happy, lost time of the stones of Licudi. I had no real desire to possess them; indeed, they didn't seem mine, or they were mine only as the past into which they led me back was mine. But like the boy looking for shells on the shingle, tiny debris that in their short lives still hold the feeling of the endless, I regained in those anonymous things, already reduced to merest matter, the touching symbols of a human whole. On foggy days, when the bad weather made me give up my absurd trudging through the suffering of the streets, with bits of drapery or tricks of light I made random pieces of decoration, then changed them or let them be; till I had too much junk for my storeroom, and took back to Stoker things I'd bought from him and asked him to sell them again; and again the past tore itself excruciatingly away. I repeated those deaths without asking myself what they meant, but not out of masochism or for a morbid stirring in the ashes. I wanted to save myself by a suffering – and I could give it a name. That other suffering was unbearable, that searching for what was perhaps my creation, my creature, but perhaps just something that had never been mine, or had already been consumed in the hands of others or in nothingness. The melancholy note of the piano hesitated before dying away.

Old second-hand dealers rummaged in the cellars, absorbed in their searches. They too were shades; and like the countless houses of London they might be obstacles to my search or they might be propitious. Binding myself to the city, area after area, I bound myself too in Stoker and Coe to the grey figures who frequented the place, as alike and as numberless as the houses. It was a way of evading the ghastly millions of men separating me from Penny. On occasion I thought she was sitting among us, that I should be able to recognise her because she too would be drawn to some object that resembled something that had once been Cristina's.

The buyers in the horrid rooms of Stoker and Coe varied no more in person than in expertise; and isolated in that microcosm, within the macrocosm of London, I saw them follow the same rules as the poor of Licudi, where everyone knew best about something, and the others left him to it. Apart from one or two who came and went, the group of rag-and-bone men stayed as homogeneous as a reef in the surf. They had their modest businesses in the neighbourhood, and this was the only source from which they could supply themselves. Constrained by the wear and tear of time, and constrained by the same needs to make the same concessions, without discussing it explicitly they parcelled out the mirrors or carpets or metalwork to one man, to another the furniture or the books or the linen, to others the tools or the lamps, the liquor or the machinery. This division wasn't openly referred to; sometimes there were arguments, but for hidden reasons which seemed to be allowed, and they were ready on occasion to lose a day's profits in such a disagreement. But they were as poor as they were proud, and once the rules of the game were accepted they were clung to tenaciously. By the nature of the goods and the system, and because of the speed of the bidding, everything proceeded most passionately, the rational and the human getting mixed up in the risks and choices. The whims of a rich man, at the auction only by chance; someone's overriding personal need; a collector's mania; the errors of the ignorant; a late train that eliminated a rival, or rain that kept someone idling there all day; being in funds or out, and the riddle of distributing your purchases throughout the auction; all these things produced the trembling anxieties, the regrets, the silent joys of this squad of the only seemingly colourless and wretched. I should have been struck by the perpetual interference and near supremacy of chance, but not forgetting Demetrio. I saw in it all an absolute balance between the tension and the response, the wish and the ultimate result. I knew too that wherever Penny was, the same vehement impulse would bring me to her.

In that human whirlpool I nursed my hopes. I was consoled by echoes in my imagination; by the exaltation as well as the melancholy of my commitment; by my affinity with the unconfessed solitudes of others. Each one of us was engaged in an interior dialogue, and act of conscience, of judging the merits and errors of what he had done, of recognising himself skilful or valiant or defeated each time Coe's hammer wearily fell.

Mixed up in all this, I gave little attention to the moment, to the grandoise social transformation I was living through. Fifty years before, in Naples, because of the decline which followed the end of the kingdom, bit by bit the great families' heritage after seven dynasties arrived on the antiquarians' tables. Now, in the London of the Commonwealth, the glories of Elizabeth and George and Victoria were coming under the auctioneer's hammer, the plunder of greater times garnered over three hundred years from all the countries and races of the earth. From all that, they had made the city of demi-gods, the society of the white columns of Belgravia, Kensington, Mayfair, Holland Park. This was now giving way to a new idea of life expressed in aluminium and plastic and plate glass.

It wasn't the spirit of the nephew of Lerici who bartered such a heritage, even if it seemed he wanted to destroy it. But as once that heritage was shipped from the dominions to the quays of the Thames, now hundreds of ships released these things, the conquerors restored to the now freed vassals the documents which country by country they had collected and preserved, so that those others could in their turn begin. The spoils were immense, in infinite pieces but alive; re-elaborated and reassessed and consumed by one culture, they now passed on to their successors in history.

I had all this in my heart, but I wanted to give it away. I was tired of meditating. I thought Penny's embraces would be sweet, and that I would have deserved them.

'The search for the one-time teachers at the Allenswood boarding-school has been difficult, but we have succeeded.' (This is still taken from the agency's thin sheets of paper.) 'From Miss Gertrude O'Neill, now retired and living in Devon, we have obtained the information we enclose (see sheets A and B). We also enclose a detailed account of her duties.'

It is dated, London, 4 July 1953. There are no blots or mistakes. The first sheet enclosed was Miss O'Neill's declaration. 'I recall Penny Marsi very well. She was the only French girl at the school at that time. I taught her in 1943 and '44, unhappy years for her because she was separated from her family. She was sensitive and clever, though also volatile and distracted. She showed talent for drawing, for dance and for acting, though she said she suffered from shyness. She read a lot, including books she should not have had, which were then taken from her. She did not particularly distinguish herself in class, but she was liked for her charm, despite a tendency to melancholy.'

Then there was the second enclosed sheet. 'Penny Marsi's close friends were: 1. Matilde Marchenein, Viennese, Jewish, of a big industrialist's family slaughtered by the Nazis. She now lives with a distant aunt in Westmoreland.' (There is a note in red by the detective: it seems she has not been able to be of help to Miss Marsi, nor, indeed, has she kept in touch with her.) '2. Miss Kemp Campbell, daughter of John Kemp Campbell of the Birmingham steel company. She lives in a flat in Knightsbridge and buys and sells antiques.' (A note in red: it would be easy to discover more, if that were desirable, by speaking to her when she attends sales at Neale's or Christie's.) I read the third name two or three times. '3. Judith, second child of Lord Anthony Percival, of Hasting Castle in East Anglia.' And then in red: everything indicates this was her closest friend. (Yes, and she belongs to the highest aristocracy of the land! A marvel!) There was the detective's last comment: we will proceed as far as we can. But if one of the young ladies is in touch with Miss Marsi, it means she helped her to disappear, and that means she knows and sympathizes with the reason for the disappearance. She would have to have the most powerful of motives for divulging a secret which otherwise she will keep. Moreover we are dealing with members of the upper class who would not be susceptible to bribery. We await your further instructions. Etc., etc.

'Very good,' Jack had said when I'd summoned him. 'How are you going to resolve it?'

'You must tell me. If in my plot I establish that it's Penny's real father who's searching for her, can I trust the detective with this fact? He could do anything!'

'It depends,' Jack reflected. 'Still, I like your story. You've got the details right far better than I'd thought.'

It was stuffy and we had opened the door. Molly's weak voice came to me. Who was it who questioned that other old exile retired in Devon, breaking her silence? And this photograph of Penny aged twelve! Was it alive or a shade? I recalled from when I wasn't yet twelve a voice from the drawing-rooms of the family tree. 'One saw a face that had suffered but that was noble, with large, shadowy, melancholy eyes.' Was that a portrait of the Baroness Egloffstein then or of Penny now? My memory went forward, leaping the decades. 'It's as if it were always the same person who dies.' I saw Uncle Gedeone's immobile face. Then I heard: 'It's as if it were always the same person who is born.'

Molly is boasting to Jack's irascible wife for the twentieth time about the excellent strawberry harvest she's had this year. One might imagine baskets of fruit – but Molly, in a miserable handkerchief of ground between the coal-cellar and the dustbins, has picked five strawberries, asking me to go with her and to help.

She is the surviving child of a large family. After three-quarters of a century of events, of unknown feelings and griefs, here she is alone in monstrous London with the violet shadow of Jack's eyes her only protection. At the beginning, I was told she'd help me with shopping and laundry. But when she says she wants to cook for me, it's clear that I must finally make her sit down, and I must serve her. I'd have to overcome her vegetarian caprices too, and her medieval ascetic's pretentions of nourishing herself only on nuts, black bread, honey and milk.

I couldn't bear any relationships except those with Jack and Molly. As a child on the Fleetwood coast she got used to the wind from the sea, when the tide came up over the sands in yellow ridges that dribbled black.

'Once the wind was so strong I was stuck for six hours in the tram-shelter,' she says. 'It was night. That was a wind that blew you inside out! The police found me there at four in the morning.'

Molly worries about my health. She suggests an almost magical potion based on unknown herbs. She has one tooth left, but she won't have it out because, she says, 'it bites like the devil'. When she thinks she has overslept, she manages to kick her own backside with a thin leg from which her stockings droop like sails from a yardarm in a calm, yelling, 'Walk, you old lunatic!' Then, armed with a small green watering-can, she goes to Nunhead cemetery, and sits down, either on the grass or on the grave of her last brother, who left her Jack's flat and mine. He came from the sea to die in the sludge of the Thames, like those vessels that after knowing the seas of half the world lie here in the anchorage for ever, lived in by an eccentric artist or a vagabond. And yet Jack tells me he saw, years ago, photographs now long disappeared which showed Molly looking marvellously beautiful in a large garden between noble columns.

> Like something fine and beautiful and alive, that falls into the sea of things, is rolled in the grey depths for years, perpetually losing infinitesimal parts of itself as time passes, till it's an unrecognisable pebble among millions of others, all as grey and inert as the sandy bowels of the sea, poor Molly lies on a London wharf. Penny will be the same if I can't find her; she may already have begun to be like that.

I pushed aside my diary. I shivered, and turned on the light in my little room, so London vanished from the window and only my willpower was left. I went out to join Jack.

From opening-time at six till well after eleven (whatever the police thought about it!) if he wasn't in the country on business he was where the river curves at Deptford, in the heart of the docks, at the bar of the Charlie Brown. It was only one stop on the tube from home, in an area where even the police ventured cautiously, and where his wife would never have dared look for him, especially after dark. On a winter's night his friends would when necessary carry him home up Telegraph Hill. The Charlie Brown, even after the war, when a lot of things were changing fast, remained faithful to the times when Nunhead was a staging-post on the way to Dover. So there's Jack, whispering something in Charlie's ear, while the latter listens intently and goes on needlessly polishing a pint mug. Above them, the lugubrious emblem of the pub hung from the ribs of the ceiling as if from the ribs of an upside-down hull. There were arrows and barbarous-looking blades, iron clubs, instruments of torture, pitchforks and whips, swords like the crosses of the executed, an executioner's gauntlet. In the middle hung a hangman's noose. Below it, Jack, protector of the innocent Molly, stood murmuring for hours with Charlie.

The first time I was lost in the maze of quays and canals of the docks, and I asked a policeman where Charlie Brown's was, he stopped short and looked me up and down.

'And what are you looking for in Charlie Brown's place?' he asked. Nor did he believe me when I said I only wanted half a pint of bitter.

The lesser decorations at Charlie Brown's were impressive too. In suitable corners, there were glass-fronted cabinets of the sort that in Italy would have held relics, but here were for boxing-gloves used in famous fights. One pair had the fists together as if handcuffed. Another pair butted against each other. One pair held out beseeching hands. They'd been used by the American champion the only time he was ever floored by a regular at Charlie Brown's. 'But that time,' a label explains, 'the stitches didn't give way.' Into the two rooms of the pub were also fitted five colossal papier mâché heads left over from some old carnival or fairground booth. In the violent colours of their fierce buffoonery, these roughly shaped grotesques winked with eyes white as boiled eggs and grimaced showing their black teeth. One, wearing a grey top hat, gazed fixedly and enigmatically, making one fear a knife in the back.

Brown's didn't appear in Thomas Cook's tours of London folklore; nor did affluent, free-and-easy parties of visitors from the Far West ever come there even by chance. The general decay, the murky grease on the weapons and the mannequins, showed that the exhibition mounted above Charlie's and Jack's heads wasn't a luna-park joke to attract tourists, but a reminder for anyone who needed his memory jogging. Once in a while one of the regulars had indeed gone to the gallows; so the noose in the middle performed the same office as the gallows set up above their castle by the counts of Gand to warn people for thirty miles around of the peremptory force of their prescriptions and ordinances.

I came into Brown's just as Jack was whispering something in the landlord's ear. Everyone accepted me silently, as they accepted everyone - probably corsairs - who came to anchor there. Jack made a sign to me. He had been waiting for a while for me to confide in him;

but like a good Englishman, he hadn't invited my confidence, though he knew he deserved it. I think that's what he meant by his gesture of propitiation each time I came in. I'd often scrutinised the others in the bar. There were powerful-looking lorry drivers and dockers, sailors with bare forearms at all times of the year like the ancients, arms tattooed by the specialists of Hamburg, if not of islands on the other side of the world. These men confided in each other; I saw them in pairs take themselves to quiet corners, perhaps under the imploring hands in the glass cabinets, where one would listen intentely while the other told what only he was capable of understanding. It was like the balm of Catholic confession, an act of conscience resolved by revealing everything to the priest, because here below there is no friend to confide in. But these men were lucky, they were taken back into humanity with the friends who were born in the slums with them, who with them had known hunger and rain, the risk of being attacked, the risk of prison. They joined against an incomprehensible, hard, vengeful world. They knew how important were the talks with a mortified, beloved working girl, standing on a windy corner with your shoes in the water. And they understood how indispensable it was to recount and to hear the difficult story of every kind of love.

That morning, for the hundredth time, I'd gone back to the dusty tumult of Peckham to see the detective. For the hundredth time he'd told me our search was at a standstill, blocked by a simple but insuperable obstacle. We had reached the end of August.

'We're convinced, sir, for a variety of reasons,' the detective had said, 'that it was the Honourable Judith Percival of Hasting who helped Penny Marsi to disappear. A governess confessed to one of our men that the two young ladies were in touch. That is all. The governess left the castle over three years ago. None of us could approach Miss Percival, given the exalted circles she lives in. None of her servants would presume to question her. Therefore the only way to get a precise answer from her is to ask her a precise question; but the question must be asked by someone who can give a plausible account of himself, and give a good reason for asking his question. We've done all we could, sir. Now you are the only person who could talk to Miss Percival. If a gentleman asks her, the young lady will feel obliged to answer.'

Jack responded to my look of appeal, and left Charlie, who watched him go with the expression of a chained mastiff who cannot follow his master. Jack came over to me slowly, so as not to spill the two brimming pints of Red Barrel he was carrying. The pub had only just opened and was half-empty. The papier mâché head with the evil expression and the grey hat looked our way menacingly. But Jack's crocodile's skin and deep-set tired eyes kept it at bay.

'Listen, Jack,' I said, 'this girl can't be found.'

Slowly I went over the whole story from the beginning, without explaining why I was telling him as truth what till then had been told as imaginary, and without apologising. London had crushed me with its mud and brick and iron; but it was London that was listening to me, Jack with his bitter eyes and his way of rubbing the back of his wrinkled hand over his dry lips. I felt the warmth of his affection, his readiness to help that melted my heart.

'And why, when all's said and done,' he asked when he had thought it over, 'why shouldn't the real father do what the detective suggests? I wouldn't tell him the truth. But she's a lady; and you're a gentleman, as the detective says. I don't believe you're just called Mr Sansa anyway.'

'Jack,' I said, 'I haven't told you everything. It's not certain that Miss Marsi is the daughter of the man looking for her. How could one explain all this to the lady beforehand? How could one explain it to Penny herself, now that her mother, whose memory she venerates, has died abandoned in an hotel in Marseilles, and Marsi, she thinks, was to blame? No, the girl still must know nothing and suppose nothing. Nor must her friend, therefore. Either we find Penny without that help, or I'll have to go on looking for her as long as I can. That's just how it is.'

'What's the lady called?' asked Jack. 'And what's Miss Marsi's real name?'

'Penny Marsi is her real name. The other is Judith, daughter of Lord Anthony Percival, Earl of Hasting, in East Anglia. I've written it here.'

'Percival?' said Jack. 'Is that the one who races at Newmarket? Last year they drugged one of his horses.'

'Yes, I think so,' I replied. 'They're almost a princely family.'

Jack rolled the piece of paper I gave him like a cigarette, and put it in a rusty tin box with two or three others.

'London?' he said. 'Barclays Bank has five hundred branches here. Smith? There are seven thousand in the telephone directory, six thousand Taylors, six thousand five hundred Browns. God help us if she's taken a name like that.'

He returned to the bar and muttered with Charlie again, who went back to polishing the same pint mug. I looked at the old lifebelt from a steamer, which had the name Brown on it, like the name of a wrecked ship. I imagined the ship rolling out of the fog and the night. I imagined a sort of ballad, something like this:

Save us the *Charlie* of Deptford has sunk.

Save our souls.

Let us go back to the old Tower by the Bridge, where the cranes raise their arms and help us with our work. Save the lives of we who carry great weights, we who hasten to offer our bent shoulders, who are bowed down by jute sacks and by crates as a ship goes down into the water. Let us suffer in the Thames mist, in the muddy tide, convicts lifting up our chains, drowning men fascinated by the last mouthful of water that kills us.

But first we want to hear the songs of home again, we want to go back in the drunkenness that soothes us to our black roots that made us free men, free to carry great weights, to sail to our shipwreck, to fight and to die without the blood being seen on our red coats. Let us be drunk once more, to magnify what oppresses us but does not overcome the water of the Thames like the diseased serum in our veins, nor the yellow stream of beer, nor the songs sung when nobody is listening, here in the foggy reaches of Deptford.

That time it was Jack who took me home to Telegraph Hill. I believe he put me to bed. And Molly came to the door; for the first time, she was surrounded by a whiteness, like an innocent ghost.

Thereafter my absurd pilgrimage began again. It was absurd because I could gain nothing by chasing a shadow without appearance or name, chasing the vanished girl materially in my imagination. Ten times a day I imagined I had found her. I recognised her in a hundred different women; I considered them all because they were all possibilities; I was downcast because they were not her. I questioned every door, and behind them imagined a different life for her. I was afraid when in the city's vile hours the evil or the impoverished or the monstrous drew near; I was filled with hope when I was passed by flaxen-haired girls who clearly lived on nothing but milk and honey. Penny was all of them and none of them. If I thought she might have left the city and gone to live elsewhere, the emptiness of the metropolis clutched at my heart. If I was mysteriously filled with confidence that she was near, and would come back to me, the evening lit up brilliantly. I trekked to all four corners of the gigantic conglomeration, to the outlying parks around Wembley, to those from Kew Gardens to Kingston and Ascot which crown Hampton Court. I went down to Dulwich, to Croydon, and up to Epping Forest. I went from common to common, ever further, to Eltham, to Dartford, to Farningham, and high up to Edgware and Watford, from name to name till the city thinned to the wide green of the countryside, the radiating cohorts of houses merged in my sight with the tossing heads of hair of the trees, everything was space, hills, sky, and I lost myself in distance, lost the sense of things and myself.

In this way, I believed I was penetrating the London of Jack and Charlie and the lifebelt that meant so many things. Looking for Penny without being able to find her, I had in my hands the key of the truth of a country that lay open and free; but which, being boundless could, equally, never be arrived at, would always be secret. Each one of the ten million men was knotted into the invisible net of his prime necessities, the scarcity of his money and the hidden haemorrhage of the pub. Freed from the serfdom of the Middle Ages, they were bound now in standardisation. Penny, vanished into the innumerable and the undifferentiated, was my symbol of what everyone was looking for without finding. Now, in this extreme experience, I was one of them, and thus accepted at Brown's with a sign from Jack.

I kept at it, I was indefatigable. I explored by tube the furthest ramifactions of Shadwell and Rotherhithe, where it goes deep under the maze of canals and basins of the Thames between enormous iron castles where water trickles. In the silence, in the draughts of the dungeons, I listened. I coasted through hundreds of markets, all alike. The butchers' were laden with rigid meat, without any character except a pinkness diluted by ice. There were strings of cockerels white as paper or yellow as saffron or lilac as the bruises left by a beating. There were the industries: cardboard, cellophane, aluminium, tinfoil. I asked the way: where's the bus, the tube, the river? They looked at me. Then the interminable explanations and gestures. You turn right, left, then right again, you go to the end, you turn left. Perhaps the bus, the tube, the Thames, were only a few yards off, perhaps far away. They didn't know or didn't remember or didn't think. Mesmerised by the immense sponge of London, they knew only the nearest infinitesimal piece. For a lifetime they used one bus only, one ride by tube, a few streets, in the evening the same pub. Passively they believed what they were told. 'In July the shops will lower their prices.' It wasn't true, but they waited till July to buy things. 'You ought to do your

Christmas shopping in October to avoid the crowds.' Enormous crowds flocked to the shops in October. 'Use the house agents if you want to move.' It wasn't necessary; but the powerful but innocent people obeyed. In the shops of Bermondsey and Camberwell, there wasn't a hint of white; just browns, ochres, greens, blues. There were coarse plastic jackets, tanned boots, belts with pitiless claws, iron helmets, dusty sheepskins, aluminium spectacles. All to defend, and at the same time oppress, the strong, unsmiling people. They laughed, though, at the tops of their voices, to get the fog out of their innards, when Charlie filled the glasses at night.

I went back to Stoker's in the gap left by the bomb. From the middle, the outlines of the houses seemed far off, already absorbed in the dark, striped by a light here and there. A malign wind scurried over the grass, which was flaccid underfoot like a dead rag. After nearly ten years, the smell of the fire was still in the air. One could see marks of burning. The evil, unexpected spirit was still in the city's memory after centuries – witness the destroyed houses around St Paul's, lopped-off columns, stone arches broken, brick stripped of its marble facing like muscle skinned by an anatomist. The London ruins were hollow, vacuous, crumbling, like the dead trunks of agave or cactus, more vegetable than mineral. The vegetation of a land supine under the rain endured in the houses, which had begun as huts of tree-trunks and clay, and had developed into dwellings of brick; but wood and brick remained earth and vegetation, and reverted to such after death. The city grew as quickly as lichen or mushrooms, and fell into ruin like a wood. The silences of men were vegetable silences. Their fear of being disturbed or removed, their affection for the limited place where they lived and for their habits, were immobile and continuous values like those of the woods. Their passion for their tiny gardens was a part of this; their fear of the evil of fire when it flares up in the wood of houses was the same fear as strikes the forest when fires sweep through the summer ravines, leaving only red gusts of ash, fertile humus for new growth.

I came back in by the already silent thoroughfare. In the shops waiting for demolition or for a new tenant, broken slabs, overturned tables, torn paper among rags of linoleum or carpet – things which had seen good service for years – were as if devastated in a sack of the city. Big mansions decayed; no one could say who the owners were, they'd left, vanished like shadows, like Penny. Great flights of bats arose from these houses at night; they seemed abandoned stretches of jungle; or in the river's foggy breath they seemed covered by water, they were sea, wave after wave rising and falling each into the next. Or the houses were ships, each one under a single owner, as at sea the captain is master. As if at sea, each one had everything necessary laid on beforehand following precise procedures, knowing that when night falls, or foul weather sets in, or the harbours are closed, each one is alone. The abandonment of everything was like the sea too, the feeling of being afloat on a whirlpool, the prospect of shipwreck, Charlie's lifebelt, my perpetual veering.

London, November 1953

A little light glimmers from the hatchway where Molly vanished. Who, as weary, debasing days went by, caused the smell of death to come from the clothes of she who had been beautiful and had known love? But the memory of a carpet salesman will redeem you in imagination, a young girl glowing with life in your garden.

All my evenings were passed in Charlie Brown's, where the sailors, often showing signs of old injuries, always powerful still, remembered silently with half-closed eyes. The old crones grew passionate over their lamentations. The young sluts pretended not to see their hungry children who came to implore them from the threshold they weren't allowed to cross. Below the noose, Jack's and Charlie's whispering and their sudden pauses seemed like priests' intonations.

This time when I came in Jack left Charlie at once, who followed him with his eyes.

'Sir,' he said, extracting his rusty box, and from it a piece of paper rolled like a cigarette, 'Miss Penny Marsi, who these days calls herself Clo Nelson, is living in a basement in Archway. This is her address.'

He looked at me with his troubled eyes like the eyes of an old dog motionless in his heaviness and his darkness, the bags under his eyes deeper in that light. I looked at him, struck by admiration and reverence, as I had known children be struck when faced with my great-uncle the cardinal. I held out my hand to him. He gripped it, bending slightly. In the sudden quiet around us, the strong, unspeaking people consecrated the defeat of London.

Some mornings, regardless of the season, the London air rises more lightly. Not in the thoroughfares martyred by traffic, but in side streets not much used, and in dead ends. The houses are all much alike with their tiny gardens adorned with a fake corner of rock, like birds' houses on a large scale. They're for men who think like birds, even though they are also great flyers, who cross oceans; but who instead of twigs and lumps of earth bring back names for their nests, names like Jawalapoor, Setchouan, Malabar, which bring a beating of wings and a smell of distances into the silence of obscure bits of London touched by a little sunlight.

From the solid white balcony with its lozenges and cut-off cones, I followed the crescent as it curved gracefully past its perspectives, the moulding of its sloping roofs, the porticos in the colonial style. Far away at the bottom was a narrow stretch of Holloway Road, but there were impassable spaces between that noise and smoke, and the quiet and security of my new lodgings. I felt like a vessel asleep in a safe estuary, while beyond the harbour mouth the angry but vanquished sea raises its clamour.

By day, for a good two miles, Holloway was as wide as a beach, and tormented like a railway. Shaken like a bridge is shaken by the multitude of heavy vehicles crossing it, it could be pretty dismaying. Clouds of foul dust danced on the black bitumen, on heaps of bricks and iron, on immense trellises, on masses of cable twined on colossal bobbins, on yards, on engines, on hammers. The evenings were oddly dark despite the number of lights. The cold wind milled the accumulating rubbish; in the public garden around the church, the wrapping-paper of the snacks eaten at midday whirled above the ancient graves. A confused humming noise rose from the pubs along with the strong smell of beer. Disquieting figures wandered, black and white in the dazzling light and the darkness.

But where Holloway rose up on the wave of the hill and just touched the back of Archway, a short way west one entered an unexpected world, a jewel hidden between the famous elegance of Hampstead, the smart paintwork of Highgate and the powerhouse of the City. It was a valley walled with houses around the perfect green of Waterlow Park. Beyond Laurier Road, going down Dartmouth Avenue, isolated houses faced Georgian mansions with neo-classical porticos reminiscent of Bath, with shiny black front doors, immaculate white walls, dim windows behind which you can just make out precious forms. It seemed a sight of beneficent mysteries, the sort of place where I had liked to imagine Penny, and where it turned out she really did live.

Before checking the place, before spying out her house, after all those sad months I gave myself the pleasure of tasting again the unknown of

London; but like one who on the slope of a hill realises from the light above him that the woodland is giving out and he has reached the peak. At last I was stronger than my circumstances, Penny was so close I could almost hear her breathing, I could almost talk to the feelings in her heart. I hesitated; perhaps I was nervous. I knew that only in the first excitement of any love is there purity and certainty. Perhaps I didn't want to take from my heart the nostalgia and longing which had been my life for many months and were dear to me. I considered the little roll of paper Jack had given me, which smelled of his tobacco. Perhaps in these few shaky letters lay the conclusion of two lives. It was like a spell that would open enchanted iron doors, that would solve an enigma that had remained mysterious for years. I read the address with my eyes only, not aloud, so the magic wouldn't be dispersed.

My colloquy with the detective, V.R. Ronald, had its piquant moments. I couldn't tell him that where his widely respected firm had spent months getting nowhere, Jack had been far quicker. Jack offered no explanation of his inscrutable powers. He seemed so confident that I never asked him. But I recalled what he'd once said. 'Lord Percival? He has a stable. They drugged one of his horses.' Perhaps the core of the problem had been dissolved as the powder vanishes in a bucket of bran. Maybe Charlie, with the incalculable ramifications of his customers who met under the noose, knew some secret of Lord Percival's stable – the sort of secret which, if adroitly handled, could be traded for another. All these were things to keep from V.R. Ronald, who was listening to me politely.

'In the end,' I told him, 'I had to follow your advice. I managed to make indirect contact with Judith Percival through a prelate of Ely Cathedral. She wasn't told the full truth; but she was given every assurance that the request for her whereabouts would in no way harm her friend, and that Giunio Marsi was nothing to do with it. That is her present name, this is her address. But your job isn't finished.'

Mr Ronald looked at me benevolently. He was a big man, wearing ill-fitting, baggy, dark clothes. He had a springy step, and wore outsize army shoes polished with excessive military shininess. His bald head was even browner than his face. All in all, a splendid fellow.

'Going through a priest was a thoroughly Latin idea,' he said. 'I'd thought that sort of thing no longer worked, but I take note it was successful. What do we have to do now?'

'I must meet Miss Marsi completely casually,' I replied. 'It won't be difficult. It would be enough if you discovered a little club or some sporting facilities she frequents anything where it's easy to join. I'll take care of the rest.'

On the last day of the year I was waiting for them to call me. Following Mr Ronald's advice, without leaving my rooms in Molly's house I'd taken modest lodgings in Holloway too. My fellow tenant, who lived below me, was a Mr Bates, a shop-window decorator whom I helped with a few continental ideas, a few pieces from the antique trade he could make use of, a little money because times were hard, all in the course of three weeks. Bates therefore, seeing I was a foreigner alone in the world, got me invited to a New Year's Eve party at which Mr Ronald assured me I'd meet Clo Nelson – Penny, in other words. I had a bad photograph of her, taken recently by someone from the agency on a windy street where people looked as if they were suffering. She was well dressed, slender; as far as one could tell her face looked refined. Bates banged on the ceiling with a stick a little too late; the house turned out to be way up by Cockfosters; it was striking midnight when we arrived. Coming into the tumult, we were kissed by a lot of people who hardly looked at us; and I shivered to think I'd come close to her in this way.

The party had the disorder and uproar and waste of all such. People were heaped on to the sofas and stretched on the floor. There were hands filthy with engine oil, pretentious clothes and shoes and boots, fourteenth-century page boys and tipsy boxers. It was a big party, people spread through the numerous rooms and upstairs too. There was dancing in a vast semi-darkness to sobbing, barbarous rhythms. For a moment I was afraid I wouldn't find her; but then I saw her where the light fell, sitting gracefully on a small circular sofa. It was her hair that was so striking: a sort of yellow straw-rick, or a Cochin-Chinese hat, then an oval ivory face and long lashes, a strange loveliness and faint melancholy. So I recognised her.

In that instant Penny entered deep inside me and stayed there. She was slender but harmonious. She was so demure that had it not been for that straw thatch she could have been one of the girls of my generation in Gian Luigi's house. She had very fine hands; her eyes were brown, and slightly veined, like Mavì's. On her little circular sofa she received the homage of an Oxford-looking young man, tall, red-headed, who wore a Canadian trapper's coat of the kind made famous by Davy Crockett. She listened, without discouraging or encouraging him. I liked her negative condescension. But then I was startled, because I'd been looking only at Mavì's daughter – but was this girl, in whom I saw the ghost of Cristina, not also Marsi's daughter?

She was sensitive enough to know she was being watched. She was clearly getting bored with the Oxford man's panegyrics, and when she'd caught my eye two or three times she perhaps saw that it would be a diversion if she could involve someone new. But she couldn't, either from natural female idleness, or flirtatiousness, or reluctance to leave her sofa, knowing that then she'd either have to stand or sit on the floor; so she endured my glances, half roguishly, half questioningly; and in the end when I sketched a faint bow she smiled at me and showed I could approach her. Going over to her, I wanted to control myself and dominate the silence and the time that had brought me there; but I was the loser, and I feared she might sense this. But at least to outward appearance she hid her thoughts well. At once she asked me if I came from Paris.

'I'm Italian, from the South,' I answered. 'My name's Giulio.'

As open as you please when talking on a social level, the English are reserved and prudent when it comes to personal matters, and direct questions are indiscreet. Therefore if you're reluctant to discuss the weather, politics or sport, an embarrassing silence falls. Penny scrutinised me from under half-closed eyelids, judging it useless to talk superficially with me. Then she decided.

'You know,' she said to me in Italian, though with a marked French accent, 'I'm of Italian origin too.' She thought for an instant, then raised her melancholy but luminous eyes to me. 'I've never been to Italy. My mother was Genovese.'

She fell quiet. I'd heard an almost imperceptible inflection in her voice when she said 'My mother' and I too was moved. The Oxford man, excluded from a conversation he couldn't understand, moved away. The silence which followed seemed to disquiet her. She examined me afresh; perhaps she thought I was shy; I'd needed to be encouraged before I'd approached. In the end she smiled again.

'Do you want to dance?' It was years since I'd taken the floor; I knew modern dance only from what I'd seen in films. She nodded, and led me away. It wasn't that difficult. I launched into an acrobatic sort of dance with the gay abandon of a boy. The improvisations which in my ignorance I came up with amused her.

At one point she stopped. 'How did you fetch up here?'

She seemed to be asking me how I had come to be at that sort of party; but she might have had me telling her a lot more.

'A man who lives in the same house took pity on my solitude. I'm in

London because it's the heart of the antique trade. I like it. And you?'

She talked in a diffuse kind of way about the Knightsbridge fashion house she worked for, sometimes as designer, sometimes as model; she talked about her basement in Dartmouth Avenue, and about other things that were light but not indifferent. She had her mother's eyes. When she raised them and then looked distractedly away I felt the same sensation as years before, so far away but never forgotten. It was rather like someone who takes your hand between his own and then goes on holding it.

'The one who was paying me all those compliments? He's quite a fellow, his uncle's Sir Charles Devil, the number two in the Conservative Party. He'll be in Parliament soon, no doubt about it. He looks like Davy Crockett to you? That's a notion. We'll call him that.'

As it grew late we seemed to be making friends. I always had to be careful to call her not Penny but Clo. She promised to tell me next time she was free for an evening or had time for a trip somewhere. 'We live round the corner from each other. London's hopeless for friends who are twenty miles away.' One or two of her acquaintances looked at me with a certain curiosity. Crockett seemed preoccupied and, hoping to conceal the fact, said so. Clo laughed. When she went out she didn't look at me.

Immediately, time, which till then had been painful and slow, woke up in a fragmentary tumult of bizarre leaps and stops. Leaving the rough majesty of the low banks of the Thames, I left too my solitude and nostalgia. Now London was precious, alive, full of commitment and plans, no longer that other city of heaviness and space and memory. From Holloway, I was always off with Penny through the City or beyond the Serpentine or to the domestic Babylon of Brompton or Sloane Square. Penny let eight whole days pass before she got in touch; I hadn't stirred, I had simply waited for her. The event I had awaited and had tried to hasten for so long found me not unprepared; but not for this reason. No actuality resembled my thousands of hypotheses. Nor were my feelings those I had imagined. Penny resembled the portrait composed then by my mind; but she wasn't the imagined woman, she was real. In the clamour of the auction room, while the hammer blows of the weary Coe assigned me objects I had bid for mechanically, without even looking at them, I saw again the yellow thatch and, beneath, the noble ivory face, the shining openings of her eyes. I drew back into the very rhythm of my obscure blood, from which she had perhaps been born. Perhaps.

Our first sentences when we saw each other again were rather more formal than at our first meeting. She seemed to be waiting, and to be prepared. We were in a large tea room in Leicester Square, uncrowded at that unconventional hour. With the light behind me, I saw her whole for the first time, minutely revealed by the crude light reflected in the plate glass. She was pale; there were faint violet shadows beneath her eyes, a suggestion of the consumptive around her mouth. The yellow wig gone, her real hair under a scarf tied below her chin, her face seemed exposed and defenceless; somehow she seemed called upon to defend herself. It was she who guided our conversation. She talked to me again about the basement in Archway where she lived.

'In the beginning,' she said, 'I lived there with a girlfriend, but she had to leave. It's handsome, though a bit damp. I've got fond of it, but I don't know if I'll be able to keep it. It's expensive for me to live there alone.'

It was an invitation to go into details about her finances. Different voices within me asked different questions. A middle-aged man who at a first meeting with a model is told of her money troubles is meant to think what? And what about the father who knows that his twenty-six-year-old daughter has spoken like this to a gentleman of fifty? By the improbable irony of circumstances, I had to suffer and judge at the same time, I had to weigh up myself and Penny and Clo.

We skirmished a long time. I was so afraid of betraying myself by letting slip her real name that I asked her if Clo was a pseudonym. She readily admitted her real name was Penelope, and found my gallantry acceptable when I asked to be allowed to distinguish myself from others by using the common English diminutive Penny. For the rest, I talked in general terms, studying her the while, as she was studying me. I offered her financial help as one Bohemian to another, so she could easily refuse with a smile. We went out into the lively, cheerful streets just before the theatres opened. She wore a close-fitting red coat, and a red scarf on her head. Most bizarre in the depths of winter, she also wore lace gloves, tight at the wrist but then belling out like those in seventeenth-century Flemish paintings. She seemed light-hearted; she certainly looked beautiful. But when we went our different ways her eyes met mine and I felt how sharp her look was.

Going back to Kitto Road that evening in the rumble and clatter of the tube, I thought of what I had said, and why. At the New Year's Eve party it had been simple courtesy to suggest another meeting. But now perhaps she had worked me out? Had she said she was hard-up so I should make plain my intentions, as people normally would in such a situation? Or was she aware of not regarding me as another Crockett, and wanted to see my reaction so she could tell if she was right or wrong? I didn't find the excellent Jack at Charlie's; he was off around the Black Country, they said, selling his carpets. And Molly was asleep.

The half-underground basements which insulated the old Victorian houses from rising damp have, in modern London, become that new institution - the basement flat.

They don't exist in the outskirts or the poor quarters, where the houses don't run to a floor underground, or are designed as if they were cottages or country houses. But at the nerve centres of the metropolis, where among the vast pleasure gardens the classical terraced houses with colonnades were built in enormous numbers, and where for about a hundred years an almost mythical people lived, there are basements everywhere. Then they were used for kitchens, service areas, store-rooms, and the family lived on the four or five floors above. These days, following changes more in social than in economic conditions, you find a different family living on each floor, if it's big enough. The owner or the main tenant will live on the ground floor; and at the top, with a view over the roofs of London, there may be a single young professional. The basement is left for someone without much money but who needs or wants to live next to those who have it. People in the theatre or in fashion, artists waiting for success, adventurers looking for their lucky break, the middlemen of luxury, pleasure or vice, students struggling to get qualified, girls dodging along between vanity and respectability, the dissolute, the humorous, the unsuccessful - all these, alone, in pairs, in groups, lived in the basements of central London. They put up as best they could with the smell of mould in winter and the smell of rubbish in summer. They arranged their bits of old crockery, and painted their squalid walls to give their poverty what refinement was possible.

English houses rarely have tiled floors; their rough wooden boards need a lot of carpets; and the resources of those living in basements are often exhausted by this first necessity. You may see the largest room covered with a good Wilton or an imaginative Axminster; but for the rest there will be haphazard beds that are more like couches, a small radio, a disorderly heap of books, clothes in suitcases. Then, because basements are cold, in the cavity where the old stove once stood there will be the gas-meter that gives out the warmth of life at a shilling a time. When the rent has been paid – always high, in the centre of town – and heating has been paid, what remains for food? Throughout the year the capital is the hunting-ground of people staving off hunger with bread rolls, sometimes for days, till a real meal comes their way. But you'll never hear these penniless folk complaining. Being young and English they live in a happy Gehenna of pride; there greatness and sorrow are being prepared, but they are not ready yet; there opulence is judged and society condemned, because the former has not yet been achieved or the latter dominated; and there Penny lived; and I was perhaps ideally suited to understand her.

Her friends – who became my judges, my objects of study and my provisional companions – were remarkable for their showy superficiality, their ceaseless play of mockery and implication, their punctilious self-love, their invincible liking for sensual pleasures. They were bizarre, open-minded, careless. English slovenliness, which grew out of abundance, survived poverty undiminished. Domestic chores were neglected, shopping done quickly and inadequately, everything done at the worst time; people turned up unexpectedly, sometimes merry, sometimes desperate, always ravenous, often inquisitive, never discreet; they twittered like agitated flights of birds in a tree. Penny stoutly defended the room she slept in, though she wasn't safe from the curiosity of passers-by which amused her, and gave her unkind stories to tell. She had a valuable rug from Shiraz; a brass bed with filigree work; linen from Flanders; an odd little table or gilded reading-desk held up by a globe, which was a rare example of transitional French neo-classical work; and a single Windsor chair with an attractive greenish patina. Satin ribbons and rosettes won by horses hung on the walls. There was nothing else.

When one went to visit her, if there was already one guest there (which was almost always the case) one had to sit on the floor, leaning against the corner, while the other person luxuriated in the Windsor chair, and Penny took the bed, like Cleopatra in front of Caesar or Antony. She was never put out, whoever turned up; but she watched every move, judging most severely anyone who when crossing the room stumbled on her slippers, which were always left right in the middle, or who was inelegant when greeting her or bowing or stretching out on the floor. She wouldn't tolerate people who made insufficient use of soap and water; so one plague that had spread half across the world since the war was happily absent from the basement in Archway.

Though one almost never met the same person twice, there was somebody who was always there, but who stayed in one of the smaller rooms or in the kitchen when there were visitors in front of the brass bed. I recognised the master of the big house where the New Year's Eve party had been held, or at least the man who had played the part of host; he had been distinguished then by his crêpe *tricolore* scarf like those worn by the people's commissaries in the French Revolution, and his Phrygian cap with its cockade from Barnum's, the theatrical costumier's; he might have been twenty-four or twenty-five, but with his sickly appearance he could have been older or younger. His name was Jeremy. He spoke little, usually just a few interruptions and exclamations. His abstraction was perpetual; his absence was barely concealed by a pallid smile or a grimace; his eyes were always distracted and vague. But his submissive loyalty to Penny was long-lasting and, I saw, inveterate; so much so that it called for no explanations or agreements. Jeremy provided for a hundred small necessities without her asking him or thanking him, still less directing him. Sometimes his ministrations were extravagant or unexpected, but she never batted an eyelid. Once he placed a lobster in a corner, as a note of colour. Another time he made a composition of chimney pots at the entrance to the basement, that made it look like an expanse of roofs at a great height. This last device of Jeremy's had Bates as an accomplice, who through me had become a regular visitor. But after a while the chimney pots were replaced by a sedan chair in front of the entrance; one had to wriggle into it from one side and then out the other. The sedan chair came from the dismantling of a shop-window in John Lewis. Penny accepted it gracefully.

Jeremy had neither a job nor even a hobby, which was rare in London; rarer still, his rich parents maintained him generously and asked no questions. He may have suffered from some inherited defect, though he was inoffensive and indeed sweet-natured. When I appeared, Jeremy showed no animosity; he hardly saw me – I was just another face. After a time, when I greeted him he responded with that grimace that might have been a smile; later still, he would glance at me, but without energy – it was the pallid, weak glance of an imprisoned bird. As for Sir Charles Devil's nephew, whom I called Crockett, he never came to the basement, and for the best of reasons. It takes a good forty minutes to drive from Knightsbridge to Archway if the traffic is reasonable. In the mornings, when Penny went to work at her fashion house, Jeremy punctually took her in his ridiculous old black Austin, which dated from 1937 and was dearly loved by his sophisticated friends from Cambridge and Chelsea. Bit by bit, I began to help him, till by tacit agreement this duty was shared almost equally between us. But Crockett had not only a Mercedes sports car but even a Bentley too; he picked up 'the enchanting Clo' after work, and took her off where he could be seen with her in smart restaurants, he took her to the theatre, or he took her dancing; and his cars only brought her back up the hill at night. She kept us precisely informed of Crockett's movements so no confusion should arise, but she made no comments. So with Crockett invisible, Jeremy abstracted, and I rapt in my thoughts, our entwined lives proceeded in utter silence and secrecy. But this gave it flavour and fascination. As far as I was concerned, it was the only situation I felt able to bear.

The days began to flow quickly; it was like floating down a delicious but dark current, the depth of which I ignored, though I feared its whirlpools. In fact I knew, and could have known, nothing. I had imagined that mysterious signs would attract me to her or repel me from her, and that thus I would have gained or lost a certainty which, if it wasn't rational, could present itself as instinct or even sentiment. I had believed the same thing would happen to her, that she might come to feel me not as extraneous but as of the same stuff from which she was made. But these notions proved chimerical. The only voices were the ones forever repeating the same questions. Worse still! For towards the evening of my life, sated with solitude, I had gathered myself together in hope of a resolution, of help of some sort; and it was truly ridiculous yet again to be catching glimpses of a woman. And what woman!

As the days passed, Penny too began to be aware of questions. She was free and unprejudiced; but she was under pressure from the circles in which she moved, and which now dominated her into a sort of atheism in love. She did not ask herself those questions to begin with. I was one of many who attempted to get close to her. Their aims were simple and the procedure monotonous. She knew their orientation, she foresaw the checks and the impulses and the crises. They wanted understanding and comforting; they suggested agreements and help. If, like Crockett, they were allowed to present her in the limelight of the social world as a useful adjunct to their own vanity, after a reasonable period that declined, was diluted by circumstance, ended by tacit consent, rarely in a break-up; it left no scars, just a distaste which in its turn vanished.

Having seen me evade the trial the first time, she therefore had waited with sceptical stoicism to see if I would surrender, to see if in one way or another I would go in that certain direction. After many weeks, she had to realise that I kept always at the same distance, asking her for nothing she didn't want to give, disguising the attention I gave to the practicalities of life she neglected. As Bates amused himself decorating and transforming her flat like a little theatre, Jeremy and I agreed to look after the basics of life. So the man who at Licudi had built the house of twenty thousand stones, went back to those old pleasures. It was made easy by Stoker and Coe, who saw me dedicate myself, with the specialists' tolerance, to new sectors: curtains, cutlery, crockery, lights. Jeremy's Austin and my Ford panted between New Cross and Holloway, piece by piece putting together a house Penny could really live in. She never knew which of us was behind all these changes, which we disguised so she discovered them only later, and sometimes never. Jeremy grew accustomed to me and I to him. We both cordially detested Crockett (from whom it seemed Penny had never accepted so much as a pin for the house). But we maintained an impassivity towards him which at the beginning seemed to her, at least on my part, in good taste; I was the only one who respected her liberty. Now she had to ask herself this other question. And finding no answer made her feel, I believe, uneasy.

Faced with the others, the ephemeral and brash and weird figures of her loving circle, whom she governed with dignity from her brass bed, I behaved as if I saw and heard nothing. They didn't think much of me. They had no idea how far ahead of them I had been, in my time, and they might have set on me if it hadn't been clear that Penny would not allow that. Slowly she was getting used to me. I wasn't the special and suitable man her mind had put together. At the start, I believe she hadn't even considered me as a possible man at her side. But subtle and strong bonds were tightening themselves between us: in the things that together we succeeded in seeing and understanding; in similar tastes; in similar repugnances; in the equal pleasure we took in a certain kind of game between things and us and other people and us. It was as if we were together while all else was to one side; or as if our particular world couldn't communicate with that of others, and for this reason they left us separated and together, the two of us.

So day by day I brought myself to pass increasing amounts of my time with her. She expected it like a service owed and enjoyed who knows why. She wasn't too tied down to her work, which, though at times it occupied her to the point of exhaustion, at other times left her free, on occasion for weeks. She liked the shops of London, big and small alike, for the way they seem to gather everything that exists, and each time show you what you have never seen before. We went from the emporiums of Soho to the specialised shops in Jermyn Street, from the expensiveness of New Bond Street to the ordinary tumult of High Street Kensington, from the antiquarians' lumber rooms of Marylebone to the refined boutiques of Belgravia and Chelsea.

In Paris, and then in a school for rich children, she had developed and preserved expensive tastes, which now she was unable to satisfy except in the smallest of ways. When I suggested some delicacy, some novelty, some trinket, she would shake her head; then thoughtfully she would tell me she liked only this or she liked only that; it was almost as if, when she didn't get precisely what she longed for, to accept anything else was completely impossible, might even be dangerous, but without her having to explain. Thus, before the marvellous array forever being offered her, she'd hesitate, shaking her head, and after long whisperings with the shopgirls, end by rejecting everything. The shopgirls appeared to understand, and I tried to.

When the fine weather came, which in a London mortified by winter arrives like a party, and fills the shops with invitations to strip off one's clothes, to spread one's arms, to fly, Penny on certain inspired mornings, among the thousand carefully chosen futilities she enjoyed, abandoned herself to a sort of dance. From a distance she pointed her finger at the hood or the jewel or the veil she found most beautiful. She exclaimed. She circled round it. She skimmed her open palm swiftly over a series of silks. She took off a shoe to try on two or three new ones; she wrapped herself in a shawl; she tried on a strass tiara. On the high stools of recondite bars we sipped like children at fruit juices and ices; we exchanged them time and again, always at her suggestion; we always found the other was the best. The expert women who manage those paradises looked at us endlessly, and avidly formed their various opinions.

They scrutinised us, those priestesses of luxury, those sellers of scent and underwear and make-up, those who hold the mystery of the hairdresser or the dressmaker. They devoted themselves to painstaking, nervous work for others' beauty or splendour, others on whom all the trade's resources were lavished for the ephemeral lustre of a fitting. They were tireless in the vigils passed preparing a royal costume or a trousseau, these bees sacrificed for the incomprehensible rights of an abstract queen. Penny was one of them too now; they recognised her. They wondered what rapport could unite her to such a man – they who were always being besieged by men, they who were defenceless and needy, who were subject to the perpetual dizzy spinning of vanity and money. The shrewdest sometimes gave themselves, and not for love. Perhaps they wondered whether she was selling herself and how unjust that was, whether I was trying to buy her and whether it was possible. They wondered if we had feelings they had known: agreement, the attempt at abuse, silent calculation, resigned passivity, a taste for vice, the determination not to know and the longing to forget. Perhaps they imagined the decision to take whatever comes that people make when they've already suffered too much – but which of us two had truly arrived at that?

In the stronghold in Kitto Road I looked at myself in a mirror that had come in a job lot from Stoker and Coe. It was a heavy Victorian oval with a plaster frame of unattractive fake gilding. The man who regarded me out of the vague vacuum looked concentrated; his hair was still dark; the scars on his forehead and cheeks looked as if they'd been deliberately sculpted. I saw ancestral traits in him that I recognised from portraits on the family tree I'd mocked so much forty years before. I had taken myself off around Europe in peace and war as they had done. But there was no magnificent armour or scarlet cloak framed in the best gold from the mint. Instead, I saw a grey shadow in the emptiness reflected in the plaster oval. I was a Sansevero, yes, though without the vigour and without the power. Still, I had my place in the tribe. But I was between the jaws of a vice by which none of them had been gripped. The ancient Sanhedrim of my ideal judges had vanished and their seats were empty. I had gone further than they had; I was alone and I had to decide not only for myself but also for them.

I was sure now that Penny was as attracted by me as I was by her. My thoughts were complicated by seeing her mother's eyes in her, by smelling again that June evening in Ferrara many years before. My thoughts were taken to lie in a shadowy void, when all I wanted was simply to be with her. I wanted to consume my perplexities at the roots of my imagination without having to explain or resolve an impossible dilemma.

How else could I stop the march of events? How could I tell her the truth, she who was not ready to hear or to understand? Could I say: 'I loved your mother, and I left her because I did not believe you were my child. Now I am alone, and I would like to know you and to believe you mine, though I will not be able to. But if you share this doubt with me, and share this secret, we can be company for each other in this bitter sea of life, you will help me to live and I will help you.' In front of the mirror I imagined these romantic things that at the same time were inflexibly true.

Obscurely but intensely she now struggled against me as I against her. Before every meeting with her I reflected on what she must have been thinking, and prepared my own thoughts. She did likewise. When we saw each other again, each combatant glanced at the other to estimate the damage suffered, at the terrain so as not to forget the detail that might be decisive for victory or defeat. We passed from easy and superficial smiles to deliberate silences, from things said that were beautiful and true, to explicit lies and insidious questions. Sometimes I felt the vice gripping us, and we both escaped with the same effort. Everything seemed at once pretence and falsification, and openness and sincerity.

Each knew the other would exploit an unguarded moment, yet didn't want the superficial victory of possession or abandonment. It was the ponderous but sublime game of assuming another's life into one's own to feel it as one's own. It was more than love. Or perhaps it was truly love.

About the middle of April, from one day to the next Penny got rid of her rather elaborate hairstyle that a French hairdresser touched up every fortnight. Her black hair had a violet shade in it, like Mavì's, and she took to wearing it in a nineteenth-century way that made her look innocent and mild. She invited me to the park beside her house so I could admire it. But she didn't uncover her head till we were settled on a bench. The day was soft as sunset approached, the place was beautiful.

Waterlow Park, one of the seven hundred in London, is remote; but it is one of the most beautiful, sloping up to a romantic crown of oaks beyond which one sees the City, vast and orderly. As the view from Telegraph Hill gives one the smoky and the dramatic, this view is almost the opposite, is defined and reassuring. Collecting my thoughts, I looked down over the countless regimented buildings where money arrives from all over the world, over the blue and green, over the peaceful flags. When I looked back at Penny I met her eyes watching me, like the first time we had met.

'Julien,' she said, 'have I ever shown you my mother's photograph?'

I started. Again in her voice I remembered an almost imperceptible tremor. I felt my own emptiness.

'Here it is,' she went on. 'I've changed my hair because I want to look more like her.'

She gave me the case with one hand, and with the other bared her head so I could judge. I gained time by looking at her. Leonardo preferred the light of evening for his masterpieces, and when Penny's face was at that moment lit by a ray of the sun, my heart was touched. Her hair shaded her face; it was nervous, vibrant hair, like you see in some symbolic images. Her tender eyes were, yes, at that moment, Cristina's. I lowered my own gaze and confronted that other gaze that smiled strongly up at me. It was Mavì as she had been when she was the focus of all Ferrara's admiring whisperings, with her heavy raven hair and the curve of her luminous face, her eyes that had chosen me and that now, from beyond her sorrow, from beyond her death, looked at me with an ironical challenge or perhaps with pity.

'Yes,' I said, closing the case. 'She's very like you. She was very beautiful.'

'Isn't that so?' she asked, her voice slightly agitated. 'You're strange, Julien, you've never asked me anything about myself or my mother, nor why I live here, nor if I have anyone of my own.'

'I'm alone,' I said after a silence, 'and maybe I think others are alone too. I feel that if I told others all about myself, they couldn't do anything. So I don't ask other people. I love you dearly, Penny, that's all.'

'No,' she said, shaking her head. 'That's not fair, and I don't think it's true either. Perhaps it's because people think like that that my mother died poor and abandoned during the war when I wasn't there to comfort her. She was alone all her life because no one knew how to comfort her, as I am alone now. So I'm like her and I want to be like her.'

'You don't have other relatives? Nobody?'

'A man is responsible for my mother's death,' Penny said with concentrated tension in her voice. 'A man who used his wealth to buy her, when she was an inexperienced girl, who tormented and oppressed her till she was forced to run away and die like that. Julien, how can I bear the knowledge that my father conceived me with evil and with violence? But I'm that man's daughter only for the sad things in me. It's his blood. But my mother is everything I want to be and am not. I know perfectly well that I'm not as I ought to be. But it's my revenge on him. He's proud and obstinate. My life is his shame, and when the right time comes I'll pillory him in front of all the world.'

She told me about herself at some length, of her melancholy childhood, of the quarrels and accusations she believed her mother unjustly suffered. She saw Mavì unsullied and Marsi a sadistic persecutor. Could I tell her the impossible truth, make her recognise me as the prime mover of the tragic train of events that ended in that *pension* in Marseilles? That would be to destroy the cult she nurtured in her mind, give the lie to her hatred of Marsi, make her see herself unjust and cruel towards him, overturn her thoughts, change the value of her memories, bring back her childhood to her in what different light?

And what about me, who in times before she could remember had moved those two souls so that they suffered and were lost? I'd judged Mavì as a man in his early twenties would; I hadn't believed she loved me, nor that she was waiting for help from me so she could redeem herself and start all over again. But later? Faced with the child that was born? I had lost all those years in which Penny began to smile and babble and walk, when she began her games, her first studies and activities. I had lost what is the parent's unutterable joy, that time before the adult to come is visible in the child, when the child still bears traces of the celestial world from which it has come. That was when if Penny was mine I had in my turn lost her; I had let an outsider come and profane her sleep with his kiss – or not, if Marsi had believed Penny was not his, and had left her alone with her mother's silence.

'Penny, where is that man now?'

'He's got another woman,' she replied contemptuously, 'probably one he finds convenient.'

She might hate me as, believing Marsi was her father, she hated him. We two were equal, faced with Mavì's death. She loathed him so much she had taken herself off, and preferred her damp basement, and the charmless attentions of Crockett, and the friendship of a defective like Jeremy, preferred these things to wealth and the beautiful land of France when made foul to her by Marsi. She acted with a determination that showed she was too deeply wounded to be healed, as I had been when Nerina died when I was young and I had turned implacably against my father. Now I was the age he had been then, his brilliant eyes met mine and forced me to lower them. Our confrontation had come to an end in the play of events, a hostile god had stamped me with the signs of the difficult, the contrary, the forbidden.

And now, because of Mavì's death, Penny was ruthless with her father – but with which one?

After that talk, when she had confided in me so I should do the same, and I had not done so, she seemed to come to a decision. It was the busiest time of year for her: presentations of new designs, publicity, trips, displays. Devil/Crockett was in Paris for the brilliant season, and luckily left us in peace. Since she had neither the time to devote to her household, nor the money for the grand hotels where her work took place, a car and some help were vital to her. Between us, Jeremy and I played the secretary, the assistant, the majordomo, the chauffeur. But it was clear that he was to look after her personally, while I was to show her off as Crockett had done. I bought a more dignified car; for her sake more than for mine I smartened up my wardrobe. Then, like an expert swimmer going into a rough sea, who trusts his own strength but also puts his trust in fortune, I plunged in, with her and perhaps also against her.

London was marvellous at that time of year, in those refined and fast-moving circles. I accepted everything; the lives of others seemed a game. Of all the thousands of courageous and beautiful women come from all over the world for that last and harshest of trials, I found none who inspired me as I was inspired following the spirit of Penny's black hair. Perhaps no one in all the city could share my lofty secret with me.

Like someone who has decided to see nothing, she reduced me to the role of a superficial accessory like Crockett. In this way she showed she assigned me his value, too; I was labelled; according to the etiquette of the world I was the *cavalier servente* of a lady in the best society. To accentuate this, Penny, who was always high-spirited, made herself aggressive and stubborn. Our way was snagged with lively incidents, in some of which she amused herself by provoking others to the point where I was also exposed.

I had abadoned Stoker and Coe. Now with Penny I attended the Mayfair auction rooms where billionaires raised the bidding by fifty thousand pounds with the slightest movements of their heads. With her I saw sold the furnishing of palace rooms, princes' china, lords' collections of pictures. Penny had nothing; she lived in a basement for which she just managed to pay the rent each week; but she examined and appraised everything, and it seemed somehow as if the others recognised in her as it were an abstract capacity for purchase. The impassive auctioneers at these alarming sales would have accepted a nod of her head, certain that she had the power and the wealth to make good her bid. She would look at an object - say, a nabob's crown worth a whole quarter of London - as carefully as a goldsmith. She asked endless questions, and no one ever wearied of explaining things to her. She was determined in her judgements; she recognised and despised reproductions; she often derided high prices paid for things not that good; and she got away with it. The ragged existentialists in black jerseys and dirty sandals, when they mocked bourgeois society's late appreciation of Van Gogh or Modigliani, found a natural ally in her, for she gave voice to protests that otherwise would have remained unspoken. She was much admired for her nervous energy which adorned the salerooms more than did the famous works shown there. I was watched too, and I was afraid I might be penetrated and revealed, so unlike her and yet so alike; for it was her blood that gave her that role and those rights - our blood.

I was spending more money, though Penny never asked even indirectly, and I always had to find new ways of offering. My storeroom near the bombsite proved to be a goldmine. The year before I had bought a mass of stuff and had dumped it there and forgotten it. What with the difference between the areas, an extraordinary leap in the market, my instinct, perhaps guided by the placated spirit of Gian Luigi, I found myself selling in Mayfair for two or three hundred pounds canvases and pieces of furniture for which in Lewisham I had paid fifteen. Therefore I could cope with my new extravagance. Penny became capricious. Perhaps she had never had the chance to act on impulse, had never known the pleasure of at once satisfying sudden wishes. Harrods' publicity tricks passed before our delighted eyes and those of the other hatless devotees, first the jewels from the Tower of London reproduced in glass and pinchbeck, then the furnishings of Tutankamen's tomb. Or we visited the fossils in Kensington or the colossal new buildings in Fleet Street. Or we took one of the lazy steamers that take three hours to go from the Houses of Parliament to Kingston, when you forget the city and slip along between lonely banks and silent boatyards and children on the shingle shores as white as gulls. When Penny clambered up to the cabin of a crane, or when she sat on the tail of a fairground dinosaur, or when she graced the grandstand at Ascot, she came back to my mind later when I'd returned to my room in Kitto Road as a symbolic or almost bewitched figure. She was my magic and my nightmare. She was challenging me, and must have known it.

London, July 1954

I've never wanted to go back to via Nullo in Milan, nor to Morea, nor to Berg. But I love going with her to the remote places I went to when looking for her. She doesn't know, she adapts, without understanding she looks at what I saw before her, when I imagined her and longed to find her. But for me those monotonous streets, those out-of-the-way quarters, those far-off parks, are the flowers on a garland I have dedicated to her.

Crockett came back in early September, having been in the sun at Cannes and Monte Carlo and therefore more freckled than ever. Penny had less work to do, and went back to lying on her brass bed. I gave business as my excuse for once more haunting Stoker's and once more looking up Jack at Charlie Brown's. He looked at me silently, rubbing the back of his hand across his drinker's lips. He sat with me and kept me company below the papier-mâché head with the grey hat, still without saying anything. Without a word passing between us, he understood all my ills. He consoled me simply by setting his exhausted spirit next to mine.

Penny, seeing less of me, asked no questions, though now and then she looked at me for a long time. She took to slightly wild gestures, like appearing in a shabby old dress she would ostentatiously say she had bought for a few shillings in the East End. Then she'd asked me to accompany her to fashionable places. But her elegant manners were enough to assure her indulgence and homage. I think she was even forgiven the bizarre way she obstinately struck with me. In the end she grew exasperated with my apparent patience, and instead of defending herself against presents she invited them, especially when it was a case of large and useless expense. She was trying to make me deny her things; or anyway to force me to ask for favours in exchange which would have degraded both of us, but at least would have cut the Gordian Knot of an impossible situation. I did great violence to both our feelings, I think; but rather than leave her I sold as much from the storeroom as was necessary and went on into the darkness. Some of her acquaintances became uneasy. Crockett tried to hurt me.

'Louis XVIII,' he said, 'thought that senile love was the most profound because it was impotent.'

Penny's eyes were clouded with a pain I could understand because it was as cruel as mine. We were in a vice, and it seemed we couldn't get free.

Coming back in the evening was often difficult, coming from south London, from Crystal Palace or Wimbledon or Richmond, with many miles to drive late at night and no chaotic traffic to distract us from confronting each other. It was difficult to find words, in the slightly sinister streets of the dark metropolis. I was aware of her scent, her young figure; I believed she made a point of never touching me, and that made it inevitable and difficult. I could have stopped, I could have taken her in my arms; I wasn't sure my masculinity wouldn't have been reawakened. 'Love her,' said the voice (from another river now, still more melancholy and exhausted), 'love her because you love her, without asking yourself who you are or who she is. She'll never know, and you must forget. You're so detached from the world you can resolve an absurdity beyond the world. You've risked everything – wasn't it so you should conquer your fear? You're already in deep. What can it mean to you, to go on further down?' She seemed drowsy. The streets of London passed and went on passing, like a nameless cabal from which I had rescued her, and which was waiting to get her back.

On one of these evenings she wanted me to go in with her, through the sedan chair guarding the door. She left me sitting in the Windsor chair, and came back carrying a jade bracelet on her open palm.

'I've wanted to show you this for a while,' she said. 'It belonged to my mother. She gave it to me before I left for England, the last time I saw her. "Only once I was loved," my mother told me, "and this is a memento of that love. I'll give it to you so it protects you in love. Only show it to who deserves to see it." '

They were minute pieces of jade, which the Chinese believe are symbols of the highest virtues, each one sculpted into the form of a small animal. I had given them to Mavì many years before. And now they brought me her message.

From behind the bar, Charlie whispered to Jack and looked at me as he polished that same mug. Now I was beyond help even from them, under the executioner's gauntlet and the fatal noose. Our silence was the silence that comes before sunrise on the allotted day.

In the fine weather at the end of September, Crockett offered his Bentley for a trip to Cornwall. Much against my wishes, I had to go with them. The English countryside, beautiful though it is, gave me the same feeling as London, of a marvellous phantom but one which eluded me. From a low hill one saw the loveliest prospects; but when one stopped it was difficult even to find a bank on which to sit or to lie. Here the way was closed, there lay a ditch, further on it was wet or cultivated or windswept. The English - all great walkers and accustomed to tough sports - stretched themselves out blithely on the wet grass without rugs or groundsheets. I delighed in clumps of trees, the counties that seemed gardens, the infinite country houses amid their gardens, the roads that fanned out in many directions, all of them attractive. The normal, the well-cared-for, the finished, were everywhere repeated. But was this all to silence the voice of truth, I wondered? What was there under the leather coat of the Oxfordian Devil? What was in Jeremy's stereotyped smile? And in Penny?

That day was the death of me. The British will spend four times the time together that we would devote to our dearest friend, and still never emerge from the dullest formality; and Penny applied this principle ferociously. She knew I couldn't stand Crockett's false enthusiasms while we dragged ourselves around the little square in Fowey, which is half the size of the one at Capri, and where a sea of people parked their cars, gathered, held forth, did business and amused themselves.

Like everyone else, Crockett hired a boat, and we went up the estuary, which branches into three and vanishes into the depths of the woods. In the heavy heat, Penny lay still and almost naked in the bows, sunbathing. An invincible unease rose in me at the sight of her slender, delicate form defenceless before Jeremy's ambiguous absence, and which Crockett neglected almost as if he knew it. I was still just a mature man faced with a young woman. My emotion and my restraint could be give many names; the confusion of my feelings grew because I was sure she was challenging me, she wanted to arouse desire in me. I didn't know. Exposed like that to the sun, reddening her slowly, she seemed almost sexless. I wanted to ask her to bunch herself up, to hug her knees between her arms and bow her head on to her knees till her hair hid her entire body. It was pity, or jealousy. But a feeling such as I could have felt for my woman, my daughter, and perhaps even for my mother?

From Fowey to Polperro the road runs between the high walls of green that give the county its name. Penny, not completely dressed again, still had the abandon and immodesty of women who come from bathing. Crockett was the most rigorous of tourists. He amused himself by exasperating me, though he got no visible reaction. Back at our tiny cottage in Lerry, nothing more than a bit of plaster and a bit of earth, I discovered the superior English capacity to pass off as choice and elegant what is merely rough and almost uninhabitable. The cottage was deathly cold. The rest of the time was passed in the restaurant, where the battered, muscular staff treated us familiarly and seemed to enjoy what they imagined to be our various loves. In the end Penny got up, said something in a low voice to Jeremy, who never batted an eyelid, and without considering Crockett, who was deep in a sporting journal, with her eyes asked me to come with her. We went outside.

'How long is it since you met me, Julien?' she asked at once, keeping at a distance from me.

The night was dark along the shores of the wide waterway making a gulf in the woods. The water was a perfect, dangerous blackness. The banks were deserted.

'Eight months and twenty-six days,' I answered. 'It's an easy calculation because it starts from the first day of the year. Or, to be more English, thirty-seven weeks I think.'

She laughed with a slightly strident laugh like Mavì's.

'I didn't think you'd know so accurately,' she replied. 'But do you just count the days since you've known me or also the days still to go before you leave me?'

'Penny, why should I leave you? Why should I want to leave you?'

She stood still, three paces from me, in that deep darkness and perfect silence.

'Julien,' she said, 'it'll soon be a year. What you're doing is incomprehensible. I'm alone, as you know, if you leave out Jeremy and Crockett; but he'll get into Parliament and marry an heiress; I could stay with him half a lifetime if I wanted - but only as his lover. Jeremy's very mixed-up; however, he adores me and he, on the other hand, would wait for me all his life. So I'm free in my thoughts and my actions in regard to both of them. It's all plain. But with you things are different. I don't like a man who hangs around me and never says what he's after. It cramps my freedom, and sometimes it wearies me.'

She imposed and I had to accept this hopeless struggle.

'Would you like me to confess a secret love for you?' I said. In that darkness she could interpret every slightest vibration of my voice. 'Maybe you'd reply that you were pleased. But if it's not like that? You've been hurt and you've retreated from your first love. Lets just call him "that man". Couldn't the same thing have happened to me? What if I too have given up a certain kind of love? And here in England what does it matter what I think or who I am? Certainly I don't want to hurt you. Where I can, I help. Do I inflict myself on you? If you want to live with Crockett or marry Jeremy, do so. You'll get a wedding present from me.'

'And what do you believe I am?' she returned bitterly. 'No, a man can't dispose of another person with his secret thoughts. That's not much good as a relationship. What have you given up? With me, you've suffered torments, I've seen! If you don't think I'm any good for you, why do you put up with it? You're not just anyone, Julien. So now what?'

Her excitement slightly calmed mine.

'Please be calm and think. This isn't a novel. I'm alone, and doubly alone here. Why shouldn't I enjoy your company? Where else should I go? How else should I spend what I earn? To me you're still a young girl. What worry is there, what's unacceptable, if I who am childless regard you in that light?'

I knew how false I was being, without hearing it in the bitter tone of her reply.

'But this is absurd, Julien, now, between you and me. Julien! It's as if I didn't know what a father was.' She quickly overtook me and began in a singsong voice. '*Il y avait un homme de Madère / qui cassa le nez à son père / lorsque on lui demanda pourquoi / il répondit, ma foi / vous ne connaissez pas mon père!*'

The quiet hung on the river, which at high tide nearly overflowed on to the road. With the faintest lapping, a white ghostly swan passed and disappeared. I went back into the house. Penny had gone to bed. The others hadn't yet come back. I left a formal note excusing myself. I spent the night in a wretched inn nearby. I went back to London on the first train, alone.

London, 6 October 1954

From my balcony in the crescent over Holloway I watch the pigeons. They're as dull and blackish as the London asphalt, despised by mankind, never tamed. Every day they have to resume their struggle for existence. They come and wait on the outer edge of my little terrace, always ready to take flight.

They have their own way of looking; they move, not the pupil, but the whole head, in the desired direction; and then it seems their red eyes give off a more tawny spark. As soon as I half-open the shutter, they go for a short flight. Then they come back, but they don't go to the bird seed; they stay still, though small starts of their heads show

how intensely they're waiting. Then they start their dance, by which one chases or repulses another, turning, cooing, showing with breast and beak what piece of ground they claim as theirs. They keep at it, feathers ruffled, the cantankerous against the despotic, and like this they stretch out their hunger. But then sprightly smaller birds jump on the whitest of the crumbs and hurl them about in particles with their beaks, they seem to gargle crumbs, and gulp them as they were singing. The pigeons make up their minds. First two, then four, then ten furiously gobble their meal. I can open the window and watch them from close up. They no longer look round, they have decided to live, and in that moment are not afraid of dying.

The pigeons had been my pastime for about two weeks, and I was amusing myself watching them when I saw Crockett's Bentley turn into the street. It seemed offensive, somehow, in that out-of-the way place; but when he knocked at the door I was ready to receive him.

'Mr Sansa,' he said, 'it's not for me to interest myself in the affairs of others, less still to ask you questions. However, I must tell you that since we left each other at Fowey, Clo is sad not to have seen you again.'

I looked at him attentively. Crockett couldn't have the slightest interest in calling me back. I thought he'd pushed Penny into that scene at Lerry so as to make a break between us two. And now?

'Jeremy's upset too,' he went on. 'Clo is very agitated now, and that's bad for her.'

'What sort of distress,' I asked, 'and why is it bad for her? Last year I didn't know her. I've been a good friend to her. What does it matter if she doesn't see me?'

'It wouldn't matter for a normal person,' Crockett said, staring hard at me. 'But it matters for her. Perhaps you didn't know that she was for a time in a sanatorium for nervous disorders?'

I shuddered, and Crockett saw. But he couldn't imagine how I'd seen the ghost Cristina restored to life in Penny's eyes, how now I saw her resurrected to menace me with her desperate sweetness.

Crockett finished his picture of the situation. 'Clo can become fixated on someone or on something. I don't know if this is the case now, but it's possible. The doctors say one shouldn't cross her when this happens; on the contrary, one should make light of it. Then she'll become calm again, and after a while will forget the people or things that have so forcibly struck her. In short, I think it would be wise for you to rejoin us as if nothing had occurred. As a gentleman you'll understand her feelings and behave appropriately. I felt I should warn you.'

Devil's car had barely turned the corner before my cares settled upon me. He was clever, he was an actor, he was ill-disposed towards me. When I had appeared among Penny's friends, he had examined me minutely. He was insolent when he could be, but he didn't make the mistake of judging me immediately; and he knew her way of seeing things well enough to know that my age was not an insuperable obstacle.

He had come because otherwise, sooner or later, she would have come herself. He had come so he could at least cause difficulties, so he could appeal to my scruples as a gentleman and stop me taking advantage of a sick girl's feelings – and only so he could abuse them himself. It was sad, but it made me laugh too. But without knowing it, he had dealt me a grievous injury. The vice was closed.

I examined this unexceptionable contraption with resigned coldness. There was something morbid in the exalted passion with which Penny detested Marsi and idolized Mavì. But I could sense that by some obscure instinct she didn't feel herself his daughter. She had looked to words for reasons which were in her blood; she had fled not from her mother's persecutor but from someone who was in fact extraneous to her.

She was not born from him, therefore. 'Once I was loved,' said Mavì's voice, while the jade bracelet took the light and I saw it around her lovely wrist. So Penny was mine. By what proof? Perhaps the evil that had carried Duke Michele, Gian Luigi's father, to his end; and then my beloved Cristina. And how many more of us?

'She had a man's courage when she shot herself with Gian Michele's pistol,' my uncle Federico had said forty years ago. 'But perhaps he didn't deserve it . . .'

Then, like everyone, I had thought that Gian Michele had opposed Dolores' love for some young fellow or other. Now I shivered to think she had wanted to die for him – for him who had been abandoned by the widow, for him whom she as a child, not being his daughter, had understood and loved for years with her whole being. He had denied her, thinking that love impossible. '. . . she knew that by killing herself she would destroy his life too . . .' Destroy? Make hers for ever. What impenetrable silences lived on in that courtyard with the well up on the hill at Paola!

I thought of the 'unhappy victims of love' on the fifth floor between the attics and the displaced tiles of the house of Santo Spirito di Palazzo. Then Gedeone and Francesca, life in a single memory. Then Checchina in the nunnery at Sora, and I myself, Nerina . . . I felt myself descending deeper into my memory, into my memory established before I was born. I came to the sad hills of Basilicata and the man who had given himself to Egloffstein, who resembled Cristina, who resembled Penny - given himself, and exhausted all his being.

If she had that ghost of theirs in her, I couldn't now deceive her. But it was more impossible still to lay that ghost without upsetting her fragile mental balance. This closed a vicious circle, but at the same time resolved it. What before had seemed unbearable or monstrous now became something to do quickly and easily. Where before I had had to leave her because she was my daughter and she loved me, now I could welcome her and love her freely. I had washed myself in that sea of sin and illusion, I had taken its rhythm into myself, I had retired into the solitary and even sinister castle of my heart, I had put on again the sackcloth I had worn in youth, to expiate love and expiate pride.

And she! Dead, absent or vanished I could never again get out of the consuming fire of her love, if she like all of us had evoked it with that same irreducible strength. But it was by a blessed destiny that our race drew towards its end like this. The circle of many centuries was being closed in our two souls, given back in silence and secret to the hermetic deities that had given it to us.

I thought she'd have lived with Jeremy. Perhaps, like Cristina, she knew her own ills. She was drawn to him because she could protect one worse afflicted than herself, and with him she didn't feel herself corrupted. Perhaps she could have lived in peace, in a precious enchanted garden, in a pact of silence. Those interminable silences of Jeremy's made me understand why in primitive magical ages the mad seemed to hold the secrets of the heavens.

'Giuliano,' said the voice, 'none of this is certain. There may be other reasons, and things may be quite different. She doesn't know; you could have met her and not known. There's nothing real here, just your mind burning like coal. She is drawn to you and you to her. You say father, or daughter, but they're only two names. Keep your secret. Love her, because she needs help; let yourself love, and the world you have lost will be yours once more.'

Four days later, V.R. Ronald, having neatly settled himself on the chair Crockett had used during his visit, and having made a point of consulting his watch, said to me: 'Sir, I have several pieces of news which might interest you. In the first place, I'd like to underline that, in the course of the undertaking you have been good enough to entrust to us, my firm has had cause to appreciate you highly. We know you have been moved by delicate and noble intentions. I would feel uncomfortable if I didn't point out to you that for professional reasons we have to inform ourselves about our clients, so as to be in the clear about what is asked of us. In short, sir, we know who you are.'

I didn't move. Within myself, everything had been decided. Events could confirm things, but not change them.

'Giunio Marsi,' Ronald went on, 'died in Paris two months ago, of a heart attack, in the grandstand at Longchamp. There is no will in favour of a third person. His bank has used its powerful connections to make minute enquiries. In short, the Paris Civil Court, through a trustee nominated to hold the unclaimed inheritance, is now looking for Miss Penny Marsi, the banker's only heir. He left something like a million sterling.'

V.R. Ronald took out a bundle of papers and the dummy of a page of a newspaper.

'This is the lay-out for the *Evening News*,' he said, 'which is already set up on the press, and will come out tomorrow in two million copies all over England. It's three o'clock now; they'll start printing at five. We got hold of it privately through a collaborator of ours. These twenty-five lines are the official court explanation of why Miss Marsi is sought, and the invitation to her to present herself. There is a good reward offered for whoever finds her. Sir, do you think I have the right to give them in advance the information they are looking for? Do you believe that Miss Marsi has now no longer any reason to conceal herself? If she presents herself spontaneously, that reward will be lost pointlessly. Or Lady Judith Percival will come forward; but she would refuse the reward.'

'Really it is Miss Marsi who is paying the reward,' I said, 'even if out of her inheritance. But for various reasons I think I can take on this responsibility. You're a good man, Mr Ronald. You could have decided not to come to me. Therefore, if you can get that money, do so. There's a telephone downstairs. Only, in exchange, make the newspaper agree not to publish the announcement and, at least for the present, not publish the story as news. I need a few days' grace.'

Ronald went off shuffling in his over-polished shoes, and ten minutes later he was back.

'My firm is safe,' he said, 'and so is Miss Marsi. They are flying over from Paris and I will see them this evening. Now let me give you further information. You and Miss Marsi have rewarded us in other ways, and we are grateful to you.'

As before I had not expected the last word to be spoken by Crockett, I didn't now expect it from him. As a father or as a lover it was already impossible for me to present myself to Penny, since I hadn't done so before. That was exactly the point - that my knowledge of the facts followed and did not precede my thoughts.

'When you asked us to find means of approaching Miss Marsi, then Miss Nelson, without it seeming intentional, we made the necessary enquiries among her acquaintances. The first person we investigated was Christopher Devil, eldest grandson of Sir Robi Pleydell Devil, who has served in more than one cabinet, and himself a Conservative candidate. You found Miss Marsi through Judith Percival of Hasting; and she is a first cousin of Christopher Devil. We therefore have reason to believe that he has known Miss Marsi's identity all along. What is more, two months ago when Giunio Marsi died, Devil was in Paris, and thus he has certainly known since then. Lastly,' and here V.R. Ronald lowered his eyes, 'we discovered by other means, through an agency connected with ours, that Devil has had enquiries made about you. I happened to see the dossier.'

Yes, this was the seal. Apart from my real name, Crockett could have discovered nothing. All traces of Ferrara had vanished from my long and troubled life. No inkling of it had reached Naples; and then I had lived at Licudi for many years; I had been to the war; I had been to Rome and afterwards to the Po. But he would certainly have believed I knew of Marsi's money, as he himself knew, and that I had simply been more shrewd and had waited more patiently. It was like that other time when Carruozzo had designs at once on the money and on the woman, and held dominion over her because he knew how undermined and defenceless she was. If I had come out against him, he would have told her he knew all about me, that I knew everything but was being secretive. I would not have been able to defend myself.

'Many thanks, sir,' Ronald concluded as he got up. 'I will leave you now. I don't know, and I've no right to know, why you were looking for Miss Marsi. But I wish her well, and I wish you well, though I come close to fearing that from an excess of scrupulousness on both sides you will put difficulties in the way of the happiness you deserve. Don't do it, sir. Don't do it, for her sake - and also for yours.'

He bowed, and noisily vanished down my wretched staircase.

It was already very late when I reached Dartmouth Avenue. Her friends must have left Penny some while ago. There was still a light shining behind her curtains. I knocked on the window and she appeared for a moment, sweeping her eyes over me in the shadows. I went through the sedan chair. In her room there were a few empty glasses on the floor, ashtrays, a faint smell of people and of tobacco.

She kicked her shoes off and lay on her brass bed. She leaned on an embroidered cushion hardly bigger than her head. It was cold, the gas stove was lit. I let the Windsor chair be, and sat on the ground in the corner nearest the fire, in that uncomfortable position which over many months had become familiar. She looked at me in that attentive way of hers, determined not to speak if I wouldn't speak, knowing that the first word would be important.

'I've come to say goodbye,' I said at last. 'I've had letters from Italy. I've got to make a quick dash there for two or three weeks.'

'Two or three weeks,' Penny said in no particular tone of voice. In London, everyone is always off somewhere for two or three weeks. Someone in the same household as you says goodbye when he goes out as usual with his bowler hat and briefcase and umbrella. You don't see him again for a month. Then he reappears, and you find out, though not from him, that he's been in Singapore or Kuwait or British Columbia.

'Perhaps more,' I said, 'perhaps less. I wasn't expecting the news I've had. I hope you'll let me ask you if there's anything you need. I'm leaving on a flight tonight, at three o'clock.'

'Perhaps more, perhaps less,' Penny said, looking at me fixedly over her beautiful arm. 'It won't be much fun. Crockett has been stifling me this last little while.'

'Why do you put up with him?' I asked wearily. 'Free yourself from him once and for all. Do you really have no one in all the world?'

'Yes, I had you,' said Penny, lightly stressing the word 'you'. 'Then there are my mother's parents, who are very old. But they've always written to me, and I've always written to them in Genoa. You don't know, Julien, but my real name isn't Nelson. It's a name I took so as to hide from my father. Crockett knows who I am, and pretends to me that he doesn't know. I've always known he knew and pretended not to, and I've despised him all the more for it. But now I reckon he can go to hell, if that's what you want, Julien. I promise you there'll be no more Crockett here.'

So she had imagined I had abandoned her because I didn't want to share her with him. A deep discomfort spread through me; the trajectory was going down as it had risen, in the immobility of irreparable error. It was like the destruction and death of Nerina.

'I asked you a question in Lerry,' Penny went on, still looking at me acutely over her arm. 'And you didn't answer. You're a difficult man to find things out from. If we go back, will you answer?'

'There aren't any mysteries, Penny, everything's as plain as a flat table. I was educated by the monks of the Lily, I think I told you. Now and then I've felt attracted by the idea of going back up there. People talk about vocations, but I don't know. Now the abbot has written asking me if I'd like to try. You're so young, beside me. I want to question myself on the top of that mountain – not to pray, I wouldn't know whom to pray to. But I'd like to find out whom to pray to, and why?'

The gas puffed heavily and then died. I shifted, put in a shilling, lit it again.

'Thank you!' said Penny. 'Maybe you'll be happier singing with the monks that going to Peter Jones with me, or to that great store for provincial types, Harrods, to amuse ourselves. We had a wonderful time together, you and I!'

The tears of things rose up and submerged me and submerged her. The vast plain of London was a sea of tears, the vale of weeping that the prophets saw on earth, and where we drank like oxen.

'A fine monk dressed in white?' said Penny as if thoughtfully following a vision that made her smile. She heaved herself off the bed, came towards me and knelt before my gracefully.

'Father Julien,' she said tenderly, 'forgive me my sins. Is it so terrible to love a fine monk dressed all in white?'

'My child,' I replied, in turn kneeling before her, 'by Our Lord's wounds we are forgiven.'

She made to bend towards me, I felt her vivid lips brush me as I got up. I tried not to look at her as I went out, turned on her stem like a beautiful flower, her passionate eyes (which I would never forget) watching me.

In my little room in Kitto Road I took the maps off the wall, the maps of railway lines, theatres, bus routes, tube lines, banks, all criss-crossed with markings. The fireplace hadn't been used since winter, and when I lit a fire the first flames were almost put out by a fall of soot from the chimney, but then they roared up again. The maps crackled and blew and writhed like living matter, like my enemies or malign spirits being exorcised.

It was truly like the old witchcraft in which, by piercing the breast of a wax image, by enchantment far away the hated person died; for that night, and at that hour, Stoker and Coe of Lewisham caught fire. Before anybody had noticed the smoke pouring from the cellars, the flames, helped by the autumn breeze, took hold of the heart of the buildings and as they spread seemed to shake them like trees. The premises were full to the brim, for the auction on the following day. A lot of linoleum and crates were stacked in the bombsite, with heaps of army equipment, tents, camp kitchens. Everything was still packed in its cardboard, straw and rags. It all blazed up like a witches' sabbath. The Victorian furniture, the carpets, the pictures, the books, the mattresses and beds and bales of cloth and sofas sent up clouds of smoke, they crackled and screeched, they roared and cracked amid the caving-in windows and the exploding cans. A silent crowd appeared out of the night and watched motionless as the hydrants fought their losing battle with the wild creature. It seemed the memory of the Great Fire of London flew back after three hundred years, when the enemy had razed half the city, reflecting its rage in the ice of the frozen Thames. Hitler had reawakened the memory, which now visited the bombsite, its darkness hardly impinged upon by the monstrous groaning and hissing. The dreadful breath leaped up each time, insatiably hungry, the crowd raised their cry like a sufferer who is reawoken by the very pain that made him lose consciousness.

Two hours later my aeroplane vibrated monotonously as it rose over the constellated lights of London in the calm night. Perhaps I thought I could distinguish a reddish dazzle down there . . . Perhaps all those drowsing down there, perhaps even she with her fixed gaze lying on her brass bed, had never existed; like all the past, just ash in an empty square; or it was only a single flickering coal burning in my mind.

THE EAR

Kalonerò di Sicilia, 12 June 1955

Clay is the primal matter. It is never transformed, though it can be baked to make bricks; and in time it will crumble and be clay again. And with clay goes lime, that was sandstone and will be sandstone again. In hot countries clay and lime endure uncorrupted by the sun. Just tufa, hardly more than compound clay, and dazzling white with lime, like a piece of incandescent marble – such is the church in flight on the high plateau, under the sun.

What hangs in the sunlight is not the scent of life. Memory turns to lime like a bone even the termites desert, Being is like the bizarre flames which dance in a fire, no longer form but the substance itself and quality of a man, in incurable flickering in the blood of the flames. I am saturated with the past, I am constrained by the present, I am waiting to die, but still asking, asking.

The sun's silences are terrible in the vermilion and white summer down here. The plain shimmers in the heat. Stricken by fear, beasts and plants and things lie supine. Birds and insects and snakes hide. The earth opens like decaying fruit and shows its lips of mud. Trees twist as if with their lean arms they were trying to protect themselves from chastisement. The sky is a wide-open eye above a punishment that wants to hide. But the church in its destined glory is indomitable, the only living thing in the blinded country. The church is the home of quietness; under its arches and in its shadows one can hide one's face, one can pray far from the hammer-blows of the sun.

The priest never comes to the church at this hour. He stays in his two small rooms just outside the immense nunnery, which is almost empty. Behind a wall six metres high, a few sisters still live, the last survivors of a closed order. Beyond the wall lie loggias, corridors, halls, rows of cells, spaces that were once orchards, courtyards around cemeteries; till the ceilings gape and the floors give way, and you make out beyond the last palings the white river rushing fearfully by, that year by year sucks at the monastery doomed by landslides.

Kalonerò is a Greek name, and there is a place in Arcadia call Kalonerò too. It means 'good water'. But here there is no water.

Perhaps in the days of Selinunte and Gela there were springs which welled up and were reabsorbed into the sandstone. In those magical times the marshes were breathed upon by monsters, giants ran through the forests imagining rustic, weird torments for men and rabbits and moles. Today the name of the place appears in no guidebooks. It is out of memory, waiting for the archaeologist or mage who will resuscitate it. The church stands above thirty houses. On the other three sides of the place there are three more churches, all big, all barred up, all without altars. The sun shines.

What was there here once upon a time? Why are there four churches in this desert, which were once illustrious and now have declined through ever more plaintive prayers within prayers to this last surviving murmur of five nuns and a confessor? They were marvellous churches with great vaults and arches; the play of perspective is cleaner now in their nakedness which brings them back to the pure, ideal lines their architects conceived. The abstract perfection of Santo Spirito in Florence is here produced in time and silence and bare whiteness. The mind wanders over these immense surfaces, turns and undulates with them, goes down again from the dome to the countless tiles that radiate and fan and mingle, and that free one's thoughts. Knife-blades of sunlight fall everywhere in the silence. If you listen you may catch the echo of psalms that have remained in the walls or under the roots of stone. Pray. Pray. Why?

Who raised these churches? In the nunnery there is a vast hall that must once have been the library. Only some bookcases remain, littered with flakes of plaster. There are no books in Kalonerò; not even the priest has books, except the odd missal yellow with age. Who had the strength to raise these immense monuments, and load them with works which then equally mysterious hands took away and annihilated? The churches have been cleaned as the sea cleans fish-bones. But beneath the white, faintly red and blue traces still shine through, fragments of frescos and mosaics. At some stage in history, the thinking that had generated these great works was distracted. The masterpieces were whitewashed. Art which briefly had glorified God returned to mingle itself with the sum of human vanities. The psalms were absorbed into the stonework, in this Beyond without Paradise, in this Licudi without that charm and that sea. Yes, this is the place for me, I who am as consumed as the things around me. I have to get back into the sun. There is one more step I must take, once more only I must struggle. The priest and I have kindred destinies, and here in this unimaginable corner of the world, where the landscape has vanished and the choirs have vanished, we must overcome our last trial.

His name is Giovanni, that holy name which belonged both to the favourite disciple and to the baptist. He doesn't come from here; he was born sixty years ago in the hills above Brescia. He has been thirty years in this impoverished place, where no one knows anything about him because all they know comes from him and he tells them nothing. He has the cure of less than two hundred souls, three-quarters of them old people or children or young people waiting, like those of Licudi, to join their relations in America. Like Licudi, Kalonerò is administered from Perla, down on the plateau. They see the mayor maybe once a year; there are no aldermen or policemen. The priest makes up for some of these lacks, he writes letters, he gets people out of work to do the small jobs that are needed, like cleaning the streets and patching up the pavements; and bit by bit, in the sun, these jobs get done.

Don Giovanni is of middling height, dignified and bony. His dark face is sculpted, but of roughly cut wood, not of refined marble or terracotta, but sad brown wood that cheap varnish has robbed of its purity without giving it lustre. His eyes are black and opaque, with large pupils. His grizzled hair is short and wiry on his skull of stone, the small iron-grey head of a highlander. He is not dreadfully poor, he has an acre or two nearby. He dresses carefully, but like a soldier afraid of the sergeant's eye. Perhaps he is afraid of the eye of God? I surprised him once in a corner of this hermitage where he had bent down to wipe the dust from his shoes. Who could be looking at him up here? Who would, I don't mean judge him, but even notice or make a suggestion? Would I? Was it for me he was polishing his boots? Does he know he'll have to fight against me? How has he discovered?

Even before dawn has touched the high, piled stones till then crowned with stars, when the night is at its most intense because it is about to die, shadow after shadow leaves the village, either with the rustling of bare feet, or with the muffled hoofbeats of horses or mules. All who can, scatter over the plateau before the implacable sun has risen, to their fields and livestock, to the mine, to various labours all the way to Perla. The light comes up quickly from the peaks and pours in mighty torrents down the gulleys. The perfect church grows whiter in the daylight. Bare-footed boys swing on the bell-rope. Don Giovanni says mass for four old women, a few dodderers, the boys.

It is five o'clock. On working days he can almost never find anyone to help him, so he does everything himself. He carries the bible. He rings the bell. He burns the incense. He is deeply absorbed. One can hear outside the hens scratching and the doves cooing. There's not a living soul for kilometres around the church in which the service is so devoutly held: only five brides of God in the nunnery, shut away to pray since birth maybe; and in the houses, the sick and children two or three years old looked after by their sisters of five, an artisan or two, and the smith. The dogs have been left outside the doors which are never shut, not even at night. The countryside is burned by the sun's patient devotion. Don Giovanni's sibilants whisper in the already torrid silence:

Domine non sum dignus!
Domine non sum dignus!
Domine non sum dignus!

He knows that in this innocent poverty there is one watchful and audacious soul, capable of suffering and of harming, the alien who came pleading ill-health, saying the doctors had told him he must live quietly. Don Giovanni was not deceived. At the first glance he knew that the person he had expected and feared was just outside the secret cell of his silence. It was the same for me. I too had come to a bare stage for a last dialogue.

10 September 1955

I've never had a house that really suited me as much as this one does, a house that didn't go against my ideas, that not having cost me any effort offered generosity and simplicity. This house has come to me in that exchange of things which I remember Arquà spoke of once, the way in which pieces of my life have been taken and nothing left in return. For some while the barracks at Ferrara, and the green room of those days, haven't existed any more. The beach of the Maronti has become a luna park, my lodgings at the edge of the foam is a whisky-a-go-go. Monte di Dio is scrap-iron twisted by the bombardment of 1942, among the ruins of Gian Luigi's house. Licudi was sold in the end and turned into a fashionable hotel. Checchina passed Uncle Gedeone's quarters over to a pious foundation who have put their administration there, so all day long there are forms being filled in and people begging for things.

Here, this big house must have been built two or three hundred years ago, along with the church. A stone over the doorway bears the motto: *Amphyon Thebas ego domum.* Inside wide surrounding walls lies uncultivated ground where a lot of plants I don't recognise grow, thanks to the great cistern which makes sonorous noises and is famous for never drying up even in the worst droughts. This year, though no rain has fallen for five months, it still has water. Inside there are I don't know how many rooms. From the windows one sees the immense grey Sicilian landscape where clouds gallop, sunlight crossed by shadows, red gashes like clotted and baked blood, smoky beneath the sailing sky.

No one has lived here for decades and there's no furniture. There's cardboard instead of glass in the windows, big damp patches where water has come in on the wind or through leaks in the roof, and dust everywhere. Don Giovanni has the disposal of the place, on behalf of who knows whom; he looked thoughtfully at the first year's rent I gave him, as at a gift from heaven. I was given tables and chairs from the houses of people who have emigrated. I made a few essential repairs. I bought a bed and one or two other things in an emporium in Perla. I've made a track through the long grass in the courtyard. I have no further needs: just time and silence. Silence above all, a hundred years of it so I can understand what I've made of my life.

The woman who comes and looks after me is called Ninfa; she's nearly eighty; the priest found her for me. She's a tiny bundle of bones and skin, dark as a bedouin, her straight hair still black. She neither understands nor touches any of the things I use. She's never seen the sea, nor Corleone, nor taken a train. She sweeps here and there, she does my bed, she looks after the laundry and runs the kitchen. I eat what she conceives one might eat, which isn't much. She has no notion of buying more than a hundred grams of cheese or a scrap of bacon-fat or a drop of oil. She brings me her own bread.

Time and silence. But this silence is resonant; and I cannot cross this time. The day passes under the weight of the mighty hand of the sun, in heat which solidifies the air. Where the sun has spared a nook, and it's possible to sit in a breath of air, one's eyes rest on the earth. It's always streaked with wisps of straw, marked by the tracks of animals; there are bits of ribbon and coloured oddments left over from children's games. I neither approach the children nor avoid them. I neither approach nor avoid any of the poor people who live here. I will not fall again into the trap that deceived me in Licudi, of thinking humanity better where I find it wretched and ill-treated. Original sin hangs over them as it hangs over me. These are not the light-hearted countrymen of Arrichetta in the happy days. They laugh little, and when they sing they only just sing. They wear severe black and brown clothes of heavy material in this scorching climate, like the Tuareg of Atlante. If a mother with her babe in her arms watches me as I pass, with her brilliant eyes like olives, I can sense her thinking: 'That's the gentleman who lives alone in the big house with the cistern. He doesn't work. He's got nobody. They say he's ill. What are you ill with?' the shining eyes ask. 'Don't you know there's only one malady in life and this babe in my arms suffers from it? The only malady is that I've got very little milk.' But I avoid that glance and do not answer. I don't look at the children, nor at their mothers, nor at the other souls of Kalonerò. I don't look at the girls when they come back from the countryside in the evening and cast their eyes up to the unlit lamp at my window. I don't look at the young men. They've stopped being men and women to me. Maybe they're just souls, as they are for don Giovanni. I look inward, into the flame of life which is all that's left of me. It burns in the furnace of the sun, it's stronger than the flames of the sun.

So the day passes. But the night? I sit in the walled garden; the fireflies flutter close by my face; one stops and shines above my arm. I listen to the village in the starlight, the barking dogs, the rustling of the weary trees as they drink the dew. There's still heat, which comes, perhaps, from the sea. The limitless river of time high over the mountains pours down and will flow over my sleep. And tomorrow?

Don Giovanni's days are far more industrious than those I idle away. The *Ora et Labora* of the Benedictines is the opposite of 'Think and Lie Down' I live by. When he says mass at five in the morning, without himself receiving the sacrament, he has already celebrated matins for the nuns in the chapel before four. At six he sets off on his mule around these mountains to the farmsteads and hamlets, perhaps to his own plot of land or to Perla. He comes back at ten when the sun is already oppressive. He goes into the sacristy to listen to the women and children, to help prepare them for catechism or arrange baptisms. Or else he writes at a corner of the big table, while the others swarm around with cheerful irreverence, seven or eight of them opening and shutting drawers, shifting vestments and chairs and candelabra.

The sacristy is big and sonorous. There are colossal wardrobes which, when the arms of their doors are opened, become brown caverns breathing out dusty smells. Each drawer would make a trough to knead dough for enough bread for a hundred soldiers. Inside there are silvery pedestals, wooden angels, black crucifixes, papier-mâché saints, printed decrees sent out by a Bourbon bishop a hundred years ago. There are candles, or blocks of wax. There are series of folded cardboard structures which when opened are mock-ups of perspectives, like stage scenery, with recessions of arches, clouds, gilded rays from paradise. The children know how to set these up with canvas and string and struts. The church is decorated for the funeral mass of someone who has died in Virginia, or to give thanks for someone who in China escaped the black smallpox. Don Giovanni is writing at the corner of the table on a moth-eaten cloth. The children run and shout. There comes the sound of the wing-beat of a dove that has got into the church. It flies all round, and goes out, white, into the sun.

Towards one o'clock the priest retires till four. Then he disappears into the nunnery. There is no point in talking to him about this period of his day, because at the grating behind the altar in the chapel he hears the confessions of the nuns hidden all their lives behind the wall six metres high. The confessions take a long time; it's evening when they are over. The villagers come back from the countryside; he goes among the houses asking, listening, advising. It is after ten when he retires to his rooms by the nunnery. On the other side of the village I do likewise. We both listen to the night, knowing the other is doing so.

There is no other life than that which turns around this priest therefore; and since it seems everyone helps him, the only thing to do is to help him too in what he does. His ministry occupies him in the morning and afternoon; he is among his flock in the evening; so the time he can call his own is the hours in the sacristy when he writes at the corner of the table. One can decipher for him the letters he gets from those who have forgotten what little orthography they ever knew, written in vile sailors' English, letters which have been to Montevideo, New York, Southampton, Le Havre, Marseilles, Genoa, Palermo, Corleone, Perla, Corleone, Kalonerò. The writing straggles all over the place on the envelopes among wrinkled stamps, stamps livid green and violet with damp. They want the office for the dead celebrated for somebody who died eight thousand kilometres away. They want ceremony number four. The countersigned, decorated postcards cross the seas dozens of times, they get worn away like old ration-cards or season-tickets. One can help, too, by restoring the creased bits of card (here where no one has a camera) and setting them up like the wings of a theatre on either side of the nave. It is quite an undertaking, in the throng of children. But then you have the whole effect, the clouds, angelic choirs, celestial light! It took all August and part of September. Then I wrote in English or French to consuls here and there, on behalf of wives who had lost their husbands, or whose husbands were living with half-caste girls in Venezuela or Costarica and never sent money orders any more. So far no mention has been made of poverty or charity. I won't go in for giving the children sweets or tips again. Still less will I give bread. I'll be like the church, which knows the value of hardship and interprets its laws.

Don Giovanni hardly looks at me with his black eyes in his wan face. Sometimes he covers half his face with an open hand like a wing, so one sees half his mouth, one eye and half his forehead. With his elbow in his free hand, he looks at me with his other eye. The visible half of his mouth is a thread only. His wooden face and stony skull are motionless. Still he has told me nothing of what he thinks, nor have I unburdened myself to him; but it will come.

The strange rocks to which Kalonerò clings have undergone the whims of erosion. What used to be a sloping crag of the mountain has become an earthy octopus stretching out five or six tentacles towards the valley. Sometimes they are gentle, sometimes they are precipitous and brambles hang in the void; there are dirty streaks where rubbish has been thrown out of the village over the decades. The road follows the only safe part of the hump of land. Otherwise, Kalonerò is inaccessible, shut off by the valley where the river flows; and thus the village, like the nunnery, can in the end only vanish in a landslide.

The houses are packed around the church, and extend only reluctantly along the more risky extremities. But from one of these there is the finest view of the spreading countryside on the Sciacca side that falls away to the African sea. At the end of the alley long ago a little fountain had been built. It was dry now, but it had a graceful stone pillar which held up the gargoyle from which the water had spouted. Then there's a curving outer wall that serves at once as a seat and a parapet, and there are the street urchins in the evening.

I sit on this low wall at sunset, rather like I did at Krano looking at the Taiyetos. The children pretend not to see me as they play; they are at once near and distant. The sun goes down; when it touches the rim of the hills hiding the sea, the heat of the day seems suddenly to give up. There is a perfect moment in which the soul, which is in one's limbs, rests. I go every evening so as not to lose that perfect moment. It's as if the sun said something I could understand. Evening by evening the children come slightly closer, though I don't encourage them, like the wild cat in Ischia. Then one time a girl maybe ten years old came out of one of the doorways and straight up to me.

'I'm Achiròpita,' she said.

Vague memories of beginning to speak the language in Greece stirred in me, or memories of boarding-school or of travelling.

'Where are you from with a name like that?'

'This is my house,' she answered with dignity, pointing to the doorway she had come out of. 'If you would do us the honour . . .'

I follow her, while the urchins pretend not to see; but there's connivance between them, as there will have been premeditation too. Achiròpita's house, like almost all the houses from Alcamo to Ragusa, has by the door a heavy iron ring for tying up horses. When there is no horse, the housewives stick their brooms through them, for they are most punctilious about the tidiness of their bit of pavement. The poverty-stricken house was very clean too, or rather the single room where a woolly old man greeted me without getting up, though he took off his beret.

'This is my grandfather,' said the child. Then she said more loudly, no doubt because he was hard of hearing: 'This is the gentleman from the villa.' Then she sat down composedly on a little seat I believe must have been her own special seat, and appeared to wait for the compliments of a regulation visit.

I found out she had lost both her parents, her father not long ago, her mother when she was born. She had been a woman of Rossano Calabro, where the patron saint is the Byzantine virgin Achiròpita. It is a Greek name meaning 'Not painted by human hand', in other words someone who has appeared by miracle, as I was inclined to believe the little child had appeared to me. When we had exhausted these topics, she got up and opened a big roughly-made wooden chest. A strong, wild smell that I recognised came out.

'My father left these,' she said. 'He was going to sell them. Do you want any?'

I couldn't suppress my confusion. The chest was full of a tangled mass of horse-hair. There were entire tails, twisted and tied; there were confused manes winding in and out of each other so homogeneously and continuously that it seemed the motionless dense whole was moving. All the colours of horses' coats were there, faint golds of sorrels and bays, reddish roans, shining blacks, pearly whites and ashen greys. Where had Achiròpita's father collected such epic relics, a hundred years after the last cavalry battle?

'My father turned them over all the time,' said Achiròpita. 'He brushed and combed them, he wound them into hanks, he disinfected them. The middlemen from Corleone came three times bringing clients from Palermo and from the mainland. But I've talked it over with Grandfather, and we want to give them all to you.'

No doubt about it, this ten-year-old Achiròpita, though she appears to be flesh and bone, is not of mortal tissue. How did she know that in all Italy there's one man so out of things that he'd buy a chest of manes and tails from a child and an old man who offer it as the most natural thing in the world? There's more of the past, more of the appearance of glorious death, in this musty heroic smell than in any museum - death in the threads of the arras of time, in that impulsive weaving, that making and unmaking.

There were no furnishings in my house; but it was turned into a Napoleonic bivouac before battle, or a parade of trophies after victory: there were shining tails and manes on the stairs, on the arches, on the doorposts. Achiròpita came to organise the moving of the chest; she indicated where the best place to put it would be; she elected herself curator and caretaker. I acquired her like someone who acquires an estate and with it the farm labourers, or a circus and with it lions and trainers and acrobats. There's a gulf of seventy years between her and old Ninfa; but when I look at the old woman doing her little jobs, and the child airing and smoothing the manes and tails, I sometimes think they've exchanged ages.

On market days down in Corleone the horses wait in a fouled piece of open ground. Their smell is rank in the scorching air, like the smell of the black horses that took Aunt Elisa away with her diamond earrings. It's the smell that comes out of the depths of the chest when Achiròpita empties it, leaving only a few dry, almost metallic hairs on the grey dust. I look at the tails and manes, when at midday the dry walls breathe a vague eroticism and remind me of youth and when the gardener's daughter at San Sebastiano assailed my innocence. I watch Achiròpita in the empty room tidying her treasure which lies around her. She has brought her seat with her, and sits on it in her cheap, threadbare, thin clothes that barely modify her taut, nervous physique. She works away as if performing a rite, shaking out the solid tails and making them shine in the blades of sunlight, while her blood flows almost visibly beneath her almond-coloured skin.

In Ferrara they gave the small, wild Maremma horses to some half-barbarous Sardinian soldiers, who tamed them. Am I now the sort of proud animal, perhaps, that Achiròpita's purity can subdue? Since she's been with me - and she comes here ever more often - the villagers, if they want to ask me this or that, do it through her. When she turns to me, I read in her eyes her devoted conviction that I will deny nothing. The priest has said nothing of what has occurred; only, if he has to mention her, he averts his eyes. When there are messages or requests, I notice he too approaches me through her.

Kalonerò di Sicilia, 25 October 1955

On Sunday I go to hear don Giovanni's nine o'clock mass. He doesn't go up into the pulpit; but from one side of the altar he speaks to those who have come to listen, respectful but free, blowing their noses and coughing, women here and there leaning towards each other's cheeks to whisper.

He harangues his parishioners steadily, as if they weren't there, following his own train of thought which is far too sophisticated for them to understand. But I believe that religion, like poetry, is always intuited or imagined; people don't understand the Latin prayers, but they catch the inspiration. His homilies are nearly always about the Old Testament's grandiose and gloomy stories of patriarchs swathed in wool or camel skins as in confused guilts. The awful deity of battle and of vengeance comes alive in don Giovanni's sermons. He thinks that these faraway things are appropriate for his primitive flock shut away in their stony hills with their burning sun and their horses' diseases. So he distils his prayers drop by drop in the white silence of the church, like an exorcism or an incantation, bowing the simple souls before a Truth which is sublime and certain exactly because it is impenetrable. In the same way, the thoughts and actions of the kings and prophets are borne up by the judgement and will and justice of an age now utterly submerged. They are abstract symbols the people bow before, as at the liturgy all the church, everlasting because separate and distinct, is the only thing that can fill the empty vaults. The church is as big as all the hovels of Kalonerò put together. There the innocent thoughts of men can be gathered and find rest.

Next to the entrance with my back to the wall I stand with a few others, among them Achiròpita's uncle the farrier, near the doorway with my shoulder to the wall. Almost by tradition, the smiths are the people's political leaders. The farrier of Kalonerò is the only person to have, if not an argument against don Giovanni, at least notions which refer to him. He says: 'Being the nuns' confessor is the main thing as far as he's concerned. There are five of them, and he's heard the confessions of all five for thirty years. Every evening. Did you know that?'

The acrid smell of the smithy fills the street; that stench of burned horn sticks in one's nostrils like the filth in the alleys sticks to one's shoes. As for the leather apron shiny with grease, the shaggy forearms, the tongs, the hammers, the irons - the gear makes one think of a crucifixion. The onlookers are out of a church fresco. The horse stands stock-still, neck arched, mysterious eyes half-closed, ears back as if attached to the skull, mouth closed almost in a sneer, while the hammer blows flash at his feet, and quivers shimmer beneath his skin. Then everyone breathes again, the horse moves dancingly away on new shoes so unnaturally nailed to his agile feet, though he'll wear them down soon like the ones before. The farrier with his tongs in his hand watches the horse to see if he's going evenly on all four feet. Then in silence he congratulates himself. This animal will go all the way to Corleone without slipping once. If they know how to look after him, he won't be back here again for seven or eight months.

The farrier bore the epic name of Montalbano. Cutting up tin-foil with mighty iron scissors - because in his free time he amuses himself making kitchen pans - he divulges his thoughts to me.

'In my grandparents' time there were too many nuns to count. When I was a lad and I left for Brazil I remember there were still sixteen. When I came back ten years ago there were nine. Now there are these five. They say one of them is nearly a hundred. On the other hand, one is young, she came after the war, she's not much more than thirty.'

'Who's seen her?'

'Nobody,' replies Montalbano thoughtfully. 'But it's what we're led to think. So in these last few years four nuns have died. Every time, don Giovanni has gone in, taking the gravedigger with him. They did everything on their own in there, because the nunnery has got its own cemetery. The gravedigger just dug and that was all. He says he went through corridor after corridor and they were all painted yellow, like gold. He says the only thing he heard was a bell sounding. Who knows!'

When mass is over, the priest turns his sculpted wooden face towards us and says the words of the leave-taking. Seen from this distance, his black eyes beneath his brows seem two bottomless holes which pass through his skull and are lost in cavernous depths among gigantic spiders and dead waters. I sense a cavity where fear moves without ever becoming concrete, or the ditch the gravedigger dug that day. I hear the bell ringing. There in the hollow of the mind are the patriarchs in their woollen robes and their long beards, the sensuous sinful women, the Lord with his anger and his lightning. Punishment! Castigation! I'm cold now. Why? I go out into the sun. It's calm and good. Achiròpita comes to tell me of a special lunch she has prepared today. There are no shades or ditches or heavens. When will this end?

The bonds which unite this priest and the people here are very different from those which, because of the twenty thousand stones of the House, united me with the people of Licudi. Many years of Sicily, of this island and this sun, haven't altered this unyielding mountaineer with his remoteness and inflexibility and unsociability. Even his smell never alters: a mixture of his dark clothes, church things, the cottages where people and animals sleep together, and where he goes in and touches the newly born and the moribund whose eyes he closes when they are dead.

He is separated, distinct, as closed as the vaults and arches and altar furnishings. In a sense, he *is* the church; and they come to him as to it, this pile of stone with its dregs of holy water. They stand uneasily but ceremoniously by the font in the same way as they walk with him in a funeral or a saint's day procession. These are all things beyond the human; but their humanity cannot live without them. They bring their miseries to him who seems, not outside such things, but beyond them. They tell him their loves, though he seems to give no thought to women. They tell him their troubles, their debts, their anxieties, though he stand unassailable with his shoulders to the nunnery wall, defended by poverty and solitude better than by any fortress. There are no *carabinieri*, no mayor, no bandits, no *mafiosi*, on top of don Giovanni. The altar is his citadel; his magical armour is his black cassock in the sun. The poor people decant their human sorrows into his ear as they might whisper them into a cavern. They talk to him as in ancient days they would have gone to a sacred image. What he answers is what must be. If he does not answer, all is over, as in the depths of a cave the smooth sandstone says: 'Only so far . . .'

Does he have pity? I don't know. He involves himself in everything, he writes, he listens, he decides. He never smiles; his face never shows interest or disdain. He watches with his dark eyes. When Achiròpita brings me a message from him, I study her. I've noticed that Achiròpita approaches don Giovanni easily, without boldness and without reverence and without fright. She's as collected as a boxwood bush. Only her hearing is directed towards him; it's as if she listened to the impersonal striking of the hour, and then came to tell me, it's nine, or it's seven.

'He wants you to give Zillo a bit of help with the crib,' she says. 'He knows there'll be time at Christmas; but Zillo is pretty slow.'

'What do you make of don Giovanni, Achiròpita?' I ask.

'He's the priest. Or do you want to know how he is? He's well.'

Zillo is the gravedigger; but here that doesn't amount to much, there are only two funerals a year. So he helps the farrier, or in church he takes round the collection or helps the children prepare for festivals. I first met him in the dilapidated nunnery; I was exploring, and he came out of a door.

'I live here. Do you want to come and see?'

Who goes willingly into a gravedigger's house? But inside there was a passage, very big and very white, decorated with a tumult of colours, an explosion of coloured paper stars, wreaths, festoons, lanterns, comets.

'Who did all this?'

'I did.'

'But how long did it take?'

'What you see here took eight years. The others I did before were burned; there were nearly twice as many.'

The little scissors with which Zillo cuts the tissue paper to obtain these prodigies are slender, needlework scissors. His great hands use them jerkily, but he always cuts precisely where he wants. The remnants fall, and he opens out a glorious flower, or an arabesque reminiscent of mosques, or a shining bunch of fruit. It's an Angelico Paradise, with the colours of sanctity on the cheeks and clothes of the blessed; and then the monochrome, murky damned, and night, and sin, and Hell.

These are the chromes of Kalonerò: the lime white in the sun; the red of blood beneath Achiròpita's skin and in the farrier's arms and in the horses' muscles; the black of don Giovanni's cassock and the holes of his eyes. There is another, hidden colour.

'What was the nunnery like inside?'

'Yellow, like sand when you're digging, if the sun's shining.'

That nun who is nearly a hundred years old has been shut up for sixty between ochre walls! Since she was thirty, every day she has recounted her charmed narcosis. Every day, when the village is empty, or resting, or pretending to rest, he goes behind the chapel, turns behind the alter, reaches the seat. He sits on the worn-out cushions and leans his wooden ear to the grating. From that other world he receives the secret balm, incomprehensible confessions of sins I cannot imagine, ground fine over decades, soaked into the walls, hallucinated under the sun.

He is responsible for that lean flock of souls; he assures them they are expiating the sins of others; their silent offerings to a silent divinity purge the guilts that stain the earth, like a swamp infected with poisonous bubbles. But does he understand what a human being is? A woman capable of conceiving, and nourishing the fruit of her womb? Would he deny all nature and all femininity in Achiròpita, to turn her aside for silence and transcendent matrimony and total, fearful sacrifice? How would he join in this? What do his five surviving nuns give him to keep him alive? (Because it is they who keep him alive, I can feel it.) That is the terrible milk he has been nourished by all these years in the desert. Now when he looks at me he is afraid that I understand, and that I may violate his secret. Each innocent message that comes to me through Achiròpita seems to give me the care of this simple people; he is burdening me with this, so I shouldn't cast my profane eyes over the untouchable wall. How is it possible there can be so much between us without anything being said? How does he know that behind Achiròpita is Arrichetta's shade? And what am I to him?

Arrichetta, yes. But after her Penny once and for all shut up sin and life in me. I know I am of this world; together with that, I know too that I am no longer alive. People might say I have been redeemed, or I am chaste, but I'm only finished. My reserve is just the inability to suffer or desire. But I'd succeed in understanding the voices from another world (this is what the priest guesses and is afraid of). Everything was over between mankind and me that night when I came out through the sedan chair; I could talk with God if I knew where He was. Perhaps he's behind the grating where don Giovanni leans his ear? Are we fighting for possession of this or for domination over it? For those words filtered from another universe without time? For His impossible voice?

Soon it will be Christmas. The wagon will come from Corleone as far as here, adorned with puppets, multi-coloured on the outside, and inside a faded and immense archaic synthesis of all Sicily with its dozens of heads, suits of armour, plumes, a hybrid of mannequins and of the epic, of the childish and also of the divine.

The master of the puppet theatre has taken us to his temporary lodgings for us to repair Guido di Santacroce. Guido lies stretched on the floor in the miserable little room bathed in the brownish light. His glittering eyes are open; he has the oval face of a young girl; his mouth is vermilion. His damascened armour is marvellous, engraved and chased on its colours of old silver and pale gold. Above his crest is a cross wreathed with sea-blue plumes. He seems a living creature abandoned to his dreams on a field that is only for others a field of battle and death. Lying on the floor, he seems raised above the clouds.

'There are still a few people who understand these things,' the puppet master says. 'In the cities it's all over, they just want to amuse themselves, and they want the paladins to be brand-new dandies. But up in the mountains, when Orlando dies people stand up and take off their caps.'

It must have been like this when in the Globe before a performance the poet prepared his audience and exhorted them: 'Imagine! Imagine!' Helping Zillo with the crib, I shall imagine the journey of the three kings following a star and bringing the treasures of the world to a babe not yet born, whom they knew of only by virtue of that star. Why should I believe it a fable? I too have journeyed all my life to bring adoration, love and hope without knowing to whom and guided by nothing. Do the nuns know, who day by day approach nearer to the heavenly gates journeying without moving, not in space but in time? What about don Giovanni, who accompanies them one by one to the gate and then goes back for the next? He reminds me of the figure of Death in Breughel's painting in Madrid, who one by one leads everyone to their end, when he guides the brides of Christ to their sunlit ochre graves.

Zillo says that when the church is empty he'll turn on the lights so the nuns can come and look at the crib from behind their grating. They are waiting for the Birth. Like the Wise Men, they are travelling in their minds, in time, going back two thousand years to remote regions to find in that cradle the infinity that is to come. The child is born to women who have renounced everything, and is transmuted into a mystical bridegroom. Then, as his beloved daughters, they will rest on his bosom. Penny!

When the crib was ready, Zillo appeared with his coloured treasure in his arms, an explosion of amaranth yellow, solar orange, beryl green, vermilion, turquoise, light playing on the thin paper in new colours and shades. Rightly has the Shepherd of the Miracle that enchanted air. Only don Giovanni's eyes pass for an instant like the shadow of a hawk on sunlit ground. And you, Guido di Santacroce, how much longer can you lie there without getting up to fight Evil with your shining sword?

Kalonerò, last day of February 1956

Without wishing to, just by passively letting things happen, I share the village's needs and distresses and even secrets. There's an odd relationship between me and those I've helped without our speaking to each other. They're accustomed to the mediation of saints, effigies, medallions, sculptures, scapulars; they talk naturally to Achiròpita, bowing before her, she who stands like an idol, upright, intensely alive. In their simple way they imagine me to command limitless willpower, charity and perhaps even magic. I feel their thoughts following me, their cupidity too, and their exhortations that could never be confessed, their conviction that I never decline because I cannot help, but because I have decided not to, all the mixed-up unsophisticated dross that is usually confided to patron saints.

'The family from Gemara,' says Achiròpita, supremely dignified in her rags and tatters, 'will never free themselves from the crook of Lercara Friddi if they can't pay off their debt. And he'll take home Zita Gemara, who's sixteen, and he'll make her serve him all right!'

I look at Achiròpita the messenger, the new little Mercury, with her skimpy dress and her plaits and her certainty. How does don Giovanni know that I don't believe in giving charity? I only agree for the sake of the tiny gesture of victorious assent which she makes for me and for herself every time I say yes. Achiròpita! It's you who have tangled the magic among the dead horses' manes and tails.

Even if I don't talk to those concerned, I have to talk about them increasingly frequently to the priest, day after day at the corner of the table, while the children rampage in the wardrobes. Don Giovanni has never asked me if I hold to the faith, or if I practise it, or if I've ever been to confession. But when the crib was ready except for the Baby he would instal on Christmas Eve, he said: 'Years of meditation are not enough to understand the mystery of the Incarnation, of God who is born again as Man to take upon Himself the expiation of sins and the redemption of the world.'

I feel he is testing me; but I can travesty my answer by attributing it to others.

'It's been said the world would explode were it not for the force that condenses it around its centre. Because of that force, there's weight, and therefore attrition, and therefore suffering. Creation must suffer to exist. It's right that its Maker should take up the burden. But where was the ransom?'

Don Giovanni covers half his face tightly with his open hand. His other eye draws me into black nothingness.

'If the certainty of eternal bliss was given us by our reason,' he says, 'who wouldn't trade in the provisional for the everlasting? We'd all accept a fleeting, futile life if that burden gained us unending happiness. Then faith would be a contract with God, from the outset there would be nothing to lose and all to gain. But God doesn't make pacts like that with us. Doubt and indeed the negation of reason are the merits of our belief. How could the apostle Thomas be a saint if he wasn't the supreme sceptic and therefore the sublime blind man? He wants to touch the sores. He asks that of the unbelievable ghostly Christ who has already been crucified, he goes against the mind and the senses. But Christ really was standing before him. He doubted the Resurrection, but the wound satisfied him. *Credo quia absurdum.* That's how it is.'

'Don Giovanni,' says Montalbano as a sort of counterpart, cutting his tin-foil with his big iron scissors, 'was out in the countryside once for three weeks. Can you believe that? One of the nuns had escaped, in disguise or with someone who helped her. The priest never stopped till he'd found her. It was the young one. They say she repented. She must live on penitence alone. Is that possible?'

I set myself to co-ordinate these elusive notions. I'll free Zita Gemara from the usurer Lercara Friddi, as before I freed Amalia from Carruozzo, Albertina from Toia and Penny from Crockett. You, don Giovanni, will number this in the annals of Good, knowing how scarred I am, knowing that you constrain me to this contact with others, almost, under the trusting eyes of Achiròpita, to their love, and all for the expiation of Arrichetta. But if reason denies the faith you admit to be absurd, I sense in your decaying soul a hurt far deeper than mine, a chronic wasting and a sin. You chased desperately to catch the escaped woman. Why? You brought her back to God with your own hands. Was it worth it? Beneath your holy words yawns a horrible vacuum. You want to use them to call me back; but I will come to fight you, and to defend – whom?

With Montalbano's complicity, Achiròpita enlivens my supper with a powerful dark ruby red wine of destructive strength. Drop by drop it exalts my thoughts and also paralyses them – unmakes, sets on fire, darkens again. It stands beside the wholemeal bread, which is yellow as saffron and the pride of Sicily, and which the baker signs with his name, Cataldo. No anchorite's water for me; I take wine as my spiritual drink for these mystical practices. It comes from the soil of Gea and transfigures vine-shoots into inspiration and the bubbles of the must into sparkling imagination. This is why it is used to signify blood in the eucharist, at once man's cross and his very life. To drink it is to take God's nourishment in form and spirit.

Who gave this dark heavy liquid the power to cloud a mind that could resist fear and passion and suffering? Is it spirit or substance in me? What do I look into, or do I only dream?

'The difference between man's excessive and impossible desires,' says don Giovanni, 'and his actual ability to achieve them, is represented in us by our sight. Our vision is so disproportionate to our needs that we can see not only the mountain-tops and the clouds but even the unreachable stars in the sky. The mind makes the same errors as our sight. It's made for a world of limits, but it asks to look into the beyond and to conceive the infinite and the eternal.'

I know he's not saying what he really thinks; he wants to constrain me or provoke me into confessing my essential self to his stony ears. I'm beginning to understand what he wants, and that I must deny him.

'The church didn't oppose Galileo,' he continues, 'out of scientific blindness, but out of a sense of proportion. Our eyes see too far away, and become burdened with what is not for them. Our ears are nearly always dealing with what is our concern and what we can comprehend. We give up remote sounds, we listen carefully to words, those that are the First Principle; in the Word Itself.'

I deny this. And it is don Giovanni's negation of it that points me to the truth, which is the very opposite. The eye commands the kingdom of man's illimitable destiny. This is how man is distinguished from the beasts ruminating on the earth. Because of his sight, he is called body and soul to the conquest of the spaces between the stars of heaven.

I see again Father Onorato's ears that bristled, like his nose, with tufts of hair through which even so came filtering the psalms of Marcello like spring water through a tangle of leafy branches. In the body of man, everything is roughed out with good-hearted liberality and simplicity: the arches of shoulders and cheeks, the loins and knees and arms are harmonised and rounded off like loaves of bread. Then there are eyebrows, the curving forehead, the eyes like little targets; lastly, the symmetrical mouth, modelled, coloured, like a painter's brush-stroke, finally satisfied with what it has done. But the ears are worse than the nostrils (which at least are hidden from sight). The ear is so convoluted, hollowed out, ambiguous and exuding wax. Often it's deformed looking like a lampshade or canopy or atrophied spike. It's filled with hypocrisy, slander, indiscretion, subterfuge. Don Giovanni's ear is a fissure that has sucked in words, thoughts, sufferings, like a rift in the clay that absorbs a river and takes it Lord knows where, leaving a whole countryside without water.

I realise that by delegating to me through Achiròpita the secular arm of his dominion over the village, but by reserving to himself the confidences of those in need, he has taken that relationship from me; and his exploring and his discovering increase in proportion to my ability to satisfy people's wants. He rejoices in this that normally would be kept from a priest. He's inhuman, the way he senses my ills: that I'm unable to listen to music or to read books; that my spirit can endure only by keeping absolutely still; that the waves of others' sufferings do not alleviate mine, but merely submerge or hide them. To take me out of my silent endurance, to reawaken me, to make me feel and see, is cruelty; and it is theft too. He shrinks from nothing to break into my reserve; ever more openly he tries to drive me out of the remote corners of my consciousness. He never relents. I don't know if he even conceives that there might be traces of tenderness left in me which are not handed over to him. He insinuates himself, he inquires; and as bit by bit my defence becomes more impenetrable, I see him preyed upon by cravings like those of the sick or those dying of thirst; and I feel repugnance, and then a mis-bred pity which forces me to lower my guard and to give.

'Bettina's family,' says Achiròpita, 'won't be able to send her to her rich cousin's wedding at Corleone because they can't dress her beautifully like the others' families.'

This once I am obliged to meet Bettina's family, almost furtively, in the dressmaker's in Corleone.

'Achiròpita, couldn't they attend to all this on their own?'

'How? They've got to choose the materials, and her veil and her shoes. They come at a hundred different prices. If you don't say what they can have, how could they take the liberty?'

Bettina keeps in a corner, rather like the Circassian slaves in the illustrations I remember from boyhood, while in the foreground their sale is worked out among paunches and turbans and gold coins. She has brown hair; her thin face is dotted with moles; she looks nervy, like a crucible of fire.

'I hope these people have been discreet,' don Giovanni says, fixing me with his eyes that shine mysteriously a moment.

'The dressmaker has been given a free hand in order to dress her up in more or less the same type of clothes as she is making for all those from Corleone going to the wedding.'

'Girls sometimes go from being even too reserved,' says don Giovanni, 'to being too talkative. I don't know if Marietta . . .'

He'd like me to talk about them, about her. He wants to hear about the big room with its beams covered with cheap paper laid over the lumps of the wood and stained with damp, about the wardrobes where the cloth smells of the new and the shut-away. He wants to hear about the lanky dressmaker with her white lace collar, her gold-rimmed lorgnettes, her high buttoned shoes like young unmarried women wore long ago. Then about the relatives, very restrained but full of longing, who talk as if they were in church and are forever glancing at each other in silent consultation. Then about Bettina, whom the assistant measures with the rule of oilcloth, so clearly numbered, 77, 78, 79, up to 101, thereafter worn out and frayed near the tin clasp at its end. Then about how they hold the crumpled, rumpled stuffs against her to see if she can wear this tea-rose taffeta, or that magenta, or that almost black violet. Each time she emerges from the shining stuff like a lily from its stalk.

'I was in a rush, don Giovanni. I sorted everything out in a word or two. They've been discreet.'

The priest says nothing. He sighs from his thin chest. He is hungry for confessions. Perhaps he will take revenge.

Kalonerò, 18 September 1956

The watch over the dilapidated monuments, the castles, the deconsecrated churches, is kept by a shepherd or by a destitute old woman or by a cripple who can't earn his living in the fields. They have the keys, they'll show you which way to go to get to the noble spaces from which the glory has vanished.

Zillo has stayed in the enormous convent, keeping life at the heart of it in his room decorated with coloured paper. He explores and he supervises; he counts the hours and the heartbeats that are wearing it down towards its end. He's rather like Achiròpita, who's no doctor, but just by looking at my face can tell the rate my heart is beating and how my inner landslide is going.

With Zillo, I got to the furthest wing, the first to lose the sun. The walls surmount a narrow arm of ground; here and there erosion has already reached and touched, the foundations overhang the precipice with the walls they're meant to hold up. There are wide cracks in the fabric, though the whole thing is still standing in one piece, as the whole thing in one piece may one day fall. But when?

'This part has been empty for more than ten years,' Zillo tells me. 'Engineers came from Palermo and walled up the ways in. I made the opening we came through. In ten years nothing has fallen, and it won't fall yet.'

In the great windowless chambers one can see patches of sky. The rooms don't seem dead, there are a few fronds and birds. At only one point the expanse of hard brick flooring has opened and revealed a mighty beam. Below, as I saw it that first time, lie the tangled brambles and the dry bed of the stream.

'See? There's nothing beneath, and yet it doesn't fall.'

Zillo goes to the edge and jumps, cracking his heels down. He laughs, he enjoys this. I stand still beside him, without believing in God but knowing myself to be in his hands.

20 September 1956

I haven't written anything in this Sicilian journal for nearly six months. I've been unwell, and I'm slowing down. At Lausanne, when I was on my way here from London, they told me my malaria might have damaged my heart. But I know what it is. I haven't strained my aorta. I've spent hours and hours with Zillo without doing a thing. Or I've sat in one of the many empty rooms in my house – empty except for the manes. Achiròpita keeps me company sitting on her seat while I doze in an armchair and sink my memories in the damp-stains on the daubed walls. They're the damp-stains in the blue room in the house at Solitaria again, when I was eight maybe.

I get ready a toy theatre for my little sister. It's a box which when emptied and turned upside-down becomes a stage. We set up the proscenium, the wings, the machinery; here we have a wood, there bright-red hangings indicate a palace. The lid of the box becomes the background. Then there are the puppets, the Royals, the fairy, the devil, the page, the cut-throat, the 'uncle monk'. 'Uncle monk' is a wonderful figure with his puce habit, his red cheeks, his flask of wine stuck to his hand. His flask is never emptied, his thirst never satisfied. Is that what life has been?

Now the stain on the plaster is black. It's the ground-floor wall of the house at Monte de Dio. I'm thirteen, just back from boarding-school, shy, introverted, with untidy hair. I'm alone against five or six girlfriends of Checchina's, all as plump and frivolous as she. Two by two they hold hands and rush in a circle faster and faster, hammering with their heels, their heads back, lips half open, panting. I watch, sulky and dazzled. A fragrant, heavy mass hits me in the face, passes on, then hits me again. It's Stefania's famous red hair. I've taken fifty years to realise that at that time she was trying to arouse me. This deep sleep has perhaps lasted all my life; and I shall come to consciousness only to lose it again.

Achiròpita gets up, comes to me, takes my hand, puts her ear to my wrist as if to check my pulse.

'How are you?' she asks.

I place her in front of my knees, upright as the stem of a plant. I hold her gently by her elbows. She looks at me like a light. It's Arrichetta. She holds a flower in her hands. I glance away for an instant and the flower has gone. Now it's Checchina, and her childish voice entreating me, 'Giuliano, you'll hurt yourself!' Now we're at Sorrento in the citrus orchard in the heat of noon although it's winter. We play bowls with fallen oranges on the uneven ground. As we play, a lot of our throws take us a long way off. She and I arrange and rearrange our game while the half-blind governess snoozes. I go early to bed with a great show of obedience. Then I run to find her, and we savour together the ineffable joys of sucking sweets in the dark.

'Are you leaving me?' say Achiròpita.

I go back to the farrier. 'This morning,' he says, 'I got a nice paper bag of biscuits from the nuns. Do you want some?'

They are big, floury biscuits, shaped like violins, like the ones you see in still-life paintings of the Neapolitan seventeenth century. Even the paper is coarse and brownish like in the paintings. Holding it up to the light, I make out a medallion with a horse in the middle and an initial. This is the cover of an old book. To please Montalbano, I try a biscuit. The sugar has almost crumbled away into the flour; these biscuits were made yesterday, but it's as if they were a hundred years old.

'How does one get these biscuits from the nuns?'

'They pass them out to the old woman who takes them their victuals. There's a wheel beside the grating where they confess.'

Some time ago, while the priest was out and Zillo was washing the sacristy floor, I went into the chapel. I went up to the grating covered by its little curtain; I examined the seat in the thickness of the wall, the marble sill where the confessor leans his elbow as he listens, worn by two or three hundred years use. When I opened the curtain on my side, the other let through a thread of amber-coloured light, and in the quiet I thought I heard a sigh.

In the eighteen months I've been here, don Giovanni has never asked me to go anywhere near the confessional, that brown monument more redolent of time and loftiness than many greater ones of stone. At the established times he goes in there; even if there's nobody in the church, he stays a long while, half hidden behind the mauve curtain, so it's clear he's waiting and is ready to discharge his duties. If someone in the obscurity at God's knees whispers to the priest's black silence, if I among others who stand aloof almost catch the penitent's words, I imagine them flowing into the incomprehensible soul that absorbs those waters of life, and I cannot overcome my repulsion and my fear. The knot between us has been tightened in these last months. The village, which for many years has had only one source of consolation, has slowly turned towards me for help. Certainly don Giovanni and his impoverished church could only ever offer advice, decorate the church for festivals, and look after spiritual needs. The newcomer from the mainland cannot baptise them, cannot join them in matrimony, cannot absolve them, but he can dress the newly born, give the brides dowries, buy back a mule or shore up a dilapidated house. Still, I feel this isn't it. As I am gradually possessed by certainty, they too in their turn sense a coldness in him. As I kept myself from him, they spontaneously keep themselves from him too, and deal with Achiròpita. The priest is aware Kalonerò is slipping from his grasp, is flaking away like the crumbling mountain that one day will engulf it. The children come and rummage in the sacristy wardrobes more rarely. When I go in, the priest's dark eyes are bloodshot with weariness, like Paolo Grilli's weariness before it was all over between us. They say my heart is pretty weak. How then can it be stronger than the man of God, if that's what he is?

'Don Giovanni,' Achiròpita conveys to me in one of his last messages, 'says the old priest wants to take out a life annuity with the Retreat at Castelvetrano and go there.'

He was here before don Giovanni, and he was already old before he gave up the parish thirty years ago. Dumb and paralysed, he lives at Prizzi with a sister as old as himself, in a big room where the floor is alive with fleas. They have a small property; but they find they can't manage on their own.

I slowly explain to the old priest how we will prepare deeds to cede the property to the Retreat at Castelvetrano, which will undertake to maintain him and his sister till their deaths. I tell him however than on the same terms don Giovanni would be prepared to do the same thing, and therefore the property would stay with the parish. The old man fixes me with his very clear, almost empty eyes. His silence seems to be assent, and what I am saying seems to come to a logical conclusion.

'So we'll arrange the annuity not with the Retreat but with don Giovanni, shall we?'

The invalid stares at me. He raises his eyebrows. His soundless lips say unmistakably: 'The Retreat!'

Distant relatives no doubt have rights on the property, so I stand surety. I don't mention it to don Giovanni; nor, this time, does he ask. I go into the empty convent, I go to the floor that has fallen away. The light comes up from below, and throws the black beam into sinister relief.

Suddenly I feel dizzy. Isn't that a shadow down there?

Kalonerò, April 1957

On his clear glassy panels the painter Cosme Tura dreamed fantastic towers, rocks veined like gems, like coagulations of blood, seaweed, roots. A countryside from another planet, poor crumbling ground, undulating at its horizon against the clearest of skies which reveal its far-away height.

Helped by the puppet master, I've followed the route of the mythical, decorated wagon of the paladins, from Rocca Busambra to Caltanissetta. I've looked for and found the castle where the Spada family came from on the plateau of Mazzarino. From far away I glimpsed its black profile in a blue gorge under a torn moist blue sky marked with dark tatters. Close up, it was vast and irregular, integrated and confused with the peak on which it stood.

'Who lives there?'

'No one. The Count left the castle and the neighbourhood years ago.'

'Count Ascanio?'

'Yes, that's right. How did you know? They used to come every year, for months at a time. Now the peasants have emigrated, their plots of land are left fallow as far as you can see. The shepherds use the castle.'

Under the archway with its coat-of-arms, the gate is off its hinges. It's difficult to get across the boggy mire in the first courtyard. The flock is out, the ground floor stinks of dung-fouled litter. Two pregnant cows, sordid with mud, are chewing the cud in a corner. The horses cropping the grass growing on the slope of the bastion make a dull sound that reverberates in the ground. The first floor is empty. The roof has gone at many points, as in Baron Castro's house at Acerenza. Joists and beams stick out, that once were useful to a man I'd no longer recognise, even if I were to remember him.

I go back downstairs and cross the second courtyard around the keep, a solid block of stone with only one way in, high up and out of reach. Below is the church. It hasn't got a door. The beautiful inlaid marble floor is dirty with loam. There are splendid altars and columns and decorative stonework, but the paintings have mostly vanished and the stucco is in ruins. In the apse the steps going down into the holy ground are blocked. There lie Nerina's forebears, from whom she took her gentle blood and at whose hands she was then sacrificed. Yes, all is well, all is just. This had to fall and come to an end; it was condemned when the thread of her life was cut. Her ancestors' pride and pomp and power could not outlive her.

But the centuries of these stones, have been embodied in her being, conveyed to me by her magical love, which, in my magical love, I have taken into the dark life-stream of my family tree in order to create life.

I see again the beach at Miseno towards evening, Nerina kneeling in the sand, her face to the sunset, her arms slack and her fingers skimming the sand. I see Nene again on the beach at sunset, and Penny on her knees with her dark eyes questioning.

Poets call it love; and it was poetry. It has guided me. I have known no other energy and no other law; reflected out of my being I have seen nothing but that in others, that or its perversion. I think of the innocent land of Licudi, my repudiation of it, then Naples soaked in its saints, then my abjuration of Rome. These acts of the heart are only love and poetry, a secret rhythm moving my life and the lives of others, and the one driving force behind all history.

I go outside again. The flock comes back. The shepherds drive their sheep by whistling, they bunch them together by throwing stones, helped by the dashing of the dogs. Three of them are carrying a new-born lamb they picked up off the grass, stained with the blood of its birth, head down as if already slaughtered, only one or two hours old.

I slip under the archway and along the overhanging wall. From an opening, a goat sticks out its chest and bends its neck down and fixes me with its yellow witch's eyes. What does it want? It seems I still have obligations . . .

But forgive me, gentlest shade. Not much time separates us now. Soon we will find each other again. Exiled from the Absolute, I will give myself up to it again with death.

July 1957

The hammer of the sun beats and beats. Defended by shadows – but even here it's baking hot – I listen, dreaming or even delirious. The thoughts which form in my mind are utterly different from those which used to live in me and which I could welcome as mine. I recognise myself against a scorched background; and the something else that is in me contemplates me with compassion.

'You looked for the truth for fifty years,' says the voice, 'without realising you possessed it already; for we all have it if we ourselves are true, if we accept the burden of our faculties and serve them devoutly. You have failed only when you doubted.'

Should I doubt now? I have a holy man before me; his sacristy is empty, the tablecloth where he writes is dusty. He sits waiting in the confessional and for days no one goes to him in the violet halo of repentance. Does the malign lurk within his holy vestments? Are they only the mask of atheism or heresy? What sort of damned man can live only by feeding on others? Have I, under an hallucination, denied and destroyed the sacrament he represents?

'Who dressed Our Lady of the Sorrows in the chapel?' It's I this time who ask the questions. For an instant the priest's face shows he is startled.

'The sisters, maybe. That image must be two hundred years old. Her dress and her mantle have been redone since.'

'That dark crêpe around her hands which are trembling as if they were about to fall! And the seven swords! Right up to the hilt!'

'The faithful,' says don Giovanni, 'do not examine the Madonna. They weep, and that is all.'

'I've been thinking a lot,' I go on. 'I don't know whether in a church I should ask such questions, but they say that doubt is the antechamber of faith. In the first Paradise' (the priest makes a faint gesture of assent, so I go on) 'everything appeared perfect and unchanging, without sin and without future. Such felicity was motionless, it was its own end. I knew a man who wondered if sin was the creation of the Devil. Because it is the opposite. The impulse that set the rhythm of the world in motion.'

Don Giovanni looks at me, batting his reddish eyelashes on his weary eyes. I am exhausted, Achiròpita feels my pulse ever more often; and he is exhausted too. We are close to each other.

'You talk a lot about the Devil,' he says, 'and less about God. No! I don't believe this is the antechamber of faith. The Rebel creates nothing. He brings only his malice and his pride. He wants to obscure creation, break its rhythm, disorder it where possible and cause anarchy. Evil is in every interruption of the Law.'

'But,' says the voice, 'he cannot interrupt the Law, which is forever recomposing itself, closing over him again, like water which parts over a body but then closes over it again. Hellish chaos each time momentarily shows how indestructible Divine Rule is. The rhythm is that of the Law itself.'

'Then Evil only knows how to yearn for Chaos,' I went on aloud, 'and uses what exists already, not what he makes. He uses anger and perverse hatred, things without intrinsic value, things not of this world, emptiness which to fill and nourish itself with life exposes that life to danger, sacrifice and suffering. Men's sins and vices are this sacrilegious food; and the impotence of the Anti-Christ in the end will be Hell. Not disorder. Evil is wherever there is heaviness and oppression, the bleeding of things, bodies, souls. Evil is the unimaginable parasite of the world.'

Don Giovanni covers half his face with his open hand. But now, in his wooden face the other eye is shut.

Kalonerò, 10 September 1957

Yesterday after five months of drought, torrential rain has struck. Two hours later the rising river overwhelmed the one road into the village, which was almost deserted because most people were in the fields. I battled against the downpour and reached the nunnery. Zillo's door was closed. The buildings trembled as the storm hit the mountain. I went along the passage towards the condemned wing. 'It'll fall,' I said to myself, 'it'll fall.' Then my heart faltered and I stopped. Someone was ahead of me; but it wasn't Zillo. Through the gaping floor I could hear the wild roaring of the river. Still somehow it was quiet, and I heard a dry creaking, then a clear crack. I waited.

I knew that if I went to the black beam outlined against the void, if I showed myself there, I would find that shade there again. But it had already disappeared. Halfway along the beam hung a broken rope. The rain poured through the ruined roof on to the floor and cascaded into the opening. It washed, it washed. I wanted to hold my wrist to my ear as Achiròpita does. My watch said it was four o'clock.

Behind the altar in the chapel, I sat on the empty seat without trembling, and leaned my ear to lose myself in mercy.

Behind the little curtain, the gleam of light is darkened. And the creature's voice comes to me and absolves me.

It says: 'I have sinned.'

Here Giuliano di Sansevero's *Sicilian Journal* ends.

APPENDIX

Report of the commissioner responsible. To the chief of police at Palermo.

Object: the disappearance or flight of the nun Carmela, called Rubina Ibla, from the closed nunnery at Kalonerò, a village under the authorities at Perla; and the disappearance or suicide of the reverend don Giovanni Baraldi, priest of that parish.

On 14 September, Sante Macaluso, popularly known as Zillo, gravedigger in Kalonerò, presented himself at the office of the *carabinieri* at Corleone. He stated that: 'On 6 September I was summoned through Father Baraldi to go to Lercara Friddi because a landslide had blocked a passage in the sulphur mine. On the fourteenth I came back to Kalonerò, where I live in the nunnery. The village having been damaged by floods, I thought the dangerous wing over the precipice would have fallen, but I found it as I had left it. I saw a broken rope dangling from the beam that spans the gap where the floor has given way. In a corner I found the priest's cassock, which was folded, his breviary, which I recognised, and a small gold cross he used to wear round his neck. All this I know for certain. When I had last seen him, on leaving, the priest had been as he always was, and he had paid me an advance.'

The people of the parish, when questioned, were unable to furnish any useful information. The flooding on the ninth cut off the village for three days, and people imagined the priest was away, or they noticed nothing. A search of the river below the rope revealed nothing; but this would be explained by the violence of the flood. Nor has it been possible to discover anything from the Neapolitan gentleman, Giuliano, Duke of Sansevero, who was in regular contact with the priest. He in fact died of heart failure during the night between the thirteenth and fourteenth of September. We know of him only that his elder brother was Ferrante, Duke of Sansevero; he was well known in political circles in Rome for his clandestine activities in favour of the restoration of the monarchy in Italy, he being a supporter of the Neapolitan house of Bourbon.

When the servant girl Achiròpita Montalbano was questioned she said: 'The day of the flood the gentleman went out only once, when it started to rain, and he retired before evening. He went out again when the road was reopened and everybody came back. That was on the thirteenth. Then in the evening he took to his bed and told me, "Tonight, stay close to me." I fell asleep in my chair and when I woke up it was nearly four o'clock. He had raised himself up and was looking at me fixedly. I asked him, "What do you want?" He held out his hand, and I gave him mine. I held his wrist to my ear to hear how he was. And while he was looking at me steadily and I was looking at him I realised that he had died. Then I called.'

When the other servant, the old Ninfa Bonfadio, was questioned, she confirmed this.

After that Count Don Michele Arquà, the senator for the Liberal Party, arrived in Kalonerò. He had been told of these events by the Corleone notary, Signor Arcangeli. As the executor of the Duke of Sansevero's will, he has taken responsibility for his lodgings and personal belongings. It appears that a number of bequests are made in the will, including provision for the girl Achiròpita Montalbano, who is entrusted to the custody and care of the senator Count Arquà.

Since it has proved impossible to establish that the priest committed suicide; let alone that he did so between the ninth and the fourteenth, we have followed up our enquiries about Sister Carmela. Through a delegate of the Bishop of the diocese we have established that: the parish priest don Giovanni heard confession in the nunnery for the last time on the day of the flood, i.e. the ninth, at four in the afternoon, as he always did.

He confessed only one of the nuns, and that was Sister Carmela. The others think that he then left because of the downpour.

Sister Carmela vanished from the nunnery on the thirteenth, the day the road was reopened. There was heavy traffic that day, and no one noticed anything unusual.

The said Sister had already vanished once from the nunnery, four years before. She is only thirty-seven, whereas the other nuns are all extremely old. Opinions which in the course of duty we have sounded out all say Father Baraldi only pretended to commit suicide, and that he has fled with Sister Rubina Ibla, the only person he spoke with through the grating of the confessional at four o'clock on the ninth. I omit the witchcraft and sorcery elaborated by popular superstition.

Photographs of don Giovanni Baraldi and Rubina Ibla have been sent to every police station in the country. Enquiries continue.

Perla, 19 September 1957
The Commissioner (signed)

Report of the Bishop's delegate. To Monsignor . . . , vicar of His Excellency the Bishop of . . .

Following the sad and regrettable events at Kalonerò, with the permission of the authorities I have questioned the nuns who still remain in the nunnery. They confirm that don Giovanni Baraldi had for a long time worthily carried out his duties as daily confessor and spiritual adviser; in this respect, nothing in the past or in the present has had to be queried. Sister Carmela lived in repentance for the lapse from which she had been recalled, and had obtained pardon for it. She disappeared on the afternoon of 13 September without leaving any indication of how she did so. She was the only one to go to confession at four o'clock on the ninth; after about half an hour, the priest went away, perhaps to escape the heavy rain, and did not come back. I have concealed the disappearance of the priest from the nuns; they believe that, as had already happened once, he has gone to look for Sister Carmela. I have given the police commissioner all information that falls within his competence.

I now come to the disconcerting truth. I have been summoned by the Liberal senator, Count Michele Arquà, who is the executor of the will left by the Neapolitan nobleman Giuliano, Duke of Sansevero, who was the last of his line after his elder brother, Duke Ferrante, died last year in an air crash in Rome without leaving other heirs. The senator enjoined me to reveal nothing without the Bishop's approval, and then gave me a manuscript, which I enclose. It is the journal kept by Sansevero in Kalonerò from 12 June 1955 till 10 September 1957.

My superiors will want to evaluate this journal; but it seems to leave one little option but to believe that don Baraldi was replaced at the grating of the confessional by the Duke of Sansevero, and it was to him that Sister Carmela unburdened herself that last time. It is impossible to establish whether she has escaped again, and, if so, whether it was with his help, but one is led to suppose this. Nor is it certain that don Giovanni Baraldi did in fact commit suicide in the afternoon of 9 September, because the journal speaks of a 'broken rope', as is specified too in the gravedigger's statement, but not of a body, But if the priest, in denial of his calling, did kill himself and then disappear in the flood, and if that is not the work of the Devil, the Duke perhaps knew what happened. On the other hand, if that is not what happened, the other hypotheses remain possible.

I have not told the nuns that one of their number, albeit a lost soul among them, saw the secrecy of the sacrament violated surreptitiously by one who had no call to be there. Moreover, we cannot be sure what form the dialogue took. The Bishop will judge the Duke, who in his manuscript reveals himself to have been an impetuous, ardent spirit, though capable of intolerable errors. So far as I am permitted, as a Christian I dare to hope that mercy will be shown his troubled soul, and that the last words of his journal, 'I have sinned,' will serve as his repentance and will earn him forgiveness.

Perla, 20 October 1957
Don Rosario . . . , priest

Rome, November 1957
Senate of the Republic
Senator Michele Arquà to His Excellency the Bishop of . . .
Your Excellency will some time ago have received the report of the events at Kalonerò. I collected from the notary in Corleone the enormous mass of the Duke of Sansevero's memoirs from his childhood up to his time in London in 1954. I felt it my duty to refer the final *Sicilian Journal* to the ecclesiastical authorities.

With regard to conclusions about him which will be formed, as his friend I must speak on his behalf. He was an outstanding man who ceaselessly in his own person paid the price of knowledge. Perhaps he believed himself a Man of God, though he never took holy orders, or that all men really are such. Or perhaps he conceived of one Truth above us all. Perhaps he went to his death as he felt he had lived, pure substance beyond all forms. His last days were a first endeavour at man's challenge to space; after the priest Baraldi's 'listening' recorded in the journal, came perhaps Giuliano's 'seeing'. He will have given us the signs of this in his story of his life. I would therefore ask your Excellency as a Christian priest to spread a veil where possible, a veil of prayer, over the uncertain facts of that life.

In accordance with his wishes, his surviving sister, Sister Francesca, and I have had him buried beside the body of another person who is to remain nameless. At the foot of the stone, as he was the last of his line, we had engraved his escutcheon with its armoured arm. Count Tèolo of Verona chose his epitaph:

GIULIANO
A MAN OF GOD WHO
WAS GENEROUS WITH OTHER
MEN

QUARTET ENCOUNTERS

The purpose of this paperback series is to bring together influential and outstanding works of twentieth-century European literature in translation. Each title has an introduction by a distinguished contemporary writer, describing a personal or cultural 'encounter' with the text, as well as placing it within its literary and historical perspective.

Quartet Encounters will concentrate on fiction, although the overall emphasis is upon works of enduring literary merit, whether biography, travel, history or politics. The series will also preserve a balance between new and older works, between new translations and reprints of notable existing translations. Quartet Encounters provides a much-needed forum for prose translation, and makes accessible to a wide readership some of the more unjustly neglected classics of modern European literature.

Aharon Appelfeld · *The Retreat*

Translated from the Hebrew by Dalya Bilu
with an introduction by Gabriel Josipovici
'A small masterpiece . . . the vision of a remarkable poet'
New York Times Book Review

Gaston Bachelard · *The Psychoanalysis of Fire*

Translated from the French by Alan C.M. Ross
with an introduction by Northrop Frye
'. . . he is a philosopher, with a professional training in the sciences, who devoted most of the second phase of his career to promoting that aspect of human nature which often seems most inimical to science: the poetic imagination . . .'
J.G. Weightman, *The New York Review of Books*

Robert Bresson · *Notes on the Cinematographer*

Translated from the French by Jonathan Griffin
with an introduction by J.M.G. Le Clézio
'[Bresson] is the French cinema, as Dostoyevsky
is the Russian novel and Mozart is German music'
Jean-Luc Godard, *Cahiers du Cinéma*

Hermann Broch · *The Sleepwalkers*

Translated from the German by Willa and Edwin Muir
with an introduction by Michael Tanner
'One of the greatest European novels . . .
masterful' Milan Kundera

E.M. Cioran · *The Temptation to Exist*

Translated from the French by Richard Howard
with an introduction by Susan Sontag
'Cioran is one of the most delicate minds of real power
writing today. Nuance, irony, and refinement are the
essence of his thinking . . .' Susan Sontag

Stig Dagerman · *The Games of Night*

Translated from the Swedish by Naomi Walford
with an introduction by Michael Meyer
'One is haunted by a secret and uneasy suspicion
that [Dagerman's] private vision, like Strindberg's
and Kafka's, may in fact be nearer the truth of things
than those visions of the great humanists, such as
Tolstoy and Balzac, which people call universal'
Michael Meyer

Grazia Deledda · *After the Divorce*

Translated from the Italian by Susan Ashe
with an introduction by Sheila MacLeod
'What [Deledda] does is create the passionate complex of a primitive populace' D.H. Lawrence

Marcellus Emants · *A Posthumous Confession*

Translated from the Dutch and
with an introduction by J.M. Coetzee
'Since the time of Rousseau we have seen the growth of the genre of the *confessional novel*, of which *A Posthumous Confession* is a singularly pure example. Termeer [the narrator], claiming to be unable to keep his dreadful secret, records his confession and leaves it behind as a monument to himself, thereby turning a worthless life into art' J.M. Coetzee

Carlo Emilio Gadda · *That Awful Mess on Via Merulana*

Translated from the Italian by William Weaver
with an introduction by Italo Calvino
'One of the greatest and most original Italian novels of our time' Alberto Moravia

Martin A. Hansen · *The Liar*

Translated from the Danish by John Jepson Egglishaw
with an introduction by Eric Christiansen
'[The Liar] is both a vindication of religious truth and a farewell to the traditional modes of extended fiction. It is haunted by literary ghosts, and English readers will recognize the shadowy forms of Hans Anderson . . . and Søren Kierkegaard' Eric Christiansen

Gustav Janouch · *Conversations with Kafka*

Translated from the German by Goronwy Rees
with an introduction by Hugh Haughton
'I read it and was stunned by the wealth of new material . . .
which plainly and unmistakably bore the stamp of Kafka's
genius' Max Brod

Ismaïl Kadaré · *The General of the Dead Army*

Translated from the French by Derek Coltman
with an introduction by David Smiley
'Ismaïl Kadaré is presenting his readers not merely
with a novel of world stature — which is already a
great deal — but also, and even more important, with
a novel that is the voice of ancient Albania herself,
speaking to today's world of her rebirth' Robert Escarpit

Miroslav Krleža · *On the Edge of Reason*

Translated from the Croatian by Zora Depolo
with an introduction by Jeremy Catto
'Paris had its Balzac and Zola; Dublin, its Joyce;
Croatia, its Krleža . . . one of the most accomplished,
profound authors in European literature . . .'
Saturday Review

Pär Lagerkvist · *The Dwarf*

Translated from the Swedish by Alexandra Dick
with an introduction by Quentin Crewe
'A considerable imaginative feat'
Times Literary Supplement

Henry de Montherlant · *The Bachelors*

Translated from the French and with an introduction by Terence Kilmartin
'One of those carefully framed, precise and acid studies on a small canvas in which French writers again and again excel' V.S. Pritchett

Rainer Maria Rilke · *Rodin and other Prose Pieces*

Translated from the German by G. Craig Houston with an introduction by William Tucker
'[Rilke's] essay remains the outstanding interpretation of Rodin's œuvre, anticipating and rendering otiose almost all subsequent criticism'
William Tucker, *The Language of Sculpture*

Lou Andreas-Salomé · *The Freud Journal*

Translated from the German by Stanley A. Leavy with an introduction by Mary-Kay Wilmers
'Lou Andreas-Salomé was a woman with a remarkable flair for great men and . . . it was said of her that she had attached herself to the greatest men of the nineteenth and twentieth centuries Nietzsche and Freud respectively'
Ernest Jones, *The Life and Work of Sigmund Freud*

Stanislaw Ignacy Witkiewicz · *Insatiability*

Translated from the Polish by Louis Iribarne with an introduction by Czeslaw Milosz
'A study of decay: mad, dissonant music, erotic perversion, . . . and complex psychopathic personalities'
Czeslaw Milosz